F
HEY

Heywood, Joseph.

Chasing a blond
moon.

$21.95

DATE			

CHASING A
BLOND MOON

A WOODS COP MYSTERY

Also by Joseph Heywood

Fiction:

Taxi Dancer
The Berkut
The Domino Conspiracy
The Snowfly

Woods Cop Mysteries:

Ice Hunter
Blue Wolf in Green Fire

Non-Fiction:

Covered Waters: Tempests of a Nomadic Trouter

JOSEPH HEYWOOD

CHASING A
BLOND MOON

A WOODS COP MYSTERY

THE LYONS PRESS

GUILFORD, CONNECTICUT

AN IMPRINT OF THE GLOBE PEQUOT PRESS

The Lyons Press is an imprint of The Globe Pequot Press.

Printed in the United States of America

ISBN 1-59228-051-X

10   9   8   7   6   5   4   3   2   1

Library of Congress Cataloging-in-Publication data is available on file.

To Michigan Conservation Officers Dave Painter, Steve Burton, and Grant Emery, who haul me around in their trucks and share their world. While the weather is sometimes lousy and the rides and roads rough, the work and company are always fascinating. Only the swimming conditions leave a bit to be desired.

· PROLOGUE: SUMMER HAZE ·

G rady Service stood at the aged brick entrance of Monroe's Custer Memorial Municipal Ice Arena and recalled that the flamboyant George Armstrong Custer had been raised in Monroe and that his life, after some exhilarating highs, had ended badly at the Little Big Horn. Perhaps the naming of the building was aimed at exhorting its teams to find a better outcome than Custer had found. Service wondered if the general's youth spent only forty miles south of Detroit had inured the youthful Custer with a time-released dose of bad luck. Detroit had that effect on a lot of people.

It was early August and humidity added to the funk inside, which smelled of generations of fans and players. The lobby was filled with rows of tarnished trophies and aging dusty photographs of players and teams. In the arena itself, scents and the sounds of steel blades scraping and cutting ice brought memories rushing back into Grady Service's mind, but he tried to will them away. He had walked away from hockey because he had brutally injured and nearly killed another player in his final collegiate game. Had he possessed a thicker skin, he would have had a shot at the NHL out of college, but after the incident his heart had been laden with remorse and was no longer in the game. It was not that he lacked the ability to kill. He had done that in Vietnam. What he feared was killing without purpose or choice. Nearly killing someone in a child's game had made him walk.

"You gotta be crazy play a game on ice," Detroit Metropolitan Police Lieutenant Luticious Treebone grumbled, walking beside Service. "No ice with hoops. Get to keep your size twelves on Mother Earth's booty."

Service smiled at his friend. He and Treebone had finished college the same year, Service at Northern Michigan University and Treebone at Wayne State. Service had been a fair student and a solid hockey player. At six-five and two hundred and sixty pounds, Treebone had lettered in baseball and football and had graduated cum laude. They had both volunteered for the marines and met at Parris Island before serving together for a year in the same long-range recon unit in Vietnam. They had been through hell and rarely spoke of it.

When they got back to "the world" they had joined the Michigan State Police and two years after completing the academy, there had been an opportunity to jump to DNR law enforcement and both had done so. After a year, Tree had moved to the Detroit Metropolitan Police and had risen to lieutenant in one of the department's many vice units. The two men had remained close for more than twenty years and when Tree called him and announced, "Get your white booty to Detroit most *dinky dau*," Service and Maridly Nantz had flown south in Nantz's plane with her at the controls. Tree had been vague on the phone, saying only that there was something that Service had to see for himself. It was the end of July and the call had come last night; now it was 11 A.M. and he and Nantz and Tree were inside the ancient arena in the rusting industrial city of Monroe.

Service ignored his friend and saw a short man with a graying goatee and unmatched dark hair standing beside the boards. He couldn't be more than five-five, but he had the facial scars, bull neck, and wide upper body of an old-time player. He wore a faded blue corduroy jacket with "Marlies" stitched in white script across the right breast. Marlies was slang for the Toronto Marlboroughs, the Junior A club sponsored by the NHL Maple Leafs.

"Coach Bernard?" Service said. A half-dozen players were on the ice, moving lethargically, loosening muscles and kinks by halfheartedly slapping pucks against the boards with staccato cracks.

The man turned and squinted with dark eyes. "You ever have to take a dump and your plumbing don't work?"

Service blinked.

"I get me that problem," Tree said. "I take the prunes."

"Prunes be go to hell," the coach said, glaring at Tree. "Nothin' to do but wait 'er out."

"Hey Hempsted, get the cement outta your *ass!*" he screamed at an acne-faced player gliding by, admiring his reflection in pitted plexiglass.

"Bloody kids all concerned about their mugs, eh? I tell 'em, you want ginch, put a right hook in the mush of the other guy's goon and the broads'll come. Some things don't never change about this game," he said wistfully. The man suddenly seemed to realize that he had strangers before him. "Banger Service?" he asked. "Yah, you'd be him, eh! I seen you play a lot longer ago than either of us wants to remember. You hit like a bloody bulldozer."

Service said, "You called Lt. Treebone."

Tree and Bernard nodded perfunctorily, leaving Service to conclude they had met before.

"Right," Bernard said. "I got this kid come out from Phoenix. Not invited, see, but he had a note from an old pal, Lig Lemieux, and Lig told me I should give 'im a close look."

Everybody who knew anything about hockey knew of Lig Lemieux, who had played for five or six NHL teams over a dozen years and fought his way the whole time. His given name was actually Herve. Lig was an acronym for "Let It Go," the words referees used to shout at him as they tried to pry him out of fights. After his playing career Lemieux had made a second and far more successful career as a pro talent scout who worked freelance; the highest bidder got his evaluations, which had become legendary in their accuracy. Lig rarely missed on a kid.

Bernard continued, "The boy's right on the bottom of junior age eligibility, but old Lig says take a look, I take a look. The kid's got it," Bernard added. "Barely sixteen, but he's six-three, one-ninety-five, three percent body fat—all muscle. Soft hands, good head, quick reactions, and he skates like a bloody five-circle twirly, eh. After three days, I pult 'im back inta da office and I tell him I'm tinkin' about takin' 'im, but he's a young pup and maybe we ought to put him in our midget feeder program. The kid says no fuckin' midgets, it's juniors or he's gonna enlist in the marines. I tell 'im he's got to have his folks' permish, one way or t'other. Kid says he's an orphan and his guardian will sign anything to get rid of him."

Service listened patiently.

"So I calt Lig and ask him what the deal is. The kid's name is Walter Commando and it turns out the kid's mother died last September. She was on that plane went down in Pennsylvania, eh? Geez, what shit luck. The kid's guardian is actually his stepdad, name 's J. T. Commando, bigshot land developer in Phoenix. Lig says the stepdad and the lad don't get along so well and all the kid wants is a life in hockey like his real old man. Lig pointed the kid to me and suggested I give you a head's up. I got a retired cop runs the fat boy leagues here, plays twice a week up in Detroit. Told me he knew a Detroit cop who knew where you were, and that's how I got to Treebone."

"We've come a long way from the U.P.," Service said, wondering if there was a point to this biography.

Bernard focused his dark eyes on Service and said, "You got a longer way to go than you think, Banger. Lig says the kid's father is you."

Grady Service didn't react, but Nantz stepped in. "Which kid is he?"

Bernard scanned the ice. "He ain't out there yet."

As players streamed through the doors from the locker room to stretch and warm up for practice, Nantz said, "My God."

The player wore number fourteen, the same Grady Service had worn. The kid was rangy, with a frame that would fill out to carry a lot more muscle than he was already packing.

Bernard said, "The stepdad says, I want him, he's mine, but when I found out he was your kid I thought I'd better talk to you."

Service said, "I don't have a kid."

Maridly Nantz poked him in the ribs. "*Look* at him, Grady."

Treebone grinned. "Dawg, that leaf didn't fall far from the tree."

"You want me to get him over here?" Bernard asked.

Service said, "You got the stepfather's phone number?"

"You betcha," Bernard said, handing him a piece of paper. "My office is second on da right. I don't got no secretary cause da club owner's a cheap fuck, so just go on in and dial nine to get the outside line. You really didn't know?"

Service left without answering. Nantz followed at his side.

He punched in the telephone number and nodded at another phone. Nantz sat at a small table by the wall and picked up the extension to listen.

"Thomas Commando Development," a woman said, answering the phone. "This is Joanne Baker, may I help you?"

"I'd like to speak to Mr. Commando."

"He's in a meeting," the secretary said.

"This is Grady Service and I am calling about his stepson."

"Walter?"

"Yes."

"Do you know where he is?" She sounded concerned.

"I do."

"I'll get Mr. Commando."

"Thomas Commando, is this Service?" The man's voice was both raspy and smooth, accustomed to giving orders and having them followed.

"Grady Service," Service said.

"Where's the boy?" Not his boy, but the boy, Service noted.

"You already know where he is," Service said. "You talked to Coach Bernard about him. What happened to Bathsheba?"

"Sheba died September 11. What's it to you?"

Sheba? "She was my wife a long time ago."

"Ah, *that* Service. Now I get the connection. Have you seen the boy?"

"A few minutes ago."

"She said you threw her out when you found out she was pregnant."

"Why would I do that?"

"Because the kid wasn't yours."

Service was confused. "How could I throw her out when I didn't know she was pregnant?"

"She said she told you and you took it poorly. Said you had a hot head, had a bad time in 'Nam."

"Who did she say is the boy's father?"

"I think his name was Parker, but I don't really remember the details."

Parker, Service thought. Bathsheba wouldn't look at Parker, much less . . . "When did you get married?"

"After Sheba finished law school at the University of Arizona. Her firm was representing my company and we started going out and you know how it goes."

"You told Bernard if he wants the boy, he's his. What's that mean?"

"The kid's nothing but trouble. Drove Sheba crazy. Me too, but I didn't take it so personally. She said he was just like his father, only out for himself and a risk-taker."

The description didn't fit Parker, who had nominally been his sergeant for a period of time, and who Service couldn't tolerate. Parker was a politicking toady and a devout coward. "The boy's barely sixteen," Service said.

"The team can work that out. He'll bunk with a family out there and then he's their problem."

"Does the boy know how you feel?"

"We don't talk. Never have and it's worse since I lost Sheba. I tried, but he wants no part of me."

"What was Bathsheba doing on that plane last fall?"

"She was back and forth to the East Coast all the time. Hell, I still can't believe it happened."

"You're the boy's legal guardian?"

"I adopted him when we married, but he doesn't listen to me. He wants to play that stupid game and get his brains scrambled, let him. The more miles between us, the better for the both of us."

"He's a minor."

"I told Bernard, send me the paperwork and I'll do what has to be done to make it happen."

"What if the boy doesn't make the team?"

Thomas Commando laughed. "Are you kidding? He can't miss. His mother and I spent a fortune on him, the right individual skills coaching, the right teams, he's got it for the game. Too bad he doesn't have it for real life. After hockey the kid will be a loser."

The stepfather did not like the boy and Service sensed the feelings were much stronger than dislike. "But what happens if he doesn't make the team?"

"C'mon, there are other teams, lots of 'em. He went out there on his own. He doesn't make it, let him find another one."

"What's he supposed to live on?"

Commando cleared his throat. "The boy is not without means. His mother was a very successful attorney. She did all the legal work for Larry Cressman."

"The movie producer?"

"More like the one-man entertainment conglomerate. Who the hell called you into this and what business is it of yours?"

"Lig Lemieux told Coach Bernard that Walter is my son."

"I don't know where Lig got that idea. His father's name is Parker."

"Lig insists he's mine, and Coach Bernard says if the boy doesn't make the team he's going to enlist in the marines."

"Either way, he's not my problem anymore. He wants to be a jarhead, I'll sign for him. Not your problem either. You're not his father."

"I'm sorry for your loss," Service said, hanging up.

The room was silent. Nantz looked at Service and raised an eyebrow. "Severely negative vibes. Charlie Parker is the father?"

"Parker and I were equals in those days and I didn't have any use for him right out of the gate."

"He the type your ex might go for?"

"I doubt it. I met her when I was a Troop and she was a student in East Lansing. She didn't date guys her own age. Troops made good money back then. One thing led to another and we ended up married."

"Did you love her?"

"I thought I did."

"She fool around on you?"

"Not her speed. She couldn't handle risk."

"But she became a lawyer."

"Contract law isn't criminal work. She couldn't handle confrontations."

"So you don't buy the Parker story."

"Not her type," he said, shaking his head.

"What if she was trying her wings with him?"

"You can't fly with a dodo bird."

Nantz laughed. "DNA tells all," she said. "If you're the father, that will be easy enough to find out."

"The question is, do we *want* to find out?" he asked.

"You don't?" She looked and sounded surprised.

"If he's my son, I haven't exactly been a force in his life before this. What good would it do now?"

"Well, his mother is dead for one thing, and more importantly, if his father is alive, that father ought to be with him."

"He's not looking for me," Service said. "He came here to play hockey."

"And if he doesn't make it, he's going to join the *marines*. My gut says this boy knows about you, Grady. I don't know where from or how, but my intuition says he's here for a reason. I mean he could go and play anywhere, right?"

"The Downriver Rattlers play in the best junior hockey league in Canada," Service explained. "They've been to the Memorial Cup three times in the past five years. This is one of the premier Tier I junior clubs in North America. All the top players want into the best programs, because they're the ones the pro scouts watch most closely."

"I doubt this is just about hockey," Nantz said. "I've never pried about your marriage, Grady. I didn't even know your wife's name until a few minutes ago. What exactly happened between the two of you?"

The question caught him by surprise. "I told you."

"As much as you tell anybody anything. You've never even called her by name. She's always been the 'ex.' I'd really like to know, Grady," she added crisply.

"Bathsheba Pope. We got married six months after Troop academy and two years later I transferred to the DNR. She lived in Lansing while

I moved around in training assignments and then she came up here with me and lasted six more months. It lasted just short of four years."

"What did she look like?" Nantz asked.

Service glanced at her. "Tall."

"Tall? That's it?"

He grinned. "She was attractive."

"Was she good in bed?"

He shrugged. "Not as good as you."

She granted him a smile of appreciation. "Good looking and good in bed—so what happened?"

"The marriage was all appearances. We were going our separate ways. She finally announced that I had a death wish and she wanted out."

"Did *you*?"

"Not any more than you."

"Not a death wish, 'tard—did you want out?"

"I never thought about it. When one party wants out, it's over."

Nantz said, "I happen to know that the name Bathsheba means headstrong, wants to be in charge, and wants the best money can buy. Bathshebas can be overly critical to the point of injuring, quick to fight, and always looking to dominate."

"You knew her?" he said, looking at Nantz, who ignored him and kept pressing.

"Did she live with you at Slippery Creek?"

"No, we lived near Newberry then. I didn't get responsibility for the Mosquito Wilderness until a year after we split up. I bought the Slippery Creek parcel long after that."

"The divorce cost you big time?"

"We didn't have much and she took most of it—with my blessing."

"And walked out of your life."

"Ran would be more accurate. She never complained, but one night at dinner she said, 'I'd like another helping of cauliflower and a divorce.' I looked up at her. She said, 'You have a death wish and I don't want to be a young widow.' She left after she finished her second helping. She was already packed."

"You didn't stay in touch?"

He shook his head. "She filed in Nevada and I signed the papers. I never heard from or of her again."

"Did that make you sad?"

He looked over at Nantz. "I was more confused than sad," he said softly. "I thought everything was going okay; you know, not perfect, but workable."

"So you just buried yourself in work, right?"

"Pretty much."

"Which is partly what prompted her to leave in the first place."

"I was never around and when I was, she wasn't. She had a degree in accounting and was a junior trust officer at a bank in Marquette. I think we just wanted different things. I assumed it was my fault."

"Which is why there was no second Mrs. Grady Service."

"I stopped thinking in those terms."

"In those terms, or stopped thinking?"

"That too."

"What I heard is that you did most of your thinking with a certain body part for a long time. Then came Kira Lehto."

Kira Lehto was a veterinarian and had been his girlfriend when he met Nantz.

"Not until years later."

"And that was good?"

"Apparently not for her."

"But you lived together."

"For about a week. She was pressing for a commitment and I just asked her to move in. She couldn't handle it."

"She's a classy lady. Maybe you couldn't handle her."

"I was willing to try."

"Even marriage?"

"We never got that far."

Nantz laughed. "Service, I don't see you as afraid of commitment. I see you being afraid of commitments that aren't significant enough to warrant your full focus. When the right relationship comes along, you'll go for it in a big way."

"I already have," he said, and since they were having a confessional, he asked, "Why haven't we ever talked about kids?"

Nantz sucked in a deep breath. "Part of me wants kids, and another part of me doesn't want any impediments, but I guess we should talk about this kid now."

"He's here to play hockey," Service said, "not to find his daddy."

"Denial leads nowhere," she said. "Just look at him. He's the spitting image of a young Grady Service. The least we can do is make sure he's settled down here with the team, and then we can get him up to our place when he has breaks."

"You leave for the academy in November."

She made a face. "There are no problems, Service, just opportunities. We can handle any challenge that comes our way."

"Together," he said.

"That's what *we* means, you big jerk. Let's go talk to your son."

He balked at the door but she pressed the flat of her hand to his back and urged him forward. "Be a good boy and maybe I'll give you a quickie under the bleachers."

Treebone and Bernard were in a detailed discussion about bowel habits when they came back.

Bernard was saying, "It's like plumbing. You gotta keep the lines cleaned out – you know, three, four dumps a day."

"I hear you," Luticious Treebone said, nodding solemnly.

The coach turned his attention to Service and Nantz as they walked up. "You talk to the stepfather?"

"He says he'll sign whatever he needs to sign."

"You want to talk to the boy now?"

When Service didn't answer, Nantz said, "He does."

The coach climbed up on the bleachers and yelled across the ice. "Commando, get your ass over here!"

The boy came swooping across the ice with remarkable grace and power and dug in his blade edges to spray the glass with snow.

"S'up, coach?" He had the body of a man, but the face and voice of a boy.

"This is Grady Service," Bernard said with a nod.

"Hey," the boy said. He had long dark hair and intense blue eyes. He avoided looking directly at Service.

Nantz leaned over the plexiglass and said, "Maybe we can talk after practice?"

The boy shrugged and skated away.

"That went well," Service said.

"He wouldn't look at you," Nantz said.

"I saw," Service said.

"Dawg, that kid's you," Treebone said.

"He's also Bathsheba," Service said.

"That ain't a good thing," Tree replied.

"I gotta get these kids moving," Bernard said. "We got to the Cup finals last year and fell on our keesters, but I'm gonna get 'em back there again."

They watched as he circled to a Zamboni door, let himself onto the ice, and started bellowing. The players reacted immediately.

Walter skated with powerful strides and a confidence that didn't betray his age. Most of the other players were seventeen to twenty. He handled the puck with a feathery touch and moved it around effortlessly. The only weakness Service saw was a slight hitch in making moves to his right, but it was hardly noticeable and virtually every player alive always had a weak side.

After thirty minutes, Bernard called the players together at center ice and talked to them with great animation. Service couldn't hear what he was saying, but Walter surreptitiously looked in his direction several times before most of the players headed to the bench. Walter stayed on the ice at left wing and lined up against another winger who was obviously older and heavier.

The opposing center drew the puck back to a winger, who rifled it ahead to the opposite fast-breaking forward, who dumped the puck off the boards. It caromed and skittered loudly behind the net.

Walter shadowed his winger down the ice, his head up, and when the winger went into the corner, Walter dipped a shoulder and pinched him against the dasher, knocking him off balance, deftly collared the loose puck, fired it out to his curling center, and dug to get back up ice to join the rush. The big winger pursued, but didn't catch up until they were crossing the far blue line and Walter's center slid the puck back to him. The opposing winger lifted Walter's stick and stuck a shoulder into him, knocking the puck loose as he drove him sideways toward the boards. But Walter's legs were strong and he was able to counter the pressure and spin off the check as the other team recovered the puck and started in the opposite direction.

Once again Walter shadowed his man down the wing and slammed him hard when the puck came to him, this time knocking him flat on his back. By the time the player was up, Walter was in the neutral zone with the puck back on his stick. He feinted outside and sharply split two defensemen, quickly firing a hard low wrist shot from the top of the slot. The goalie swept at it with his blocker, but missed, and the puck clanged off the metal goalpost and into the net. The goalie slapped the blade of his paddle on the ice in frustration and all the players hooted.

Bernard changed lines. On Walter's bench his teammates were butting his helmet. On the other bench the players were obviously ridiculing the opposing winger.

The next time Walter's line came out, they came over the boards on the fly and Walter's defensive mark got the puck and raced for the middle, but dug in his skate edges, let the puck slide on, and made a ripping backward motion with the butt-end of his stick, catching Walter high in the stomach.

Walter dropped to his knees, but immediately popped up, shaking off his gloves, and was on top of the other winger immediately, clawing to get his helmet off and punching with bare knuckles against hard plastic.

"Tell me that ain't your son," Treebone said gleefully. "Check it out. He come from the shoulders on that busta."

Bernard let the boys wrestle and punch until they were spent, then banished them to the bench. When play restarted, one of Walter's teammates started shouting and waving at the coach. Walter was nowhere in sight. He was crumpled on the floor by the bench and the team trainer had to hop over the wall between them to get to him.

Everything stopped and before he could think, Grady Service was pushing the trainer aside and on the floor, cradling the boy's head. His eyes were closed, his breathing labored, and he was clammy.

"Call 911!" Service roared.

Four hours later, they were in a hospital. The doctors diagnosed a seriously damaged spleen, with more than a thousand milliliters of intraperitoneal blood and a rapidly falling hemoglobin concentration. A surgeon explained that he usually took his time with spleen injuries in youngsters in order to try to preserve the organ, but Walter needed immediate surgery. After a quick phone call to Thomas Commando, Walter was wheeled into an operating suite and the rest of them settled in to wait. Coach Bernard was in the hospital the whole time, which impressed Service.

"He don't need a spleen," the coach said.

"He could've been killed," Service said.

"Goes with the game, Banger. C'mon, you know that. Kid give 'im the short stick is Fitzhenry. Projected to be a top-ten draft pick this year. Your boy's been kicking his ass every day since he got here and things just come to a head. You embarrass any player long enough, he's gonna try to get his pride back."

Service said, "Somebody ought to run a short stick up that kid's ass."

Nantz squeezed his arm.

Bernard said, "I talked to the doc and he says they're doing this thing with a laparoscope, same as a knee, eh? He'll be out of the hospital in a day or two and he'll feel better in a few days, but he can't do anything strenuous for two to six weeks. Take a lot longer to get him back to full play. Truth is, I can't carry an untested kid. He had the team made, but now I can't take 'im. Next year he'll have a spot for sure. *If* he don't join the marines," he added sarcastically.

Service was dumbfounded. The boy had had a future and now he was out. How would he handle it?

Bernard started to leave. "Where you going?" Service asked.

"Gotta talk to the stepfather," he said.

"His stepfather doesn't want him back," Service said.

"I still gotta call him. He's legally responsible."

After Bernard stepped down the hall with his cell phone, Nantz pulled Service aside.

"I don't know the game, Grady, but even I can see that this kid seems born to do this."

"Not this season. You heard Bernard."

"We can't let him enlist."

"It's his choice."

"Like hell," she said, her voice hardening. "Sometimes a kid has choices but no brain to use in making them. He goes off to the marines now, well . . ." She didn't finish her statement.

"What am I supposed to do?"

"Tell him who you are, take him home with us."

"Are you crazy?"

"Just like you," Treebone said, chiming in.

When Walter Commando came out of the anesthetic he found Grady Service and Maridly Nantz in the recovery room.

"Thirsty," was his first word.

Service gave him a cup filled with cracked ice, which made the boy smile. "Just the way Scotty Bowman likes it," he said.

"I guess I'm your father," Grady Service said.

"I know," the boy said, avoiding his father's eyes.

"You knew?" Nantz said.

"Sheba told me a long time ago."

"I didn't know," Service said.

"She said you didn't deserve to know," Walter said.

"Your mother told your stepdad that your father was a man named Parker," Nantz said.

The boy shrugged. "My stepdad is a jerk. Sheba gave him a name, knowing he'd check it out. She said the Parker guy was a total loser and that J. T. wouldn't be threatened."

"Why didn't she tell me about you?" Service asked.

"I'm just her son," Walter said. "Sheba Pope did things for her own reasons. She didn't confide much in me. She gave me what she thought I needed, but that was it. We didn't exactly sit down for a lot of heart-to-hearts," the boy added, his voice cracking.

Service touched his son's shoulder. "We'd like for you to come home with us."

The boy said, "I've got hockey."

"Not this season. Bernard said you had the team made, but you'll be out too long to help the club."

"That's not fair," the boy said, his eyes reddening and tearing.

"Welcome to life," his father said. "Next time you go to a new team, try not to humiliate their best player."

"What was I supposed to do? I wanted to be noticed."

"You got noticed all right," Service said. "Then you got targeted."

"I kicked his ass," the boy said with a grimace.

"You won the battle and lost the war."

"I didn't lose the war. I made the team."

"You made the team, but you got hurt. That's hockey."

"This sucks. Now I'm supposed to pack up and go with *you?*"

"You can always go back to Phoenix."

"It would almost be worth it to see Tommy-boy squirm."

"It's your choice," Service said, immediately earning a sharp knuckle in his kidney from Nantz.

"What about Northern Michigan?" the boy asked. "They have a pretty good club."

Service sighed. "Maybe you ought to think about finishing high school first."

The boy rolled his eyes. "I *have* finished."

"At sixteen?" Nantz asked.

"Sheba talked to somebody who said it didn't really matter about a grade point if I got a GED and took the ACTs. I got a thirty on the ACT, which means I can pretty much go wherever I want."

Service was trying to process all the bits of information and come to grips with the reality of talking to his son, still not quite believing it. "Okay, we'll talk to Northern and see what they say."

"Northern's got a new coach, right?"

"Rick Comley left to take the job at Michigan State." Comley had been at Northern forever.

"What about Michigan Tech and Lake Superior State?"

"Northern's got the best program up our way right now."

"But Tech has the best academics, right?"

Service nodded.

"Let's talk to Tech then, see what they offer." The boy certainly didn't want for confidence and clearly was used to getting his own way.

"Phoenix or the U.P.?" Service asked.

"I guess I'll go with you," Walter said without enthusiasm. "But I want to give Coach Bernard a piece of my mind before we leave."

"That's not a great idea," Service countered. "In hockey you can't burn bridges."

"Is that supposed to be fatherly advice?" the boy asked with a sneer.

"It's common sense," Service said.

"Like you haven't burned any bridges in your life?"

"My life's my business," Service said.

"You're my biological father," Walter said, "not my real dad. That makes my life my business."

Nantz's knuckle was grinding into Service's kidney again, "If you're with us, you'll play by our rules," Service said.

"Your rules? Are you two married?"

"No," Service said.

"Great, I get to live with the man who abandoned me and his live-in scromp."

"You might want to keep that smart mouth of yours shut some of the time."

"Same for you," the boy said defiantly.

Nantz again poked Service.

"You'd better get some sleep," Service said. "We'll be back."

The boy put a pillow over his face as Service and Nantz backed out of the hospital room.

"That didn't go so great," Service said when they were in the corridor.

Nantz patted his hand. "He's sixteen, he's disappointed, and he's got a hard head like somebody else I know. But Grady, he's gone to the trouble of finding out about you and that has to mean something. We can make this work. I know we can."

"Maybe we'd better start by getting married."

Nantz began to laugh and shake her head. "You embarrassed, living in sin?"

"No."

"He's a big tough hockey player. He can live with us as we are. When we get married, Service, I want to do it right."

"This is not going to be easy," Service said. If he was to be a father, he had thought it would be with Nantz, having a baby and watching the kid grow over time, not having a fully grown hothead dumped on his doorstep.

"The roller coaster is king in the land of the merry-go-rounds," Nantz said.

· 1 ·

The sight of condominiums flanking Navy Street along the boulder-lined Portage Shipping Canal made Grady Service wince. The Upper Peninsula was Michigan's last remaining wilderness, and as more downstaters and out-of-staters discovered it and decided to retire here, they were moving north and bringing their flatlander lifestyles and values with them. Condos in the U.P., he grumbled in the late August darkness.

The entrance to the primitive two-track, which led to the place many locals simply called "the fish house," was hidden at the end of a low concrete wall behind some condo garages. Gus Turnage had told him it was a little less than a half-mile to the fish house and that the road was often used by kids and miscreants seeking privacy. Above him he could see the blurred lights of the town of Hancock, the so-called Gateway to the Keeweenaw, but the surroundings along the two-track remained wild and untamed. Hancock had once been the epicenter of copper mining in the Upper Peninsula, but the ore had petered out and the mining companies had moved west, leaving ruins and descendants of Finnish miners to fend for themselves. The area had never recovered.

This should be Gus's case, Service reminded himself, but Gus Turnage was home in Houghton recovering from gallbladder surgery. Service, Nantz, and Walter Commando had come to Houghton for Walter's orientation at Michigan Tech. The boy had been accepted, but had not yet decided to enroll. They had been visiting Gus when the call for assistance had come in from the Houghton County dispatcher. Walter had lived with them for nearly a month, and had come to the campus at the invitation of the varsity hockey coach. As an unknown and because of his age, Walter would not have an athletic scholarship, but he had been asked to camp as an invited walk-on. Service had expected his newly found son to reject the invite because a scholarship had not been offered, but Walter had accepted graciously, leaving Service scratching his head.

Service and Nantz had picked Walter up from campus last night for an evening with Gus, who had regaled Walter with outlandish and embellished stories of his father's exploits. He had wished Gus had shut up or stuck to the facts because his friend was making him seem larger than life. As a boy his own father had been a legend, and he knew how hard it was to grow up in such a large shadow. At fifty, he was still hearing comparisons to his old man.

If law enforcement staffing had been normal, another CO would have filled in for Gus, but Governor Sam Bozian's ham-handed budget cutting had left DNR law enforcement short and, in some large counties where four officers should be covering, there was only one.

Easing his way down the two-track in his unmarked green Yukon, Service shut off his interior and exterior lights. When you were in the dirt at night, you came upon more things running dark than by advertising your presence. With less than a year as a detective in the DNR's Wildlife Resources Protection Unit, he welcomed any chance to operate the way he had for nearly twenty years as a conservation officer. At night, that meant all lights out except the sneak light that let him see the ground, but could be seen only from inside the vehicle.

After a while the pitted, rocky road ascended a steep hummock and dropped down the west face. To his left he could faintly discern the outline of an old boathouse, one of the landmarks Gus had told him to watch for. The boat garage held three dilapidated 36-foot wooden boats once used for fishing in the area. Like many things in the U.P., whose economy had been in a steady slide for decades, stuff that couldn't be used or sold quickly usually got left to the whims and ravages of nature. The people of the U.P. didn't get much better treatment, but you rarely heard them complain. People up here might be trapped by circumstances, but they were stoical and endured what had to be endured, including a crapped-out economy, a three-month growing season for agriculture, and seven-month-long winters.

Eventually the undulating narrow road led into an open area and Service left his lights off, stopping to peer ahead. It was a fairly large parking lot of dirt and gravel, something clearly not graded or taken care of in years. Puddles of water stood in low areas and the steady rain danced on the surfaces, prickling the water.

To the left there was a large dark building, perhaps a hundred feet long. This would be the place the locals called the fish house. It had once housed the Superior Coastal Fishery Company, a typical Yooper brainstorm. The owners had been determined to market Lake Superior fish throughout the Midwest—lake trout, whitefish, pickled herring, whitefish roe—but the owners found the actual marketing more difficult than the idea and the business had gone belly-up. Now the building housed the fishing boats and gear of Native Americans who carried tribal IDs and could fish both on commercial and subsistence fishing licenses. COs referred to them most of the time as tribals.

Beyond the structure, Gus had briefed him, there was an old stone wharf and a series of decaying hundred-year-old pilings that the tribal tugboat tied up to in order to offload catches. It was not clear anymore, Gus said, who actually owned the building—perhaps the tribals, perhaps the state—but the business was called Lake Superior Fisheries, and despite operating from such a pathetic site, seemed to be making it. It periodically fell to Gus to work with a tribal commercial fisheries officer to perform various inspections on the fishing tug and facilities. There had once been fifty commercial fishermen spread from Baraga to the tip of the Keeweenaw. Now there was one Native American commercial fisherman operating out of Hancock, and the waters in the area had been so severely depleted by overfishing and lampreys that tribal netters from Baraga didn't waste their time or fuel coming up this way anymore.

Away from the building he saw the flickering gumball of a police vehicle. Beyond the squad car there was another vehicle. Off to the other side there was the silhouette of a pickup truck.

Service waited until he was less than fifty yards from the police car to announce himself by toggling his blue lights. He was met by an officer wearing a drenched dark slicker, with HOUGHTON COUNTY SHERIFF'S DEPARTMENT airbrushed in yellow block letters.

"You guys always seem to pop up outta nowhere," the officer said as he got out of his Yukon. "There's a better road down from the hospital," she added.

"We prefer the scenic routes," Service said. It always pleased him to take people by surprise, especially other cops.

"Limey Pyykkonen," the officer said, extending her hand.

"Grady Service."

"How's Gus?"

"Recovering."

"You one of the replacements?" she asked. The state legislature had put the kibosh on the governor's plan to not authorize replacements for officers who took an early retirement package designed to reduce the state government payroll. As a result, a small number of replacements were in the pipeline, but it would be a year to eighteen months before some areas had coverage again, and even then the force would not be at full strength.

"I'm out of Marquette. I was visiting Gus."

"Sorry," she said.

"What do we have?"

"Stiff," Pyykkonen answered, turning on her flashlight, lifting the yellow tape she had strung around the area, and leading him to the vehicle.

Grady Service stared at the bloated corpse in the blue Saturn. It had been raining off and on for days and the car was mud-spattered. Under the red beam of his MAG-LITE , the corpse looked larger through the windows. The dead man's arms were raised in front of him, like he had died reaching for something. "Why the DNR?" Service asked. "We don't investigate dead bodies."

"The body's mine, but it looks to me like an animal took a dump in the backseat," Detective Limey Pyykkonen said, adjusting the hood of her rain jacket. "The shit's yours," she said with a smile.

Service shone his light and saw the dark pile. "Got an ID on the vick?"

"Not yet," she said. "They found him," she added, nodding at a couple in rain gear standing in front of a Ford pickup away from the Saturn. "The M.E.'s on the way. I got the door open, checked for a pulse, took one sniff, and called for help. I don't want to soil the scene."

Service grunted. She had already cordoned off the dead man's vehicle and immediate area.

"No signs of violence," Pyykkonen said. "Natural causes maybe. Or a suicide. The doors were locked."

"Arms in the air," Service said. "That mean anything?"

"Possibly," she said. "He could have died somewhere else and been placed in the vehicle, but let's not let our imaginations fly until we see what we have."

Service stared at the stiff's distorted features. Native American or Asian—it was hard to tell with the body so swollen. "I guess we wait. You new?" Pyykkonen was a strapping, angular woman with a small round face, close-cropped hair, and worm-thin lips.

"Larry DeNover retired and I got his job. I was doing school liaison before this."

Service knew DeNover. He was Houghton County's longtime homicide detective, a slow-thinking, deliberate man whose workload fit his style. The county had few homicides. "School liaison?"

"D.A.R.E., listening to kids caught in hormone hurricanes, that sort of thing. The kids refer to me as Saint Narc."

"Good job?" he said, passing time and trying to decide if Saint Narc was positive or negative. He also considered asking her for insight into the mind of a sixteen-year-old, but said nothing. Walter and he were still trying to work things out, which meant they were polite and answered when spoken to. It was uncomfortable for him, but Nantz seemed to have fared better and Walter yacked away with her. The first night the boy was in Gladstone, Nantz had given Service signals that she wanted to fool around, and he had told her they couldn't with Walter in the next room. She had only laughed and pressed the issue, whispering, "He'd better get used to it."

"The job sucked," Pyykkonen said, "but I liked the kids. If you take the time to really listen to them, they have a lot to offer," she added. "I was a patrol officer before the school job, but I kept dinging vehicles. The sheriff put me in the schools to keep me off the roads."

"Why'd they send Homicide?"

"The department didn't. The kids called me when they found the body. I knew them from my liaison work."

"You trained for homicide?"

"Three years as a Lansing cop, and three years in homicide. I blew it in a case involving the daughter of a city councilman and got the gate."

"And you came here?"

"Followed a boyfriend. He moved on. I stayed."

"Must be the weather," Service said.

"You bet," she said, cracking a weak smile. "Especially the driving."

"Anybody else around?" he asked, tired of small talk.

"What we see is what we get," she said.

"You talk to the kids?"

"Yeah, they came down here for a little backseat aerobics. The stiff was already here. They waited for him to leave, but when they saw he wasn't moving they figured he was a drunk sleeping it off and decided to wake him up. They knocked on the windows and when he didn't respond, they called me. The boy is Jesse Renard. The girl is Jeannie Miltey."

"As in Miltey Boat Company?" The company was located in Chassell, and when fishing was in its heyday, M.B.C. had built many of the tugs used by commercial fishermen. Now the company built a line of aluminum sportfishing boats and some custom wooden jobs. Joe Miltey, who ran the boat company, had been busted more than once for fish and game law violations and was a vocal critic of the DNR.

"That's her father, but her parents are split and she lives with her mom. Mother and daughter are both pips, eh."

"Pips?"

"They don't walk on the wild side, they *sprint* it. Enthusiastic pole vaulters."

Service looked around. There were no lights nearby. A few twinkled dimly on the Houghton side of the canal, two hundred to three hundred yards across from them. The fish house was isolated, yet no more than ten minutes from downtown Hancock or Houghton. Service walked to the brick building and used his light. The construction was shoddy and a not-so-professional light-colored facade had been affixed to the front of the building; in back and on the ends, the bricks were mottled black and white and falling apart. Brick shards littered the ground. He went to the old wharf and stared down at the pilings in black water. There was a stench of fish. He didn't know the area and he wasn't much interested in getting involved. He would do what he could, pass what he had on to Gus, and let him deal with it when he was back on duty. One thing seemed certain. If you wanted privacy, this place had it.

He wondered if Tech students knew about the place and decided that college kids always knew about such places. He was curious about Walter's first day of orientation but had not had a chance to get any feedback. Their relationship was forming slowly, but was still difficult to describe. The boy didn't seem to bear grudges and when Nantz needed something done, he couldn't do it fast enough. When Service asked, there was always a negotiation. His own old man had issued orders and expected them to be obeyed, but his father had died just after his sixteenth birthday. If the old man had lived, maybe their relationship would have changed. The irony of the situation didn't escape him: He had unexpectedly lost his father at sixteen, and now all these years later had gained a son who had just turned sixteen. Had he been philosophical or religious he might have tried to make something out of this, but he was neither; mostly, he was concerned about doing things right for the boy. His *son.* The thought still made him dizzy and the word stuck in his throat. Why the hell had Bathsheba not told him about Walter? There had been no angry outburst when she pulled out; she had seemed more disappointed and tired than pissed, another example of how badly he had misread her.

"Your name?" Service said. "Limey. That's a new one."

"Finn all the way, eh? I grew up near Jacobsville where the limestone was quarried. That's where the Limey come from."

"I thought they quarried red sandstone there."

"The limestone operation wasn't as well known."

Service grunted acknowledgment. A local girl who had been a cop in Lansing, now back in the U.P. Service made the observation, didn't pursue it.

The medical examiner arrived in a muddy black Suburban. He looked harried. A vehicle with three technicians followed close behind him.

"What we got?" The doctor was young, short, and plump, with a slicked-back mullet. A tiny snowflake of toilet paper clung to a razor cut on his left jawline.

"Oriental male, forty-five to fifty-five, five-six or -seven. Been dead at least twenty-four hours, judging by the smell," Pyykkonen reported.

The doctor packed Vicks just below his nostrils, pulled on latex gloves with a snapping sound, and carefully opened the door. "Ripe," he said without emotion. It struck Service that people who handled human remains handled them with the same detachment that conservation officers handled animals, proof that death leveled all living things. The doctor's deliberate, efficient movements told Service he was experienced.

"We need the air temp and humidity both inside and outside the vehicle," the M.E. said to one of his techs, sniffing. "You smell that?"

Service had no idea what the man was talking about. The gasses from the body made it impossible for him to smell anything else except the pervading stench of dead fish. "Just the body," the tech said.

"I thought I caught a whiff of ammonia," Pyykkonen interjected. "But I could have been mistaken. This is starting to be a real stinker."

"Bitter almonds," the examiner said.

"Cyanide?" Pyykkonen said, perking up.

The doctor leaned into the Saturn and used a Popsicle stick to open the dead man's mouth, illuminating it with a penlight clamped between his teeth. "I'm guessing HCN or KCN," the doctor muttered over his shoulder. "Want to take a look here?" he added.

Pyykkonen leaned forward.

"Corroded," the doctor mumbled, holding the mouth open. "See the blistering?"

The detective nodded.

The M.E. stepped back and widened the beam of his flashlight. "Skin's red as cherries," he said. "Consistent with cyanide and this temperature, but we'll do the slab-and-lab and let science keep us off Wild-Ass-Guess Boulevard."

Service shined his light on the scat pile in the backseat but made no attempt to collect it until Pyykkonen gave him the go-ahead. The site was hers and his job was subsidiary. Over the last year, he had encountered too many stiffs in the course of duty. His boss, U.P. law boss Captain Ware Grant, was constantly reminding him to stay focused on fish and game law—which was what he wanted, too—but sometimes you ended up far afield.

The homicide detective stood with her hands on her hips, studying the car. "We'll call this a crime scene until we determine otherwise," she said. "Death under suspicious circumstances. Rigor is present," she added. "Which probably means death twelve to thirty-six hours ago. And his arms defying gravity suggest he died somewhere else."

The M.E. grunted.

Service was impressed at the detective's pragmatism and wondered what had gone wrong in Lansing for her to lose her job there.

Pyykkonen fetched her camera from her vehicle and began to take photographs of the scene, starting first at the corners of the area she had taped off with long-range shots, and working her way up to mid-range, then close-up shots. She worked silently and methodically, her camera clicking in the dark, the flash illuminating the surrounding area.

"Don't forget the shit," Service said over her shoulder.

"It's all shit," she said back to him.

After the photographs were taken, another deputy arrived and helped her to lift fingerprints. They then began a long, slow inspection of the interior of the Saturn, using tweezers to collect fibers and hairs and anything else they could find that might help in the investigation.

Eventually Pyykkonen cleared Service to collect the animal scat, which he placed in a plastic evidence bag in a cooler in the back of his vehicle. He found several long hairs mixed in the feces and several scrapes on the leather seating. Scratches? He wondered.

"Got a learned opinion?" she asked.

"Bear shit, I'd say. I'm not sure about the hair. Feels and looks like bear, but the colors are wrong. These are blond, almost white." He added, "Out West black bears range in color from light to dark, but ours are all deep black."

"Maybe this fella found a polar bear shitting in his backseat and his heart stopped," she said.

"That would do it for me," Service said. "If you don't mind, I'll ship the samples off to our lab and Gus can give you a bump when we have results."

"How long?" she asked.

"Couple of days," he said, not sure how much work the Rose Lake Lab had these days. "Maybe a week," he added, amending the estimate.

"No prob," she said. "The shit's not likely to be crucial here." Maybe, Service thought, but you didn't often find bear scat inside a vehicle. *On* them sometimes, but not *in* them. The scat might not be critical, but it meant something, his gut told him.

Pyykkonen went through the man's wallet. There's a Tech ID in here," she said. Michigan Technological University had been founded to produce mining engineers but had since branched out to become one of the country's premier engineering programs.

"Pung Juju Kang," she said, examining a business card, "Professor, Department of Structural Engineering. Probably we ought to get over to his house, notify his next of kin. You want to come along?"

Nantz would be whipping up a breakfast for Gus and Walter around now. "Sure," he said with a shrug, cursing himself for letting his curiosity have its head.

The house was made of cedar logs that glowed a flamboyant orange in the rising summer sun; it was more tall than wide and looked relatively new. There was a detached one-car garage. The severely pitched roof of the house had been built to ward off heavy winter snows and was lined with green ceramic tiles. The lawn was trimmed but there were few flowers or shrubs out front.

Pyykkonen knocked on the door several times and rang the bell, but got no response.

Service stood behind her, shifting his weight from one foot to the other, bored with the whole thing, wishing he had gone back to Gus's.

"I've got a search warrant coming," the homicide detective said not more than a minute before a beat-up Jeep Eagle clattered up the driveway. A towering man with white hair got out with a paper clenched in his beefy fist. He had a ruddy face and needed a shave.

"Judge Pavelich. I could have had somebody pick it up, Your Honor."

The judge grunted dismissively. "On my way over to the Hurons to annoy some trout," he said. "This is right on my way. No sense sending somebody else."

"Judge, this is Grady Service," Pyykkonen said.

"Otto," the judge said, extending his hand. "Heard of you, Service. Twinkie Man, right?"

"Guilty," he said with a nod, trying not to grimace. He had arrested a poacher a couple of years ago who tried to claim that sugar had made him temporarily insane, which then led to his violations. The man had lost in what was becoming a legendary court case that Service saw as just another bout with an asshole violet, his term for a violator.

"You found the guy dead?" the judge asked Pyykkonen.

"In his car down to the fish house in Hancock, eh," she said. "The M.E. thinks it could be cyanide."

"Poison," Pavelich said. "The tool of chickenshits." The judge ran his hand through his thick hair and rolled his shoulders. "Guess I'll be getting on."

He left without further comment.

Before Pyykkonen could open the door, a Houghton County patrol car pulled into the driveway. COMMAND was painted in gold script on the door by the driver's side. A red Jeep Liberty pulled up behind the squad car.

"Sheriff Macofome," the detective said to the approaching officer, who was short, squat, neckless, and hatless, his hair trimmed in a military whitewall.

"Thought I'd see if I could lend a hand," Houghton's new sheriff said. He had been appointed a couple of months before, replacing the chief who had held the job for nearly fifteen years before he died suddenly of a heart attack. The way Macofome looked at Pyykkonen made Service wonder if his helpfulness was something more than professional. Not his business, but she clearly had been rescued from school liaison to get the homicide job.

The man behind the sheriff looked antsy. "I'm Adams," he said. He was of medium height and balding, with a shape that suggested he spent too much time behind a desk.

"Harry Pung works for me. I got a call that I might be needed here. Is something wrong?"

Service thought of correcting the tense, but kept his mouth shut.

"Is it doctor or professor?" Pyykkonen asked, impressing Service with her political savvy.

"This ain't MIT. Call me Steve."

"Steve," Pyykkonen said tentatively, "I'm sorry to be the one to tell you, but Pung Juju Kang was found dead this morning." Adams stared disbelieving at the detective. "Is he married?" she asked.

"Was," Adams said. "The ex lives downstate somewhere, Detroit, I think."

"You called him Harry Pung," Service said, confused by the name. "His ID says Kang."

"Standard Korean naming convention," Adams said. "The family name is always listed first. He adopted the American name when he moved to this country. What happened to Harry?"

"We're looking into that," Pyykkonen said, offering nothing specific. "How was his health?"

"Harry? Fine; ya know, like the rest of us. We could all lose a little weight, eat better."

"History of heart problems, anything like that?"

Adams said, "He hunted and fished and hiked a lot. He was a tad overweight, but he seemed to be in good enough shape."

"What was his reputation up to the college?" Pyykkonen asked.

Adams contemplated the question. "Harry isn't one to make a good first impression. He's a bit gruff and direct, but when you get to know him, he's fine. First week of classes I had students bitching, but then they settled in and his student evaluations were excellent. He worked the kids hard. In Korea, it was tough to get slots in good schools and Harry thought students here ought to be as serious about their work."

"His colleagues like him?"

"Harry pretty much sticks to himself. He serves on department committees and does solid work. People think he's a bit eccentric, but hell, that's almost a badge of honor in academia."

"What did he hunt?" Service asked. Adams was still in present tense, had not processed the reality of Pung's death.

Adams shrugged. "Beats me. Lots of hunters and fishermen on the faculty, but Harry pretty much does his own thing."

"You said he was divorced?" Pyykkonen asked.

"Before he came here," Adams said.

"When was that?" Pyykkonen said.

"A year ago this month."

"From where?"

"Virginia Tech. He was a real catch for us. He has an international reputation in structural materials."

"Like cement?" Pyykkonen asked.

Adams showed a hint of academic superiority. "He's working on heat-resistant materials to be used for heat-shielding in high-speed aircraft."

"Government contracts?"

"No, but they're most certainly in the offing. His work is just getting recognized by the Department of Defense. His work to date has been more involved with the chemistry than applications, but he was moving into applications."

"Sounds like a smart guy," Pyykkonen said.

"He was," Adams said after a pause.

"He have kids?"

Adams again pondered the question. "One son I know of: Tunhow. He was a student here last year, but transferred to U of M this fall."

"The son have problems here?" Pyykkonen asked.

"Not book-wise. The boy made dean's list both semesters. Came in with great credentials."

"Engineering?"

"Zoology," Adams said, glancing at his watch.

Service said, "You said no problems book-wise. Were there other kinds of problems?"

"Standard stuff—booze in his dorm room, fake ID—nothing major. The kids here hit the books hard and the competition is tough. Some students play hard to offset the pressure. Is there anything else?"

"No, sir," Pyykkonen said. "We appreciate your help."

"You need anything else, you be sure to give a shout, eh?"

"Yooper?" Pyykkonen asked.

Adams looked embarrassed as he turned back to face her. "Slips out, ya know? Yah sure, born and raised over to Rock."

Pyykkonen's question didn't surprise Service. Yoopers had a tendency to try to identify each other, as if place of birth conferred a certain level of verisimilitude.

When the professor was gone, Pyykkonen and the sheriff exchanged glances. "Not all that broken up," Pyykkonen said.

"Let's get on inside," the chief said.

The foyer was standard western, with a closet and a high ceiling. From the foyer they moved into a long room with a rough-hewn wood floor.

Pyykkonen said to nobody in particular, "Should we take off our shoes?"

"Nobody to bitch if we don't," Chief Macofome said.

The first room was huge, perhaps twenty by forty feet, with a squat black enameled table in the center. The table was surrounded by embroidered black satin pillows. There was a huge digital TV in one corner. No books, no flowers. The ceiling was covered with jade green colored paper. There was a sliding glass door at the end of the room, looking out on a garden that seemed to be a collection of small twisted trees, plots of raked sand, and boulders of various sizes, shapes, and colors. The base of the walls on both sides of the room were lined with low chests of drawers. Some of the chests had pillows on them.

"Not my idea of cozy," Service said, the barren interior reminding him vaguely of how he had lived in his own place before he had fallen in love with Maridly Nantz and moved in with her. Nantz had brought a distinctly positive change to his life. What effect his son would have remained up for grabs.

There was a bedroom that was barren except for a wide low bed with nightstands and bulbous brown lamps on them. The bed was centered on a mat that looked to Service like varnished paper. Behind the bed there was a large, stark painting of a creature that had a lion's mane and a longish snout, like a combination of a lion and wolf, but it was not so much a wolf as something else, which Service couldn't place. He studied the painting for a few moments and gave up. As in the main room, there were cumbersome wooden chests along one wall.

"Homey," Pyykkonen said, wrinkling her nose.

Service was disturbed by the place. He'd always prided himself on not accumulating stuff when he lived in his cabin on Slippery Creek, but this looked barren and sterile, and he wondered if this was what people had seen when they came to his cabin. It was not a reassuring thought. There was nothing here but bare necessities—no personality, no decorations, no joy—just that peculiar painting.

The kitchen was small and equipped with all the conveniences, but it was so clean that it looked hardly used. Like the rest of the house it was virtually empty save a package of chocolate-covered figs and an untouched six-pack of OB Lager Beer in the fridge. Service looked at the bottles with the blue labels: Bottled by Oriental Brewery Co. Ltd. Seoul, Korea. "Never seen this brand before," he said.

The figs were in separate compartments like chocolates, and three compartments were empty. The fruits were each wrapped in gold foil.

She said, "Tough to be overweight when there's no food."

"Maybe he ate out a lot," Service said. The idea of a steady diet of restaurant food turned his stomach. He might not be adept at much, he told himself, but he knew good food and put a high value on it. Cooking was a way to lose himself in something that didn't involve work and carried an immediate payoff.

The other two ground-floor rooms were empty, though one of them had some scrapes on the floor, suggesting recent use; perhaps the son moving out? But hadn't the dead man's son lived in the dorm? Not your business, he reminded himself.

"See anything interesting?" Pyykkonen asked.

"One thing bugs me," Service said. "He's supposed to be an avid hunter and fisherman. Where's his gear?" Outdoor enthusiasts were rarely far from their equipment.

The homicide detective shrugged.

Macofome came up from the basement, shaking his head. "Better take a look."

Service and Pyykkonen followed him down the steep steps and found the basement empty except for a large cement statue. It was the same ugly animal as depicted in the bedroom painting.

"Lion built by committee," Pyykkonen joked.

Service nodded, but he had lost interest in the statue and painting as he pondered why there were no guns or fishing tackle in the house.

Pyykkonen looked over his shoulder. "If he had a bear in here at least it didn't shit," she said. Then she sniffed the air. "Ammonia. Somebody did some heavy duty cleaning down here."

"The whole place looks too clean," Macofome said. "Sterile."

"Well," Pyykkonen said, "We've had our walk-through. It's time to go over the place inch by inch and get photos."

"Nothing more here for me," Service said. "If you don't mind I think I'll shove off."

"Good idea," Macofome said, breaking a smile. "Thanks for the help."

"Gus will give you a call when the lab results are back," Service told Pyykkonen, who followed him upstairs.

"Thanks," Pyykkonen said at the front door.

Gus Turnage was one of Grady Service's best friends. An elf of a man with the shoulders and arms of a blacksmith, Turnage had once been voted CO of the Year in Michigan and nationally in the same year, but had shrugged off the honors. He was also the longtime scoutmaster of a troop that won national recognition every year, but you would never hear this from him. Gus's wife, Pracie, had died in a head-on collision with a logging truck almost ten years ago, and he had raised three sons on his own. All of them were away at college now and Gus was alone. He and Service had become COs the same year, and over the past twenty years their paths had crossed continuously. They'd had a lot of fun together, and both knew they could rely entirely on the other in a tough spot.

Gus lived east of Houghton, not far from their friend Yalmer "Shark" Wetelainen, who managed the Yooper Court Motel and spent the bulk of his time tying flies and reloading shotgun shells for his two passions in life. Shark was forty, short and thin, and partial to beer and any and all food. Despite copious drinking, neither Gus nor Grady had ever seen their friend drunk, and once, in disbelief, they had administered a Breathalyzer only to find that he barely registered a blood-alcohol level. They decided there and then that he had the metabolic system of a shark and the name stuck.

Since Pracie Turnage's death, Shark was at the house as often as at his own place in the motel, and this morning was no different. His beat-up pickup was parked at the end of the driveway and one of his scrawny bird dogs was stretched out on the porch working over a bone.

"Just in time for breakfast, babe," Maridly Nantz said when Service walked into the kitchen. Shark had a leaning tower of flapjacks on a plate and a stack of toast in front of him. Gus was sitting at the table looking pale, but grinning. Walter was at the counter, manning the toaster. He did not acknowledge his father's arrival.

"Big night?" Nantz asked, giving Service a lingering hug.

"Found some shit," Service said.

"Normal night," Gus said, grinning.

"Bear shit in a Saturn," Service said.

"*In* the car?" Shark asked.

"Backseat."

"There's a story begging to get told," Gus said wryly.

"You get to tell it," Service said sarcastically, putting the plastic bag with the bear scat in the refrigerator. "I'll send the bag to Rose Lake for you. When the report comes back, it's all yours."

"The work of a game warden," Gus said. "Pracie would've hit the roof if I dumped shit in the fridge."

"She'd have had a right to," Nantz said.

"You sleep all right?" Service asked his friend.

"Your woman was at my bedside all night," Gus said with a mock frown.

"Easy boys," Nantz said, setting down a cup of black coffee for Service. "Lorelei called early this morning," she said.

State Senator Lorelei Timms was running for governor against Sam Bozian's handpicked toady and surprising everyone by suddenly jumping up in the polls to pull even with the three-term governor's anointee. "She got a problem?"

"Of sorts. She wants me to fly for her," Nantz said.

"Not sure that's a good idea," Service said.

"Me either, but I'll make a good decision." She kneaded the small of his back.

"Sounds cool to me," Walter said, placing a dish stacked with toast on the table and sitting down.

"Thanks for the support," Nantz said.

"This isn't your business," Service said, immediately sorry that the words had slipped out.

Walter rolled his eyes, took a piece of toast, and grabbed for the butter.

Nantz shot a surreptitious scowl at Grady.

Service had met the aspiring governor last fall during a particularly nasty sequence of events in which two men and a bear died on a highway near Seney. Lorelei Timms had been taken by his actions at the accident scene and had been singing his praises publicly every since, a situation that made him grind his teeth every time another CO teased him about it. She had also become a constant phone pal, calling to ask him about the minutiae of fish and game management and trying to get him to act as her inside informer in the DNR. So far he had refused to help her, but this hadn't stopped her from calling, or dropping by every time she was in the U.P. on her way to her place at the exclusive Huron Mountain Club north of Marquette. He didn't dislike the senator. In fact, he liked her, but he didn't have time to hold her hand and get himself sucked into a political vortex. He had experienced two run-ins with Sam Bozian, both of which had nearly cost him his job and career. In fact, just before his unexpected and unwanted promotion to detective last summer, he had been suspended without pay for two months—on direct orders from Governor Bozian. As far as he was concerned, he never wanted to be close to anyone whose job rested on the gullibility of a bunch of uninformed fools.

"Lorne called and said he thought it might be a good idea," Nantz said.

Lorne O'Driscoll was the DNR's chief of law enforcement, the state's top woods cop. Last fall Nantz had begun training as a conservation officer and was at the top of her class when she was pulled out and thrown into a post-September 11 task force in Lansing that never materialized. While living at a motel she had been viciously attacked by a man, and the chief and his wife had taken her into their home to help her convalesce. She was scheduled to restart the DNR academy again in November, and since healing from her injuries had been a part-time con- · tract pilot for the department in the Upper Peninsula.

"You mean the *chief* called," Service said. O'Driscoll had backed him up in some important ways over the past two years and had proven to be the best chief in Service's twenty years, but like most COs he didn't care for Lansing and felt the further away he stayed, the better it was for everyone. Nantz loved to call the chief by his first name, knowing that Service found it grating.

"Lorne said to say hi. He thinks it won't hurt to have one of us with the senator."

"That's political espionage."

Nantz laughed. "Don't be paranoid. It's not healthy."

Service sampled his coffee. "Paranoia I can handle. It's help from Lansing that creeps me out."

Nantz shook her head. "The great Grady Service, afraid?"

Gus and Shark laughed as he turned red and changed the subject, relating what he had seen during the night and what promises he had made in Gus's behalf.

"Macofome show up?" Gus asked. "He's always around Pyykkonen."

Shark grinned and held up a forearm. "Boom-boom," he said. "It's all over town."

"She seems to know her job," Service said, noticing that Walter was listening carefully, taking it all in.

"No question, but you know how things can be up here, eh. The local cop house don't see a lot of serious shit, so gossip falls like January snow."

Just before Service, Walter, and Nantz got ready to leave, Gus got a phone call. He nodded at the phone and handed it to Service.

"Bearclaw." Betty "Bearclaw" Very was the CO stationed in Ontonagon.

"Hey," Sevice said.

"Think you could make a run down this way?"

"I really need to make a stop at Tech and get back to Marquette tonight."

"I think you'll want to see this," Very said. "Last night I was out by the West Branch of the Firesteel River and I found an old guy wandering around. He's blind, got only one leg, and insists he knows you. He calls himself Trapper Jet."

"He smell like fermented skunk?"

"That would be him."

"I know him," Service said. "How the hell did the old coot get way up there? His place is a hundred and twenty miles away."

"Not much of a talker," Very said. "Announced he wants to see you, end of conversation. I've got him at my place."

"What the hell was he doing?"

"He acted lost. I was out checking bear movement, fruit crops, old baiting sites, and such, and there he was. He seemed pissed that I showed up. I brought him to my place, but he clammed up on me."

"Nantz and I are rolling. It'll take us about ninety minutes, give or take." Trapper Jet might be blind, but it was not possible he was lost. The old bastard was in his late seventies, and had lived alone in a shack in northern Iron County since the mid-1950s. He looked and smelled like he was at death's door, but the old trapper could be the poster boy for self-reliance.

When they got to McInnes Arena, Walter announced that Coach Blanck wanted to see Service.

"*Blanck?*"

"He's one of the assistants."

The name jarred Service.

Following his son, they made their way to the coaching offices and there he saw the man who had been the reason for his decision to not pursue professional hockey. Toby Blanck was older, but looked fit. The last time he had seen Blanck he was being carried off the ice bleeding profusely, his skull fractured. Blanck had been critical for a week before pulling through.

When Blanck looked, up a huge smile spread across his face as he stood up and extended his hand. "Geez, Banger himself."

Service had no idea what to say. He had once nearly killed the man.

Blanck's voice was warm and inviting. "Hey, that stuff way back when? No hard feelings, Grady. It was just hockey, eh?"

Service nodded dumbly.

"So *you're* Walter's dad?"

Another dumb nod.

"You and Walter have a chance to talk?"

"I was out on a call all night," Service said.

"Yeah, woods cop; good for you, but I wouldn't want your job. You were a cop on the ice and you're still one, eh? I admire that. Listen, Walter and I had a candid talk about his future here."

Grady Service had no idea where this was going.

"You want me to leave?" the boy asked the coach.

"No, I'm not gonna say anything to your dad I haven't already said to you."

Service felt trapped and not sure why he was feeling so.

"Have a seat," Blanck said.

Service sat, staring across the desk at the man he had nearly killed in his final collegiate hockey game.

"We had Walter on skates," Blanck said. "Our doc cleared him. We're impressed as hell, eh? But his age is a concern. He's just sixteen. College players are older than juniors and there're academics to consider. This is a tough school and jocks don't get cut a lot of slack. We think it would be in Walter's best interests to redshirt him this year. He can skate with the team, but no games to preserve his eligibility and he won't be traveling with the club, so he can use that time to pound the books. We'll give him a full ride next year, so no money worries. This year we'll let him get settled in. He got his GED, and he scored out of sight on the ACT, but he hasn't been in a classroom for two years. We think it will be good for him to get that part of his college life well under control. Truth is, as soon as the scouts see him, he's gonna get drafted, and if he performs like we think he will, the offers and pressures will start coming. It's not like when we were playing, Banger. The NHL's expanded so much that they are desperately looking for talent and pushing hard to get players into the fold as early as possible. There's one other thing. Coach Forrester is going to retire at the end of this season and I've been offered his job. If Walter redshirts, we can start out together."

Service was at a loss for words. The man he had nearly killed was now coaching the son he never knew he had.

Service looked at his son. "How do you feel about this?"

Blanck spoke for the boy. "Walter said you're his dad and it's your decision."

"It's Walter's game and he's the student. It's *his* decision."

Walter said nothing and Service got the impression that he was being set up, but he couldn't imagine how or why. "Does he need to make a decision today?"

"Not till the players officially report later this month."

Service stood and reached across the desk to shake Toby Blanck's hand. "I'm glad you're here," he said, meaning alive, not necessarily as a coach.

"Me, too, and we'll be really glad to have your son here."

On the way out of the arena with his son beside him, someone shouted. Service turned to find Dr. Kermit "Rocky" Lemich, a former hockey player and now a professor at the university. Last fall Lemich had helped him solve a difficult case.

"Hey, Banger. Your kid's enrolled, eh?"

Service nodded. "Thinking about it."

"Listen, you bugger, you promised you'd get involved with kids and do some coaching, but you haven't, so I took the liberty of talking to Walter and Coach Blanck. He's gonna help me coach a bantam team when he's not practicing with the Huskies. It'll do him good, and one way or the other I'll be getting your family back into the game." Lemich laughed, pivoted, and walked away whistling.

"He's crazy," Walter said. "In a good way."

"Goaler," Service said, drawing a chuckle from his son. "Why do you want me to make the decision?"

"You're supposed to be my father. Aren't you up to it?"

"That's not the point."

"Isn't it? You invited me into your life, so I figure if you're my dad, you should do your job."

"How do you feel about redshirting?"

"I don't like it, but it makes sense and I like Blanck. Did you really beat him up?"

"That was a long time ago."

"He said you were a great player."

"I've got to get moving," Service told his son.

"You'll pick me up tonight?"

"We'll be here."

Nantz was sitting in the truck. Service got into the driver's seat and Walter stood by Nantz's window. "See you tonight," he said.

"We're late," Service said, putting the truck into gear and pulling away.

"That was abrupt," Nantz said.

"I told Bearclaw ninety minutes."

"Family comes first," Nantz said. "The job will always be there."

Her tone was so soft that he wasn't sure he had just been chastised. "You ever feel like you're in the Twilight Zone?" he asked her.

"Every day—with you, Service."

· 2 ·

"You look like you swallowed a bucket of lemon drops," Nantz said as Service raced south on the two-lane M-26.

"I don't understand him," he said.

"You mean your son. His name is Walter," she said.

"He told me the assistant coach wanted to see me, so I walked in to find a guy I nearly killed back in college. He's going to take the head coaching job next season and he wants to redshirt the boy so he can get his academics in order. The boy hasn't been in class for two years."

"Walter, not 'the boy.' What's your objection?"

"They want me to make the decision."

"So make it."

"It's the boy's decision."

"You make decisions for others all the time."

"I won't make this one for him."

"You're not being rational, Service."

"First the kid tells me I'm not his father and now he tells me to act like his father. What the hell does he want?"

"Jesus, Grady. He's sixteen. He lost his mom last year. He's got a step-father who doesn't give a shit about him. He wants what we all want. He wants stability and he wants to be wanted. This isn't rocket science."

"So he dumps the decision on me to test me?"

She raised an eyebrow. "Exactly."

"You think this is all right?"

"Jesus, Grady. Stop whining. Walter can't come right out and ask you to be his dad because he's afraid of being rejected, so he gives you a little test to see how you handle it. Didn't you test your own father?"

"*Nobody* tested my old man—not if they wanted to still have their head attached."

She smiled. "Well, I don't think Walter is looking to get the shit kicked out of him as a sign of affection, though with you men it's often hard to tell," she said.

"What's that mean?"

"It means that men get bent out of shape over the oddest things."

Service began to grind his teeth and stopped talking.

"What exactly does Betty want?" she asked after a suitable pause to let him calm down.

"She found an old guy last night. He's more than a hundred miles from home."

"So are we," she said, grinning.

"It's not a joke. He's blind and got one leg. Everybody calls him Trapper Jet, but his name is Ollie Toogood. He was a pilot in Korea, shot down, a prisoner for two years. He came back to the U.P. after the VA cut him loose and he's been here ever since. My old man used to take me to visit him. He makes his living off a small pension and trapping. Been up on Mitigwaki Creek since the late 1950s."

"Violet?" Nantz asked.

"He feeds bears year-round and rumor is that he lets people come in and pop the bigger ones for a fee."

"You've investigated?"

"It's only rumor about the fee, but it's a fact that he feeds bears. I've seen as many as a dozen around his shack at one time. I think every bear biologist in the state has been to see him at one time or another. Great chance to study the animals, and in the shape Jet's in, it doesn't hurt to have people out there from time to time. He's never applied for a bear permit."

"So we're rushing to his rescue."

"His and Betty's. The two of them are likely to tangle before too long. If Blanck hadn't been in such a yank to talk, we'd almost be there."

"Relax. An extra hour won't make a difference."

"I know, but since Joe died last year, I've been feeling like there's more I could have done to look after him." Joe Flap was a longtime DNR pilot who had lost his FAA license but continued to fly. During his career he had been in so many accidents that his nickname was Pranger. Last fall his luck had run out and so had his gas, and he had died in a crash near Escanaba. Service had found him and called for help, but his old friend hadn't made it. He had felt remorse ever since.

"We all die," Nantz said. "You can't save everybody, Grady."

"I can try," Service said.

"Not everybody wants to be saved."

"Horseshit," he said.

Nantz laughed. "Whenever you get into a discussion you don't want to have, you always say 'horseshit.' "

"Horseshit," he repeated. She rubbed his arm, leaned over, and kissed him on the shoulder.

"When you get old and frail, I'll save you," she said.

"Horseshit," he said.

"Really," she said, "it only seems like there's suddenly so many things to think about, but Jesus, Grady, you live in perpetual chaos. What's different about this—that it's not job-related? That you have a son to think about and now maybe you are thinking about this old guy, too?"

"Something like that."

"Well, I guess that makes me part of the trinity of burden."

"You're not a burden."

"No, but we have responsibility for each other, so that puts me over on that side of the scale."

"Goddammit, don't twist everything around," he snapped.

"I don't have to twist anything. I just let you spit them out and spin until they choke you."

Another period of silence ensued.

"You want to save the old man," she said, "and I wouldn't want to interfere with noble ambitions."

"Because they're so rare?"

"I'll take the fifth on that," she said with a coquettish smile. "Seriously, what would he be doing so far north?"

He looked over at her. Even after their fourteen months together, he still found himself watching her. Her long neck had a bit of a curve, which she didn't like, and her lips, according to her, were too thin. Sometimes she was merciless in self-appraisals, withholding credit where it was obviously due. Like her blue eyes that had a range of intensity equal to an industrial laser (too big, they bulge like a bug). She constantly fretted about her hair (too fine and did it seem to him that it might be thinning? It had happened to her mother), her legs (all thigh, calves too damned thin), her fingernails (why couldn't she stop chewing them?), her feet (like a damn duck's). The list was endless and he had learned to simply listen, understanding that she was venting feelings, not looking for his ham-handed attempts at making her feel better.

Sometimes he tried to look at her objectively, but such efforts invariably failed and he always reached the same conclusion: The sum of her was bigger than the parts and she was the most beautiful and interesting woman he had ever known. What he loved most was that she was alive, engaged in life, willing to stick her nose wherever curiosity led and to hell with consequences.

"With Jet, you can't tell," Service said. His father had always said that there was some deep secret in the trapper's life and that it had been this that sent him into the backcountry to live alone. "When I took over my old man's territory, I inherited Ollie Toogood." Service's father had been a conservation officer before him, and by chance Service had ended up standing guard over the same area that his father had taken care of for so long.

"He's nowhere near your territory," she said. "And?"

"His story checked out. He had a nasty war. Air Force jock. He got the Silver Star, two Distinguished Flying Crosses, a passel of Air Medals, and a Purple Heart. The Silver Star was awarded for his behavior as a prisoner of war. He was an example to others and frustrated the hell out of the North Koreans."

"Maybe he got tired of serving as a good example," Nantz said.

"Who knows? He's a strange old bird, but he knows bears and trapping better than any man I ever met. Maybe he signed off to get a break from people, got set in his ways, and couldn't find his way back."

"Like you?" she said.

Service shot her a look. "We're not talking about me."

"It will be a pleasure to meet your friend," she said with her customary optimism.

"It will be something," Service said, "but I doubt pleasure is the right word."

Betty Very owned a small farm south of Rockland, on the precipitous banks of the Ontonagon River. Pure copper had been discovered in the craggy hills around 1840, and fifty years later the population was a thousand souls, complete with Michigan's first and then only telephone system. A fire before the turn of the twentieth century had been a major setback, but the decision by copper mining companies to abandon the area and push west was even bigger, and brought the town's death knell. Now there were fewer than two hundred people in the village and land was so cheap that one local bought an entire city block just to grow flowers.

Service considered many of the residents to be of the artsy-fartsy persuasion, most of whom spent summers on the Rock and fled at the first burp of winter. Service thought of them as aging hippies who were time-trapped in the sixties. With only two bars in town the only persistent problem for local law officers were bush dope farms, and even these seemed to be on the decline.

Bearclaw dealt with more problem bears than any other CO in the state and had the scars to prove it. She was forty and lived alone on the old farm with a menagerie of goats, sheep, llamas, dogs, and cats. When she retired she planned to open an animal rehab sanctuary.

There was a small brick house in disrepair and a new pole barn gleaming beside an older wooden one that leaned precariously toward forty-five degrees. One of these winters it would finish falling.

Very came out to greet Service and Nantz. She was in civvies and did not look happy.

"The sooner you get that sonuvabitch out of here, the more likely he is to keep living," she said loudly enough for it to be heard a hundred yards away. She gestured toward the old barn, making a chopping motion of her hand.

"What's the deal?" Service asked.

"I was scouting and I ran across him. He was sitting on a blow-down not far from the river."

"Did he seem disoriented?"

"Nope, just irritated. I could see he was blind and there was nobody around and we were a mile from the road, so I told him I'd help him out, but he didn't want to come. I wasn't about to leave him. He wouldn't say why he was there alone or how he got there, so I dragged him out and he demanded to talk to you."

"I'll take care of it," Service said.

"You know him?"

Service nodded. "He lives in north Iron County. My old man used to take me to see him and now and then I stop by to see how he's getting on."

"What's he do?"

"Used to trap. Mostly he just doesn't like human company."

"Is he the one who baits in bears for biologists to study?"

"He baits them in because it pleases him. Doing something for others isn't part of his modus operandi. Jet is for Jet, period."

"The smell of him's enough to make a vulture trombone," she said, wrinkling her nose.

Which explained why she had him in the old barn. Betty Very was one of the most polite and considerate officers he had ever met, able to accept people for who and what they were, but she was also a believer in cleanliness and the old man would never meet her standards along those lines.

"I smelt youse comin'," Trapper Jet rasped when Service stepped past a door hanging from a rusty hinge. The old man was wearing faded, tattered brown Carharts. The stench radiating from him almost made Service retch.

"You got coose with you," the old man warbled before Service could speak.

Maridly stepped in beside Service. "I'm Nantz," she said.

"How do," the trapper said. "Got the curse, have ya? Smelt blood soon as youse gotten outten da truck."

Nantz stared at him. "You like to shock people, do you?"

"I'm thinkin' youse ain't of a kind to shock," the old man said with a mischievous chuckle.

"You wanted to see me, Jet?" Service asked.

"You, not the coose."

Nantz stuck out her jaw. "I have a coose, but I am not *the* coose. Nor am I *his* coose."

"Got a mouth on her," Trapper Jet said.

Nantz parried, "I can't figure how'd you'd trap anything smarter than a spruce grouse." A spruce grouse was generally considered the dumbest animal in the forest, a fact attested to by how few remained.

Trapper Jet stared up at her through darkened eyes and grinned. "Coose with fire," he said, shaking with silent mirth. "I didn't think it possible."

"You'd have to double your smarts just to be stupid—" Nantz started.

"Stop!" Service said, raising his hands. "Jet, what the hell are you doing here and what do you want?"

"You could start with givin' me a lift back to my place."

"That's not exactly on our way."

"You think my being up here is on my way?"

"Why *are* you here?"

"Got no idea."

"Why'd you call me?"

"Who else I'm gonna call, eh?"

The trapper obviously wasn't ready to talk. They loaded him in the truck, rolled the windows down, got a smile of relief from Betty Very, and headed out.

They saw smoke when they were a half-mile from the trapper's cabin on Mitigwaki Creek, a three-mile-long ribbon of water that connected Mitigwaki and Paint Lakes.

Service spied the smoke and seconds later the old trapper announced, "Somepin's burnin'." The something was Trapper Jet's cabin.

"Dowdy Kitella," the trapper said with a snarl when they got out of the Yukon.

Service knew Kitella. He was a bear dog outfitter out of Trout Creek with more run-ins with the law than Service cared to count. Kitella was an officer in a national group that promoted bear hunting with hounds, and the sort of man who didn't care to share. If other guides set up too close to the imaginary lines that defined his hunting territories, he poured gasoline on their baits and sand patches. Guides spread sand on bear trails and smoothed the patches in order to see if animals were coming to their baits. The scent of gasoline and other chemicals pushed bears away. Kitella was known to be ruthless and equally difficult to catch. Most of Kitella's arrests had come on domestic violence charges, but not once had a spouse or girlfriend pressed charges.

Once Service had read an arrest report where Kitella told the arresting officer that women were like dogs and had to be trained; if you went too easy on them, they'd never do their jobs. That time he'd broken several of a girlfriend's ribs.

"You think Kitella did this?"

"It's him," Trapper Jet said.

"Why?"

"People like him got their own ideas."

"What the hell does that mean?"

"I guess he don't want me here."

"You tinker with his baits, maybe?"

"I don't hunt bruins," the trapper said. "I entertain 'em. Besides— illegal to have baits out right now, am I right?"

"Maybe you encouraged some animals away from him?"

"Free country. Bears and people both got the right to choose, eh?"

"Maybe you'd better talk to me about this, Jet."

"No time to yap. Gotta rebuild."

"Alone?"

"Hell, I built her alone. I can rebuild her."

"Blind?"

The old man shrugged and grimaced. "Don't do no good to whine when you gotta eat shit sandwiches. Out here you work or you don't make it."

"What were you doing up on the Firesteel?"

The old man opened the door to the truck and got out. "Time I got to work."

Service grabbed his arm. "Do you have a problem, Jet?"

The old man sneered and pulled loose. "Bein' alive is the problem. I can take care of myself."

"You're welcome for the lift," Service said.

The old man didn't bother to approach the smoldering ruins. He walked straight into a cedar swamp and disappeared.

"You're going to let him stomp off into the bush alone?" Nantz asked.

"He's not totally blind," Service said.

"What?"

"I watched him. He plays at blind, but I saw his hands moving when we approached turns. I baited him by making him think I was going the wrong way. He didn't say anything, but he moved his hand or leaned in the direction he wanted to go. Maybe it's unconscious, but I'm sure he can see something and he's clammed up over why he was up on the Firesteel."

"Who is this Dowdy Kitella?"

Service shook his head. "Bad as they come."

"Worse than Limpy?" she asked.

Limpy Allerdyce was the leader of a tribe of poachers, mostly his relations, who lived like animals in the far southwest reaches of Marquette County. Limpy's crowd had been known to kill bears and sell gallbladders and footpads to Korean brokers in Los Angeles for shipment to the Far East, where such things sold for prices most people would have trouble comprehending. Allerdyce and his clan killed dozens of deer, took thousands of fish, and got substantial money for their efforts from buyers in Chicago and Detroit. Despite their income, the clan lived like savages. Service had put the leader of the clan in prison for seven years and since his release last summer, Allerdyce had become a strange breed of informer for him, claiming that he had done the same for Service's father.

"Not exactly worse than Limpy," Service said. "More like a competitor."

Service picked up his cell phone and punched in the number of CO Simon del Olmo, who lived in Crystal Falls. Simon had been a CO for five years now, and they had become pals over the past year. Like Gus, he was an officer who could be relied upon in any circumstances. The younger officer had been born near Traverse City to Mexican parents, migrant workers who spent summers in Michigan and winters in Texas. Simon had a degree from the University of Michigan and had been in combat with the Air Cav in the Gulf War.

"This is Grady, where are you?"

"Snake Rapids on the Net River. Got tips on some early baits—dirty to boot. Why?"

Dirty baits were those that used illegal materials or illegal amounts, or weren't properly presented. No baits could be out until a certain number of days before the season began. "You know Trapper Jet?"

"Wish I didn't. What's up?"

"His cabin burned down today. Nantz and I are on site now."

"Too bad," del Olmo said sarcastically.

"Bearclaw found him up on the Firesteel last night. Wouldn't say why he was there or how he got there. Nantz and I brought him back and found the fire. Can you get hold of the Troops and get the Arson unit out to the camp?"

"Roger that, but the thing was a firetrap and the old bastard's as stubborn as he is blind. Billy Klesko cuts wood for him sometimes and Jet's always bitching that the stuff's too long and some day there's gonna be a fire."

Klesko was a fish technician out of the Crystal Falls District DNR office. "Soon as we found the fire, Jet started making noises about Dowdy Kitella being responsible. When I tried to question him, he clammed up."

"He still with you?"

"Nope, he limped into the bush, said he's gotta rebuild."

"Crazy bastard," del Olmo said. "Kitella and Jet, there's a combo for you. I'll call Arson and get on up that way to meet them. You check out his dugout camp?"

"What dugout camp?"

"It's on the east side of the high country just east of that little pisshole lake about a half-mile south of his cabin."

"Never knew about that."

"I think it's his hideaway. I found it a couple of years ago when I was running surveillance on some of Kitella's baits. I think I'll check it out after Arson gets through."

"Kitella's baits are close to Jet's places?"

"Damn straight."

"Have there been conflicts?"

"Mostly carping and bitching, but I've always thought that sooner or later those two would tangle and we'd have us a major wreck to deal with."

"Be careful," Service said. His father had once declared when he was drunk that Trapper Jet was potentially the most dangerous man in the Upper Peninsula.

"Hey," del Olmo said, "do I issue a congrats to the new daddy?"

Obviously word was making its way through the force. "The jury's still out. He's sixteen."

The younger officer clucked in sympathy. "You can handle it, *jeffe*."

"Knock off that *jeffe* shit."

"Yes, Detective Dad," del Olmo said.

Service clicked his cell phone closed and stared out the window.

"How's Simon?" Nantz asked.

"Cute," Service said.

"He can't help that," she said, smiling, "though I'd call him drop-dead buff."

"Is everything a joke these days?" he said.

"What joke?" she responded.

They met Walter in front of his dorm. When he slid in beside Nantz, Service said, "You want to go to school here?"

"No problem," Walter said.

"What does no problem mean?" Service asked. "You want to or you don't?"

The boy rolled his eyes and glanced at Nantz. "No problem means no problem. Yes, I want to go to school here."

His father said, "Good. I'll call Blanck tonight and tell him you'll redshirt for the year."

"Don't you think I should have a say in this?"

Service glared over his shoulder at his son. "Today I asked you point blank and you said you didn't like the idea of redshirting, but it made sense and you like Blanck."

"I didn't say I agreed with it."

"Well, you asked me to make the decision and I have, and there it is."

Walter Commando rolled his eyes. "I wanted us to sit down and talk about it."

"When? I had a call to handle."

"No problem. But what about today—like now?"

"Okay, let's talk."

"Forget it," Walter said, "You already made the decision."

"But I haven't told Blanck."

"Your mind is made up. I have better things to do than argue with somebody whose mind is set and who doesn't have any time to talk."

"Don't be an asshole," Service growled.

"Boys," Maridly Nantz said gently.

"I don't need to go back to Gladstone," Walter announced.

"Why, because you're pissed at me?"

"It has nothing to do with you. Classes start tomorrow and I have enough clothes for the week. Let's just grab some dinner. I'll come back to the house next weekend."

"Are you sure you have enough for the week?" Nantz asked.

Walter grinned. "Shorts, T-shirts, flip-flops and socks, light jacket, baseball hat—the off-ice hockey uniform. Can we eat? *Please?*"

Being a father was a lot more difficult than Service had ever imagined. How had Gus raised *three* sons by himself?

They ate dinner at a café called the Steelhead Grille. Walter didn't have much to say and ate fast. Nantz tried to engage him, but was unsuccessful. After dinner they drove him back to the dorm.

"Do we get to see where you live?" Nantz asked.

"No problem," the boy said, leading the way up to his third-floor room.

The dorm was old, the brick face covered with ivy that wasn't quite making it. The room was small, recently painted, fumes lingering. Walter flopped in a chair under the two-by-four loft, his bedspring above him.

"Looks like home," Nantz said.

Walter shrugged and slouched in his chair.

A short boy with wide shoulders and long black hair came into the room carrying a McDonald's bag. He wore a new Tech cap backward.

"S'up, Waterbug?" Walter said. To Nantz, "He's a centericeman."

The boy had a thick mustache that curled down to his jawline. "Halifax DeRoches," the boy said, offering his hand. A gentle grip, nothing to prove. Service liked that. "Hi," the boy added.

A young woman hung back in the doorway, looking awkward.

"Karylanne Pengelly," Waterbug announced, nodding for her to come in.

"Hi," the girl said. She was thin with long, straight black hair. She wore a loose T-shirt, no bra, denim cutoffs with holes, no makeup.

Service saw that she had eyes only for his son.

"Where are you from?" Nantz asked.

"Thunder Bay," the girl said. "Other side of the lake, eh?"

"Engineering?" Nantz asked.

"Zoology." Her eyes were definitely on Walter, not his roommate.

"Well," Service said. "Guess we ought to be going. You sure you've got everything you need?"

"Not a problem," the boy said, glanced at the girl and added, "Yeah."

"Hug," Nantz said, reaching out her arms.

Service watched them embrace. "We'll come get you Friday night."

"Cool by me," Walter said.

Nantz poked Service in the back. He held out his hand. Walter shook it, his grip like a limp fish.

"He's gonna be okay," Nantz said on their way down the stairs.

"No problem," Service said. "What kind of fucking English is that?"

"Nouveau cool," Nantz said. "That girl is gorgeous. They're together. Did you pick up on that?"

Service didn't want to think about it. His first girlfriend in college had been Paige Quatrine, from St. Paul, Minnesota. In those days the university had separate dorms for male and female students. He copped a rink key from an equipment manager and early Sunday mornings used to take Paige to the equipment room, which had a bed and a shower, both of which they used regularly for nearly six months. The relationship never grew. It was strictly about sex and eventually Paige had drifted off with a senior mining student, married him after her freshman year, and moved to Alaska.

"Wouldn't it be something if we just met Walter's future wife?" Nantz said.

"Rein it in," Service said.

That night in their bed Nantz lay with her arms wrapped around his neck, snuggling close. "You did pretty good today," she said.

"He was pissed at me."

"It's just a bump in the road. He's glad you made the decision."

"How could you tell?"

"I just could, and eventually you will too."

"He had already delayed our getting to Betty's. Was I supposed to take him to lunch while we talked?"

"Remember, his mother felt left out by your focus on the job. She probably told him about it, so he's trying to find out where he fits into your priorities."

"At the top," he said.

"Just keep remembering that," she said, giving him a lingering wet kiss and sliding out from under the covers.

"Where are you going?"

"To pull my cork," she said. "I started my period last night."

When she got back under the covers she said, "Now, where were we?"

After making love she went back into the bathroom, brought out a warm washcloth and handed it to him. "It freaked me out, that old man smelling my period."

"He was just playing with your mind."

"I don't think he plays, Grady. He gave me the creeps."

He knew better than to argue with her feelings.

"You want to go again?" she asked.

"No problem," he said, running his hand up her leg.

"You," she said, pressing against him, adding, "I'm not kidding about Trapper Jet, Grady. I don't trust him at all."

· 3 ·

Walter had been at the college three days and had not called home, which bugged Grady Service. He had gone into Gladstone to gas up his truck at the Happy Rock Shell station, and when he pulled into the driveway he saw Maridly Nantz and Nathaniel "She-Guy" Zuiderveen sitting on the back steps, talking animatedly. Their dog, Newf, was pushed up close to the man, demanding noogies. The dog was a female Canary Island mastiff, a breed developed in Spain to protect cattle and known there as *Presa Canario*. She was one hundred thirty pounds and all muscle, but she looked like a lap dog against the man petting her. Zuiderveen was a retired state trooper and three-year offensive tackle for the Miami Dolphins. He was dressed in his signature costume: form-fitting black jumpsuit, above-the-knee black leather boots with three-inch heels (which made him six-foot-nine), gaudy leather Dolphins jacket, and a sequined baseball cap proclaiming PROUD TO BE A SISSY.

"You hitting on my woman, Nathaniel?" Service greeted the man.

Zuiderveen grinned. "I've got enough people wanting to kick my ass."

"With those boots, they'd need a stepladder," Service said. "Is this social or business? I expected you'd be gearing up for the season." Zuiderveen had retired from the state police, begun dressing like a woman, and had become a bear outfitter. People were unsure of his sexuality and called him "She-Guy," but always behind his back. At six-foot-six and two-fifty, he was an imposing figure with a legendary temper and strength to match. Despite his eccentricities he was considered one of the top guides in the Upper Peninsula, booked two years in advance. Grady Service had known him for ten years.

"How's the season shaping up?" Service asked.

Zuiderveen shrugged and moved his hand away from Newf, who immediately poked his hand with her massive snout, demanding continued attention. "Probably be okay," the bear guide said.

Nantz went inside and came back with two beers. "You boys want to move inside?"

"Outside's fine," Zuiderveen said.

"Too chilly for me," Nantz countered.

"Mind over matter," Zuiderveen said. "And warm duds."

The retired Troop took a long pull on his beer and belched quietly. He was usually ebullient, the center of any gathering, but today he seemed pensive.

"Everything okay?" Service asked.

"If you don't count the fact they don't make pantyhose in my size and that some scum-fuck is stealing bears, things are just peachy."

"I don't care about your pantyhose problems. What about the bears?"

"You didn't hear about Bearclaw?"

"We saw her last weekend. What about her?"

"She had a culvert trap out for a troublemaker over by Victoria and found it empty."

"Traps are empty more than filled," Service said.

"There had been a bear in this one, only it was open and gone when Betty got to it."

"When was this?"

"Monday night. An old boar has been marauding camps. She wanted to trap and move him."

"She didn't report it."

"I was with her," Zuiderveen said. "She thinks it just got out."

"But you think differently."

"No evidence," the big man said, tapping his nose. "Just this."

"You know how smart bears are. Some of them just can't be trapped. Why tell me?"

"You're the guy-in-a-tie, and you know damn well that no bear is smart enough to get out of a culvert set once it's inside." Guys-in-ties was the sometime term for detectives.

"I don't hear anything to detect." Bearclaw was the best when it came to trapping black bears.

"This isn't the first culvert trap to be sprung," Zuiderveen said.

"Yeah?"

"No shit, yeah."

"What about others?"

Zuiderveen grunted and chugged the remainder of his beer. "I've said my piece."

Service understood. Bear guides were highly competitive and some—like She-Guy and Griff Stinson out of McMillan—were fanatics about following the rules. Other guides were not, especially once the season began for running bears with dogs. But even Zuiderveen and Stinson wouldn't rat on other guides. It was part of the strange code of the often zany outfitters. "Griff have similar suspicions?"

"Could be," She-Guy said.

"What about Dowdy Kitella?"

"Fuck that little psychotic piece of shit," Zuiderveen said, spitting out the name like it was poison. "He ever touches my baits, he'll end up as bait."

It was not a threat Service took seriously. For all his reputation, She-Guy was essentially a gentle giant who loved to hunt bears. "Thanks for dropping by," Service said. "I'll give Bearclaw a call, see what she has to say."

"Push 'er a bit," Zuiderveen said. "She doesn't think it's a big deal."

"I'll remember that," Service said, watching the giant amble to his truck and back out of the driveway.

Early the next morning Service and Nantz were in the garage doing their morning weight regimen. "Do you think Nathaniel is on to something?" she asked as he spotted for her.

"Maybe. He had to be pretty worked up to come all the way over here from Baraga."

"If a bear gets into a trap and it's faulty, it can get out, right?"

"Sure, if it was faulty, but Betty doesn't use faulty traps. She's the best at using culverts and she's got a whole range of baits. She wanted to, she could go into business making them. If an animal was in her trap it's not likely it got out because the trap failed."

Service left her doing push-ups and sit-ups and went up to the bathroom to shower. When he came back down she was still at it.

Nantz followed him out to the truck and gave him a kiss.

She kissed him again. "See you tonight, babe."

"Count on it."

The office was fifty miles north of Gladstone, just outside Marquette, and Service found Captain Ware Grant staring north out at Lake Superior when he knocked on the doorjamb and stepped into his boss's office. Grant was the senior law enforcement officer for the Department of Natural Resources in the Upper Peninsula. "You wanted to see me, Captain?"

"Yes, thank you."

Service pulled out a chair at the captain's small round conference table and sat.

"That body of the Tech professor?" The captain began.

Service nodded. Why was the captain bringing this up?

"The preliminary shows evidence of a large dose of cyanide in the victim's blood. The medical examiner has ruled it a homicide, but they are not releasing this to the media yet."

Service knew that homicides were not the responsibility of DNR law enforcement. He also knew better than to try to guess where the captain's peculiar mind was taking him.

"You saw a package of chocolate-covered figs in the refrigerator at the victim's home? Some of them were laced with cyanide."

"Figs," Service said. "Not your usual murder weapon."

"It's more complex than that. What interests us is that the package containing the figs also contained two freeze-dried bear galls."

"What about the hair samples from the scat?"

"Rose Lake sent them on to Fish and Wildlife Forensics in Oregon."

Fish and Wildlife was the U.S. Fish and Wildlife Service, the federal agency charged with overseeing the nation's fish and game interests. Their forensics laboratory in Oregon was top-notch, but slow in responding to most state requests.

"Why?" Service asked.

"Rose Lake couldn't identify the samples other than to confirm they are ursine."

"This could be a tough one," Service said. There had been bear poachers off and on in the U.P. for years, but they were difficult to nail. "I don't like bringing Fish and Wildlife into this so early."

"We're not. Rose Lake told them the hairs were gathered during a vacation and they wanted ID as a favor. Right now the whole thing is scientist to scientist."

"That will take forever," Service said.

"Once we have more evidence, we can change the nature of the request."

As usual, Captain Grant was thinking ahead.

The captain added, "Officer Turnage asked if you might be available to assist him. The two gallbladders are enough for me to make this your case, but you two can decide how you want to handle it."

"Figs," Service said, shaking his head.

"You understand what the freeze-dried gallbladders signify."

"Yes." It meant poachers. The main markets for bear parts were in Asia. The dead man was Korean and Korea was one of the largest markets. Service wondered if the professor's work gave him access to cyanide.

The captain said, "We're in agreement. If we make a solid case in this arena, it will go a long way toward discouraging similar incursions."

Service understood. Some watchdog groups claimed that global trafficking in animal parts was second only to narcotics in profitability, a fact that seemed to escape the attention of the media or maybe they were as dubious as he was. It was hard to believe that such a market was real and global in nature. "I'll let Gus know I'm on my way."

At the doorway, Service stopped. "The homicide belongs to the police. We're only concerned with the gallbladders." Service had been involved in four murders and a fatal police shooting in less than a year and the captain had reminded him more than once that homicide was outside their brief.

The captain smiled. "Bravo, Detective. Let me know what you fellows find."

Service said, "Cap'n, I heard yesterday that Betty Very thinks somebody released a bear from one of her traps."

"She is studying it," the captain said. "No conclusion has been drawn."

"Have there been other trap incidents?"

"Not that I'm aware of."

"I think I'll give Bearclaw a call."

"Suit yourself," the captain said, snatching a sheaf of reports from his in-basket.

Grady Service fully intended to call on Gus in Houghton and to make contact with Betty Very in Ontonagon, but instead found himself drawn east to the small community of Ridge near Munising, which was forty miles east and out of his way. It was early September with soothing sunny days now and cooling nights. It wouldn't be long before autumn snapped into place and the air took on a bite.

He stopped at the long driveway up to the massive house, took a deep breath, and drove up the half-mile-long paved driveway lined with maple trees. At the end of the driveway there was a loop and a large new house made of cedar logs. The lawn around the house was carefully manicured and cut.

Ralph Scaffidi was in his seventies. He was short and slightly built with silver hair, a deep tan, and alert brown eyes. Before Service could get out of the truck the man was down the steps of the house and grinning.

"Your timing is impeccable," Scaffidi said. "The brookies are in full spawning colors. I was just going out back to the pond to give them a little aerobic exercise. We'll have our espresso down there."

Service didn't object and followed Scaffidi through the cavernous house. The man's background was murky. A year ago Service had met him while he was investigating a case and the old man had taken to him. Rumor had it that he was a retired mobster—perhaps banished to the U.P.—but Tree had done some checking on the man and learned that he was a CPA who had done work for the mob, but was not a made man. At one time Scaffidi had been linked to Jimmy Hoffa's legendary disappearance, but the FBI had never been able to find any evidence and eventually decided that the Mafia family in New Jersey had floated Scaffidi's name as a red herring. The FBI told Tree that Scaffidi had gotten fed up after the New Jersey mob's little game, closed his business and moved to the Upper Peninsula. Still, the old man always had three or four muscular young men around him, presumably his bodyguards.

The word was that Ralph Scaffidi could have been a world-class diplomat. He had a steel-trap mind and the demeanor of Mister Rogers.

Having reached the pond Service saw that Scaffidi had done more work on it, adding a sluice on both ends. Service could see a gravel bottom between the two sluices. There were large, dark shapes darting and jockeying for position on the gravel. The water level in the pond was usually seven or eight feet deep, but the level was down to three feet now.

Scaffidi handed Service a rod. "Five-weight. Try not to pick off the females," he warned.

Service watched the fish. The females could be seen cleaning gravel, their sides flashing in the mid-morning light. The males were lined up behind them like cars in a freight train. Service saw that his host had tied a small orange yarn egg on the tippet, and added a couple of split shot to get the egg down.

Ralph Scaffidi bowed and smiled. "After you, Detective."

His first cast was close, but the males darted out of the way of the egg bouncing along the bottom. His second cast was better and a male brookie swung over a foot and took the egg; Service lifted the rod and gave it a sharp snap to set the hook and the fish started to fight.

Scaffidi sat at a fancy lawn table and sipped espresso.

The brookie charged all over the place. It took ten minutes to bring it to the edge of the pond, extract the yarn egg, and release the fish with the gaudy orange belly and green vermiculations on its back. It was a wild fish, better than two pounds, not the sort that you often found anymore in U.P. waters.

Fish released, Service sat down and rubbed lemon peel around the rim of his small cup and tasted the bitter coffee.

"Nice?" Scaffidi asked.

"Terrific. Italian?"

The old man's eyes twinkled. "I met a gentleman from El Salvador. He does this especially for me, which costs, but it's worth it, right? What brings you over on such a beautiful September morning?"

"I heard that the global poaching of animal parts is second only to drugs in profitability. You know anything about that?"

Scaffidi made a face. "Scumbags makin' a profit off endangered animals. You know that two of the world's eight bear species are damned near extinct, with another on the brink? What's that about? For money!"

"It's true?"

The old man shrugged and slowly shook his head. "The Asian mobs are run by psychos. The families here, they don't get involved."

"But Asians don't exactly blend into the Upper Peninsula."

Scaffidi laughed. "They hire people who blend. This isn't the business of the families' personnel, you understand, but something done by punks and losers. The Asians got it organized down to the dime. Hunters acquire, sell to a middleman who, in turn, collects from several hunters and sells to a distributor on the coast. With bear populations dropping in Asia, the gangs have moved to North America. Most of them are in Canada and Alaska, but they work the other states too, if they can find the right deal."

"What's the right deal?"

Scaffidi smiled. "How about that brookie?"

"Beautiful fish."

"Right. The fish are spawning, which makes them easy to get to. That's the right deal, see. It always reduces to supply and demand. With all that September 11 crap you got tougher gigs at the borders nowadays, am I right?"

Service nodded.

"Which means security is focused outward, not inward to the woods. They're running around looking for Islamic terrorists. What better time to crank up business than when the opposition is looking elsewhere? I mean, you aren't trying to ship nukes, am I right? We're talking little stuff—galls, paws, teeth, claws. They don't weigh anything and they don't take up much space. Is this an academic tutorial or are you here on a specific case?"

"No case," Service said. Yet, he thought.

"Anything I can do, you only have to ask."

"I appreciate that."

"Okay, let's see if you can get a bigger trout out of that herd."

"I have to get on, but thanks for everything."

The old man walked him back to the truck. "Word is that congratulations are in order."

Service didn't ask Scaffidi where he got his information. He was better connected than anybody he knew.

"A son," Scaffidi said. "That's a blessing for a man. Nothing against girls, but a son . . . " His voice trailed off. "You bring him over, let him have a go at the brookies."

"He's enrolled at Tech. Maybe we can come by in the spring."

"It's an open-ended invitation." Scaffidi leaned against the truck with a furrowed brow. "These bear guys, they're elusive as hell. They hit a place and move on. They don't homestead. If you think there's a crew working here, take my advice and get expert help."

"You have someone in mind?"

The old man pursed his lips thoughtfully. "I thought you said you don't have a case?"

Service weighed his answer. Scaffidi was officially clean and a self-proclaimed conservationist who gave generously to various causes and programs, but there was always an air around him that made Service want to be cautious. "Maybe the start of something." •

"Such as the figs in the Houghton homicide?" Scaffidi said.

"That's not public knowledge," Service said, recoiling.

"Things don't have to be in the public domain to be known, Detective. Word travels through a lot of circles and some of them overlap. I'm hearing cyanide."

"No comment," Grady Service said.

Scaffidi smiled and squeezed Service's elbow. "A no comment *is* a comment, my friend. We are in the days of spin, which means you want to cover your tracks, you gotta use words, not silence. Plead the Fifth, you're guilty by inference. I might have somebody knows something about this business we've been discussing. Maybe he'll talk to you, maybe not. Worst he can say is no. You want me to make the call?"

"Thanks," Service said. As usual Scaffidi suddenly looked and talked like something more than his official record suggested, and Service did not feel comfortable about it. Frontier Alaska had once attracted society's extremes; he wondered if this applied to the Upper Peninsula as well.

"Probably take a little time to make the arrangements," Scaffidi said. "You'll probably have to go to him—this okay by you?"

Service nodded. "Thanks again."

Scaffidi smiled. "My pleasure to do my duty as a law-abiding citizen."

· 4 ·

It was mid-afternoon and Service and Gus Turnage were in the late professor's office at Michigan Tech. Steve Adams sat with them at a small table, looking glum. Homicide detective Limey Pyykkonen stood in the doorway. Service was impatient, wanted to get the interview going. He had driven almost two hundred and fifty miles today and would log more than a hundred more on the way home.

Service found it interesting that Pyykkonen chose to stand at the door. This was definitely an interview set up to put some pressure on Adams, but he wasn't sure why. With her in the door, almost at the man's back, he would be forced to keep looking back and forth from the homicide detective to the conservation officers who were seated with him. It was not an arrangement designed to make an interviewee comfortable, and as far as Service knew there was no reason to suspect Adams of anything. Is this what Lansing homicide cops were taught?

"Dean Adams," Service said.

"Acting Department Head," Adams said, correcting him. "Leave it at Steve."

"Okay, Steve," Pyykkonen said from behind the man, forcing him to turn to see her.

"I can't believe someone murdered Harry Pung," Adams declared.

"Are you aware of anyone who might have had bad feelings for Pung?" she asked.

"No."

Pyykkonen smiled benignly.

"When we met you at Professor Pung's house, you told us he was a hunter and fisherman," Service said. "But there are no guns, no rods, no gear of any kind at his place."

"So he must've kept the stuff elsewhere."

"Are you aware of another place he might have kept his equipment?"

"Like I told you before, he was a loner. Maybe he had a camp. Everybody up here seems to have one out in the bush. If there's other property, I assume it would be in his will, or with his attorney."

"We will be talking to his attorney," Pyykkonen said, "but he lives downstate in Ann Arbor and we thought Professor Pung's associates might help us get some answers quicker."

"Sorry," Adams said, with body language that told Service he wanted the interview ended.

"Thank you for your help," Pyykkonen said. "If you think of anything that might help us, even if it seems remote, you can call me at home or at the office." She walked over and put her card on the table and Adams palmed it without looking at it.

"You might ask around about a camp," Service said. "We need the help."

Adams nodded, got up and left without further comment.

"We kinda chucked him in the pit," Gus Turnage said when the three were alone.

"I just wanted to let him know that we're serious here—without threatening him," Pyykkonen said. "Subtle pressures often pay the biggest dividends. These academic types seem to think local cops are a bunch of Barney Fifes."

"The scat sample is definitely ursine," Service said, "as were the hairs, but our lab sent the stuff on to USF&WS Forensics in Oregon for more detailed testing. It's gonna take some time to get answers."

"Six years in Lansing and I never had a case like this," Pyykkonen said.

"None of us have," Grady Service added.

Gus opened the dead man's desk drawer and slid his hands inside, pawing around.

"What're you doing?" Service asked.

"Poking."

"We gave the whole office and the house a pretty good going over," Pykkonnen said.

Gus grunted and pulled out a photograph, carefully holding it by the edges. "Hand me a plastic bag." He slid the photo into the protective envelope. "It was stuck to the top, inside the drawer," he said, staring at it with a curious look.

"Taped?" Service asked.

"Nah, she was just stuck. Maybe humidity. Stuff always gets stuck in desks." He handed the snapshot to Service.

Harry Pung was dressed in a black robe. A small black hat was perched jauntily on top of his head, but tilted to one side. The hat was secured in placed by a chin-tie. He wore a red sash above his waist. Attached to it was a bow quiver. He held a bow at the draw, an arrow nocked. The bow was severely recurved.

"Not your standard compound bow and cammie-jammies," Service remarked. "So he owned a bow. Again, where the hell is it?"

Pyykkonen shook her head. "We haven't found anything."

"Hunters always keep their weapons close at hand," Service said, studying the snapshot more closely. "There're some sort of Chinese characters in the background of the photo." He passed it to the homicide detective.

"How do you know they're Chinese?" she asked

"I don't, but don't all written languages in that part of the world derive from Chinese?"

"So you're guessing?" she asked with a smile.

"Basically."

"We can try to find somebody from the college to translate," Pyykkonen said.

"We could, but I have another idea." Service looked at Gus. "McCants."

Turnage nodded. "She reads Chinese?"

"No, but she speaks and reads Korean, and if this is Korean then she can help. If not, we go to plan B." Candace McCants had been born in Korea and was adopted by Americans. She was a CO now and had responsibility for the Mosquito Wilderness Area, which had been Service's until his promotion, and his father's before him.

"I'll give Candi a yell and get back to you both," Service said.

Service lived in Gladstone, McCants a bit north of there, but closer to him than to Houghton.

"Okay," Pyykkonen said. "Time I got my butt down to the station."

"I'll give you a bump soon as I hear something," Service said.

The two men called Betty Very and arranged to meet her on a primitive two-track off Victoria Road west of Rockland, which was fifty miles southwest of Houghton. A sign where they entered the track said SEASONAL ROAD, meaning it wasn't plowed in winter. They took two vehicles so that Service could head for home when they were done. It was hilly, rocky country, with slag left from the mining days. Small orange butterflies gathered in flocks in the remainders of puddles in the ruts of the road. His trip counter now read nearly three hundred and fifty miles for the day and he was feeling weary. By the time he got home tonight he would have logged close to five hundred miles.

The barrel trap was a hundred yards up the two-track. The dark green steel canister was eight feet long and three and a half feet in diameter. Bearclaw had set it up on the lip of a small ridge leading down to a creek bottom in a thick cedar swamp, classic bear habitat.

Betty was sitting on a log by the trap, smoking and looking thoughtful.

"What was She-Guy doing with you?" Service asked.

"He rides along sometimes. He knows the animals and he's a big help."

"He says somebody let an animal loose."

"That's his conclusion. I'm not so sure."

"Are you sure you set the trap right?"

"I thought I had."

"Have you ever had one get loose before?"

"Once, ten years ago. A huge sow managed to bend the metal grates. The weld was bad. That's the only one."

"Any sign that this one tried to break out?"

"No," she said.

"Are you sure an animal was inside?"

"Absolutely. I clean the traps thoroughly after every use. There was scat in the cage and some hairs. The bait was gone."

"Has anybody else had a similar problem?"

"I heard a rumor that Griff Stinson had one get out on him. He borrowed a trap from Joe and Kathy Ketchum." The Ketchums were married COs who lived in Newberry. Joe handled the north end of Luce County and Kathy handled the south. Stinson was a bear guide and outfitter.

"Did you talk to them?"

"Haven't had a chance."

"Last fall Griff found a bear taken for its gallbladder just north of McMillan," Service said. "I went over to take a look and I thought it might be the start of something, but nothing more came along."

"Until now," Gus said.

"*Maybe*," Very cautioned. She was an excellent officer, but not one to jump too hastily to conclusions. As a result, the cases she made usually stuck.

The three officers examined the trap. Service even crawled in to see if he could find a flaw from inside. Bears were not just strong, but extremely intelligent animals who could solve a wide range of challenges. After a half hour the three of them had no answers. Something had been in the trap, but that something was long gone. *How* was the issue.

"What kind of tracks around the can?" Service asked.

"All rock up here," Very said.

"The recovered hair sample look normal?"

"Plain old *Ursus americanus*," Bearclaw said. "Black as a crow's behind."

"Scat?"

"The usual for this time of year, chokecherries and some crab apple fragments. Nothing remarkable. He or she was just working the usual chow line for winter."

Back at Service's truck, Bearclaw said, "I haven't heard anything, but you might give Elza Grinda a call. She gets her fair share of nuisance bears, but you know how she is talking about what she's doing."

Service grunted acknowledgment. He had worked with Grinda the previous fall. She had shot and killed a female assassin only seconds before the woman could shoot Service, and he felt deep gratitude to the young officer. He had also learned later that Grinda had been up for the detective job he had gotten and disappointment might have explained her initial reluctance to work with him. But Grinda had come through when it counted and that's what mattered most to other officers.

"Maybe I'll give her a call."

Betty Very said, "You'll be in a long line of gentlemen callers."

"I'm offended by sexist innuendo," Service declared.

"I'm not," Gus said.

The three agreed to stay in touch and to talk to other officers to see if anyone had encountered a similar problem. Service doubted routine inquiries would yield anything. Whatever they were dealing with was complex and very, very well planned. And Betty Very's trap escapee might not have a damn thing to do with anything other than bum luck.

On his way back to the office in Marquette, Service called Simon del Olmo on his cell phone. "Any word on Trapper Jet?"

"Arson says it was definitely an arranged deal, not an accident. They have the point of origin, but not the exact cause yet."

"Jet been around?"

"Nobody's seen him. I checked his other camp and no sign of him there either. Should we be concerned?"

"Not officially," Service said.

"Gotcha," the younger officer replied. "I'll let the county and Troops know to keep an eye out for him."

Service had just gotten home when Ralph Scaffidi called. "Did I wake you?"

"No, I just pulled in." Nantz was standing at the bottom of the stairs, waggling a finger for him to follow her upstairs.

"I got a guy might know something about the business you and I were discussing today. You got a pen?"

"Let me have it."

"Name is Vaughn Sager."

"He in the business?"

"You'll have to ask him. He tries to hit you for grease, you remind him who called him."

"Where do I meet him, and when?"

"Tomorrow at two o'clock at the Sons of Italy Club in Soo, Ontario. That work for you?"

"Why Canada?"

"I don't know the details and I don't wanta."

"Thanks, Ralph."

"Remember what I said, the little schemer tries to shake you down."

"Two o'clock."

"Let me know how it goes."

Service wrote down the man's name and thought about Scaffidi's voice. He had obviously put some pressure on this Sager guy. Pretty impressive for a retired CPA.

He bounded up the stairs, shedding clothes as he went.

"Good," Nantz said from the darkened room. "I almost started without you."

· 5 ·

The Sons of Italy Club in Sault Ste. Marie, Ontario, sat on a narrow street in view of a small gray stone Catholic church. The row houses on the street were well maintained, but it was clear that more effort was needed every year to keep up with decay and age. Service stood outside in the warm sun and had a cigarette, inhaling slowly. Why Scaffidi had sent him here without explanation was strange at best, but he had made arrangements to meet Griff Stinson on the way home, so the day wouldn't be a total write-off. There were only a half-dozen vehicles in the club's newly paved parking lot.

Service went inside. It was dark, the lights low. He walked into the bar, which was long with dark paneling. The table layout was haphazard. The bar itself was a two-fister's standup with no stools. The bartender was a woman with peroxided hair. She wore a red, white, and green vest stretched tight over a swollen bosom, and had a matching ribbon in her hair. She was stacking highball glasses and paid no attention to him. A couple of men sat at one of the tables arguing about Soo Greyhound hockey. One man sat alone in the corner, nursing a glass of wine and smoking a thin black cigar.

Service approached the man, who looked from his watch to the detective. "Service?" the man said. "I'm Shatun."

"Sorry, sir, wrong person."

"Sit," the man said. "You're looking for Vaughn Sager, right?

Service nodded. "Take a seat," the man said.

"You're Canadian?" Service asked.

"I lived in Chicago until I graduated high school. You know Chicago?"

"Not really." Service noted that the man had no fingers on his left hand.

"Hog butcher for the world, the fog comes on little cat feet," the man said, deadpan.

Service had no idea what he was talking about.

"I bore you with Sandburg," the man said apologetically. "People say I'm a flake. I just like to keep them off balance, know what I'm sayin'?"

Service nodded. The man had one eye that stared off to the side and made it difficult to look at him. "You in the parts business?"

"You can say I got retired early. You want to hear about the paw?" he held up the fingerless stump.

"Not if you don't want to talk about it."

"Hey, people like this shit, especially women. Kunashir is an island in the Kurile Islands, north of Japland. It's a dink of an island, maybe a hundred miles long, a place full of mountains and no more'n three hundred people and even more bears. The subspecies there is *Ursus arctos yesoensis*, the same animal that inhabits the Japanese far north of Hokkaido. This is one kooky bear, not like others, get me? It has a long, narrow head and a reddish collar. It hunts and kills people for sport, though this is popular bullshit and not science. Are you scientifically trained?"

"No. What's this got to do with your hand?"

The man smiled. "Some people call me *Shatun*, do you know this word?"

"No."

"It's Russkie. In some parts of Siberia bears depend on certain mast crops—ya know, nuts and shit. If it's a lousy harvest, the animals begin killing people. They move around until they kill and eat enough to get fat and only then do they hibernate. I think this is a real life illustration of Maslow's theories. *Shatun* means wanderer, and these fuckin' bears won't stop until they've gotten what they want."

Maslow? Service thought. "You're a *shatun*?"

"Fucking-eh, right. I been around, see," the man said. "It's not exactly a complimentary handle, but we don't get to pick what others call us."

Service felt a lecture coming, and wondered what the hell the man could contribute.

Shatun/Sager signaled the bartender and held up two fingers on his right hand. She soon came with two glasses and a bottle of clear liquid, a plate of Italian bread, a bowl with olive oil to dip the bread, and a bowl of black olives. Her skirt was too short and Service saw that she had a nasty bruise by her left knee. Sager pushed a glass to Service and lifted his own. "Stoli," he said. "The primo shit." They touched glasses and drank. The man's hit was much more substantial than Service's.

Service wondered how much high-test vodka it would take to be over the legal point-one blood alcohol level. "What did your father do in Chicago?"

"I never knew my old man. I grew up on the street with a bunch of Croatians. I was born a wanderer and I ain't bitchin'."

Service tore off a piece of bread and dipped it in the olive oil.

"I had a consignment for one of the Kunashir animals, but the fuckin' Russkies got tipped and they play the game rough. By the time all the fingers were gone I figured I'd better make a deal, so I bought my way out. I like the Russians: They got black fucking hearts, but peel the black back and it's pure green. Which reminds me, information ain't cheap."

"Mr. Scaffidi said to remind you that you're not supposed to shake me down."

Shatun/Sager laughed. "You're right, Service. Mr. Scaffidi says it's on the house, it's on the house." He shrugged to let Service know it wasn't a problem.

"Why are we here?" Service asked, wondering once again what sort of clout Ralph Scaffidi had.

The man held up his hands. "Hey, crossing the border ain't no picnic these days."

"You can't come? Or you choose not to?"

"We're here, let's leave it at that."

Service nodded.

"It's been said that maybe you're finding some . . . weird shit among your bear population, am I right?"

"What exactly can you do for me?"

"Who knows? God, maybe. I'm just a retired stiff on a fixed income, but maybe I can give you a name."

"Telephone books are filled with names."

"Let's not joust, Service. I went to Kunashir for a chink named Mao Chan Dung. He's a major parts dealer on the Siberian–Mongol border. He sent me to the island, said it was a sweet deal, and then the cocksucker set me up." He held up his hand. "I keep score, know what I mean? You don't keep score, people take more than some fuckin' fingers."

Shatun/Sager took another swig of vodka and popped an olive in his mouth. "I give you a name, maybe you take somebody down, and I get a little payback."

"We scratch each other's backs."

The man held up his glass of vodka. "You tell me what shit's been going down and we'll see where a little talk leads us."

The man was an enigma and Service was having a hard time getting a feel for whether he was real or full of shit. "Last year one of our bear guides found an animal shot, its gall removed. The rest was left to rot."

"They take a paw?"

"No."

"When these people take a gall, they usually take a paw with it—to prove freshness. This sells well in Asia," the man said. "What else you got?"

"We've had at least one bear released from a barrel trap and there seem to be rising tensions among some of our less-than-kosher guides who run hounds." He made a mental note to call the Ketchums on his way to visit with Griff Stinson.

"You got more?"

"A professor from one of our universities was found poisoned by cyanide. The poison was in figs, but we also found two galls in the fig container. The professor was Korean."

"Born here or an immigrant?"

"Immigrant."

"Name?"

"Pung Juju Kang."

"Okay," he said, pouring more vodka into Service's glass. "You believe all this stuff is connected?"

"I don't have any evidence; it's just a possibility."

"Right, and the common denominator is bear. Usually you don't hear shit about bears. They keep to themselves and suddenly people who got interest in bears start some funny business."

Service nodded.

The man drained his glass in one long swallow and wiped his lips with his napkin. "A man's gotta honor his hunches. If the money mavens understood just how much stiffs like you and me operated on intuition and hunches, they'd ignore us and hire witches and warlocks."

"I wasn't really at the stage where I was looking for help," Service said. "I have these things, but no evidence."

"Are you a musician?" the man asked.

"I like music, but I can't read it."

"When I was young I loved jazz. I was a *tapyor*. That's Russian for tickler." The man arched his good hand and tapped on the table as if it were a piano. "Hey, I had no talent to play even when I had all my fingers, but jazz took my soul, ya know? You dig jazz?"

"Some of it," Service said. What the fuck was he talking about and why all this Russian shit? "I thought you were from Chicago."

The man sighed. "I'm from Chicago, sure. Other places, too. They got music in Chicago, right? To understand jazz is to understand investigation—the ability to see and feel what's underneath the obvious. People who don't appreciate jazz tend to hear the melody, but they never feel the underlying chords and discordant notes that drive the music, see? When you study jazz you begin to appreciate levels."

Service understood, but had no interest in discussing the philosophies of investigation.

"You sound like an investigator," Service said.

"Hey, you're in a business, what separates the big boys from the jerk-offs? Competitive business intelligence, marketing research and such. We do the same shit, right? Do you know the word *maskirovka?*" the man asked.

"I think it's Russian for camouflage," Service said. He had learned this in the marines.

The man smiled benignly and shook his head slowly. "That's a definition that equates to listening to the melody. Camouflage comes from the French *camoufler,* meaning to blind or to veil. *Maskirovka* is more encompassing. It means deception and entails concealing activities by means of deception, including camouflage, but also including misdirection and misinformation. *Maskirovka* was at the heart of Soviet defense during the Cold War—hiding from America not so much what they had, but that which they didn't have. Follow?"

One minute the man sounded like a professor and the next like a chump. "Meaning that you have to listen to what you're not hearing with as much interest as what you are hearing," Service said.

Shatun Sager snapped the fingers of his right hand. "Bullseye! You're a smart guy—just like Mister S says. The people you're looking for aren't easy to see. The barest of clues is often all you got to go on—that and the feeling that claws at your guts and makes your balls burn. This is an ancient trade, well organized. You can't know until you investigate further, but it's not unusual for the organization to create turmoil as it moves into a new territory—to deflect the attention of competitors and the authorities from its activities. As for its own operations, these are usually quiet and efficient—damn near invisible. These people operate around the world and they've learned by trial and error what works and what doesn't work."

"Are you telling me there's a Russian poaching operation here?"

"Russian, Chinese, Korean, fucking Martian—it don't matter who, get it? They all use the same methods cause they *work*! Why reinvent the fucking wheel? All I am sayin' is based on your wimpy evidence, you could have an operation in the early phases here, and it's now you have the optimal opportunity to intercede. Wait too long and you lose."

The man refilled his glass and swigged his vodka and pointed a crooked finger at Service. "You, my friend, gotta look at what you're not seeing and hearing."

"Feel the chords, not listen to the notes."

The man held up his glass. "You understand."

"You have a name for me?"

"There's this asshole down in Grand Rapids. His name is Irvin Wan. He took the name of the great jigaboo roundball player and he's known now as Magic Wan. He owns several clubs, is involved in drugs, numbers, skin, all that shit. Makes his dough off human weakness."

"That's not much."

"Wan owns a lodge in the Upper Peninsula of Michigan and he's an avid hunter."

Service's logic told him this was unlikely to take him anywhere, but he had no evidence and no other options. "Where's his camp?"

"Don't know, but I can ask around if you're interested." The man suddenly held up his hands—"on the house for Mr. S, just so we're clear on that, right?"

"Magic Wan."

"That's him. Sleazy little prick."

"What're the names of his clubs?"

"The main one is called the Nude Inn. It's in a burg called Kalamazoo, can you fuckin' believe that's a *real* place and not just a fuckin' song title from the brown shoe army days?"

"He lives in Grand Rapids, but has a club in Kalamazoo?"

"Right. Skin trade guys sometimes don't like to stir shit where they live."

"You obviously want Wan."

"He works for Mao Chan Dung."

"You know this or this is a hunch?"

"I make it a point to know shit I need to know."

"What do you get out of this?"

"Dung likes to open new turf. Asia and Russia suck. Dung set me up and hey, all's fair, right? But now maybe I get him back where it gets him most—in his bank account. Like Ralph said, it's our duty as citizens."

"But you live in Canada."

"If you say so. Forget superfluous and irrelevant shit, man. You don't need to know where I live. It don't matter, see? They don't got no category yet for world citizen. One more thing. You need to talk again, don't look for me here. You call Ralph, *capisce?*"

"*Va bene,*" Service said.

The man spit his vodka out laughing.

O n the drive from the Soo to McMillan, Service kept thinking about Ralph Scaffidi, who had never been a mobster but seemed to know a helluva lot of people who knew a helluva lot about shit mobsters knew about. He tried to call Joe and Kathy Ketchum, but couldn't run them down. Then he called Treebone and asked him if he had somebody in Grand Rapids who could do some research for him. Tree said he would get back to him with a name. Service knew he could always call in another detective from the Wildlife Resources Protection Unit, but the lead was so thin right now, he didn't want to get a lot of DNR people involved.

Griff Stinson's camp was a few miles north of the village, on the south bank of the Tahquamenon River. Unlike most Yoopers, who lived in towns and kept remote camps (usually for R&R from their wives and kids), Griff's camp was his year-round home. The small log cabin had been built around the turn of the twentieth century with the trademark small doors of that era. Small doors kept heat inside. Griff's wife was sprawled beside the driveway on a chaise lounge. She wore a red two-piece bathing suit.

"Hey, Vernelia," Service said, sliding out of the Yukon.

"He's out back in his shop, hey," Vernelia said. She was a generation younger than her husband, a woman in her late forties who still turned heads in town and had a colorful history of hell-raising before inexplicably and suddenly settling down with Stinson. Her hair was piled on top of her head in a topknot, and the couple's brown miniature dachshund, Cootie, was laying at her feet. Cootie looked at Service and began wagging her tail.

Stinson's shop was a metal outbuilding with a concrete slab floor and oil heat. The outfitter used it to store equipment and to tinker with new bait recipes.

The bear guide was a veteran of Korea. He wore a faded Red Wings cap and had a pipe clamped between his teeth. The wiry Stinson was in his mid-seventies and clean-shaven. He was in the center of his work area with a large barrel that gave off a sweet scent.

"New formula?" Service asked. "Vernelia said you were back here."

Stinson grinned. "She sittin' out there in her underwear?"

"Looked like a bathing suit to me."

"Underwear, same thing," Griff said. "She likes to sit out there in that chair givin' the pulpy drivers hard-ons." He didn't seem particularly bothered by what she was doing.

"Seems like you gotta try something new every year," the guide said, using the cut-off handle of a canoe paddle to stir the slurry in a stainless steel drum. "Take a whiff." Service stepped close to the barrel, sniffed tentatively, and backed away.

Griff said, "Mashed Brazilian waffle cones, red gummy bears, bulk black maple syrup, day-old stop-and-rob freeze-burgers, and mini-PayDays."

"They'll smell that for sure," Service said.

"Mr. Bear always sees the world through his nose," Stinson shot back. "It's gettin' 'im to stop and eat interests me."

A horn roared from a passing truck. "That's three," Stinson said.

"Three?"

"Vernelia gets them truckers all worked up and then they get her all worked up. Six honks and she'll be back here beggin' me to give her some sweets."

"Maybe one of those drivers will slam on his brakes and step over to talk to her."

"Her choice, what she does," Stinson said. "Here 'cause she wants to be. Someday, she don't want, she'll be gone."

"You're okay with that?"

"Fully growed woman got the right to choose. What can I do for you?"

Service was not so sure he could be so nonchalant about Maridly having a dalliance, though he had to agree with Griff that people had the right to decide what they did and who they did it with.

"You borrow a trap from Joe and Kathy and have a bear get loose?"

Stinson sat down, took a foil pouch of tobacco out of his shirt pocket, and loaded the bowl of his pipe. "You hear that from?"

"Bearclaw."

"How's Betty doing?" Stinson asked. Griff and Bearclaw had been an item many years back.

"Still doin' her job," Service said. He had no idea how serious it had been or why it had ended.

"Will till the day she packs it in," Griff said. "That gal's got her a big dose of dedication and an ironclad notion of right and wrong. She liked sex, you know that? Loved it, but not with the lights on. Lights on was wrong, but anything went with the lights out. How does a person get to thinking like that?" Griff looked up and seemed to ponder his own question.

"No idea," Service said.

"Vernelia, she don't ever want the lights out."

Strange day, Service thought. "You had a bear get loose on you?" Service asked, trying to steer Griff back to the point of their meeting.

"Don't believe it *got* loose. I'm thinkin' maybe somebody give it some help."

"Evidence?"

"Lock pin was scraped and bent."

"Bear's work?"

"What bear's strong enough to bend three-quarter-inch steel? What happened was I had this big old boar over to Gimlet Creek and he tore up couple of my satellite camps. First time I put it down to fate and lousy hinges on my window shutters. Second time I figured he'd keep on tearing stuff up less I moved him, so I put out a barrel."

"And you got him."

"Sat right there in a tree stand and heard him go in and the gate come down. I climbed down, checked the cage, and come home to have dinner and sweets with Vernelia. Next morning the animal was gone, the trap busted."

"You're figuring tampering?"

"Wasn't an animal did that to steel. Somebody *took* that animal."

"Took it?"

"I found the trail. Had Cootie with me and she followed the trail to a tote, where it disappeared. Way I read it, somebody dragged the animal out to a truck and drove away."

"When?" Service asked. It would take a tranq gun and drugs to do this, and neither was readily available. He decided to add this fact to his list.

"August 22."

"How big an animal?"

"Dandy size, four hundred, I'd say. Four hundred easy."

"First time this has happened to you?"

"Won't happen again," Griff Stinson said with a determined nod. "I gotta trap another one, I'll move it at night and be done with it. Vernelia will just have to wait."

Another passing truck sounded its horn with three long, loud hoots and Griff grinned. "That's six. You best be movin' along, Grady."

"Why would somebody steal a bear from a trap?" Service asked.

"Griff, honey, I got some sweets waitin' for you inside," Vernelia called from the side of the cabin.

"Got some for Service?" the bear guide yelled back.

"Sorry, hon. Just enough for one today."

Stinson grinned at Service and winked. "Who knows why somebody'd steal an animal? Not like they can make 'im a house pet. Some mysteries ain't to be figured out, like why somebody steals a bear, or a woman like Vernelia gets wet between the legs from the horns of logging trucks. Is what it is, eh?"

Service watched Stinson duck to get through the low door of the cabin, got into his truck, and headed west.

Treebone called in on the cell phone as Service stopped in McMillan, getting ready to drive west on M-28. "There's a woman in Grand Rapids—Kentwood. She's an ex-Chicago cop, a real pro."

"She expensive?" Service asked.

"Dawg, don't you people have budget for anything?"

"Only for smoke and mirrors."

"Shit. I'll have her give you a bump."

"You got all my numbers?" Service asked his friend.

"Cell, office, and home, dawg. Later."

· 7 ·

He tried to call the Ketchums again, but they were still unfindable. East of Munising he called Candace McCants on her cell phone. "You on something right now?" he asked.

"If that's a professional question, the answer's no. If it's personal, the answer's, I wish," she said.

"Meet me in Trenary, forty minutes at SBT?"

"See you there," she said.

Andy Ecles, a retired businessman from downstate South Haven, had moved to Trenary the previous summer, bought an old café, spiffed it up, and renamed it the Star & Bucks Toastatorium—which locals called SBT. The village was famous for Trenary toast, which had the consistency of hardtack and was edible only when dipped in hot liquid, preferably hot black coffee.

McCants was already seated when Service arrived.

She waved a cigarette at him and smiled. "How's wifey?"

"We're not married," Service said.

"On paper," McCants said. The Korean-born officer was in her fifth year of duty, five-six and one hundred sixty pounds of muscle. She wasn't afraid of anything and had an inordinate amount of common sense. She had been adopted by a family in Detroit when she was twelve and joined the DNR after finishing a police academy at Kalamazoo Valley Community College.

"What up?" she asked.

Service gave her the plastic sleeve containing the photograph.

"Who's this?"

"Was. He's dead," Service said.

"That prof over to Houghton?"

"How'd you guess?"

"Not a lot of Koreans living in the Yoop. Even fewer dying. Why the heck are you carrying the photo of a suicide?"

"It's a homicide, which hasn't been announced. There's a sign behind the guy. Can you read it?"

"Can't you?" she asked playfully.

Service rolled his eyes.

McCants held the photo in front of her. "The characters are Korean. The sign says *Jung Gahn*, which means Righteous Room. This is integral to traditional Korean archery. Archers always meet at a place called a *jung*, which in Korea is an elaborate building, a sort of cross between a temple and a country club. When they arrive, they bow toward the entry sign. In this country, it's usually just an elaborate sign."

"In this country?"

"There are a few *jungs* around."

"In Michigan?"

She shook her head. "Closest is in Wisconsin, I think. You dogging another homicide?"

Service ignored her. "Why righteous room?"

"Korean archery is intertwined in the country's history. It's serious business and *very* formal. To be an accomplished archer you're expected to be a righteous person. If you're righteous, your arrows fly true. It's all about discipline and living correctly. See the flower on the bow cover? That's *Moogoonghwa*—Rose of Sharon. Each level of archery is called a *don*. The highest level is ninth *don*, but few people ever get that far, maybe two or three in the world at a given time."

"This guy is ninth *don?*"

She smiled. "What's his name?"

"Pung Juju Kang."

"Not ninth," she said with a grin. "There are only two at that level right now and everybody of Korean descent knows their names. It would be like a Canadian not knowing Mario Lemieux or Wayne Gretzky. How old was the guy?"

"Fiftyish."

"He could be fourth through sixth *don*. Each level is unbelievably demanding and you can only advance two levels a year, which in itself is rare. Most people take five to seven years to move up one."

"How do you know all this?"

"In Korea, archery is *the* sport—for men and women. We all learn to shoot early in school."

"What's with the weird bow?"

"It's traditional, handmade, designed to be shot from horseback. Only a few people in Korea are qualified and licensed by the government to make the bows or the arrows. They make the bow from a composite of water buffalo horn, bamboo, oak, mulberry, or acacia.

Everything is joined by a special glue made from some kind of saltwater fish, and the back of the bow is covered with a special birch bark from China to make it waterproof. It takes four to six months to make one bow."

"Do people hunt with them?"

McCants shook her head. "Like I said, Korean archery is steeped in history. Buddha's teachings discourage the use of the bow for killing."

"Even in war?"

"Buddha doesn't really address war, which makes for a sort of philosophical and theological loophole. In that belief system, war is to be avoided. If traditional archers used their bows to hunt animals, they'd fall off the righteous path."

"Seems like people would have hunted with the weapons."

"They did early in the country's history, but as bow training became more formalized and regimented, it became exclusive to the military and hunting with the weapons was no longer allowed. Soldier archers were sent after animals to hone their skills before they could be formally declared qualified as soldiers, but hunting was banned for civilians."

"There's no hunting in Korea?"

"Sure, but only with firearms, and even that's pretty limited. Even so, a lot of Koreans are interested in western bow hunting. Some Koreans believe that their ancestors were the first Native Americans and they're very nostalgic about how American Indians lived." She tapped the photograph of the dead man. "What's your interest?"

"There was bear scat in his vehicle when the body was found."

"You mean inside the veek?"

"Yep."

"How did he die?"

"Food poisoning."

McCants scrunched her face.

"Some chocolate-covered figs he ate were laced with cyanide."

"In other words, you *are* dogging another homicide," she chided.

"The bear shit is my sole focus. Plus there were bear galls in with the figs. I just go where the cases take me."

"Who's got the homicide?"

"Houghton detective named Pyykkonen."

"The one boffing the new sheriff?"

Service stared at his friend. "Is there some sort of central repository for Yooper gossip?"

She laughed and said in a conspiratorial tone, "There aren't that many women up here. We operate like the Borg," she said, "all part of one hive."

He shook his head. "What do you know about the outfit in Wisconsin?"

"*Jung.*"

"Right, *jung.*"

"I heard there was one between Milwaukee and Madison. The town's called Jefferson, I think."

"Are these *jungs* organized like clubs?"

"More like religions, and they all report back to Korea. This is deadly serious stuff. For the ninth *don* you have to score 39 of 39 at one hundred and forty meters."

Service looked at the photo and quickly converted the distance to almost four hundred and fifty yards. "With that toy bow?"

"Don't let the size fool you, Grady. That bow pulls more than fifty pounds and good shooters regularly plug targets with small bamboo arrows. The bow may look like something out of *The Lord of the Rings*, but it's lethal as hell."

"How do I get in touch with the Wisconsin outfit?"

"Why don't you let me call them? Speaking Korean will probably make things go faster."

"I want to know if Pung was a member, or if he was a member in one of the outfits anywhere in the country."

"Or Korea?"

"Okay, right," Service said with a nod. "I need to know more about him."

"I'll give it a try," she said, dipping a piece of concrete toast into her coffee.

Andy Ecles came over to the table as they were getting ready to leave. "Howdy, officers. You two looking for bad guys?"

"Always," McCants said.

"You didn't hear this from me," Ecles said, "but if you want a bad guy, give a visit to Bryce Verse."

"Verse?" McCants asked.

"He's from over to Manistique, but he's got a camper-trailer parked out on the back side of the Pavola farm."

McCants said, "Why does Mr. Verse qualify as a bad guy?"

"I hear he just got out of Kinross," Ecles said. Kinross was a Level II state correctional facility in Chippewa County in the eastern Upper

Peninsula. "He was in here with a couple of young girls a couple of days ago. He was packing and the girls were bragging how they'd been shooting deer."

"You *saw* a weapon?"

"The three of them were high and rowdy, but I saw enough to know what I saw."

When they got outside, McCants slid her 800 MHz radio out of its holster, and set Channel 20. "Station Twenty, this is Four One Twenty Three. Can you run a file?"

"Go ahead, Four One Twenty Three."

"Last name is Verse: Victor, Echo, Romeo, Sierra, Echo. First name Bryce: Bravo, Romeo, Yankee, Charlie, Echo. No middle name known. Allegedly just out of Kinross. Run the name, see what we come up with."

"Bryce Verse," the dispatcher in Lansing said. "Right back at you."

"You can go," McCants said.

"Think I'll hang for a while," Service said.

"You missing this part of the job?" she asked.

He nodded. "Sometimes."

Station Twenty called back, "Four One Twenty Three, Bryce Verse just finished three years at Kinross, paroled three weeks ago. You want his PO's name?"

"Go ahead."

"PO is Jenna Traffic, out of Manistique. You want her numbers?"

McCants wrote down home, office, and cell phone numbers, switched to her own cell phone, and tapped in a number. "Jenna Traffic? This is Candi McCants, DNR. You got a problem child named Bryce Verse?"

Service watched his colleague making notes on a small pad. "Okay, Jenna. We heard today that he's got a camper set up near Trenary. He was seen in town a couple of days ago in the company of two minor females, allegedly high and packing." McCants listened, then smiled. "I hear ya. Think I'll head out to his camp and have a chat with your boy."

She flipped the phone shut and looked at Service. "Supposed to check in with his PO within forty-eight hours, but she hasn't heard a word from him. She says he's a genetic dirtbag. He went up for aggravated assault, two OUILs, and statutory rape. Moody also busted him several times over in the Manistique area for fish and game before he got sent away. Apparently Moody was also the arresting officer on the aggravated assault beef." Eddie Moody, a CO for part of Schoolcraft County, was also known as Gutpile because of his spectacular ability to find the remains of poached white-tail deer.

"A Renaissance man," Service said.

McCants grinned.

Service followed her back into the restaurant where they found Ecles behind the counter. "The girls with Verse," she asked. "You know them?"

"Everybody in town knows all the kids—especially Cathalina Sector and Tina Kangaho. Both of 'em are fourteen and both of 'em are trouble."

"One of them related to the Pavolas?"

"Not that I know of."

"Is Verse related to the Pavolas?"

"Doubt that," Eccles said. "Never seen him till ten days or so ago. Old man Pavola died some years back and his wife moved downstate to live with her daughter. Pavola's sons and son-in-law come up for deer season, but most of the year the place is empty."

"Posted?" Service asked.

"Not since I lived up here," Ecles said.

"You said the girls are trouble," McCants said. "What kind?"

"Out of control. Sex and booze, out all night, skipping school, all that. They run with older men."

"Families?"

"Technically, but they don't seem to pay much attention and the girls do pretty much as they please."

"You mind if I tag along?" Service asked when they were outside again.

"Ought to let your missus know."

"Cut that out."

McCants grinned. "Our boy probably won't even be there." She dug out her Alger County plat book, and found the location of the Pavola farm. It touched up against the Delta County line and had been part of his old territory, which was now hers.

Service followed her in his truck.

A mile from the farm she pulled over and ambled back to his vehicle. "Let's hide my wheels and take your unmarked."

"You got a good hide in mind?"

McCants smiled. "I learned from the best."

She parked off a two-track in a copse of pines, covered the grill and hood with downed branches and leaves, and the two officers drove on to the farm. As predicted, nobody appeared to be in the old house, which badly needed paint. A rutted track veered away from the house across a hay field. The two of them stood on the running board of Service's truck using their binoculars to scan the surrounding fields.

"Ten o'clock," Service said. "Looks like a straight line. Something's back there."

McCants said, "Let's leave the truck behind the barn, go in on foot."

Service pulled behind the barn and locked the vehicle.

The two of them headed across the field, circling so as not to telegraph their intended destination.

At two hundred yards they could see a beat-up green trailer and a 2002 double-cab blue Ford 150 truck. "Let's move closer, get a plate number," McCants said.

They moved cautiously, staying low and using natural barriers to block their approach. When they were close enough, McCants used her binoculars, got the vehicle license number, and called it in to Lansing.

The answer came back, "2002 Ford 150, dark blue, reported stolen."

"When?" McCants asked.

"Twelve days ago."

"Stolen," McCants said to Service. "Two days after Verse got out of Kinross, and from Pickford, which is pretty much right out the back gate. This is starting to get interesting."

They could hear music blasting from the trailer.

"Hip hop," Service said.

McCants shook her head. "Rap."

"Same same," he said.

"You are *so* white. Let's get up close and personal."

"Want to pay a call now?"

"No, let's let the sun get low. He comes to the door, he'll have to look due west. That'll put the sun in his eyes. Let's use what God gives us."

Service checked his watch. "Ninety minutes, give or take."

"Wifey expecting you?"

"Knock it off, Candi. Why're we going slow on this?"

"Not sure," she said. "A feeling, and not one of the nice ones, ya know?"

He did, though he felt nothing at the moment.

The two backed off a hundred yards and set up near some tamaracks. Service used his cell phone to call home.

"Nantz."

"It's me."

"Thank God," she said excitedly. "Kate Nordquist is in the hospital in Escanaba. She and Gutpile stopped to get a snack this morning in Rapid River. She stayed in the truck while he went inside to get sandwiches and coffee. When he came out he found her on the ground. One of her legs is broken in two places, Grady. She has to have surgery. It looks like somebody nailed her with an iron bar, then drove over her. Gutpile can't understand what got her out of the truck. I called Vince. We're gonna meet at the hospital and talk to Kate's doctor." Vince was Vince Vilardo, an internist, Delta County's medical examiner, and Service's longtime friend.

Kate Nordquist was a young officer who had trained with Moody and been recently assigned to Schoolcraft County with him. She was Nantz's friend.

"Witnesses?" he asked.

"None. Gutpile called 911 and the city, county, and Troops are investigating. He followed Kate to the hospital. Where are you?"

"With Candi. We're waiting for the sun to go down to pay a call on a parolee."

"Be careful."

"Count on it. See you later tonight. Tell Gutpile I'll give him a call, and say hi to Vince for me."

"I almost forgot," she said. "You also had a call from Sheena Grinda."

"What's with her?"

"Said she found a bear with cable wrapped around its neck. She wants to talk to you."

"Dead?"

"No, alive, but she sounds uptight. Tell Candi no poaching my man."

Elza "Sheena" Grinda was an extremely self-contained officer. It was unusual for her to call anyone and he had not gotten around to contacting her. A bear with cable around its neck?

"How's Nantz?" McCants asked as he eased back beside her.

"She says no poaching her man," Service said.

"I rest my case," the younger officer said. "Married in her mind. Got her claim all staked out."

Service waited calmly. If Bryce Verse came out of the trailer, they would be ready for him. Experience had taught him to respect fear and wear it like an outer skin attuned to threats and acting like an early warning system. Just about everything he'd done in his life entailed various degrees of physical risk—hockey, the USMC, state police, DNR—but physical risk alone rarely activated his early warning system. Physical risk was more a matter of applying a skill to the challenge. If any fear persisted for him, it was the fear of not acting, rather than trepidation over results. In this way, it was like regret—which for him grew only out of things not done.

McCants slid over to him. "We've already got the stolen veek," she said. "If we want to get Verse with weapons in possession, we need to take him inside. He could claim he didn't know they were there. I wish I could look in his truck."

"Still too light," Service said.

McCants got to her knees. "I'm going to look around, see if there are other two-tracks out this way. If there's only the one road and he's not spooked, he'll come out the way he came in."

It didn't matter how many roads there were, Service told himself. They were not going to let Verse get to the blue truck. Service watched her move away in a low crawl. The first time he'd worked with her they had stopped three snaggers. One of them had swung his rod at her and buried a one-ounce lead silver spider deep in her cheek. She had not hesitated or backed off, but tackled the man and took him down with blood running down her face. She still had a small scar.

While McCants scouted, he sat so he could keep an eye on the trailer and thought about recent events, starting with Walter. Why had Bathsheba not told him about their son? He told himself if he had made an attempt to maintain even a superficial relationship with his ex-wife, he might have found out about him sooner. Something not done: regret.

He cautioned himself to keep his mind on the trailer and what might be inside, but his mind kept wandering back to other things.

Ralph Scaffidi was perplexing: wholly harmless on a superficial level, but there was always something deeper and more sinister just below the surface. Still, he felt attracted to the man. Was Magic Wan part of something real, a lead worth following? This whole bear thing was a lot of nothing so far. Hairs in a car, galls mixed with poisoned figs, some game-playing among guides, a couple of empty traps, old Trapper Jet up to something . . . None of it amounted to anything he could really work with, which was not unusual, but lack of hard evidence and direction always irritated him. And now there was possibly a bear-napper with access to drugs, meaning a link to a vet? And Grinda had a bear with a steel cable around its neck. Were any of these things connected? Was the peculiar informer right—were these symptoms of an international bear parts ring moving in?

McCants returned right at last light. "We've got a good one," she said, her voice tight, words clipped. "Windows blacked out, crawled under the trailer, coffee filters stained red, dozens of empty boxes of Nyquil, evidence of dry ice, a cylinder of liquid ammonia, and a box of empty twenty-pound propane tanks. Behind the trailer, empty case of lithium batteries," she said, finally stopping to catch her breath. "You know what this means?" she asked him.

"Drugs," he said.

"Meth lab," she said, "Your basic Beavis and Butthead operation. The lithium batteries tell me they're making Nazi meth."

"How do you know?"

"In-service last summer while you were on suspension. Didn't you read the lit? It was put in your mailbox. We pretty much shut down Cat up here, now crank is moving in." Cat was methcathinone, a home-brewed amphetamine-like drug made from battery acid, Drano, and nonprescription asthma meds. It had emerged in the U.P. in 1990 and five years later had spread to ten states, as far west as Colorado.

Service had been so caught up in life with Maridly Nantz that he had barely glanced at the information that had accumulated during his suspension.

"We need backup," McCants said.

"Shouldn't we look inside first?" he asked.

"That would be nice, but Grady, the shit laying around here can add up to only one conclusion."

"Okay," he said. "Call help." He immediately regretted saying anything because it sounded like he was her superior, approving her actions and giving orders, which was not the way it was.

"I'm going to bring them in quiet and dark," McCants said. "A lot of these meth cooks are also users. What we don't need is a tweaker. After a while users go paranoid and don't react well to anything they might mis-interpret."

While McCants withdrew to use radio, Service decided to take a closer look at the trailer.

Slithering on his belly, the first thing he noticed was the stench— like there were a thousand pissing cats living in the trailer. The debris was as Candi had described it, but there was also a pile of deer viscera and a rancid skin crumpled against the side of the trailer skirt.

He got carefully to his feet and checked the windows of the camper. Blackened, as she said, but the paint was on the outside of the glass, not the interior. Why? He used his fingernail to peel a tiny hole in the paint and look inside. The paint had not been on the glass long. A naked man was standing beside a table filled with clear mason jars. A naked teenage girl stood beside him, wearing a small revolver in a holster. A jam box was blasting. The man had long hair down to middle of his back. Blurred tattoos covered his right shoulder and upper arm. Another blurred tat was on his right buttock. It looked like a name, but he couldn't make it out. When the girl turned to stare at the window, he dropped to the ground and crawled away from the trailer.

McCants was there when he slid back into their hidey hole. "Help's rolling," she said. "ETA, twenty minutes. They're bringing the drug and hazmat teams—and Grady, they want us to wait."

"Not a problem," Service said, the words bringing a grin to his face.

"What's so funny?" McCants asked.

"Nothing," he said, shaking his head. "Should one of us go greet the posse?"

"No. The Troops will give us a bump on the eight hundred."

"Looked to me like they're making something in there right now," Service told her. "You smell cat piss?"

"That's the ammonia," she said. "I hope they're not using while they're cooking," she added somberly.

"Is there a plate on the trailer?" he asked.

McCants scowled. "I didn't notice."

Service was adding charges in his head. The more they had, the better to stick Verse with and hold him against bail. Failure to report to his PO within forty-eight hours, stolen vehicle, paroled felon in possession of firearms, adult with and giving intoxicants to minor girls, maybe a drug lab, an illegal deer—the charges were stacking up. By the looks of Verse, he'd not surrender easily. Too much to lose.

Time passed slowly. The trailer continued to shake under the barrage of music, the bass thumping like the heart of a giant beast.

"Five minutes," Service said, checking his watch.

"The sooner the better," McCants whispered.

There was a sharp crack and the tinkling of glass. Both COs tensed.

"Shot," McCants said. "Move!"

Service was on his feet and advancing before he could think through the situation. McCants had been a good officer since he'd first met her, always charging into trouble, never pausing to cogitate.

"Only one door," she said as they jogged forward. "Both of us on the front side, one to an end," she said.

When they reached the trailer she took one end and he took the other.

Two more shots cracked and the music stopped. Silence overwhelmed the scene.

The front door flew open, slapping sharply against the side of the trailer.

"You crazy fucking *bitch*!" a male voice keened angrily. "What is your fucking *problem*, man!"

"You said you'd do *me* first," a female voice answered. "*Me*. But you did her first!"

"Dude, you were cooking," the man said, his voice part defiance, part pleading.

"You promised," the girl said resolutely. "You do me, *then* you do her. That was the deal, *man*!"

"You *shot* the bitch," the man said.

Another gunshot sounded and the man toppled out the door and hit the ground hard on his back. The girl appeared in the opening, a revolver in both hands. The man tried to crawl away, but collapsed face down and stopped moving.

The girl raised the pistol over her head. "I shot the fucking monster, the monster is *fucking* dead!" she screamed.

The girl was naked, and no more than a kid. Lethal force was called for, but Service hesitated at drawing his weapon. He looked toward McCants but it was dark and he couldn't see her. He tried to listen in the direction of the farmhouse and barn, but heard nothing. Still no posse, goddamn them.

"I'm gonna cut the fucking monster's head off!" the girl said. Service recognized the tone: pure fear, driven by adrenaline and anger. He had heard this too many times in Vietnam to forget it.

"Oh shit!" another female voice said. Then, "Oh, just *fuck*!"

The girl in the door turned back to the inside.

"You supposed to be dead," the shooter said, her tone almost one of curiosity.

"You shot my *tit*, man!" the other girl said loudly.

"You did my man," the shooter said calmly.

"You watched," the other one said in her own defense. "What's the deal, man? We *both* been doing him, ya know?"

"Me first," the shooter said. "You went out of turn. We had a *deal*," she argued.

Service didn't dare move. Too far to go with the light shining out of the trailer. He hoped Candi was closer.

Another shot cracked and there was a scream, but the shooter suddenly came windmilling and flailing out of the trailer. McCants had the girl by a leg and was wrestling with her. Service jumped on the pile.

Candi was trying to pin the girl, but she was fighting and wild.

Service felt something hard strike him in the upper left arm, but got hold of one of the girl's hands and twisted it behind her. Candi had the other arm and cuffed the wrists. The two of them lay still for a second, breathing hard, not talking. The girl cursed, her words muffled because her face was pushed into the grass.

A flash of light burst from the open door of the trailer and one of the front windows, followed almost simultaneously by the thump of an explosion, the sound a sibilant *boompf* rather than a bang. The trailer erupted with white light and fire and was followed by a loud secondary explosion. Bits of glass, pieces of metal, plywood, and other debris rained down them, some of it burning and igniting fires in the nearby grass.

Service covered his head.

Someone hurtled out the door opening and hit the ground, screaming, her head on fire.

"I've got her," Service said. "I've got her."

He took off his coat, put it over the girl's head, and rolled her to put out the fire.

He heard McCants on the radio, calmly calling for help.

The girl inside his jacket was whimpering and moaning.

Lights jounced across the field toward the trailer.

McCants left the first girl and went to the man, who had not moved.

Service watched her check his pulse as the approaching vehicles illuminated the area.

"Fuck," Candi said.

Service carefully removed the coat from the second girl's head and looked at her with his MAG-LITE. Her face was black, burned severely. She still had hair, but only in patches. He turned away without making a further assessment.

"Candi?"

"I'm okay," she said.

When she walked over to him he saw that her head was covered in blood. "You're bleeding," he said.

"You too, *kemo sabe.*"

He looked down at his left arm, saw blood dripping down. "Verse?" he asked.

Candi McCants shook her head. "Let's get these two away from the fire."

The drug team came in, dressed in black, weapons at the ready.

EMTs took the burned girl. Cops began batting at fires with some sort of bags.

One of the drug team members checked Bryce Verse. A call went out to the Alger County medical examiner. He was attending a medical meeting in Wisconsin. Delta County's M.E. was covering for him. Service listened to the call to Vince Vilardo. Poor Vince. Getting close to retirement and still catching the shit.

"Let's take a look at that arm," a Troop said.

Service didn't resist as the man rolled up his sleeve, then asked an EMT for scissors. The EMT came over and cut the sleeve to expose the wound. "You're gonna need some stitches," the EMT said.

"Just clean it and tape it up for now," Service said. If Vince was coming, he could do the real repairs.

"Not a good idea," the Troop said.

"Just do it," Service said, holding out his arm and watching the blood pooling.

Before Vince Vilardo arrived, the drug team commander called a quick meeting. He was a sergeant who had just moved up from a downstate post, tall and businesslike.

"You two were supposed to wait," he said.

"Bite me," McCants said. She had cut her head in the scuffle, and had a bandage wrapped around her forehead.

"I'm not accusing you of anything," the commander said, holding up his hands.

"Fuck off," McCants repeated. Service squeezed her arm gently and calmly explained. "We waited, but we heard a shot and had to move to it. The guy appeared in the doorway, the girl we cuffed shot him, then she turned and popped the other girl. Then the trailer went up and the second girl came flying out on fire."

"You *saw* the girl shoot the man?"

"No," Service said. "We saw him in the door, heard the shot, saw him fall out. Then she appeared in the door brandishing her gun. She said she'd 'shot the monster.'"

"Why were you two here?"

"We had a tip that Verse, the dead guy, was just out on parole, in town with two minor females, that they were high and he was armed and bragging about shooting deer."

"Why didn't you call for help?"

"Call who and for what? There's one county car and one state car on duty at night," McCants said with obvious irritation. "As soon as we realized it was a meth lab, we called you guys."

"I just wish it had gone down differently," the team commander said.

"It went down the way it went down," Service said. "The burned girl?"

"Not good," the commander said. "GSW to right chest and third-degree burns to the head and shoulders."

"Man," McCants said.

"The truck over there is stolen," Service said. "We called it in."

"Okay," the team commander said. "Let's all stand down, let hazmat get to work on the site, not that there's a hell of a lot left."

Service watched three people in special suits move into the ruins. They looked like spacemen.

"That's *our* fault?" McCants snapped.

Service squeezed her arm again.

"I didn't say that," the commander said. "Did either of you draw or discharge a weapon?"

"No," Service said.

"No," McCants said.

Service was relieved that neither of them had drawn.

"Relax," the commander said, offering a pack of cigarettes. Service took one and let the man light it for him. "Rough?"

"Rougher to be dead," Service said. "Everything was quiet and then the shit hit the fan."

"Welcome to the drug war," the cop said.

When Vince Vilardo arrived he took one look at Grady Service and his jaw dropped.

"Grady?"

"Present and still accounted for."

Vince's normally steady hand was shaking as he looked at the wound. "You want to go back to the hospital so I can do this right?"

"Can you do it here?"

"You're going back to the hospital," his friend said in his doctorly voice.

Service didn't argue.

One of the team members brought over a hunting knife. There was blood on the blade.

"It was where you had the scuffle," she reported.

Service thought back. The girl had said she was going to cut off the monster's head. He should have picked up on that. The presence of a gun often blocked out the presence of other threats. Rule one of cop work: Pay attention to everything you see *and* hear.

McCants sat sullenly next to Service. "You okay?" he asked.

"Headache," she said. "Did we fuck up?" she whispered.

"No way," he said. "It just went down and we did what we could."

"Still," she said. "One dead, maybe two."

"Forget it, Candi. Move on."

They both rode behind the ambulance in Vilardo's Suburban. Verse's body and the injured girl were in the ambulance. The other girl was in a squad headed for Munising to be booked. Members of the drug team said they would follow with the officers' vehicles.

"How's Kate Nordquist?" Service asked.

"What *about* Kate?" McCants asked, perking up.

"She's got a seriously injured leg," Vilardo said. "She could lose it."

Service winced at the thought of amputation.

"*Kate?*" McCants said.

Service explained what he knew.

"You didn't tell me," she said.

"We had other things to think about," he said.

"Don't patronize me," she snapped at him. "If you knew, I should have known."

"Can it, Candi."

"Did you see Nantz?" Service asked Vilardo.

"She was still at the hospital when I left. She'll still be there with Moody."

Vince took both of them into the emergency room and stitched them. McCants got four, Service got eleven. They both got tetanus boosters and a bolus of antibiotics.

McCants was acting poochy and Service left her alone, knowing she needed to come down from stress in her own way and her own time. She would come out of it.

He saw Nantz standing outside the emergency room. When he walked out she came over to him and hugged him. There were no tears, only the warmth of her touch.

"I called Walter," she said, "as soon as I heard."

"He doesn't need to know."

"He's *your* son," she said, "and when his father gets hurt, he deserves to know."

"You shouldn't have called him," he said.

"Afraid somebody might care?" she said.

They found Gutpile Moody sitting with McCants, who was shaking her head.

"Guess what?" she said.

Service shrugged. He was in no mood for guessing games.

"The vehicle that hit Kate was a 2002 dark blue Ford 150."

"Plate verified?"

"It was Verse," she said. "Probably afraid to directly confront Eddie, so he took his vengeance on Kate."

Moody sighed. "Verse is yellow. I busted him several times. Too stupid to learn. Worst combo in the world, no brains and high ambition. I wish I knew they'd released him. He wasn't supposed to be out until next winter. Guess I won't have to deal with him anymore."

Service shook his head in disbelief. What were the odds? Then he smiled in resignation. When it came to crime and coincidence, odds often went out the window.

"You still want me to check on that Wisconsin thing?" McCants asked.

"I'm sorry I held back on Kate," he said.

"I probably would've done the same," she admitted. "I'll get hold of Wisconsin soon as I can." She offered her hand in a gentle high five.

Service wanted to look in on Kate Nordquist, but she was doped and out. "Tomorrow," a nurse said.

Moody said he was staying put in the hospital until she was out of the woods.

"Could be three or four days before they know about the leg," Vince Vilardo said.

"I'm staying," Moody said.

As they got to the hospital lobby, Captain Ware Grant was coming in. He looked tired, his skin color gray and dull. "You and McCants?"

"We're fine, Cap'n."

"Officer Nordquist?"

"Her leg is bad. They've done surgery, but it's still touch and go that she'll keep it."

The captain's eyes blazed.

"They got the man who did this," Service said.

"Who?"

"Name is Verse. He was in a meth lab. A fourteen-year-old girl shot him."

The captain patted Service's shoulder gently and walked into the hospital.

In Nantz's truck heading for home in Gladstone, she rubbed his leg and said nothing.

"The Cap'n doesn't look healthy," Service said, thinking about the stroke the captain had had last year. Doctors had returned him to duty, declaring he had no deficits; still, his color wasn't normal.

"Everyone's tired," Nantz said. "You pick up on any vibrations from Gutpile?"

He shook his head.

"He's in love with Kate," she said.

"*Gutpile?*"

"Yut," she said. "Mr. Solo himself."

"Does she know?"

"Yut."

"And?"

"Let's just say the feelings are not unreciprocated."

N ewf came to Service's side when he walked into the house, bumped his thigh, and lifted her head for his hand. "Have you seen Cat?" he asked Nantz, looking around. It had been days since he had seen her. He had found the animal years ago in a cloth bag of eight kittens somebody had drowned in Slippery Creek near his cabin. Why this one survived was beyond him, but she had lived and turned into a feline misanthrope. He had never gotten around to naming her, which made her an animal he could relate to.

Service checked the answering machine. There were two messages, the first from Walter. "Just checking to see how things are over there."

"Now we're things?" Service grumbled.

Nantz held up her hand. "Your son *called*. He's concerned."

"He didn't need to know," Service grumbled.

"You can be such a jerk," Nantz said, "but a funny one." She was smiling.

The second message was from Gus Turnage. "Hey, Walt called and said you'd hit some shit. Give me a bump. Walt has some ideas we both ought to hear. He's a great kid, Grady."

"Walt?" Service said to Nantz.

"Your son, fool."

"It's not his place to call Gus," he grumbled.

"Stop being an asshole."

Service started for the stairs but saw lights flash in the long driveway.

Nantz looked out the window. "It's Lorelei," she said.

"Aren't we lucky," Service said. "Shouldn't she be out kissing asses and babies?"

"*Grady*," Nantz said with a warning growl.

State senator and gubernatorial candidate Lorelei Timms stepped into the foyer. She was tall and a little heavy, with intense eyes and medium-length hair streaked silver. She wore a dark dress and high heels that made her even taller.

"I heard about today," the senator said.

Service wondered how she'd learned so quickly, but as a senator gunning for the top spot in state government, she was a full-blooded member of the Lansing tribe, which had its own drums and ways of passing information. He responded with a nod.

"You look like shit," she said, "if you don't mind my word choice. You, on the other hand," she said, turning to Nantz, "look like someone just off a Milan fashion runway."

"Too short," Nantz said. The women smiled at each other.

Timms turned back to Service. "I don't like police officers getting injured in the line of duty."

"Get used to it," Service said.

"I know the reality, but I don't have to like it." Service expected her to spout some kind of campaign slogan, but she turned to Nantz again. "Whit and I got a sitter for the kids so we could have a night alone. It's going to be campaigning every day and night from here on. But when I heard about what went on up here, we decided we could take our night at the House of Ludington." The House of Ludington was an Escanaba landmark, a Queen Anne–style resort hotel that had been built before the turn of the twentieth century—at a time when Great Lakes steamships brought tourists from Chicago and Milwaukee. The hotel still had one of the best kitchens in the Midwest.

"You've pulled even in the polls," Nantz said.

"Crossing the finish line first is what matters," the senator said. "Whit and I brought Jill Yonikan with us. She's an old friend and an orthopedic surgeon in Traverse City. She was at Henry Ford for ages. She's going to help your friend Kate."

Nantz smiled.

"Kate will be in good hands," Senator Timms said.

"Our doctors aren't good enough?" Service said testily.

Timms turned and stared hard at him. "In a word, no. You have some good people up here, but not nearly enough, and not enough specialists to make a difference."

"You're going to change that?"

"I'm going to try. I'm at least going to give this area some of the attention and respect it deserves. You heard what Kwami called the U.P.?"

Kwami Kilpatrick was Detroit's current mayor. He had been quoted as calling the U.P. "Michigan's Mississippi." The remark had riled a lot of people, not just in the Yoop, but the mayor had not apologized.

"He's in your party."

"Yes, he is, and he has a right to say what he thinks; but if he keeps kicking parts of the state that aren't Detroit, it's Detroit that's going to suffer. We have to get people thinking together—as one state—not Detroit, et cetera."

Good luck, Service thought. He had never heard Lori Timms speak with such conviction. Before this he had thought of her as a naive, middle-aged do-gooder from old money, but there was a hardness in her voice that suggested she was more capable of real convictions and command than he had ever imagined. But she'd have to win before anyone would know if she had what it took.

"You belong in bed," the senator said. "And Maridly and I need to talk."

Service shrugged, went up to the bedroom and called Gus Turnage. "It's Grady. I got your message."

"You okay?"

"NBD, some stitches and some wrestling."

"Fourteen-year-old tweaker, I heard. How's Nordquist?"

"They're worried about her leg."

"Man," Gus said. "Any leads on who did it?"

Gus wasn't as well informed as he was making out. "They got him." He didn't volunteer any details. These would come out soon enough. "You talked to the boy."

"Walt had dinner with Shark and me a couple of nights ago and I told him about the professor at Tech. He called me this morning and said he's learned some things about the professor's son."

Service was irked. "Dammit, Gus. Why did you tell him? It's not his concern."

"He's interested in what we do."

"It's not your place, Gus."

"Don't be stupid. Your son's taking an interest. I think we should hear what he has to say."

"He's just a kid."

"He's his old man's kid—only smarter."

"It's not his business."

"How many times have you stuck your nose into stuff that wasn't your business? He's just trying to help. When can you get over here?"

Service thought for a moment. "I need to talk to Grinda in the morning, then I can drive up. Dinner at six at the Douglass?" The Douglass House Saloon was the oldest bar and restaurant in Houghton and a hangout for the students and faculty from the university.

"Six it is. Don't go hard on Walt, Grady. You going to call him?"

"I'll take care of it."

Service called his son's dorm room and was relieved to get the answering machine. He told his son that he and Gus would meet him the next night at the Douglass at six.

Some time during the night Nantz slid into bed with him and spooned. "You awake?" she whispered.

"I am now."

"Did you call Walter?"

"Are you checking up on me?"

"Just asking," she said gently. "I told Lori I'll fly for her. I'm going to take my bird to TC tomorrow and leave it there. I agreed to one month, that's all. I told her I need a month to get ready for the academy."

"Are you okay with this?" she asked. "And don't say, 'not a problem.'"

"You're a fully growed woman."

"Jesus, you sound like Jed Clampett."

"It's your decision."

"I'll get home every chance I get," she said. "I'm not going to do anything to jeopardize the academy. What did Walter say?"

"He didn't. I left a message on his machine."

"Grinda?"

"I'm going to see her in the morning." But he had not talked to her, so he got out of bed, took the portable into the hallway and punched in her cell phone number.

"Officer Grinda," she answered, her tone all business. Grinda was a thirty-something Swede who lived near Bruce Crossing in Ontonagon County. She had fashioned a record of getting the job done well, but was also known for not willingly cooperating with other officers. She was pathologically polite and reserved, with wild brown hair that always looked windblown. She had physically tangled with many lawbreakers and was known by other officers as Sheena. Although she had ended up saving his life the previous year, he hadn't worked with her since. What their relationship would be now remained an open question.

"Service. I got your message."

"Thanks for the call back. Sounds like you and Candi had a nasty day."

"You've had worse," he said.

As usual, she got right to business. "I had a complaint about some freeloaders at Burned Dam Campground on the Tamarack River. Just before I got there a bear ran across Forest Highway 4500. It was trailing something, so I stopped, followed it, and found it tangled in some cedar roots along the river. It was exhausted. There was steel cable around its neck—like some sort of snare set. I got Doc Emmarpus from Watersmeet and we darted the animal. It's caged at the vet clinic now."

"Joe Emmarpus? I thought he retired to New Mexico." Emmarpus had been a vet in the western U.P. for more than forty years.

"He did. This is Doctor Rosary Emmarpus, Joe's granddaughter. She was practicing in Alaska, but when Joe decided to call it quits, she bought his practice. She's a little odd, but people like her. She told me she had seen cable used like this up in Alaska—by bear poachers. After we talked I tried to back-track the animal, but I lost the trail and had to call it quits. I'm going back in at first light."

"You mind if I join you—say five?"

"I could use the help," she said. "Let's meet on 4500 where it crosses the Tamarack."

She wanted help? This was a stark change from the Grinda he had first worked with last year.

"See you then."

"I'll have the donuts," she said. "You sure you're okay from today?"

"Just sore. See you at five."

He set the alarm for 3 A.M. when he got back in the bedroom and got into bed.

"Can we cuddle?" Nantz asked. "I need to be close, skin to skin."

"I'll need to get up at three," he said, "to meet Sheena."

"I'll make sure," she said, settling into the pillow.

He fell asleep basking in the fragrance of her skin and the shared warmth of their bodies.

The alarm startled him awake. When he moved his legs to get out of bed, Nantz hooked his waist with her arm and pulled him back.

"You're leaving and I won't be here when you get back tonight." Her hand was on his thigh and then higher. "There," she said, fondling him. "Up at three, just like you said."

She rolled on top and guided him inside and he didn't care if he was going to be late. "You just lay still and let your nurse do the work," she said, but it was over for both of them too quickly to savor their lovemaking. "That'll take the edge off," she said. "Get dressed and I'll get the coffee."

He found her in the kitchen, as usual, clad only in panties. Newf was following her around, hoping for people food. His double thermos was full and she had two pieces of rye toast in the toaster. A glass of OJ was on the counter, along with his vitamins. He threw all the pills down at once and she grimaced. She hated to swallow pills, especially anything larger than a BB. When the toast popped she put them in his hand, gave him the thermos, kissed him long, and squeezed his butt. "Don't forget me."

"Not likely," he said.

Cat was outside, anxiously waiting for somebody to let her in. He opened the door for the cat and called back to Nantz, "Miss Walkabout has returned."

The cat was already growling for food. Newf gave the temperamental animal her space and watched her make her demands.

· 9 ·

He crossed into the central time zone during the two-hour trip to meet Grinda, driving with his window open, the predawn air cool, but comfortable. Grinda was standing beside her truck staring down at the black Tamarack River. His upper arm ached from his wound, but he worked the old trick of telling his mind to ignore the pain. Each year the trick got harder and harder to pull off.

"Got some risers?" he asked as he got out.

"You fishermen," she said. "I was just staring."

"You don't fish?"

"Can't stand their smell or their slime. My mother tried to raise a lady with alabaster skin, untouched by the sun. Except for hating to fish, she failed on all counts."

In the time he had known Elza Grinda, this was the most she had ever disclosed about herself. He poured coffee for both of them and they drank and ate donuts in silence.

"Might as well get moving," she said after a while.

"Still pretty dark."

"I thought we'd get down to where I lost the trail and be ready to track at daylight."

He didn't ask her if the trail was marked. Some COs used various physical markers while others relied on their instincts, and if either method worked, it was fine by him. So far, few woods cops had taken to using Global Positioning System units. He knew a few officers who had terrible senses of direction, a deficiency that sometimes interfered with their ability to do their jobs. Grinda wasn't one of them.

"You know the guides who work this area?" he asked as they put on their packs.

"A couple of dog-chasers from Kentucky, but they're not up yet. I've never had any serious problems with them, and they at least pay lip service to the rules."

Grinda moved like a snake, weaving through the slash without sound, finding her way through the dark without a light. Service followed a few yards back, trying not to snap branches or trip. As with his ability to deal with pain, his night vision at nearly fifty-one was not what it once was, and the idea of losing his night vision petrified him and made him cranky.

One morning in bed Nantz had been pawing at his head.

"You've got a bald spot," she said.

He'd leaped out of bed and got one of her hand mirrors.

"It's not a bald spot," he insisted.

"Don't let it bug you," she said.

"Doesn't bug me," he told her, and she had laughed. He had added, "We'll see how funny it is when you start graying."

She had poked him in the ribs and thrown a leg over him, which had ended the conversation.

It took nearly an hour to find the place where Grinda had last seen sign, and when they reached it, they found windfalls to sit on and got out the thermos again. He calculated they had walked a bit more than two miles.

"National Weather Service is calling for El Niño," she said. "Another light winter, at least to start with. But a lot colder than normal."

The previous winter had been virtually snowless until March when five big storms swept down from the Canadian prairies. After the snow, the air warmed, it began to rain, and most of April the western U.P. was beset by floods. Over the winter, the snowfall had been so low that the DNR had not run any group snowmobile patrols. By the time the snow came, downstaters were starting to turn their minds to spring sports, and the Yooper economy had suffered another disastrous winter.

"Even Mother Nature seems to want to kill our economy," he said. Some U.P. businesses were more dependent on winter tourists than their summer brethren. When the snowfall was down, the economy tanked.

"Maybe she just doesn't want to share," Grinda said. "You know how women can be."

They both laughed.

"What's this Doc Emmarpus like?"

"Earthy," Grinda said. "I asked her to join us this morning. She'll follow our sign."

"Her grandfather couldn't find his car in a parking lot."

"Joe is one thing, Rosary is another."

They started searching at first light. Working together, they were able to follow the animal's trail, mainly because the cable trailing from it had nicked and scarred the branches and rocks it had whipped against.

It was just after 9 A.M. when they slid down into a cedar bottom land. It was dark and wet and Service grumbled as they crawled over logs and blow-downs. Several times they crossed well-traveled bear runs and saw scat piles, some of them fresh.

Service thought about how bears had prospered in the state, the population increasing nearly 50 percent to an estimated fourteen thousand animals over a ten-year period—and that estimate was now several years old. In the U.P. bears were everywhere, and often nuisances. The animals had done even better BTB (Below The Bridge), where they were now being reported as far south as the suburbs of Grand Rapids.

"Grady," Grinda said. She was just ahead of him.

He saw her point to their right. There was a large white cedar branch about eight feet off the ground. Small brown plastic bottles were hung from from the branch by wire. Such baits were illegal now, though they had once been lawful.

Service sniffed one of the bottles and made a face. "Anise," he said. "Fresh," he added, jiggling one of the plastic bottles to slosh the dark liquid around. Unless it was an airtight container, anise evaporated.

They both stood still and studied the area. Grinda lifted an arm and pointed. There were kernels of corn all over the ground. Bear baiters were supposed to bury and anchor their baits, either in holes or in hollowed logs, covering the bait sources with boulders or logs to discourage foraging deer.

"Dirty bait," she said. This year Lansing had sent down a directive urging all officers to be aggressive on bait violations for bear and deer. Corn was outlawed for bear baits because if it got spread out or scattered around, it caused opportunistic deer to congregate and feed in herds. The regs against corn for bear baiting were designed in part to prevent deer from spreading bovine TB. More importantly, Chronic Wasting Disease had been discovered last year in southwest Wisconsin and had already moved into northern Illinois.

He knew CWD was a prion disorder, and that it was related to mad cow disease, but he had no idea what a prion was. The disease destroyed the brain and central nervous systems of stricken animals, and was thought to have come into Wisconsin from infected animals on a game farm. So far it had not appeared in Michigan, but Service and other officers felt it was inevitable and, when it came, there would be wholesale changes in all baiting regs, and no doubt some sort of massive panic to eradicate the disease by killing thousands of animals, as had been done in the region of

Wisconsin where the disease had struck. The last figures he had seen reported more than nine hundred commercial game farms in Michigan; he knew for a fact that the state Department of Agriculture, which had the responsibility for policing them, did not pay a great deal of attention. CWD would come, either naturally across the border or from an infected animal imported from another state. So far scientists had shown no linkage between CWD and humans, but if that proved to be the case, the effect on the state's herds would be catastrophic. He remembered TV reports of British farmers shooting and burning their cattle and shuddered.

No steel cable could be seen, but the broken condition of the soft ground beneath the branch made it obvious that something had been in a struggle there.

Grinda climbed up a tree. "The limb's grooved," she called down to him. "The cable must've been here."

"If it snapped, there ought to be something left," he said.

"Not if somebody cleaned the site," she said.

"Wouldn't they take the anise bottles?"

Grinda didn't have an answer, which was not unusual. You rarely got a neat package of evidence that all fit together.

After searching methodically and taking down the bottles to dust later for fingerprints, they found no human footprints in the area and sat down to rest and think. A hunter using dirty bait was smart enough to wear gloves in handling things to avoid leaving any prints, but this was Grinda's case and she liked to follow the book. Service lit a cigarette.

"Nice picnic spot," a voice said, startling them both.

They had not heard or seen Rosary Emmarpus approach. One second they were alone and the next she was standing not ten feet away.

She didn't look anything like her grandfather, who was tall. She was short with frizzy black hair, wearing cut-off jeans, and a sleeveless olive drab T-shirt. Her legs, arms, and neck and shoulders were literally covered with dozens of tattoos that ran together and made him dizzy to look at. She had a gold ring in a nostril, two more in her left eyebrow, and the countenance of a turtle sticking its head out of its shell.

"Hey, Elza," the vet said.

"Morning, Rose. This is Grady Service," she said, "our detective out of Marquette."

The woman nodded.

"Any trouble finding us?" Grinda asked.

"I could smell his cancer stick a hundred yards back," she said.

Service wet his fingers, extinguished the cigarette and put it in his pocket.

Rosary Emmarpus was so strange looking that he found it impossible not to stare.

The woman looked directly at him. "You're sitting there wondering how such a freak got through vet school, right?"

Service shrugged.

"Animals don't give a shit what people look like," she said. "Neither did the people in Alaska, and I'm hoping it's not going to be an issue here. Alaska's okay, but the winters are too damned long and I hate flying with bush pilots to take care of clients. Anything else you want to know?"

He shook his head.

Emmarpus looked at the cedar limb. "That's where the snare was," she said with a nod.

"How do you know? You saw this in Alaska?" Grinda asked.

"Several times. Up there they used bottles of maple syrup to draw the animals in. The cable hangs down in a big loop. The baits are above it. The animal has to stand up in the loop and when it pulls the bait, there's a trigger that tightens the cable. Then the bear is usually caught. Sometimes the snare gets the neck, sometimes the trunk of the body. The neck kills pretty quick. The body eventually kills because the animal struggles until it crushes its ribs or spine. Either way, it's not pretty."

"Professional poachers?" Service asked.

"They all poach for money up there," the vet said. "Poachers are thieves and they all kill in any way that will work. The advantage of this gimmick is that it's quiet." She looked up in the tree. "They had the cable up there, right?"

Grinda nodded.

"You find the trigger?"

"Nothing."

"They won't be back," Emmarpus said. "They seldom hit the same place twice, especially if somebody gets on to them."

"How's the animal?" Grinda asked.

"He'll survive, but he's not that big. The bigger the animal, the more valuable the parts. They'd found this one they would have been pissed."

Service walked over to his truck to get a pack of cigarettes and as he reached for the door, he heard Rosary Emmarpus tell Grinda, "Great buns."

Grinda said, "Not available."

The peculiar little vet laughed. "That's always the case. The good ones are always married or gay."

The three of them were back at the trucks by 2 P.M. and the vet left them. Grinda said, "Gus told me about the prof at Tech—cyanide in figs, and bear galls in the same box?"

He shook his head. "It's a beaut."

"Somebody went to a lot of trouble to make sure your professor passed on," she said.

She was right on in her assessment, but how did the murder connect to the other stuff going on in recent days and weeks?

Grinda reached into the bed of her truck and pulled out the remains of cable she had recovered last night. "I'm going to check around, see if anybody around here sells this kind of material," she said. "If this stuff snapped, it might come from a defective spool and there could be reports of others. I also dusted for prints. Nothing."

It was about ninety miles north to Houghton and Service drove at a steady sixty-five, having plenty of time for the meeting with Gus and Walter.

He parked in the lot behind the Best Western and walked down Shelden Avenue. The Douglass House Saloon was in a brick building with towers on the corners, its bricks a brilliant orange in the low afternoon sun. He walked inside to a cloud of smoke and liked the smell. There were lots of towns in the process of banning smoking, but so far U.P. bars were being exempted. Good thing. When people couldn't smoke in bars, the bars would go belly-up. Or there would be a revolt.

The interior was made of wood, darkened by smoke and age. Tiffany-style glass chandeliers hung from high ceilings, creating atmosphere but delivering little light.

Gus was at a booth in the dark back bar, dressed in civvies.

"How'd the meeting go with Grinda?" he asked.

"Good. She was cooperative."

"I told you a long time ago she's good people. You just have to earn her trust."

"Somebody snared a bear with steel cable down in the Tamarack River country."

"A first?"

"For us. Apparently it happens in Alaska."

"Says who?"

"Joe Emmarpus's granddaughter."

"The one who took over his practice?"

"Am I that far out of touch?" Service asked.

"If I lived with Maridly, I'd be out of touch too," Gus said. Service knew his friend still missed his late wife, Pracie. He had occasionally dated other women since her death, but had not connected for any length of time with anyone. He spent most of his time with his sons when they were home, or with Shark Wettelainen.

Gus checked his watch. "Any minute now." Looking up, he said, "There he is."

Service turned and saw his son in the outer bar. He was accompanied by Karylanne Pengelly, whom he'd met at Walter's dorm. As then she wore a loose T-shirt, no bra or makeup, and frayed denim cutoffs. They had another girl in tow. She was dressed in a black blouse and capris and had a bright pink sweater wrapped around her shoulders. Karylanne was talking animatedly to the other girl and Walter was looking around.

Gus waved and Walter Commando nodded and guided the girls into the back room.

"This is—," Walter began.

"Karylanne Pengelly," Service said. "We met at the dorm." He took pleasure in the surprise on his son's face.

"This is Enrica," Walter continued, introducing the other girl. She had long hair tinted with blonde streaks and a thin, lopsided face that made her look both vulnerable and sexy. "Grady Service and Gus Turnage—both out of uniform," he added as they slid into the booth.

The two officers slid over to make space.

"I talked to Maridly," Walter said. Service assumed this was the boy's way of preempting him, by letting him know that he knew his father was unhappy about his actions. Having signaled that he knew, Walter launched into the purpose of the meeting.

"Gus told me about Professor Pung and his son, Terry. We did some asking around and Karylanne found Enrica." He nodded at the girl, who looked nervous.

It was cool in the tavern, but Service saw that the girl was perspiring.

She spoke haltingly. "Last year I was, like dating this football player from Wisconsin. His uncle has a place up on Lac La Belle, near Mt. Bohemia?" the girl began. It irked Service how some young people turned declarative statements into questions.

"Go on," Karylanne said.

"Okay, but like, do I have to get into, you know, like the *details?*"

"Just tell them what happened," Karylanne gently urged.

"Okay, like last spring this guy, he took me up to his uncle's place, and we like, you know?"

"What's the uncle's name?" Gus asked.

"Masonetsky. I think he lives in Iron Mountain."

Karylanne squeezed the girl's hand.

"We like, ate some stuff and got a little drunk and smoked a little weed, ya know, and the next thing I knew it was morning, and like, I didn't feel so good?"

"Hangover?" Gus asked.

"Well, yah," she said, "that, but I like, felt like stuff happened during the night I couldn't much remember and I thought it was like a really bad dream, but like, I was really sore . . . *down there*, ya know?" She glanced at her lap.

Her face was red, and she wouldn't make eye contact. "So I said to the guy, the football player, did we like . . . ? And he said, 'Yeah, three times.' I was upset and I told him I'd never done it before and he said, 'It didn't seem that way last night.' I was like, really bummed, but it was done and hey, ya know you're gonna do it sooner or later, right?" She raised an eyebrow at Karylanne and implored support with her hands. "Anyhow, he made us breakfast and I tried to go along with it, ya know? But the next thing I know, I'm feeling dizzy again and I'm back in bed and this guy is on top of me and I told him to get the hell off me, and I started hitting him. I made him take me back to campus. I yanked all day and all night and I still felt bad on Monday for classes."

"Did you tell anybody about this?" Gus asked.

"Just Karylanne."

"What's this got to do with Terry Pung?" Service asked, interrupting. He felt bad for the girl, but the whole story seemed pointless. It wasn't DNR business.

"When we got up to the cabin he went a couple of doors down and brought back this guy and he said his name was Terry Pung. This Terry, he sold us some weed, and my date, he said the guy's father was a prof at Tech and I told my date that I had a kid named Terry Pung in one of my classes, but this Terry didn't look like the same dude, ya know?"

"What's the football player's name?" Gus asked.

"Rafe Masonetsky," she said. "He played in back of the line or some-thing, I don't know football."

"Where's Rafe now?" Gus asked.

"He dropped out, said he was tired of school. He wasn't on scholar-ship or anything. I guess he went home to Wisconsin."

"Where in Wisconsin?" Gus asked.

"Some town near Madison, I think. I told him that this Pung dude didn't look like the Pung in my classes and Rafe laughed. He said Pung was cool—he brought some kid over from Korea and enrolled him in school under his name so that he didn't have to go to class. Terry likes to hunt, I guess."

Walter suddenly spoke up.

"Tell them what you ate at Rafe's uncle's place."

"We had some fruit and he grilled some veggie burgers? In the morning we had fruit and yogurt. I'm like a vegan, I don't eat living flesh?"

"What kind of fruit?" Karylanne said.

"Berries, grapes, orange slices, peaches, bananas, ya know?"

"And?" Karylanne prompted.

"You mean the figs and prunes?" she asked, seeking guidance.

Gus snapped to attention. "Figs?"

"Rafe said Terry brought them to us as a gift. I think they were in the fridge? I never looked. Even though they were chocolate-covered, I didn't like how they tasted, but I wanted to be polite, ya know?"

"Is the Pung boy in school now?" Service asked.

"No, I heard he transferred to U of M." This checked out with what Service had heard from Pung's boss.

"You haven't seen Rafe since then?"

"No, he kept calling and I told him if he didn't stop I was going to tell the school what had happened."

"Did you?"

"No," she said, looking down at the table. "I figured it was my fault. I never shoulda gone out there with the dude. Can I go now? I've got a lot of studying to do."

Gus said, "How can we reach you?"

"I don't want to be involved?" the girl said. "I've got like, this hu-mongous load this semester and I need to stay on schedule. I made a mistake—can we just leave it at that?"

Service was glad that Gus didn't push any harder. If they needed to talk to her, they could find her easily enough.

Walter and the two girls got up and started to leave. Service followed and caught his son's arm. "Are you going to have dinner with us?"

"No, Karylanne and I have to study. Next time, okay?"

Service wanted to chew out his son for poking his nose where it didn't belong, but the information was promising and he was too much a detective to niggle.

"I guess Maridly's gonna be gone a lot?" Walter asked.

"Flying for Senator Timms."

"So you let her go?"

"I don't *let* her do anything. She makes her own decisions."

"That's cool," his son said, heading for the door. "See you soon?"

"Absolutely," Service said, not wanting to fail the test and thinking he needed to get the boy wheels, if the university would allow it.

Back at the table, Gus asked where Walter was. "He went with Karylanne," Service said.

Gus smiled. "Don't blame him a bit."

"Chocolate-covered figs," Service said. "Too damned much coincidence here to not follow up."

"Pyykkonen talked to Pung's lawyer. There isn't any camp or other house and he's worth about four hundred grand, mostly in the house and stocks, all of which goes to his ex."

"What about the son?"

Gus shrugged. "No mention of a son."

"We'd better take a look at that cabin on Lac La Belle," Service said, wondering what the deal was with Terry Pung.

They left Gus's vehicle at his house, loaded some of his gear into Service's Yukon, and headed across the bridge through Hancock.

"You figure the figs were laced?" Gus asked as Service drove up US 41.

Service said, "Maybe GHB or whatever it's called. I think our boy Pung is a wannabe chemist."

"GHB or whatever," Gus said. "Listen to us. We don't know shit. Let's give Pyykkonen a bump. She worked school liaison. She'll know."

Service didn't argue.

Lac La Belle was way out on the Keeweenaw Peninsula in Keeweenaw County. On the way there, Gus hauled out his county plat books and found a property registered to a George Masonetsky. There were several cabins on the east side of Mount Bohemia. None of them were directly on the lake, but were high enough to have a spectacular view. The mountain was more than eight hundred feet tall, steep and pocked with boulders. Some of the local X-sports types tried to ski it from time to time—usually with disastrous results.

They waited on the county road for Pyykkonen.

"Hi, guys," she said as she unfolded from her vehicle.

Gus told her about the girl and what they had heard, and she listened without interrupting. He ended by telling her that Service thought the girl might have been slipped GHB.

"Possibly," she said, "but roofies would be better."

"Roofies?" Gus asked.

"Rohypnol. It's a sleeping pill. Take the stuff, crush it, put the powder in a liquid. You won't smell it or taste it. It kicks in within a half-hour, even faster if you're drinking. It sticks in the blood for thirty-six hours if you've mixed it with booze."

"Could you load it in figs?"

"Sure, like I said, dissolve it in water, inject the fig, and you're on your way. Simple and effective."

Service shook his head. Yesterday it had been a meth lab, now something called roofies. Things might take time to migrate to the U.P., but they always got there.

"The girl said Pung's cabin was a couple of doors down," Service said.

"We can't go in without a warrant," Pyykkonen said. "We'll have to call in the K-County sheriff. This is outside my jurisdiction."

"She's right," Gus said, glancing at Service.

"But it's not outside ours," Service said. "Don't worry, we'll keep everything nice and clean," he added, knowing you could always enter a private dwelling if you thought there was a problem or an emergency. You couldn't search around and root through things that weren't visible, but if you saw something in plain sight suggesting a crime, you could get a warrant on that. Up here it was easier to get warrants than in some downstate jurisdictions, where judges stuck to process to avoid the ever-present eyes of the ACLU and other watchdog groups.

They split up, Gus volunteering to go with the Houghton detective, leaving Service to do what he needed to do.

The house they were looking for was not a couple of doors away, but four cabins down. Using his flashlight Service could see all weapons safes inside. An arrow was in a vise on a table by the window and for a moment it looked like someone might be there working, but his probing light got no response and he went to fetch the others.

Back at the cabin he showed them a broken window. "Looks like somebody tried to break in," he said.

"I wonder who," Pyykkonen said, her voice thick with skepticism. "You two can cut the bullshit tag team act. I'm a big girl."

"Door's locked," Gus said. "But maybe somebody banged against it and weakened the lock."

"No goddamned way," Limey Pyykkonen said. "This is as far as it goes. Let's get the County out here."

The two conservation officers did not protest. Service wondered if her insistence on adhering to protocol got her tossed in Lansing.

Gus whispered, "Did you have to bust the window?"

"Hey, I found it that way," Service said. He didn't add that it had been cracked and only partially broken and that it had collapsed when he tested it. It had been an accident, but he could have been gentler.

It took thirty minutes for Keeweenaw County to send a deputy. His name was Dupuis, a weary man who looked to be in his sixties.

The deputy looked at the broken window and cursed. "Bloody kids are always breakin' into cabins out this way."

"We ought to look inside," Pyykkonen said.

"Wait," Service said, feeling an unexpected surge of caution. "Let's see if we can get the owner out here." If they were into an evidence stream he didn't want to lose the case on a procedural technicality. Now he was being cautious and the realization made him smile.

Dupuis gave him a look that said he wanted to get back to what he had been doing and that this was an unneeded distraction, but he agreed after some initial stalling.

The name on Gus's plat book said R. BROWN. "You know the owner?" Gus asked the deputy.

"Met 'im coupla times. Lives ta Houghton, works ta college."

"Let's get him out here," Pyykkonen said.

"Tonight?"

"Soon as he can get here," she said.

"I'm t'only uniform on duty in da county tonight," Dupuis whined as he shuffled off to his patrol car to make the call.

"This may be nothing," Pyykkonen said.

"Maybe," Service said, but two incidents involving laced chocolate-covered figs and both involving the same family name made him think they'd caught a break.

R. Brown turned out to be Reinhardt Brown, who was assistant head of maintenance for Michigan Tech's Student Development Center. It was close to fifty miles from Houghton to the cabin, all along twisting, narrow, and unlit roads, and it took the cabin owner more than an hour to get there. He drove a several-years-old Toyota pickup with bad suspension and an engine that was spewing blue exhaust and sounded ready to cough up a rod.

He pulled up in the trees below the cabin and waddled up the wooden steps. Service saw a wide-bodied small man with a shaved head and long neck, with the overall effect of a lightbulb on steroids.

"Da blazes is dis?" Brown greeted them as he huffed up the stairs. He had a high-pitched, cartoon voice. His face was flushed from the short walk up from his truck.

"Looks like somebody tried ta break into your cabin," Keeweenaw deputy Dupuis explained. "We need ta get inside and look around, make sure everyting's okay."

"Dis couldn't wait? You know what's on da tube tonight?"

Service, Turnage, and Pyykkonen introduced themselves.

Brown grunted. "Youse like da fuckin' Untouchables or somepin'?" He took out a key and opened the front door. He stepped inside, turned on the lights, and held the door open for them.

The officers pulled on latex gloves before they went inside.

The first thing Service noticed was that the interior was too dust-free to have been unoccupied long. There were no cobwebs along the windows or in the corners. Pyykkonen went directly to the small kitchen and opened the refrigerator. It was empty.

"That would've been too easy," she said over her shoulder.

The room he had seen through the window looked like the main living area. Service stood by the table with the vise and looked at the arrow. Graphite, not bamboo. It looked like someone had shaved some of the fletching.

"What's in the gun lockers?" Service asked the owner.

"Don't got a clue," the man said.

Gus stared at him. "What did you say?"

"Don't got a clue," the man repeated. "None a dis junk's mine, hey? I leased da place last spring." He quickly added, "If Deputee Dog woulda gimme half a chance, I woulda tolt 'im on da Bell, hey? But no, he makes me drive all da way out. Youse know how much gas costs?"

"Who leased it?" Service asked.

"Gook prof from da college."

"Professor Pung?"

"Yah, guy croaked on da canal Hancock, hey?"

"Was there a contract?" Pyykkonen asked.

"We done cash, month at a time," Brown muttered.

"How much a month?"

"Why I gotta tell youse?"

"We can get a court order," Pyykkonen pressed. "This is a felony investigation."

"A thou."

"One thousand dollars a month? That's way over local prices for a place like this," Service said. Even with the view the place was old and too modest in size for a thou.

"Now I'm gonna have to pay bloody taxes on it," Brown complained.

Service stayed out of it. The U.P. had a well-established barter-and-cash economy that existed outside the official economy. Some Yoopers would go to great lengths to avoid paying taxes.

"Did you write receipts for the professor?" Pyykkonen asked.

"Shook on 'er, man to man," Brown said. "Don't need paper for dat, eh?"

Gus Turnage said, "Play ball with us and maybe your cash business stays yours."

Brown looked at Gus. "For real?"

"*If* you play ball," Gus said.

"If you *don't* cooperate," Limey Pyykkonen chimed in, "I will personally go to the IRS."

Brown quickly raised his hands in surrender. "I'm in da game, guys." He made a pained face, said, "TV's shot all ta bloody hell anyhow. I got beer inna truck. You guys want one?"

They said no. Brown and Pyykkonen left the cabin together. Service lit a cigarette while Gus disappeared through a door and down some stairs.

"Come down here," Gus shouted up at him.

The basement was one room. There was a large low rectangular object in the center, covered with a paint-spattered canvas drop cloth. Whatever was underneath looked to be six feet by four feet.

Gus picked up a corner of the tarp and looked underneath.

"Geez," he said, carefully peeling off the entire tarp.

The box turned out to be a collapsible cage made of half-inch stainless steel tubing. Gus knelt to click open the release mechanism. He looked around inside, took out tweezers and a plastic evidence bag, and began picking things up.

"Got something?" Service asked.

His friend held up a clump of hair. "Looks like the same you got from the professor's car."

"I hope the cap'n uses this to light a fire under the fed techies."

Gus grinned.

About forty minutes after they began, Sheriff Macofome showed up at the cabin and Service immediately wondered who had called him and why. He was dressed in cut-off sweatpants and a tank top in the style most cops called a wife-beater.

Sheriff Macofome carried a leather bag filled with special tools and old keys. He had the first gun cabinet open in ten minutes. The other two took even less time. All of them were empty.

Macofome and the two DNR officers helped Limey Pyykkonen dust the cabin for fingerprints. The local deputy sat outside on the stoop with the owner.

They covered the cabin methodically and it was nearly 3 A.M. before Pyykkonen and Macofome declared they had had enough.

"No point sticking around," Pyykkonen told them. "We'll clean up and you can all call it a night."

Brown had finished two six-packs while they worked, and Gus told him he'd drive him back to Houghton. "Bunk at my place?" he asked Service as he and Brown were getting ready to depart.

"See you there." Service paused before getting into Gus's truck to follow the Toyota.

When they got to Gus's, Shark was there, tying flies on a small table in the kitchen. There were bits of feather and fur all over the floor. Shark barely looked up. "Salmon," was all he said.

Service peeled off his bulletproof vest and shirt, unlaced his boots, and curled up on the sofa. He did not think about the case. He wondered where Nantz was and hoped she was being careful.

A phone was ringing just out of his consciousness. Service rolled over and squinted at the time on Gus's VCR: 7 A.M. He groped for his cell phone, but couldn't find it, heard Shark's voice in the kitchen, then nearer, pushing the phone at him.

"It's Walt," Shark said.

"Sorry to wake you up, but Karylanne and I were up all night with Enrica. We're at the Sheriff's Department. She's giving a statement to an officer. We promised her that if she told the cops, they'll do something to get this creep."

"Okay," Service said, wondering what the hell Walter was thinking, making deals with a witness. Emotion, he reminded himself, got in the way of police work. Still, he was impressed that the boy had not stopped with the meeting last night. He had shown initiative and doggedness. He wasn't happy Walter had gotten involved, but if he hadn't, things might be completely stalled. Because of Walter, they had direction again. It might pan out and it might not, but movement was better than stasis.

His son said. "When she's done here, we're gonna take her back to campus."

"You did the right thing," Service said, feeling the words stick as he spoke them. Had his old man ever been happy with anything he'd done?

"Your life really weirds out, doesn't it?"

"Sometimes."

Service called Pyykkonen at home. She answered on the first ring. "Enrica is at the station right now, giving a statement."

She hesitated. "I'm Homicide."

"I know that, but all of this is connected and right now Rafe Masonetsky's our only link to the Pungs."

"Fair enough," she said. "I'm headed down there now. I've already talked to Foxy Stevenson," she added. Stevenson was Michigan Tech's longtime football coach who had earned his nickname by recruiting lesser athletes than his opponents and somehow winning games through unorthodox leadership, flawless preparation, and creative game plans.

Coach Stevenson put a premium on players learning to think for themselves and perform under stress.

"What did he have to say?"

"Masonetsky failed his second drug test last spring. Anabolic steroids. Foxy gave him the boot and the boy didn't bother to finish the semester."

"You get an address?"

"Jefferson, Wisconsin. I guess his old man called Foxy and thundered like hell. He threatened to sue, but never followed through. Foxy said the kid's a loose cannon and we need to exercise caution."

Jefferson, Service thought. Things were beginning to come together, at least geographically. "You'd better get a move on," he said.

"I'm walking out the door now. Talk to you later."

He checked in with McCants. "How're you feeling?"

"Sore. I took yesterday off and called Wisconsin. The *jung* director's name is Randall Gage. He's not Korean and he's not interested in talking to cops. He says *jung* membership is a private matter and if we want names, we'd better bring a subpoena."

"You tell him we can do just that?"

"No, I figured you'd take care of that."

He made toast for breakfast and later called Captain Grant in Marquette. "We've found more of that hair and Gus'll get it off to the fed lab. I think it's time to turn up the burners."

"Are the samples similar?"

"They look identical: ursine and blond."

"Get the samples in the mail to the lab and consider the heat to be up."

"Thanks, Captain."

"How's your arm?"

"Fine." It had ached when he had awakened, but he had willed the soreness away and it felt fine now. He took the captain through the circumstances of the investigation, the coincidence of the figs, and the connection to the Pung family.

"Where's the son now?"

"Supposedly enrolled at Michigan, but maybe he's playing the same game he played here."

"Keep me informed," the captain said.

Pyykkonen showed up just after he finished eating.

"Want breakfast?" Shark asked, showing a connection to the world for the first time since last night. It wasn't like Wettelainen to react to women he'd not met before, but he certainly was reacting this morning and Service found it amusing.

She smiled as Shark pulled back a chair for her, took an order for eggs over easy and bacon, and started assembling the breakfast.

"Walter promised the girl that the cops will follow through on this," Service said.

"His name is Walt," Shark said from the stove.

Limey Pyykkonen said, "I called the prosecutor and Judge Pavelich. They're talking to people in Wisconsin about extradition. I'm going to drive down there and be in on the arrest. The sheriff talked to the university about Pung's son and his surrogate. They don't buy it at all."

Service wasn't surprised. "You want company in Wisconsin?"

She seemed to hesitate. "Sure."

"Call me on my cell phone. I'll meet you in Crystal Falls and we'll go from there."

On his way to Watersmeet he called Jimmy Crosbee, the student who looked after Newf and Cat when he and Nantz had to be away. Jimmy had first worked for them last year, was now a senior at Escanaba High School, and one of the top football players in the Upper Peninsula. The boy didn't hesitate and said he'd take care of the animals after practice, and if Service's absence ran into Friday, his cousin would fill in for him. The team had a Friday night game in Traverse City.

He located Sheena Grinda on the Automatic Vehicle Locator computer, called her on 800 MHz, and arranged to meet her at a coffee shop in Watersmeet.

Grinda arrived after him, dressed in shorts, a halter, and tiny white sandals. It was apparent that her uniform hid a lot and he wondered if this was by design.

"You didn't tell me it was a pass day," he said. Like most workers, officers got off two days a week, and called them pass days. Weekend was a term that didn't exist for them, and holiday was rarely more than a word in the dictionary.

"It's not. I'm working later tonight. I've got a dork running a trot line in one of the back bays of Beatons Lake."

This was the Grinda he knew, always working, always pushing. "Any luck on that cable?"

"There are nine places west of Marquette selling it. I've made phone contact with all of them. Now I have to go visit and show them the sample. They tell me there's a way to identify the brand and from that we might get a back-trail. I'm headed down to Menominee as soon as we're finished."

"Nice outfit," Service said.

"Bait is bait," she said, giving him the hint of a smile. "I had lunch with Simon yesterday," she said.

Simon del Olmo was in adjacent Iron County.

"Still no sign of that trapper you've been looking for, but he says he has a lead on another of his hidey holes. Does that mean anything to you?"

"He had a cabin on Mitigwaki Creek. It burned. But Simon found another place. He wasn't there. The guy gets around pretty well, considering he's blind and on one leg."

He watched Grinda drive away after a quick coffee and went into Watersmeet's nondescript post office. The postmistress was a tall, gaunt woman. She looked to be around his age, had long straight hair and freckles. He explained who he was and what he was doing.

"I'm not out to violate federal law," he said, "but I need to know if Oliver Toogood has a mailbox here, and if so, does he get any mail?" He knew that Trapper Jet didn't have a mailbox at his camp. He had looked and never seen one.

"He doesn't have a mailbox here."

"I guess the other question is moot," he said. He'd try Iron River next. It was on his way to Crystal Falls.

"He *had* one here," the woman added, "but I insisted he give it up so I could assign it to somebody else. We only have so many and there's a lot of demand."

"Reassign it? Because it didn't get used?"

"I think I've said all I can say."

"Thanks," he said. If Trapper Jet never got any mail, how was he getting a disability check from the government? Maybe he wasn't? If not, why? His mind began to flood with questions all leading off in uncontrolled and unproductive directions.

"You might check Mailboxes Forever. It's a private business. They opened in June. They've got some boxes, but mostly they mail packages and do packing."

"Great," Service said. Mailboxes Forever was in a small gray pole-barn near the intersection of US 2 and M-47. Service walked inside and found a man at the counter. He had a dozen yellow perch on a sheet of newspaper comics and was cleaning them. The man didn't look up.

"They biting?" Service asked. There was no size limit on yellow perch, but most people who chased them preferred the fat jumbos, ten inches and longer.

"Were this morning," the man said. "Hope they will be again tonight."

Service took out his badge and waved it under the man's nose to get his attention. "You got a customer named Oliver Toogood with a box?"

The man looked up. "Ought to arrest that sonuvabitch," he said, with a hard voice. "Came in here last year stinking to high heaven, demanded I give him a mailbox. Can you imagine that shit? *Give* him one! Said the feds didn't have room for him no more."

"Did you rent him one?"

The man's lips curled up in anger. "I told him to get da hell out. I'm in business here and I don't need some stinking cripple in here ranking out my customers."

The man's hands were covered with blood and the smell of fish was wafting through the place. "Yeah, it pays to keep a clean business."

"Right," the man said, returning his attention to his fish.

A quick stop at the main post office in downtown Iron River got him the same answer. Ollie Toogood did not have a mailbox. If not Watersmeet or Iron River, where? He was forced to conclude there was neither box nor checks, which raised the question of what the man lived on. Was the rumor true, that he was baiting bears for hunters willing to pay big fees? Or was he truly self-sufficient?

Just outside Crystal Falls he pulled into the District 4 office in time to see a small black bear lope through the parking lot, headed north toward the cover of a cedar swamp. It looked over its shoulder at him and accelerated as he pulled into a parking slot.

Margie, the district's dispatcher, waved as he passed by. He stopped into the office to see the district's lieutenant, but he was out. Service asked Margie if he could use a phone and she told him that since Yogi "Wolf Daddy" Zambonet had retired in the spring, his office was temporarily open. Zambonet was the state's wolf expert and had been involved in a case with Service the previous fall. Wolf Daddy opted for the early retirement engineered by Governor Sam Bozian to reduce the state's work force. As with other Bozian initiatives, he had gone for sheer numbers with no thought about institutional memory or expertise needed to provide continuity to state programs. His plan called for the replacement of only one in four who took the early out, but the legislature, led by Lorelei Timms, had risen up and vetoed this. All the early-outers would be replaced, but it would take eighteen months to get the force back up to some semblance of strength. It was one of the few wins against Bozian in his long tenure.

"He come around much?"

"No, he's been fishing and getting ready for bird season."

Yogi's office was empty, devoid of all the wolf posters, equipment, and gizmos he used in managing the U.P.'s wolf packs. The place looked sad to Service.

He called the captain again and told him he was going to Wisconsin with Pyykkonen.

"Explain," the captain said with his customary directness.

"Pung was involved in a Korean archery group. There's a club in Wisconsin, which happens to be where the Masonetsky kid lives. I asked McCants to talk to the archery club, but the director went hard-ass on her. We found a photo of Pung in traditional archery gear. It had to come from someplace, and the Masonetsky kid and the Pung kid are connected, or so I'm thinking."

"Have the Wisconsin authorities been contacted?"

"By the prosecutor and Judge Pavelich in Houghton."

"What about Wisconsin Fish and Game?" the captain said.

"Not yet," Service said. He added, "you've got contacts in Washington?"

"Fewer each year," the captain said. He didn't seem dismayed by the fact.

"There's a man lives in Iron County. His named is Ollie Toogood. My father introduced me to him when I was a kid. He's a decorated Korean war vet, on full disability, a former POW. When he got out of the VA hospital system, he came up here and has been here ever since."

"It sounds like you already know everything there is to know about him."

"I thought I did, but could you use your contacts to pull his service record for us. And, if possible, the address where they're sending his checks?"

"Priority?"

He didn't really know, but Trapper Jet's disappearance was beginning to bug him. "Not overnight, but soon should do it."

"Anything else?"

"No, that'll do it." He thanked the captain, hung up, and tried to call Nantz, but got her voice mail. "Hey, it's me. I'm headed to Wisconsin, near Milwaukee. I'll have my TX along. I miss you, Mar. By the way, Walter did good. I'll tell you all about it later." TX was cop jargon for telephone.

He parked at Simon del Olmo's house near Crystal Falls. Simon's truck was gone. His personal truck, an old Ford, was in the garage. It was nearly 3 P.M. and he called Pyykkonen and asked if she needed directions.

"You gave them to me once," she replied. "Not all women are directionally challenged. I should be there in ten minutes."

Jefferson, Wisconsin, was an attractive little farm town and county seat about halfway between Milwaukee and Madison. It was close to three hundred miles south of Crystal Falls. Pyykkonen didn't have much to say as she concentrated on her driving. They grabbed burgers at a fast food joint south of Green Bay and kept going.

En route he called Roger Guild, a Wisconsin game warden who had responsibility for the county that butted up against Iron County. Wisconsin wardens were limited to fish and game work and did not have full police powers. He had known Guild for several years.

"Rog, Grady Service. I'm headed down to Jefferson. Who's the warden down that way?"

"Wayno Ficorelli, why?"

"I need to plumb his mind."

"You won't need a long string," Guild said. He gave him the warden's cell phone number.

"Somebody else I should talk to?"

"No, Wayno's okay, just a little unorthodox."

"Thanks, Rog."

"It's cool." Service stared at the phone. Why was everyone talking like a sixteen-year old?

"What?" Pyykkonen asked, seeing the look on his face.

"Never mind," he said.

He immediately called his son. "Hey, I thought you ought to know — if you get down to the house, there's a high school kid named Crosbee taking care of the animals. He'll be coming in every night." It was strange to think that his son was in college and younger than Crosbee.

"Thanks, but I've got homework and hockey."

"Just thought you ought to know so you wouldn't think we had a break-in." The words sounded feeble in his mind. "Okay," he concluded. "I gotta go."

"You seem distracted," Pyykkonen said.

"Aren't we all?" he countered.

She looked down the highway and nodded.

He reached Warden Ficorelli on his first try.

"Your dime, start talking," Ficorelli answered.

"This is Grady Service. I'm a DNR detective up in the U.P. Roger Guild gave me your number."

"You know Roger?"

"For a few years."

"Okay, he's one of the good guys."

"The good guys?"

"He doesn't have his tongue surgically fitted to the bureaucratic butt-cracks in Madison. You a Packer-backer?"

"No."

"Good, I hate those fuckers. What kind of team can you build wearing yellow for chrissakes?"

"Lombardi did okay."

"He was a fucking Nazi. Since then, nothin' but pansies and players in yellow."

Ficorelli wasn't one to let his opinions lay dormant.

"I'm headed down to Jefferson. You know a guy named Masonetsky?"

"Rafe or his old man?"

"Either. Both," Service said.

"Coupla loudmouths," Ficorelli said. "I been bustin' Rafe since he was twelve. Everybody thought he was gonna go into the NFL, but he went off to some dink college up your way and hurt his leg and that's the end of that tune."

Ficorelli didn't know what had happened. "I don't think that's how it went down."

"No?"

"He failed a drug test. Steroids."

"Dumb fuck," Ficorelli said, sounding delighted. "Big dumb fuck."

"Do you know a guy named Randall Gage?"

"I thought you wanted to know about the Masonetskys."

"Gage too."

"Gage is a prick. He runs some archery shit up toward Oconomowoc. Bastard trucks in rabbits and cats and his members have night shoots."

"That's legal?"

"Fuck no, but the members are a tight-lipped buncha assholes and so far I haven't been able to make a case."

"You got a tip?"

"Madison got an anonymous letter."

"I have business with Gage and I also want to talk to Rafe Masonetsky."

"What business?"

"Gage's membership list."

"What about the big dumb fuck?"

Ficorelli didn't sound particularly stable, but he decided to confide some of the reasons.

"There's a warrant for his arrest. Drugs."

"Steroids?"

"No, something else."

"You want my help?"

"That's why I called. We'll be in town in about ten or so. Got the name of a good motel?"

"Hell with that motel shit," Ficorelli said. "You can bunk with Mom and me."

Service fought a snicker. "You live with your mother?" The man sounded like he was in his early thirties.

"You got a problem with that?" Ficorelli asked.

"No, no. But there's two of us."

"We got room." Ficorelli gave him directions and promised to meet them at ten.

"We have a place to bunk tonight," Service told Pyykkonen. That will give us all day tomorrow to do business. We can talk to the cops tonight, get everything coordinated, make sure the warrants are in, check on subpoena status."

"Sounds like a plan," she said.

Ficorelli and his mother lived in a farmhouse a mile north of town. It was surrounded by fields filled with dried field corn that rattled in the breeze.

The warden was no taller than five-six and small-boned, but jutted out his jaw like a feisty dog ready to do battle over anything. His mother was frail and gentle with blue hair, and blue veins showing through her pale cheeks.

Ficorelli met them with glasses of red wine. "Made this myself," he said, beaming with pride. He was still in uniform. His mother had loaded a table with snack food and made pasta while they munched.

"How can you eat like that and stay so skinny?" Pyykkonen asked their host as he hoisted spoonfuls of food and swallowed without chewing. He ate like some sort of constrictor, Service thought.

"I fuck a lot," Ficorelli said, breaking into a laugh.

Pyykkonen glared at Service, who raised his eyebrows in answer.

Service stepped onto the porch to try Nantz again and heard Ficorelli yip.

When he stepped back into the house, the warden's cheek was red and he was eating silently, his attention focused on biscotti.

Pyykkonen stared at Service. Her look was not one of amusement.

· 11 ·

Mama Ficorelli was up early the next morning and when Service came down to the kitchen she was already piling food on the table. The aroma of baking bread filled the house like an airborne intoxicant.

"Did you sleep all right?" Mama asked.

"Yes, fine." But he hadn't. He had left another voice mail with Nantz and still hadn't heard from her.

Sometime during the night he also thought he heard voices in the next room—Wayno and Pyykkonen—but he decided that was ridiculous and went back to sleep.

Limey came down to breakfast before Ficorelli and sat on the side of the table, next to an open chair. Her hair was frazzled, and she looked like she hadn't slept much. An insipid smile was pasted on her face.

"Good morning," she said with more enthusiasm than Service was accustomed to.

Mama Ficorelli was serving blueberry pancakes when her son came bouncing into the room and plopped in a chair beside Pyykkonen. The antagonism of last night seemed to have dissipated.

Service ate in silence, thinking about the day ahead, wondering if Rafe Masonetsky and Randall Gage were going to help give the two investigations new directions and impetus. When he tuned in, Pyykkonen and Wayno were talking about porcupines and ladybugs. Service tuned them out and tried to get Limey's attention, but she was locked on to Wayno and it took a while.

"What?" she asked.

"We set on a subpoena for the archery club?"

"No," she said. "The prosecutor says we don't have enough to justify one."

"Not even if Pung was a member?"

"He's a prick," Ficorelli said, joining in. "Don't worry, Service. I've got a plan. We don't need a fucking subpoena. We'll get the list."

Pyykkonen smiled supportively.

Service exhaled and returned his attention to a cup of hot coffee.

After breakfast they thanked Ficorelli's mother and Service thought he saw Wayno's hand on Pyykkonen's rump, touching her like this wasn't the first time.

Outside Wayno gave them directions to the *jung* and told them he had some things to do before they joined up at 10 A.M.

Service and Pyykkonen cruised into town and checked out a place called Bipedal Bowling, where Rafe Masonetsky worked. The sign said, ONLY TWO-LANE BOWLING EAST OF WYOMING. BURGERS: FIVE FOR A BUCK. The parking lot for the bowling alley was behind the building with the red brick facade. It was small, unpaved, and there were few lights.

"What the hell does that mean?" Service asked, pointing at the sign.

"We're in Wisconsin," Pyykkonen said. "They think differently down here."

"Why the hell won't the prosecutor cooperate?"

"He's cooperating—on the warrant for Masonetsky. We'll have an extradition order by tonight. It's all set."

"Good. But what about Randall Gage?"

"Don't worry, Wayno has a plan."

Wayno? "Last night you looked ready to kill the guy."

"I was. He grabbed my ass while you were outside."

"And you slapped him. I saw the mark."

"Not that hard."

"And now the ass-grabber is Wayno?"

"Leave it alone," she said. "When I was a rookie in Lansing, my first supervisor was a woman, the first female sergeant in the Lansing force. I had another officer grab me one night on patrol, so I asked her what someone should do when that happened."

Service watched her while she drove.

She glanced at him. "She said, 'First, decide if you like it.' "

"So you didn't like it?"

"I liked it just fine," she said, "but I didn't want him thinking he was in control."

"What was all that talk about porcupines and ladybugs?"

Pyykkonen looked over at him and smiled. "Porcupines have sex every day of their lives, and the orgasm of a female ladybug lasts up to nine hours."

Service mulled it over for several minutes as they moved through town. The slap and antagonism had been replaced by bedroom hair and red eyes, and the sex habits of porcupines and ladybugs. "Jesus!" he blurted out. "You slept with him?"

"Not that it's any of your business, but yes. It was my decision and now you're wondering, am I Macofome's regular squeeze, or what? Again, that's equally none of your business. I sleep with whoever I please, when I please. As I understand it, you've gotten around yourself."

Service stared at her. Had she been checking up on him, and why? The thought made him wince.

"If men can do it, women can do it," she said. "Welcome to the twenty-first century. Sex is just sex."

They met Ficorelli about a mile south of the *jung*, which had the formal name of Oconomowoc Korean Archery Center (OKAC).

The little warden was jacked up on adrenaline. "You make your request. If he cooperates, fine. If not, step back and let me take over."

"What's you plan?"

"I'll take care of it," Ficorelli said.

The OKAC was an old barn that had been re-sided and re-done. The range itself was built at the back of a housing development, with a tree-line to the north and homes on both sides. Service saw a large sign with Chinese characters. The one he had seen in Pung's photo? He felt encouraged.

Randall Gage came out to meet them. He was a short, dumpy man wearing a padded black coat and black felt boots that stretched up to his knees. He wore a Fu Manchu mustache, carefully trimmed, and had dark eyes, which made him look menacing.

"Mr. Gage, I'm Grady Service. You talked to my colleague, Officer Candice McCants."

"I figured I'd see somebody," he said. "I've talked to my lawyer. You can't have our list. It's an unwarranted intrusion of privacy."

Ficorelli didn't wait for Service to react. "Okay, Randy, let's talk a different matter. State law does not allow the discharge of an arrow within one hundred and fifty yards of an occupied dwelling. This is called the safety zone rule."

"I *know* the law," Gage replied. "It applies only to hunting and we are not a hunt club. We are an archery shooting range."

"Did you or did you not complain to the Jefferson County Sheriff's Department about someone who shot a deer on this so-called range?"

"I did, but I did not file a complaint. We took care of that through club rules."

"Where did this happen?"

Gage pointed to a side of the long range.

"There?" Ficorelli asked, seeking confirmation.

"Yes, I just said there."

"What happened to the member?" Service asked.

"As a consequence, you dumped him?" Ficorelli said.

"Our members are very serious about rules." Gage looked confident. "He was dismissed."

"A club rule was broken," Ficorelli said.

"Yes," Gage said. "What point are you so ineptly trying to make?"

"This," the little warden said. "A rule was broken on your property. In breaking your rule, two state laws were also violated. A deer was killed out of season and an arrow was discharged within the safety zone."

"I never filed a complaint," Gage said, his eyes beginning to dart.

"I'm filing the complaint. You've just confirmed the violations."

"It was not inside the safety zone," Gage insisted.

Ficorelli pointed to a tree and a fence behind it to the east. "See the green roof beyond the fence? It's fifteen yards from the house to the tree, and from that tree to your first target is one hundred and twenty yards, meaning you're fifteen yards short of the required safety requirement. I am going to ask the prosecutor to close you down for safety violations."

"We're a range," Gage said.

"You admitted to the killing and to the distance. I have no choice but to act."

"You little bastard."

"As a matter of fact," Ficorelli said. "I am a bastard. My mom never married my dad. I don't consider that a negative."

"I am going to call my attorney," Gage said.

"Good. I'll call the prosecutor and we can get the both of them out here, and while we're at it, we'll need your membership list in order to talk to those involved. Once they're under oath we'll be asking them about night shooting of rabbits and cats."

"You think you're pretty smart," Gage said, holding his cell phone.

"C'mon," Ficorelli purred. "You do, too. Your ass is against the wall. My colleagues from Michigan want to confirm the names of some of your members. Is that too much to ask in return for looking past your transgressions?"

"What are the names?" Gage asked.

"They want to read them on the list for themselves," Ficorelli said.

"Are you calling me a liar?"

"No," the warden said. "I'm trying to save you from lying. If you don't show them the list, I'm gonna go forward on charges and then we'll get the list and then we'll charge your ass with perjury and conspiracy."

Gage pivoted and went quickly into the building.

Ficorelli stood calmly.

Gage returned and held out a folder. Ficorelli nodded at Service.

Service took the folder, went to an outdoor table and sat down with Pyykkonen standing beside him. Both Pungs were members. There was a line drawn through Terry's name. The Masonetskys were both members; Rafe Masonetsky's name also had a line drawn through it. The elder Masonetsky was a member of the club's board of governors. His kid had been suspended in college and kicked out of the club. He was undoubtedly an unhappy parent.

"Rafe Masonetsky shot the deer," Service said.

"I don't have to disclose that," Gage said, trying to maintain some dignity.

"Terry Pung's name is crossed out."

"At his father's request," Gage said.

"Is there a record of that?" Service asked.

"No, it was a personal conversation."

"When?"

"Early August."

"Why?"

"That's between father and son," Gage said.

Which was not long before the elder Pung turned up dead. Cause and effect? "Thank you, Mr. Gage."

"Shove it," Gage said, snatching the folder back and stalking away sullenly from the three officers.

Service looked at Ficorelli and smiled. "You nailed that one."

"Told you I had a plan," he said.

The Wisconsin State Police insisted on being in on the arrest so as to facilitate the transfer under the extradition order. After processing, the prisoner would be officially turned over to Pyykkonen, who would take him back to Houghton. They spent most of the day talking to various officials and getting a tactical plan in place. In the end it was decided that there would be a city cop named McYest, a county deputy named Mawbry, a trooper named Kalminson, along with Service, Pyykkonen, and Ficorelli, whose role was primarily that of observer.

McYest drove by the bowling alley around 9 P.M. and reported that Rafe Masonetsky's truck was in the parking lot. The alleys closed at eleven and employees were usually gone by 11:30. The decision was made to assemble in the parking lot at 10:45. After some debate, the team also decided that Kalminson and Pyykkonen should enter the premises and make the arrest inside as close to 11 P.M. as possible. McYest would position himself out front on the street. Mawbry, Service, and Ficorelli would be in the rear parking lot as backups.

Service had been involved in hundreds of arrests during his career and knew from experience that while most situations went as planned, some went down the toilet, and almost always without warning. He had no feelings one way or the other about this one.

It was dark, the parking lot poorly lit. Pyykkonen and Kalminson were inside less than thirty seconds when a tall, powerfully built man came striding out. He wore dark baggy pants that hung around his hips and looked ready to fall. He ambled deliberately, showing no haste. Ficorelli whispered, "Rafe."

What had gone wrong and where were Pyykkonen and the Wisconsin trooper? Service asked himself as he stepped forward from the shadow of the truck to block the man's path.

"Rafe Masonetsky?" Service said.

"Dude, who wants to know?"

Service jiggled the badge hanging from a chain around his neck. "Detective Grady Service, Michigan DNR, Mr. Masonetsky." Ficorelli moved along the far side of the truck to get behind the man. Deputy Mawbry headed for the door to let the others know Rafe had somehow gotten outside.

"How's it goin'?'" Masonetsky said. He seemed calm.

"You're off early tonight," Service said.

"I got a date, dude." Masonetsky pivoted to look at Ficorelli. "What is your *problem*?" The football player looked back at Service. He was no more than three feet away and made Service feel small.

Service had been waiting for Pyykkonen and Kalminson but sensed he had to act before the man bolted. "Rafe Masonetsky, you are under arrest." He carefully listed the charges and quickly moved into Miranda, reading the prisoner's constitutional rights from the plastic card he carried at all times.

"You're creepin' me out fuck-head," Masonetsky said menacingly.

"Lay down on the ground and put your hands behind you," Service said.

"Fuck you, the ground's cold."

"Do you want a lawyer?"

"I don't need a lawyer, dude, that bitch wanted it," Masonetsky said. "She couldn't get enough of it."

"You put roofies in figs."

"That was Terry. The bitch wanted it. The roofies were to help her relax."

"Terry gave you the figs?"

"Whole thing was his idea, dude."

"Did he join in?"

"Dude, he just wanted to watch, know what I'm sayin'?"

"I've got it," Wayno Ficorelli said. He held up a small cassette recorder.

Service felt his adrenaline rising quickly. Masonetsky was in the process of making a decision. Service wished he could see his eyes.

"Down on the ground, Rafe," he said. Using first names sometimes softened arrest situations.

There was a flash of white light and pain surging through Service's face and head and he felt himself going out and clutching.

He awoke with a throbbing head and face in a white room with masked faces above him.

"You're in a hospital, Detective," one of the masks said.

"In Madison," another mask added.

Madison was forty miles west of Jefferson. "Where are the others?" Service asked.

He tried to sit up, but hands kept him down. He reached for one of the restraining hands, but pain shot up his arm and he let his right hand drop back to his side. "You've had a pretty nasty bump," a mask said. "We're going to put you to sleep now and do some repairs."

"What am I, a damn Chrysler?"

Nobody laughed. A plastic mask was placed over his face. He heard a hiss in the background.

Service saw Ficorelli sitting next to the bed, flipping though a magazine. Pyykkonen was standing by the doorway. Nothing else registered.

"He's waking up," Pyykkonen said.

A nurse came into the room and fiddled with an I.V. drip beside the bed. Service felt like an object. A doctor came in after the nurse. He was young and tan. "How do you feel?"

"Numb," Service said.

"We give great dope," the doctor said. "Do you know where you are?"

"Hospital."

"Right, in Madison. You were transported from Jefferson. Do you re-member that?"

"No."

"You have a severe concussion," the doctor said. "We put twelve stitches into your upper lip and fifteen into your forehead. Your nose is fractured and we played with getting that straight, but you may need more attention later. You had some gravel lodged in the back of your head, but I think we managed to get all of that. Your right pinkie is frac-tured and splinted. That should heal fine. It was a clean break. We're not worrying about an infection, but we are going to keep you here tonight. We are going to be waking you up periodically to make sure your brain doesn't try to take a vacation. If you need anything, press the button under your left forefinger. Please press it now."

Service pressed the button.

"Okay, good. I'm sorry we'll have to wake you up, but it's for the best. I'm sure you understand." The doctor left the room.

Service tried to adjust his body position, but couldn't. "What's going on?" he asked.

"Wayno?" Pyykkonen said.

"Masonetsky head-butted you. Blood went everywhere, but you didn't go down. You grabbed him by the throat and head-butted him back, two or three times. It sounded like a concrete block dropped from the ceiling in an empty gym. He started to go down, but you wouldn't let go. You had your hands locked on his throat. I grabbed at you and yelled at you to let go, but you were on automatic and I couldn't get through. I had to snap your finger to break your grip. I'm sorry about that."

"He kept you from doing more than hurting the boy," Pyykkonen said.

"Masonetsky?"

"He's a mess," Ficorelli said. "Broken cheekbones, fractured nose, frac-tured jaw, concussion, cuts and abrasions. It was like two big bucks going head to head. We've called your captain." Good, Nantz would know.

"They're going to hold Masonetsky until the day after tomorrow," Pyykkonen said, "then I'll drive him to Houghton."

"Why did he come out early?"

"Gage called his old man, and his old man tipped his kid that we were asking about him."

"There's a plane coming to fetch you, Mr. Big Shot," Ficorelli said. "Some senator is sending it."

Timms. "She's a *state* senator," Service said. "Not a real one."

"Real enough to run for governor," Pyykkonen said.

Service nodded.

When he awoke he felt pressure beside him, shifted his head and found Maridly Nantz cozied up against him, outside the covers. Walter Commando was asleep in the chair where he had last seen Ficorelli sitting.

He tried to move his left hand, but it hurt. He lightly nudged Nantz with his elbow.

"Not tonight, honey," she whispered. "You have a headache." She slid her hand up to his face and let it rest there. No words were necessary. He went back to sleep smiling.

· 12 ·

Walter Commando was back in Service's room, sitting in a chair, a book in his lap, but he was not studying. Nantz had gone out to make arrangements.

"What are you staring at?" Service asked his son.

The boy drew in a deep breath, seemed hesitant to answer. "You look, like . . . heinous."

"That's bad?"

"Like, mega."

"Is that bad as in bad or bad as in cool?"

"Way cool. The bad guys won't be able to look at you."

"You're not helping my self-image."

"Fathers don't have self-images."

"This one does."

"You really don't remember what happened?"

Service exhaled. "There was a little wrestling." Which was hearsay. What he remembered was a flash of white, spiking adrenaline, silence.

"Wull, Peel-grim," Walter said, with a bad impersonation of John Wayne. "We all know yore tough. You don't gotta be humble too."

"I'm not humble."

"You said it, not me," Walter said.

"Finish your sentence," Service said.

The boy looked puzzled. "Dude," Service said.

"Dude," Walter said. "Did the doctor happen to mention permanent loss of brain function?"

"Not a problem," Service said.

Walter looked at him. "Does that mean yes, it's not a problem, or yes, he talked to you?"

Service smirked and wanted to laugh, but his face was too sore and swollen. "See how it feels to talk to you?"

Walter rolled his eyes.

Nantz came into the room. "How it feels to talk to who?"

"Stay out of this," Service and his son said in unison.

"There's a driver waiting to take us to the airport," Nantz said.

"In Madison?" Service asked.

"Madison is where we are," she said.

"I need to make a side trip on the way to the airport."

"Is there something I can do for you?" she asked.

"Not unless you can beam me over to Jefferson, Scotty."

Walter Commando and Maridly Nantz exchanged glances. "Are you all right, Grady?"

"You tell me."

"I don't think you're all right."

"Can we go to Jefferson now?"

"Why?"

"I want to talk to Masonetsky."

"That idea sucks," Wayno Ficorelli said, walking into the room. "He's in the hospital there."

"You broke my finger," Service said.

Nantz tapped Walter on the shoulder. "Let's go."

"You broke a finger on my right hand," Service said.

"There wasn't time to assess handedness," Ficorelli said.

"You need a remedial class to improve observational skills."

"I observe that you guys are leaving. Am I going along?"

"So you can cripple my other hand?"

"Let's *all* move," Nantz said sternly.

"Tell the kid it was just some wrestling," Service said.

Ficorelli looked at Walter. "It was just some wrestling."

"Was there a winner?" the boy asked.

They were in the corridor. "The law," Service said.

"Is that the same as justice?" his son asked.

"Rarely."

"This is not uplifting for a young college student."

"It gets worse as you get older."

Nantz said, "Okay, *boys*."

They stopped at the discharge desk so that Service could sign out and continued out into bright sunlight.

Ficorelli said, "Like, am I invited, or am I wasting steps here?"

"Next time we work a case maybe I'll have the finger re-broken before we start," Service said.

Nantz opened the side door of a black super cargo van.

Service looked at Ficorelli. "Mount up, finger-snapper."

When they were all seated and belted, Nantz said, "You can all shut up now."

Walter said, "It's them, not me."

"We're bonding," Service said.

"The Mars thing," Ficorelli chipped in.

"No bonding in this van," she said.

"Does that mean sex is out of the question?" Ficorelli asked.

Service cuffed him on the back of the head with his left hand.

Rafe Masonetsky was lodged in the Jefferson Hospital. Pyykkonen was already there, waiting for him to be handed over so she could haul him back to Houghton.

As soon as Ficorelli saw Pyykkonen, he abandoned Service.

Rafe sat on a bed, his face swollen and bandaged. His first words: "I want my lawyer."

"Terry Pung's father is dead," Service said. "We're gonna find Terry and I have a hunch he's going to implicate you."

"Dude, I know nothing about that," Masonetsky said shakily.

"Where's Terry?"

"Ann Arbor, I heard, but I don't know, man. He called me in August and asked if I could help him with something, but I had to work."

"Where did he call from?"

"I don't know, man. Ask his mama."

"His mama?"

"He's a mama's boy. He don't do shit unless he checks with her."

"You've met her?"

"*More* than met, dude." Rafe shuddered when he spoke.

Service decided that Rafe was afraid of the woman. "You have a problem with her?"

"She's like, hot, man."

Service switched directions. "Cats and rabbits at the archery range."

"What?"

"I figure you know who supplies Gage. Gage gave you up to us to get Ficorelli off his back. Who supplies him?"

"Fuck, I should tell you?"

"Let's count the reasons: resisting arrest, assault and battery against an officer of the law, attempting to flee, criminal sexual conduct, drugs—you want me to go on?"

Masonetsky moaned softly. "What do I get?"

"Payback on Gage, and we tell the prosecutor you cooperated fully."

"Jubal Charter," Rafe said.

"Does Ficorelli know him?"

Masonetsky nodded. "Everybody knows him. He's the county's animal control guy. You busted me up good," Rafe said.

"We'll call it even on that score," Service said, his face aching.

Ficorelli was outside, sticking close to Pyykkonen. Service looked at him and shook his head. "Jubal Charter supplies rabbits and cats to Gage."

"Hah," Ficorelli said. "They hire Wisconsin wardens up there in Michigan?"

"It happens. Tell your mom thanks for her hospitality."

On the drive back to Madison, Nantz said, "You'd recommend he be hired?"

"He's unorthodox, but he gets the job done."

Service was surprised to see Nantz's Cessna on the tarmac. "I thought the senator sent her plane?"

"Sent her pilot. Actually she didn't have a choice. I was coming whether she approved or not. I wanted to bring Walter and I couldn't justify burning her fuel."

Service sat in the right seat while Nantz did her preflight check and started engines. Walter sat in the jump seat just behind and between them. "You never called me back," Service said.

"Her pace is a killer," Nantz said. "We were on the go constantly and we had some mechanical problems in Saginaw. Grady, the polls show her moving ahead. I think she'll win."

"You never called me back," he repeated.

"She came as soon as she heard," Walter said. "Cut her some slack."

"Put a sock in it," Service said over his shoulder. "This is between us."

"What he said," Nantz said, asking for taxi instructions.

As they turned over Lake Michigan and began to climb, Nantz looked over at him. "That girl who was burned? She didn't make it. Candi says they're gonna petition to try the other kid as an adult."

"Fourteen," Service said, shaking his head. It sometimes seemed that God's only interest in mankind was body count. "Are we dropping the kid in Houghton?" he asked with a nod toward Walter.

"Duh, I'm coming home for a couple of days," Walter said. "Remember?"

Nantz looked at Service. "The captain says you *will* take a couple of pass days. He also says he has the information you wanted, but not to think about any work until you've been off a couple of days."

"What about you?" Service asked.

"Lori said we can take as long as we need. Have you heard what Sam is going to do when he leaves office?"

Die, Service thought. "No."

"Lori says that there's some inside talk that he may move to Washington and take a cabinet job."

"His reward from the Republicans for destroying the state?"

She shook her head and called, "Level at angels fourteen."

Service looked at her. "Why do they call it angels? If you put the plane a thousand feet into the ground, do they call *smashed at devils one* or something?"

"Is he always like this?" Walter asked.

"Sometimes he's worse," Nantz said, adjusting the throttles.

· 13 ·

S ervice's home office was still a work in progress and consisted mostly of an old oak door across two sawhorses, a rickety desk chair, a battered metal file cabinet, and two huge wall maps. Nantz was constantly threatening to bring in a builder to construct a proper office, but he preferred the basement as it was and asked her to leave it alone. So far she had. One map was of the Mosquito Wilderness, the other of the Upper Peninsula. Since putting up the U.P. map the previous summer, it had hung untouched. By contrast, he was constantly making new notations on the Mosquito chart. For Service the Mosquito remained alive in all ways, though his notations had tapered off since Candi McCants had taken responsibility for the area.

He got out a box of red pushpins, lit a cigarette, and stood in front of the U.P. map, which was mounted on a floor-to-ceiling cork wall. He started inserting pins, one for each event that could be connected—at least in his mind. The pins stretched from McMillan in the east, to Iron and Gogebic Counties in the west, a distance of almost one hundred and eighty miles. He inserted pins for Griff Stinson, Betty Very and She-Guy Zuiderveen, Sheena Grinda, Trapper Jet, Dowdy Kitella, and finally, a red pin at the location of Pung's body on the Portage Canal. He wrote off the events in Trenary with Bryce Verse and the girls as separate and unrelated.

He balanced an unlit cigarette in his mouth, put his feet up, and studied the pattern. Griff lost a bear—confirmed. Bearclaw probably lost a bear. Sheena found a bear caught in steel cable. There was ursine hair in Pung's Saturn and more hair resembling it in the Brown camp at Lac La Belle in the Keeweenaw. Trapper Jet's presence on Betty Very's turf remained unexplained, and his grousing about Kitella probably was no more than a gripe. There was no pattern to be seen. The only pattern he had to work with was ursine hair in the car in Hancock and hair and a steel cage at Pung's rented camp at Lac La Belle. Had a bear been kept at the camp and moved to a boat in Hancock? This was the only way to read it at this point, and the main thing he wanted to focus on.

"Hon?" Nantz said from the stairs.

He looked over at her. "Captain Grant is here," she said. "You okay?" No, he was frustrated.

The captain came down the stairs stiffly, his uniform freshly pressed. Service gave him the only chair and stood by the wall. The captain sat stiffly with a manila folder in his lap, looking more uncomfortable than normal as he surveyed the Mosquito wall map.

"Hard to let go?" the captain said.

"Any word from the federal lab?" Service asked, changing the subject.

"Not as yet. You will take more than a couple of days off," his boss added in a tone that told Service it was not a request.

"I'm fine," Service said. He didn't want people fussing over him. He had been hurt many times and he had always eventually healed.

"Grady," the captain said, looking directly into his eyes. The use of his given name jolted him. "At our age we can't be involving ourselves in physical confrontations. Over time we have to learn to use our brains instead of our muscles."

What was this about? Service wondered. A reprimand?

"By every measure of performance, you should be a captain now, or at least a lieutenant, but until last year you were still a working warden."

Was he looking for an explanation? "I always liked my job, Captain." Which was the truth. It was hard enough to look after himself and the Mosquito without having to worry about a bunch of officers.

"That has been self-evident," Grant said. "It is equally clear to me that you have taken creative steps to ensure that you would never be considered for promotion."

What the hell did the captain want?

"You have over the course of your career gone out of your way to annoy Lansing and to isolate yourself from the center."

"Not intentionally," Service said, beginning to feel defensive. "They didn't like me. I didn't like them. It was balanced."

"Rationalize it any way you like," the captain said, "but your past behaviors ensured that the overall mission of the department was compromised."

"Sir?"

"For an organization to function at maximum efficiency and to discharge its mission, it needs to have the right people in the right jobs. You haven't been in the right job for a long time and despite your denials, I believe that this was a matter of choice. Your selfishness, Grady, affected all of us."

The rebuke stung. He admired and respected the captain, and was confused by the captain's disappointment in him. "Sir, why are you telling me this?"

"I am going to retire, Grady. I have recovered most of what was lost from the stroke, but frankly I don't have the endurance I once had, and I can't concentrate the way I once could. It's time for me to step aside and make room for someone who can fully perform."

Grady Service didn't know what to say.

"If I were a betting man," the captain went on, "I would wager on Senator Timms capturing the gubernatorial helm. After she takes office, I will step down."

"What if she doesn't win?"

The captain smiled. "She will, Detective. But here is my concern: She is extremely smitten by you and I fear that she will move to appoint you to a position that you do not deserve. You have been a polarizing personality throughout your career."

"Sir, I haven't done anything to encourage her attention."

"I understand that, but I am telling you that while I think you could perform any job in the department, you have not earned it and I expect that when the time comes, you will reject her patronage."

"Captain, I don't want another job. You have my word on that."

Grant nodded crisply. "Good." He held out the folder. "This is the information on Mr. Toogood."

"Anything interesting in it?"

"I haven't looked. I have no idea why you wanted it, or where your mind is these days. You asked for the record and I have now delivered it. I do not want you back on duty until you can assure me that you are feeling closer to normal."

Service was tempted to object, but said simply, "Yessir."

He walked upstairs with the captain, who made small talk with Nantz and Walter, and then escorted him to his vehicle. "Our conversation today is a matter of honor," the captain said. "Just the two of us, man to man. I trust you and depend on you and I know you will never let me down."

Service found himself staring at the driveway long after the captain was gone.

Nantz prepared a lunch of ravioli with rosemary walnut sauce and brought two bowls down to Service in his basement office. He opened a bottle of 1999 Cima Merlot Montervo and splashed some in two glasses. The wine was new to them, the color rich and red.

"I didn't have Kasseri," Nantz said apologetically. "I used Asiago and I didn't have time to pick up fresh *pane*."

"This is great," Service said with his mouth full. It hurt to try to eat.

She sipped the wine. "Nice."

Walter came downstairs sniffing. "I'm hungry."

"Pasta in the kitchen," Nantz said.

"Do I get wine?" he asked. "Sheba always let me have a glass of wine."

"No," Service said.

"I figured you'd say that," Walter mumbled, going back upstairs.

"He's always pushing," Service said.

"You didn't when you were that age?"

"If I had, I'd have looked like I do now."

"I pushed my parents all the time, especially my dad," Nantz confessed.

"Look how you turned out," Service said.

She smiled. "Not too shabby, hey?"

He nodded and pushed his bowl aside. Half the ravioli was still there.

"You're hurting," she said. "It always shows in your appetite."

"The swelling makes it hard to chew."

She put her hand on his leg. "It will go away."

She shook her head with worry and took a swig of wine. "What did the captain want?"

"He brought me some stuff I asked for."

"He was here quite a while."

He had made a promise to the captain and, given what his boss had confided and Nantz's closeness to Senator Timms, he couldn't tell her. "It was just work stuff, and he thinks I should take a few more days off."

"Will you?"

"I can't sit round on my keester all day, babe."

"You're holding back on what you and the captain talked about."

"He said it was just between us."

"So if Lori says something is just between her and me, I shouldn't tell you?"

"A promise is a promise," he said, wondering what the senator had told her.

"I thought we were always going to tell each other everything."

·"Mar."

"I know, I know, but I'm dying to tell you something and I can't."

"Maybe there'll be times when we have to accept a delay in telling each other things," he said.

Nantz laughed. "God," she said. "Lori is right. You have the instincts of a politician and don't even recognize it."

"She doesn't know me."

"I think she knows you better than you realize. Don't be fooled by her appearance, Grady. She's sharp and she thinks, quote, Grady is underutilized, end quote."

He leaned over and kissed her. The captain might be right about Timms, he decided.

"Is that a dismissal?"

"I really have to work."

"You're supposed to be resting."

"I am resting."

"Okay, spoilsport." She collected the wine bottle, bowls, forks, and glasses and went upstairs.

Newf padded down the stairs, came over to the table and lay down underneath.

"What're you?" he asked the dog. "Second shift guard?"

The dog wagged her tail.

· 14 ·

Service heard the telephone ring and ignored it.

"I need to get back to school tomorrow," Walter told his father.

"My truck's in Crystal Falls," Service said. "Nantz can drop us there in the morning and I'll run you up to Houghton."

"How come you call her Nantz?" Walter asked.

Service had never thought about it. "Habit, I guess."

Walter nodded and paused. It seemed to Service that he had more on his mind, but the boy went upstairs and Service heard the TV come on.

He put his feet up and tried to think. Violets who committed crimes always left trails and wakes; sooner or later you picked up a strand, and if you were lucky, it let you make the case. All cases had this in common—threads. But habitual criminals were generally more careful than the impulsives. The trick was to find the threads you needed and stick with them. In the Pung case, he still felt blind. He liked Pyykkonen, though her behavior with Wayno Ficorelli had taken him by surprise and made him wonder if she was also impulsive on the job. If so, she'd be jumping from this to that without making progress, letting velocity substitute for direction. Again he wondered about her dismissal from Lansing.

"You look unhappy," Nantz said from the stairs. "That was Lori on the phone."

"Just thinking," he said. The homicide was Pyykkonen's and the shit belonged to Gus and him. But if she didn't get off her ass and start picking up some of her threads, neither case was going anywhere. He hated being dependent on others, but as a detective this was becoming the rule rather than the exception. Did the captain understand *that*? The more he thought about it, the more irritated he got. "What did the senator want?"

"She wants me back downstate tomorrow. She's going to introduce a bill, hold a quick press conference, and get back on the campaign trail."

Service's mind was elsewhere.

"This bill," Nantz said, "will provide a mandatory ten-year sentence in any case where a police officer is injured."

"There are plenty of laws on the books now," he said.

"She feels strongly about this."

"In any case—misdemeanor or felony?"

"That's what she says."

"As it stands now most people plead out on misdemeanors, because the time and money aren't all that much. But you slap ten years on stuff and they are gonna fight like hell in court, and that's a disaster for us." Most conservation officers spent little time in court, in large part because they made good cases, which defendants and their lawyers couldn't fight effectively. He had spent less time in court than other officers, but if a law like this went on the books, all officers would be spending a lot more time in court than in the woods. With staffing already low, that would put even fewer people out where they should be.

"Lousy idea," he added. He explained the unintended effects that might accrue.

Nantz listened attentively and when he had finished talking, she asked, "Do you mind if I share this with Lori?"

"Your choice," he said, quickly adding, "but let it be your response, not mine."

"Why? Lori respects you."

"I don't like politicians leaning on me."

"You might consider it a sign of respect; and in any event, I brought this up, not her."

"She's playing you."

"You're underestimating me, Service." And her face made it clear that she didn't like it.

"A politician trying to get elected uses everybody and everything they can to get what they want."

"Like a detective?" she shot at him.

"I guess," he said. " The boy needs to get back to school tomorrow. Can you drop us at Simon's? I'll drive him from there."

"Simon's?"

"I left the Yukon there when Pyykkonen and I went down to Wisconsin."

"I can just fly him up to Houghton."

"No, I can drive him."

"You know what he'd really like? To fish with us."

"We don't have time," he said. "Neither of us."

"You're supposed to be relaxing, and I can *make* time," she said with a tone of voice that told him he was going to be fishing tonight. "I'll fly you guys to Crystal in the morning and then head for TC. Let's run up to

Slippery Creek. Fresh trout on the grill sounds good," she said. "All we need is bacon, a little brown sugar, some salt, pepper, and fresh lemons. I'll run Walter into town to get him a license and then we can get this show on the road."

Service knew better than to argue. Once she got a plan fixed in her mind, that was the end of discussion.

She bounded up the stairs, yelling Walter's name.

He called Pyykkonen at home and she took a long time answering.

"You alone?" he asked.

"Not that it's any of your business," she said, "but your friend Shark just left. He made breakfast for us."

Shark? Breakfast? In all the time he'd known Wetelainen, he'd never known him to go on dates. He might pick up a woman at a bar and bring her home, but no dates. He was too cheap and focused on other things to tolerate the time demands of romance.

"He's a good guy," she said.

Shark Wetelainen, Chief Macofome, Warden Wayno Ficorelli, he thought. Pyykkonen was a woman who got around. "What's going on with Pung's lawyer?"

"Near as we can tell, he doesn't have one. He has a firm in South-field and I never get the same lawyer twice."

This information took Service aback. "What about finances?"

"Told you earlier . . . the house, stocks, but no domestic bank accounts, savings or checking, and no credit cards. He got paid once a month and took it to a local bank to be cashed. We were able to determine that. This guy was the original greenback man."

"How much did he make at Tech?"

"Right at ninety thou."

"You find out who he rented his house from?"

"A woman from Painesdale named Maggie Soper. He paid cash, one grand a month."

Painesdale was six miles south of Houghton, along the iron range of old mining villages. "One thou for the camp, another K for the house— that's thirty percent of his monthly income."

"Twenty-seven percent," she said. "But he stopped paying rent in August and bought the house for one fifty K, all cash."

"Jesus. What did he make at Virginia Tech?"

"One fifteen."

"Meaning he took a twenty-percent cut to move here?"

"Eighteen percent," she corrected him.

"Doesn't that strike you as odd in this day and age?"

"From what we know, the late Harry Pung was a very odd man."

"Somebody who lives a life of cash is about money," he said. "Where the hell did he get a hundred and fifty grand for the house if he doesn't have bank accounts? Did he keep cash in the house?"

"We sure didn't find any in the house or on his person," she said.

"Which means robbery could be a motive here." The words immediately gave him a sinking feeling.

"What about insurance beneficiaries?"

"He had a policy from the university for a hundred thousand. His ex-wife is the sole beneficiary. Are you trying to tell me how to do my job, Service?"

"No way."

"Well, it feels like it."

In fact, he was not happy that she hadn't shared some of this information before now. "I'll be in Houghton tomorrow around noon. You want to grab some lunch, see where we are?"

"I'll be at the station," she said abruptly.

"Tomorrow," he said, hanging up.

He immediately called Simon. "Nantz is flying us to Crystal tomorrow. We'll plan to land about eight. Can you pick us up? I need to grab the Yukon."

"No problem. I'm not on duty until five tomorrow. We can talk then."

"You got something?"

"No, Toogood seems to have disappeared."

"See you at nine."

Service immediately pulled the files on Ollie Toogood and began to read.

The records were old, frail and yellowed, copies made on some sort of ancient mimeograph. They were smeared and dark, hard to read. Obviously nobody had looked at them in a long time. There was a space for Toogood's photograph on the service record. The space was empty.

Oliver Franklin Toogood was born in Lansing, Michigan, on 4 March 1930, and graduated from Lansing High School in June 1947. He spent two years at Purdue University and in 1949 was accepted into the Air Force Aviation Cadet Program. He was assigned to the 51st Fighter Interceptor Wing in Korea at Base K-14, on 3 December 1951. Or was it

K-13? The printing was blurred and dark. Shot down on 12 February 1952 and captured near Hoengsong. This was about six weeks after he arrived.

His medals and decorations included the Distinguished Service Medal, Silver Star, two Distinguished Flying Crosses, three Air Medals, and the Purple Heart. He was credited with shooting down four MiG-15s, one short of ace. For only being in combat for six weeks, Trapper Jet had made quite a record for himself. Maybe his youth had made him aggressive.

Lt. Toogood was repatriated at Freedom Village, Panmunjom. Was he among the first to be released, or among the later groups? Service wondered.

The second sheet listed citations from his medals. The one for the Distinguished Service Medal was the most informative.

> Lt. Toogood was a prisoner first of the North Koreans and later of the Chinese Communists from 12 February 1952 to 21 January 1954. During his 23 months of captivity, Lt. Toogood was held in solitary confinement for 20 of his 23 months. He was tortured throughout captivity and lost a leg as a result of injuries suffered during captivity.

So the injury was from the camps, not from his shoot-down. He was lucky to be alive, given what Service knew of the conditions of camps in those days.

> Lt. Toogood devised a communications system for prisoners and as he was moved from camp to camp, he taught the system until most prisoners in Korea were using it. Despite unrelenting torture and privation, Lt. Toogood was cited numerous times by fellow prisoners as setting an example of resistance that others adopted. For intrepid behavior and courage, Lt. Oliver Toogood is awarded the Distinguished Service Medal."

A hard-ass, even then. That fit the Trapper Jet he knew. The signature on the citation was that of General Curtis LeMay. To earn the DSM required genuine heroism—or insanity: sometimes they were too close to distinguish between in combat. In Korea, the next honor after the DSM was the Congressional Medal of Honor—usually awarded posthumously. That's how it had been in Vietnam too. He had not known about Toogood's DSM.

Service flipped to the next page. Trapper Jet had been in a hospital in Japan, and then in VA hospitals in the Washington, D.C., and

Baltimore areas until May 1956. Twenty-nine months was a long convalescence, a clue as to how severe Toogood's injuries had been. There was no mention of a medical disability or a mailing address. Were those bits in a separate file? With the military you never knew.

Sometimes investigations were easy. This one wouldn't be, but there was a thread: Lansing. If he got desperate, he would try to wend his way into the Department of Defense system, but only as a last resort. If Toogood was from Lansing, why had he come to the U.P. and remained here? Were there relatives in Lansing? Had he had contact with them after his release? So many questions and no good answers.

He was studying the map again when Nantz returned.

"Gear's loaded," she said, hardly able to contain her excitement.

"Do me a favor in Lansing?" he asked.

"Sure."

He handed her the folder. "Oliver Toogood, Trapper Jet. He graduated from Lansing High School in 1947. There ought to be an old yearbook with a photo."

"If they haven't cleaned the attic," she said. "I'll give it a try."

She nuzzled his neck. "Let's move it, big boy! We're burning daylight!"

Walter looked at the unpainted cabin as they put on waders and asked, "What's this?"

"Where your father lived before I dragged him back to civilization," Nantz said. "The term 'lived' is figurative," she added with a wink.

"Looks like a hermit's place," Walter said.

Service shot a dirty look at his son, but saw that the boy was smiling. "Chill, it's a joke," the boy said.

Nantz said, "Some joke. It looks even more pathetic inside."

Slippery Creek was difficult to fish with a fly rod. It was overgrown with wild grapevines and tag alders, but there was a promising riffle about two hundred yards downstream. Service led them to it through several groves of white birch, letting Walter lug the portable grill and cooler.

Nantz took rods out of their tubes and put them together while Service checked the grill to make sure they had gas. "I checked it at home," Nantz said. "Let's fish."

She handed two rods to Service, both of them eight-foot 4-weights. "Rig Walter," she said. "I'm gonna fish."

Walter's initial casts were clumsy, and like most beginners with a fly rod, he broke his wrist like he was trying to throw a ball. Service showed him how to point his forefinger down the rod and to lock his wrist. "It's a lever," he explained. "The weight is in the line, not the fly. The line takes the fly out to the target. It's like a slap shot. The trick is timing, not back swing or force."

"*Yessss!!!*" Nantz shouted.

She had a fish on and was letting it run, enjoying the tug.

"You don't have to exhaust it," he reminded her.

She laughed. "It's gonna be in our bellies in an hour. This is catch-and-digest night."

He loved watching her fish. She took it seriously, learned quickly, and over time had become a pretty good caster.

Walter hooked a small brook trout after about fifteen minutes of trying. His son fished with a singular focus and made corrections without comment. The trout slashed at a Size 18 royal stimulator, a dry fly that did not mimic a particular insect. He played the fish pretty well and got it to his leg. "It's a trout," the boy said, "maybe eight inches."

"Let it go," Service said. "Let's shoot for ten-inchers." He looked over at Nantz. "How big was yours?"

"Big enough," she cackled.

Service never rigged his rod. He watched Walter and Maridly and coached, and they groused and laughed, but in an hour they had six fish gutted and ready for the grill.

He sprinkled them lightly with brown sugar, inside and out, salt and pepper, and set them aside on tin foil. He fried bacon slices in a small pan until the bacon was beginning to firm up, then put one strip inside each trout and another on top. He cut lemons into thin slices and put slices inside and on top of the fish and pinned them with twigs he had whittled. When the fish were ready, he put them on tin foil on the grill.

Walter and Nantz continued to fish, releasing what they caught.

"Smells good!" Nantz shouted. "There's wine in the cooler."

He opened the cooler and dug around. Not wine, but champagne, Taittinger. There were also three glass flutes.

"Three?" he called over to her.

"His first fish with a fly rod. We're gonna celebrate as a family. Firsts matter."

"Why the brown sugar?" his son asked as he stared at the trout on his paper plate.

"Takes out the iodine flavor."

The boy inhaled the two fish and wanted more. "Cook a couple more if I get 'em?" he asked his father.

Nantz poked Service. "Sure," he said, "but they aren't always so cooperative."

It took the boy fifteen minutes to catch two more of the right size and clean them.

Service cooked them, then sat back with Nantz and watched the boy eat.

Nantz poured champagne and handed out the flutes. "To your first fly-fishing success," she said, raising the glass. "May this be the first of many!"

"I *really* like this," Walter said, staring at the reel. "Can I take a rod back to school?"

"Season closes end of the month," Service said.

"I want to practice casting all winter."

"Take the one you're using," Service said. The champagne bloomed nicely in his belly and made him feel warm. Nantz leaned against him and kissed his neck. "If it was earlier we'd slip into the woods," she whispered.

He kissed her and ignored the pain in his lip.

"I did good," she said, "didn't I?"

"Always," he said.

"All ways," she added. "I'll find that photo for you," she said. "Has Simon seen the old man?"

Service shook his head. "Not yet."

"That's not good," she said.

She was right about that.

"I loved watching you guys," she said. "You were really patient."

"He learns fast," Service said.

"Like his old man," she whispered.

· 15 ·

Limey Pyykkonen grabbed Service by the shoulder, thrust him into an office with a half brick and glass wall, facing into an open bay, and slammed the door behind them. Veins stood out in her neck and her face was bright red. "Just play along," she said, her voice in total contrast to her body language. "Sit."

He sat down across the table from her, his back to a yellow cinderblock wall. He saw Sheriff Macofome in the office bay, his arms crossed, watching.

She swept her hands upward in a flamboyant motion and slammed a fist on the table, causing him to jump. Her voice said, "Macofome's wife knows about us. She's kicked him out. Now he's all over my ass about the Pung case."

"What's part A got to do with part B?" Service asked.

"The chief also found out about Shark. He wants to move in with me and I told him no."

"Getting a little messy," he said. "Why the dramatics this morning?"

"Macofome is crazy jealous and he doesn't want you around. All of this will work out," she said, gesticulating again. "But as long as I'm in the office, he's going to hover, so I think we should get the hell out of here."

"For lunch?"

"This has wiped out my appetite. There's a complaint I need to follow up on."

"Related to Harry Pung?"

Her facial expression hardened. "No. I've been ordered to ream your ass and to tell you to stop interfering in county law enforcement matters." Her hand swept dramatically up again. "Do you feel duly chastised?"

"Totally humiliated and duly warned," he said.

"Okay, leave and I'll meet you outside the coffee shop across from Shark's place. Now get the hell out!" she roared, her voice suddenly rising.

It had been the strangest meeting he could remember. He sat in the Yukon and lit a cigarette before heading for the rendezvous. Initially he smiled when he thought about her theatrics. The detective's proclivities had landed her in a mess, but he couldn't help but admire her style, especially her cool. He also couldn't help wondering again if her style got in the way of her work and the thought made the smile fade.

She pulled up alongside him and told him to jump in with her. "Don't bother with questions," she said as he buckled his seat belt. "I've been down this road before."

"Lansing?"

She nodded solemnly. "There was a city councilman. There had been kidnap-murder of a kid, the daughter of a friend of his. He promised the friend he'd put pressure on the department."

"Did he?"

She rolled her eyes. "He was a practitioner of honey. We had coffee, we had meetings. Later it was dinner and drinks. He'd stop by my office, call me at home, send flowers. It went on for weeks, and I had to admire his sheer persistence. He asked me to take him to the crime scene, a motel. We ended up in bed."

"In the room where the killing took place?"

She sighed. "It just happened. He wore me down."

"And the wife found out."

"Everybody found out. The motel manager had illegally crossed the police line and reinstalled a videotape for the motel security system. We were stars. Word got around and the wife found out. The manager's tape disappeared and I got canned."

"What happened to the boyfriend?"

"The media never got the real story, but his wife was given a copy of the tape and she divorced him. He didn't get reelected." She looked over at Service. "I make no apologies. We were consenting adults and sometimes you just do what you do. It didn't affect the investigation."

"Except to interrupt your focus." She didn't like the comment and he decided to back off. "They get the guy who killed the kid?"

She nodded. "I got a tip from a snitch after I got canned. I passed it on and they found the guy. He had some of the girl's clothes in his apartment. He was a student taking a semester off and working at a store where the kid went to buy pop."

"And, of course, you got the credit," he said sarcastically.

"It wasn't about credit, Service. It was about taking down a dirtbag. Then I moved up here with the boyfriend and I made another bad decision and he lit out. Macofome was a lieutenant when we first hooked up."

"When he made sheriff, you got promoted."

"I know it looks fishy," she said, "but I was also the most qualified. I just hoped the thing would end differently."

"Where are we going?" he asked, noticing that they were driving south.

"We're short of people—like all cop shops these days. I have homicide, but we all have to do vake fills. There's a complaint from a woman who lives just inside the city limits. The city could handle it, but I don't want to be in the office. The woman claims there's been a lot of kids in and out of a house near her. The old suspicious activity call."

"School liaison gets you the short straw."

"You've got it." She looked over at him. "You're probably wondering about your friend, Shark. He's a great guy," she said, "but he's also totally consumed by his fishing and stuff. It is what it is," she said. "Am I being clear?"

Service wondered if Shark could handle it. His friend tended to go all out with anything he got interested in.

"Not my business," he said.

"Bull," she said. "You penises always stick together," she said, matter-of-factly.

"That's a kinky metaphor," he said.

The complainant was in her late forties, severely thin, well dressed and pleasant in an oily way.

"I don't know if it's anything, but traffic down the road at the yellow house has been pretty unusual," she explained. "Nights mostly. Kids. They don't raise the dickens or nothing. They're just there."

"Do you have kids?" Pyykkonen asked.

"Grown up, gone," the woman said, with a tone suggesting she was relieved that they weren't around for this.

"You recognize any of the kids?"

The woman shook her head.

Service was skeptical.

Pyykkonen made notes, didn't ask a lot of questions. The woman had obviously gotten herself worked up, but she was organized and gave them some license plate numbers, and times of activity—a lot more detail than normally came with complaints. Whatever the house's draw, it had been underway for just over two weeks.

"Why didn't you call us earlier?" Pyykkonen asked.

"Din't want to make trouble, hey. I thought it would go on for a weekend and that would be that. You know how kids are. But it din't stop, so I started thinking something's just not so right at da yellow house, hey."

"Who lives there?"

"Don't know. It's a rental. The owner's Maggie Soper."

"From Painesdale?" Pyykkonen asked.

"Ya, youse know her?"

Pyykkonen nodded and glanced at Service, who nodded to let her know he'd also picked up on the name.

"You don't know the renter?"

"No. I just got back from Duluth couple weeks ago. My sister's sick. Before that I was in Montana all summer, with my son and 'is wife. The place was empty when I left."

They thanked the woman and drove by the house. It sat on Portage Lake, just west of where Torch Bay angled sharply. Further south, just above Chassel, the shipping canal cut southeast through to Keeweenaw Bay and the open waters of Lake Superior. Ore boats had once used the canal to steam east to the Soo locks so they could deliver their cargoes to lower Great Lakes ports.

The house was a small yellow cottage with an addition that didn't blend well. There was green mildew on the white shutters and roof. An aluminum dock was out front in the water and an orange plastic buoy beyond the dock. The lawn was torn up by tire marks. Several beer cans flashed in the grass in the early afternoon sun.

"I think we should wait until tonight, see what goes down," Pyykkonen said. "If we approach now, somebody is liable to see us."

"Pung rented and bought his house from the woman in Painesdale."

"This probably doesn't have anything to do with Pung."

"Let's call the landlord," he said.

She looked at him. "Better yet, let's go see her," Pyykkonen said, checking her wristwatch. "We've got time."

Copper was discovered on the Keeweenaw Peninsula thousands of years before Europeans arrived. Early explorers found primitive mining pits that were later dated back five thousand years. The Chippewas did not use copper, but respected it for the spirits contained in the reddish ore. The real copper boom began in the middle of the nineteenth century when ore was discovered in the rugged greenstone spine of the peninsula, stretching north and south of Houghton. The area below was known as the Copper, or south range, the area above and across the shipping canal as the Keeweenaw, or north range. The activity below Houghton had been centered in what became the village of South Range, whose houses were old, the weary remnants of Copper Range Company structures built more than a century before.

Painesdale was the village below South Range, different from its neighbor only in size.

Maggie Soper lived in an original mining house across from old Painesdale Jeffers High School. The house was distinguished from surrounding houses by its faded red barn paint. The battered yellow cowling of a snowmobile lay on its side in the yard among broken and bent brown weeds. There was no lawn.

The owner came out on the porch and showed no interest in inviting them inside. She was short and plump with a silver pixie haircut and wire-rimmed glasses. She had long, manicured fingernails, freshly done, and small soft hands.

"Mrs. Soper," Pyykkonen said.

"It's Miss," the woman said. "I never had time to marry."

"I'm Limey Pyykkonen," the Houghton detective said. "We talked on the phone."

"About the professor. I remember," the woman said.

"You sold your house to him."

"I tolt youse that," the woman said.

"Do you own other rental properties?"

"Do I need my lawyer?"

"No ma'am, we're just doing follow-ups. This is Detective Service of the DNR."

Maggie Soper didn't bother to acknowledge him.

"Do you own other properties, Miss Soper?"

"What do you mean by 'properties'?"

"Real estate, houses, cabins, that sort of thing." Service admired Pyykkonen's patience.

The woman didn't pause as she ticked off the list: "Da house in Freda, 'nudder in Redridge overlook da dam on da Salmon Trout. Two here in town, two more in South Range, one in Atlantic Mine, three in Houghton, two in Lake Linden."

Twelve, Service counted. It seemed like a lot of real estate for an old woman whose home looked ready to collapse under the next snowpack.

"Are all of them occupied now?"

"All but da one the professor bought. How long you tink it take for da probate and da will? Somebody gonna get da house?"

Service understood. The woman's life was money. She'd sold high and now hoped for a cheap buy-back so she could rent or sell again.

"Do you have the names of your renters?"

"All public record."

"What about the house on the canal in Houghton?"

"What's this about?"

"Like I said, we're just doing routine follow-ups."

Maggie Soper looked skeptical. "I rent dat to such a nice, polite boy. His name is Terry Tunhow."

"Korean?"

The woman curled a lip. "Dey all look alike to me, but he's polite. 'Course he doesn't speak our language too good. Got da heavy accent."

"When did he start renting?"

"July."

"What does he pay?"

"Tousand a month."

"Seems like a lot."

"You've seen da place?"

"Yes, ma'am."

"If it's on da wadder, dey'll pay it and I'll take it."

"Cash?"

"Twentieth of the month. He's always on time. He comes to da house, hands me cash money, and dat's it."

"Did he pay for August?"

"Right on time. He'll be back twentieth of dis month."

Pyykkonen turned to Service. "Any questions?"

"You've got a lot of real estate," he said.

"Just like a man to wonder how a woman gets her money. I'm frugal and I know real estate. I buy some places and fix them up. Others I build, do all da work myself."

"You've got a contractor's license?"

The woman puffed up. "If dere's nothing else, I've got work."

Pyykkonen and Service bought pasties and coffee at Mother's Load in South Range and ate in the car.

"I doubt she's ever held a hammer," Pyykkonen said. "You see her hands?"

He had and he was encouraged that she had noticed them too.

"Terry Tunhow," he said. "Tunhow Pung went by Terry. Maybe we're catching a break here. Not too clever using two first names."

"I don't know," Pyykkonen said. "There's something going on in all this," she added. "Some kind of undertow, but I can't tell if it's pushing us or pulling us."

"Doesn't matter," Service said, "as long as it keeps us moving."

Pyykkonen laughed and said, "We're gonna crack this."

"If you say so."

"Did I ever mention I've never had an unsolved homicide?"

"No, you didn't."

" 'Course, that was downstate and this is here."

"There is that," he said.

"You ever have any unsolveds?"

"In my business most of my violets are habituals. They can't stop. Sooner or later we get them."

"Violets?"

"Violators."

"I like that," she said.

The house was empty until after dark. Only then did cars and pick-ups start to roll in quietly. From where they stood, behind a neighboring house's storage shed, they couldn't make out anything more distinct than blurred movement. Occasionally a flashlight beam moved around inside. Then some candles began to flicker. The place was quiet.

They waited an hour until the traffic seemed to clear. A couple of times there was a muffled shriek inside, the sound immediately cut short. Somebody came out the back door and lit a cigarette.

"Weed?" Pyykkonen asked.

"Odds are," he said.

At 9 P.M. she said, "Shall we dance?"

"Front door, back door?" he asked. All of the traffic had been through the back door. "I'll take the front," he said, wishing they had compatible radios. Troops and the DNR were on the 800 megahertz, counties on another system, which required Troops and DNR personnel to carry two radio systems in order to be fully coordinated.

He stood beside the front door with his MAG-LITE, moved to a screened window, peeked inside. Candles everywhere, shadows of movement. What the hell were they doing in there? The scent of dope wafted through the screen.

Somebody inside hissed, "Everybody fuckin' *chill*!"

He saw movement come to a stop, heard Pyykkonen rapping on the back door.

"Cops!" somebody said in a panicked whisper.

The stampede came at the front door.

Service stood to the side, waiting for the door to open. When it swung inward, he stepped across the opening and was banged into by someone, who bounced off him and fell back into the darkness. "Police!" he said. "Everybody freeze." He clicked on his light, scanned the room, and counted eight people, all of them cowering. One of them began to sniffle. He tried to figure out who had collided with him. His upper lip felt numb, then started to hurt again.

"Service?" Pyykkonen yelled through to him.

"Secure here," he answered.

The lights came on.

He had miscounted by one. There were nine kids in the room. "Everybody sit where you are," he said. Pyykkonen herded three more in from the back of the house.

The musk of dope hung in the air.

"What's going on here?" Pyykkonen asked.

The question was met with silence.

"I'm going to look around," she said.

Service moved to the middle of the room to see front and back. Some kids stared at him, but most of them studied the floor or gazed past him, avoiding eye contact.

One girl had her blouse off. "Put on your shirt," he said. She started groping for the garment.

Pyykkonen came to the end of the hall that opened into the room where Service had the kids. She lifted her radio and called for backup, starting with the ten code for an emergency.

Service saw that she was red in the face, the lines tight around her mouth.

She looked at him, said, "You're bleeding."

He licked his upper lip, tasted salt and iron. From the collision in the doorway? He hoped the stitches were holding.

They heard sirens, saw lights outside. The kids inside looked shaky and huddled together, staring at the floor.

A city cop was first to arrive. He looked to be the same age as the kids in the living room.

A Houghton County deputy came next. Pyykkonen talked to the two officers, who moved into the living room, took out notebooks, and started taking names. A girl against the wall suddenly vomited, causing the others to draw up their legs and scrunch away from her.

Pyykkonen tugged Service's sleeve, led him to the bathroom, urged him inside. The smell from the door told him what was waiting.

Dozens of empty yellow plastic ice bags were on the floor, and more were piled in the corner by a closet. There was water on the floor and muddy footprints.

The shower unit was a modular model, the type builders and do-it-yourselfers could pop into place and attach to the plumbing. Pyykkonen pulled open the shower door. There was a plastic board across the inside of the door, up about three feet. She nodded for him to look.

The body inside was naked, curled in the fetal position inside plastic. Bags of ice were piled around it. Some of them had melted. The body's skin was blue.

"Don't inhale too deeply," Pyykkonen said. She slipped a small jar of Vicks from her pocket, dabbed some under her nostrils, offered the jar to him.

Service tried to memorize what he was seeing. The body was male, Asian. Eyes closed, no overt signs of violence. Pyykkonen had put on rubber gloves and was pushing down on his skin. She said, "Long past rigor."

He didn't ask what all the kids were doing in the house with a body that had been dead long before tonight. In due course, they would find out. His job was to stand clear and let the cops do their work. He remembered a case in downstate Newaygo County where some teens had found the body of an old man in a trailer and charged friends admission to see the corpse. The U.P. was not exclusive domain to anti-social and macabre behaviors. He'd thought then it was a once-in-a-lifetime case. It was disturbing that he couldn't remember where his keys were from one minute to the next, but he could recall the details of years-old cases he'd had nothing to do with. Gus called it "cop mop"—a cop's brain absorbing all sorts of dirty water and letting it float around inside the brain for years.

"I'm gonna get out of your way," he told Pyykkonen.

He went outside and lit up. There was a dark pickup near the porch. It had two stickers in the back window: I PLAY HOOKIE FOR NOOKIE, and THUGS DRINK BLOOD. He rarely worried about people with such stickers.

It was the ones without decals he worried about: The bad ones didn't have to advertise.

Sheriff Macofome was fifteen minutes behind the others and stopped like he wanted to confront Service, who just pointed through the door. "She's in there."

EMS arrived along with a van with the same crime lab techs he'd worked with in Hancock when all this started. The same medical examiner arrived after the techs.

Flashbulbs popped inside. At one point Pyykkonen came outside, took a cigarette, smoked silently, and went back inside.

Adults began arriving in vehicles. Parents, Service assumed. Cops brought out kids, handed them over to the adults, told them to go to the station in Houghton. Just after eleven, Pyykkonen came out, nodded for him to come in.

A boy and a girl were sitting at a table. They both looked shaken.

"Daran Cencek and Sally Grice," Pyykkonen whispered. "He's a junior at Houghton High School and she's an eighth-grader."

"You know them?" he said. The girl was well developed, and looked at least twenty. Her mascara and eye makeup had run and left her with the mask of a raccoon. The boy had acne, his hair spiked and dyed purple and green. He had a gold post in his left nostril, another in his right eyebrow. If he spoke, Service expected he'd hear another one in his tongue, clicking against his teeth.

She nodded. "Daran claims he was buying dope from a Tech student here all summer. He brought the girl here because she wanted to fish for salmon."

"Salmon *here*?" This was news to him.

"No," she said. "He just told her that. Thought they'd do some weed and beer, get it on. The night he brought her there was an aluminum boat tied up to the dock and a bigger boat, a twenty-five- or thirty-footer with a cabin. Daran went up to the house and bought a couple of dime bags just like he says he always did. The college kid came out afterward, took the aluminum boat out to the bigger boat, hitched the aluminum to it, and headed south down the lake."

"The guy in the shower?"

"I'm getting to that. Daran and Sally smoked and fished and drank, then came up to the house. It was locked, but Daran jimmied the lock and got in. They used the bed. The bathroom was empty. Afterward he took the girl home and came back alone. He wanted to snag a salmon."

"But there aren't any salmon."

"He was high. He claims he was flinging a spider and it got hung up by the buoy. It felt like it was draped over the line, and he didn't want to bury the hook because he had only the one spider with him. So he swam out to retrieve it, but the spider wasn't hung on the line. It was way over the line and hooked down below. He swam down to pull it loose and felt something. He panicked when he realized what it was. He went back to get a couple of friends and the three of them pulled the body up. It was in plastic and weighted in about ten feet of water. They took the body inside and put it in the shower until they could decide what to do. Then they started worrying about the cops blaming them. One of them got the bright idea that this was an opportunity. They went out and bought ice, put the barrier inside the shower door, and packed the body. They've been re-icing it a couple of times a day since then. The next day at school Daran told a couple of kids he had a dead body. He charged them each thirty-two bucks a look and provided beer. Daran fancies himself a real entrepreneur."

"Thirty-two bucks?"

"It's his lucky number. He's a hockey player. They've been running their little sideshow since then. He says he's cleared almost four grand."

"And no rumors got out?"

"You know how kids can be when they want to."

"When did they find the body?"

"August twenty-sixth," she said solemnly.

"The night we found Harry Pung," Service said.

"Right."

"So who's the dead kid?"

"They don't know, but it's not the guy who sold the drugs."

"Did you get a description of the other kid?"

"Asian," she said, "about five-ten, maybe six-foot, heavy build. The big boat had a blue hull."

Parents took their kids to the station for processing. Police took Daran and Sally. The ones over eighteen were being held at the county all night; the others were taken to Juvie. They would all be arraigned in the morning on charges of unlawful entry, failure to report a dead person, possession and distribution of illegal substances. There were so many potential charges and so many statements to sort out that the prosecutor would work all night getting everything ready for court in the morning.

Service and Pyykkonen got to the hospital after 2 A.M. They were both tired. The medical examiner showed them into a room. "We've done the gross and prelim tonight," he told them. "Labs tomorrow."

"What do we know so far?" she asked.

"Not a helluva lot. The body's in good shape, considering how long it's been, but we'll need the labs to point us. No signs of violence and no defensive marks or anything like that. Could be natural." The M.E. saw Pyykkonen's look and amended his statement. "That's just theoretical."

"You mean CYA," she said.

The M.E. grinned. "They're synonyms."

Service and Pyykkonen went outside for a smoke. "We got all sorts of prints from the house. It's gonna take time to sort it all out. We tried to take prints off the stiff, but I don't know how good they are. The skin was beginning to come apart. We'll put them into AFIS later today." The FBI maintained AFIS—Automated Fingerprint Identification Systems.

"I hate waiting," she said. "I'm thinking about getting Maggie Soper down here. You think that friend of your son's could look at the body for us?"

"Let's set it up for seven in the morning," he said.

He went to Walter's dorm and knocked on the door. His son opened the door with sleep in his eyes. "Got a place for me to bunk for the night?"

The boy opened the door and let his father in. "You're bleeding."

Service said, "We need Enrica to come to the hospital tomorrow."

"Why?" The boy tossed a hand towel to his father.

"There's another body."

"She's pretty delicate right now."

"We need her to do this."

"I'll call Karylanne."

"Six," Service said. "We'll pick her up."

"Karylanne and I better go with her."

Service wondered if the boy could handle it, but didn't challenge him. He needed this to go as smoothly as possible. Walter took his cell phone into the hall. Service curled up on the floor and went to sleep. When he awoke there was a blanket over him and a pillow under his head. He found a bloodstain on the pillow case. Damn stitches.

Maggie Soper took one look at the body and said, "That's him—Terry Tunhow."

"You're sure?" Pyykkonen asked.

"I don't forget people who pay me," she said.

Enrica came in next. She was shaky and teary. Karylanne and Walter helped her into the viewing room.

She stared at the body and began to sob.

"You recognize him?" Service asked.

"It's the guy from my class," she said. "What happened?"

"Terry Pung?" Pyykkonen asked. "Not the Terry Pung from the lake?"

The girl nodded, shook her head, and began to faint. Walter caught her before she hit the floor and carried her into the hallway.

Service and Pyykkonen got coffee out of vending machines and went outside to light up.

"Harry Pung's dead," Service began, trying to focus his mind. "Bear hair in the car, and at the camp. Dead at a boat ramp on the same body of water where we found this last guy."

"Terry Tunhow, which is an alias, and not Pung's son."

"Presumably," he said. "Is there a police artist here?"

"Get real," she said. "There's a Troop in Negaunee, if we can get her."

"We need to get something on paper we can start working with. So here's how it looks to me. Somebody had a bear in the cabin at Lac La Belle, brought it down to the canal by the fish house."

"Harry Pung," she said.

Service nodded. "As far as Hancock. He loaded the bear in a boat to motor down here."

"But Harry missed the boat," she said.

"Right, and then Terry gets in the big boat here and disappears, leaving his stand-in to a nap with the fish."

"You think it all fits?"

"It never all fits until you have somebody in custody and can work it through," he said. "I'm too tired to think. My brain is fried."

"You gonna hang around town?"

"I've got to get back to Marquette."

"I'll call you as soon as we have something," she said. "Thanks for the help. Remember, I've never lost a killer."

There's always a first time, he thought.

· 16 ·

He was just across the Marquette County line when a Troop came up on the county radio. "Shot fired, in pursuit, officer needs assistance, westbound US Forty One, two miles east of Champion." It was a female voice, calm, almost detached. In the U.P. cops were few; even so, all officers in the various police jurisdictions had discretion in responding to calls of other agencies, based on location and other factors. But *shots fired* was one you went to, no matter what you were doing. You went because the day might come when you'd be making the call. He toggled his mike and told the Marquette County dispatcher. "DNR Twenty-Five Fourteen responding."

"Where are you, Twenty-Five Fourteen?"

"Forty One, eastbound, just passing the county line."

Another voice chimed in and Service recognized Marquette County Deputy Sheriff Linsenman. Almost a year ago, in the same area, the two of them had responded to a moose–vehicle collision. Linsenman had dispatched the animal, which was at the bottom of a ditch on top of the driver, who had been thrown out of his pickup.

"Suspect in green Ford pickup running eighty-plus," the female Troop reported, her voice up only slightly. "Westbound on Forty One, approaching Van Riper."

Van Riper was a state park, six miles ahead in his twelve o'clock position. Suspect in what? It would help to know. His adrenaline began to spike. Shot fired and pursuit. Next to domestic disputes, it was the worst call of all.

"Suspect is turning north on the Pesheke Grade Road," the Troop radioed. "Following," she added, her voice beginning to betray the strain of the chase.

There'd be no eighty-miles-per-hour pursuit on that road, Service told himself. It was steep, washboarded, studded with large rocks, narrow and winding as it snaked over the southwestern slabs of the Huron Mountains. At the first summit there was a deep gouge in the road between two huge stone abutments, a precarious squeeze even when you were going slow and had the vehicle under control.

Linsenman reported turning up the grade.

Service began to slow for his turn to the north, searching his memory for a shortcut to an intercept, but there wasn't one. He'd have to go all the way around by Skanee and come back south and it was at least a hundred miles around, which is why the Pesheke grade was a popular cut-through for locals.

The washboarded road pounded his undercarriage, making the vehicle lurch and fishtail. The vehicles ahead of him were kicking up heavy dust, which hung in the air like a cloud of cocoa powder. He switched on his headlights, but they made no difference, and his blue lights seemed to bounce off the dust and make visibility worse.

The Troop came back on the radio. "Suspect out of vehicle," she said, her words clipped.

Linsenman radioed, "Vehicles in sight."

Service kept his eyes on the road, both hands firmly on the steering wheel.

Loose gear in back of the Yukon was flying all over the place, bouncing off the windows and roof. For weeks he'd been telling himself to put things away, tie it all down, but he'd never gotten around to it.

Service bounced out of a severe left turn and saw emergency lights ahead on a long, rising straightaway. Two police vehicles were on the road, their doors open. Dust lingered in the air. He saw Linsenman behind the open driver's door of his squad, looking ahead. A blue state police cruiser was ahead of Linsenman, but Service couldn't see the driver. The Pesheke River was on their left, just over the lip of a steep, boulder-strewn berm that looked like it had sprouted teeth. It was good defensive cover for a shooter.

"Shot fired," the Troop reported on the radio.

Service braked, got out, opened his door, and used it as a shield while he studied the situation. He had heard no gunshot.

What he heard was Linsenman yelling at the Troop, "Where is he?" *He*, Service thought, evil's gender always assumed to be male and usually true. The recent fourteen-year-old shooter had been an anomaly, though his experience said the gap was narrowing between males and females in the arena of violence.

"Left side," she yelled back. "Above the river."

Service tried to will the two of them to get on their radios. Yelling only helped the suspect know where they were. He started to call out to Linsenman to tell him to get on the radio, but stopped. What was Linsenman's first name? All these years and he'd never known. He'd always been Linsenman. Service reached into the back seat and uncased his rifle. It was new, issued to all officers in mid-summer. He'd shot about twenty rounds through it. The sights were true, but the weapon would be too heavy to lug around. It was intended officially for dispatching large animals, but every officer knew that handguns or shotguns were not matches for perps with rifles.

He bolted a round into the chamber and checked the safety on. A shot sounded while he was hunched over with the rifle.

He popped up to see Linsenman aiming his sidearm toward the berm.

Two more shots popped. Handgun, Service thought. Big bore.

A third shot answered from the Troop's position.

Linsenman was holding tight, the pistol in his right hand, his left palm under the butt, his left thumb flat against the barrel for stability, exactly as it was supposed to be.

Sirens were bleating behind them on the grade. The radio was alive with voices and static.

Linsenman remained still.

Service found himself mesmerized.

The next shot was blended with another—two shots merged as one. Linsenman's windshield exploded and Service saw the deputy's arm jerk in recoil. His mind did the replay: windshield, then the arm. A fire-back, a response. Nobody moved. Sirens drew closer. What sick dickhead invented modern sirens?

Linsenman stayed by his door, his weapon still pointed across the road. Smoke snaked out of the barrel and blended with lingering dust particles. The Troop from the car ahead of him hustled low in the ditch on Linsenman's right, reached his vehicle, pulled open his passenger door. Linsenman never looked at her. Service could hear her trying to talk to him, but couldn't make out her words.

Focused, Service told himself, watching Linsenman.

Two Troops, including a sergeant, came up behind Service.

Nobody spoke.

A gentle breeze lifted and rattled through the tamaracks to Service's right. Soon their needles would yellow and fall. Beyond the trees there was a small pond. He hadn't noticed it when he pulled up. See it all, he chided himself. Be here, nowhere else.

A ragged formation of geese started to descend toward the pond, looked at the situation and scrambled to climb back out, making a lot of noise. Service admired their good sense. There were lots of times when he wanted to fly away from the shit. Like now.

A white-tail doe and her fawn had crept to the far edge of the pond. The fawn was small for this time of year, late birth probably. It would die this winter. The mother watched across the pond while the little one stood in the water drinking delicately, its little tail flicking nervously. A raven in a dead tree beyond the pond yawped forlornly. Its call went unanswered.

The two state policemen didn't ask him what was going on. They flattened themselves against his Yukon, weapons drawn, bodies tense, all eyes locked on the berm.

The Troop with Linsenman waved the pair forward. They waddled awkwardly, hunched over to reduce their profiles.

Two deputies crept through waist-high bracken ferns on top of the rocky berm to Service's left, their eyes focused ahead. A few small white birches were twisted and wind-bent among the rocks, too small to provide effective cover. The men worked together, the front man focusing forward, the second man watching the sides, stopping occasionally to scan behind them.

"Secure," someone proclaimed over the radio. "Suspect down, get the EMTs up here." A male voice, not female.

Linsenman finally lowered his weapon, letting his hand hang limply by his side.

Service heard voices where the officers had converged on the berm.

Linsenman slumped to his seat, sat with his legs extended and splayed on the ground, the posture of a dishrag.

A squat EMS truck crunched up the narrow road, its emergency lights blinking, its grooved tires spitting small rocks that peppered the landscape. Service closed his door to make it easier for it to pass. When it stopped just past Linsenman's squad, Service eased forward, watching his friend light the filter end of a cigarette, unaware of the stench, the taste, smoking on automatic, needing something, anything, to settle his nerves.

Linsenman looked up at him. "Are you everywhere?" It was an old joke between them. "This ain't the same as a moose," he added. Service saw the deputy's hand shaking, carefully took his weapon, unchambered a round, slid out the clip, placed it on the dash.

EMTs hustled a stretcher up the rocky berm, slipping on the loose scree.

A Marquette County deputy stopped and squeezed Linsenman's shoulder. "Afraid?"

"I was too damned scared to be afraid," he said. It wasn't a joke.

The words stuck in Service's mind. Too scared to be afraid. Only people who worked in the shit would appreciate the distinction.

The EMTs came back down the gravel berm, juggling the stretcher in the bad footing. Two deputies were on either side, helping stabilize the patient. "Alive," the front EMT called out, tapping his right shoulder. Suspect to patient, Service thought, a severe change in status. No cop would call the man a victim. That would be for lawyers to debate.

Linsenman shook his head, sighed deeply. "I'm the worst shot in the department," he said.

"Not today," Service said.

The female Troop came back, looked down at Linsenman, stuck out her hand. "Thanks."

She was young, Service saw. Her voice had remained relatively controlled throughout the situation, but a calm voice could sometimes betray or mask what was really going on inside.

Linsenman nodded, exhaled smoke, ignored her hand.

Service pulled her aside. "Why the pursuit?"

"I got a call to stop a green Ford. When I tried to get him over, he let one loose out his window."

Service looked at the vehicle ahead of her squad. Its nose was askew in the left ditch, its ass sticking up like a feeding duck. It was a green Chevy, not a Ford. She'd tried to stop the wrong vehicle and gotten a violent response by sheer chance. "They give you a plate number?"

She shook her head. "Just a green Ford."

He kept quiet. At some point somebody would ask questions, sort out the mistake, try to apply logic to it, fail. Serendipity sometimes had a violent side.

One of the county's sergeants came forward. His name was Don and his deputies called him "Padre." His shirt was wet with sweat, his hair matted. "Get somebody with Linsenman," Service said. "He's in shock."

Padre said, "We have a procedure."

Service bit his lip. There was also a procedure for identifying vehicles, and it had failed.

"Get help for him." Shooting another person was not like a movie shooting. You couldn't put a bullet into a human being and walk away feeling normal.

"Look," a cop said from the growing knot of uniforms. He pointed across the small pond. A deer was floating in the shallows. Service saw a fan of blood staining the dark water.

"Write the fucker for a deer out of season," a voice said. The cops laughed nervously.

Service didn't laugh with them. He waded the perimeter of the pond, getting wet to his knees, got the fawn by a leg and dragged it to dry land. There was a gaping hole in the neck, unaimed bullets as lethal as aimed ones. In more than twenty years in law enforcement he had rarely pulled his weapon and never discharged it at another person. History aside, he knew the day might come when somebody would leave him no choice. He looked at Linsenman sitting with his head down and understood what he was feeling. In Vietnam he had done it too many times and it had exacted a price. He sat down on a patch of reindeer moss and lit a cigarette. Better him than me.

Why couldn't he remember Linsenman's first name?

Fern LeBlanc, Captain Grant's secretary, looked disapprovingly at Service's muddy boots and pants. She held out several call-back slips, did not speak to him. Fern had worked exclusively for the captain for a long time and seemed to resent Service's presence. Sometimes she seemed frazzled by his ways, all the calls that came in, his abruptness. The feelings were mutual. LeBlanc was chemically blonde and fifty-two years old with the figure of a thirty-five-year-old. Men and women around the office talked about her, but nobody challenged her. She was the captain's gate guard.

Service sat in his cubicle. The captain stopped in the doorway and Service cringed, expecting a rebuke for being on duty and not at home, but the captain said only, "You're bleeding," and walked on. Service touched a tissue to his upper lip, found blood.

He set the slips aside, punched in the code for his voice mail. There were several messages.

Nantz: "Crazy schedule, honey. There're two high schools down here, Everett and Eastern. I have to find out which one used to be Lansing High. Love you."

Del Olmo: "The missing remain missing. Sorry I wasn't there this morning. Something came up."

Gus: "Thirty-two bucks to see a stiff? Sorry I missed I that."

Deputy Linsenman: "Thanks, man. You *are* everywhere."

Walter: "Enrica's okay. Thanks for the fly rod."

Chief O'Driscoll: "Give me a bump, Detective. No rush."

Service picked up and read the call-backs, shoved them into his in-basket, which was already full.

He called Pyykkonen, got a busy signal, and was switched over to her phone mail.

"It's Service. I'm in my office."

When the phone rang, he expected Pyykkonen, but it was Nathaniel Zuiderveen.

"You hear about Dowdy Kitella?" She-Guy began.

"Hear what?"

"Somebody beat hell out of him last night outside the Amasa Hotel."

"You sound pleased," Service said.

"Don't try to mind-fuck a mind-fucker."

Pyykkonen called after Zuiderveen. "We put the prints through AFIS and we got a hit. The prints are those of Tunhow Pung. They were in the immigration file."

"But that's not Terry Pung in the morgue."

"It becomes curiouser and curiouser," she said. "I'd say Pung had his stand-in fully covered with paper and that he actually came through immigration in Terry's place."

"When?"

"Most recent entry was July 2001."

"Pung was a student at Tech '01–'02, right?"

"Somebody was," she said.

"You get the ex-wife's name and address?"

He heard her shuffling papers. "Here," she said. "Siquin Soong." She spelled the first name, pronounced it again, "That's *She-quin*. She's remarried."

He wrote down the name. "Address?"

"Nine One Two Two, Orchard Apple Circle, White Lake. It's in Oakland County. She owns a business in Southfield, White Moon Trading Company. I talked to her lawyer in Ann Arbor. She is quote, unavailable, end quote. It's the same firm as her late husband's."

"Did you ask about the son?"

"Ms. Soong is in seclusion," one of her lawyers says. "End of quote."

"I bet," Service said. "Talk to you later."

He dialed his friend, Luticious Treebone.

"Hey," Tree said. "What up?"

"The usual," Service said.

"Yeah, scut. I talked to Nantz. She told me about Wisconsin. Said you are a busted up old man."

"She'd never say that."

"That don't mean it's not true."

"I need information."

"You mean you need it again. You lived in civilization you wouldn't need to call me all the time."

"You'd be lonely."

"I'd find a way to deal with it. What's the name."

"Siquin Soong," Service said.

"White Moon Trading."

"You know her?"

"Big donor to the Democrats, beaucoup money into the Timms campaign."

"Never knew you to follow politics."

"This is Dee-troit, dawg. We breathe that shit. Got to keep you pale-skinned barbarians outside the gate."

"There's no gate there," Service said, "but that's an idea worth thinking about."

"Racist," Tree said.

"Soong's squeaky clean?"

"Ain't nobody squeaky clean, brother. Not even us."

"You gonna give me the Paul Harvey?"

Tree chuckled. "The rest of the story. . . . Feds think White Moon is a front, that the lady is into a lot of shady shit, but nothing sticks."

"Her husband's name is Soong?" Service said.

"Her old man's Buzz Gishron." The name meant nothing to Service. "He was a deputy ambassador to the UN under Carter. He teaches constitutional law at Wayne State, where he has also been a major donor. If anybody's squeaky clean, it's Gishron—patron saint of individual rights and lost causes."

"Married to her?"

"It got people shaking their heads when it happened. He's an old fart. She's late forties, major bootie and high maintenance. Got all the moves and the looks and money to make the moves work. Local society queen and the rights king—a marriage made for *People* magazine."

"They covered it?"

"*Everybody* covered it. You don't get news up there? What do you want with Siquin Soong?"

"You got a cup of coffee close by?"

"Jolt Cola. Shoot."

Service walked his friend through the case, starting with the finding of the body in the Saturn, through the discovery of the second body in the shower in the house in Houghton.

"People think cities got all the savages," Treebone said. "The bodies still in a cooler up there?"

"Pending release by the prosecutor."

"Don't sound like nobody wants those folks."

Tree's statement struck a chord. A respected professor had been murdered and who had come forward to speak for him? "Can you get me some details on Soong, her business, all the stuff the feds think?"

"Can try, but Snoop-Doggin' a big-time Democrat could raise a few hackles and get my very black ass kicked, sayin'?"

"Whatever you can do."

"Nothing in writing, okay? I don't want no paper trail."

"I'll come to you."

"Good, and bring Nantz. We'll have dinner with Kalina."

"Your wife is culinarily deprived."

"Man, I wouldn't subject nobody to Kalina's cooking. We step out. How's that boy of yours?"

"Settled into school, I think."

"You see much of him?" his friend asked.

"Stayed with him last night." He didn't amplify with details.

"I knew you had that father shit in you. You hear anything from Eugenie in Grand Rapids?"

"She the P.I.? Not yet. Yell when you have something on Soong," Service said.

"Semper Fi," Tree said.

Service got a cup of coffee and stepped outside to light a cigarette. Fern LeBlanc saw him and flashed a look of scorn. She neither smoked nor drank and saw both habits as signs of moral weakness.

How could he dig up information on Harry Pung?

Lieutenant Lisette McKower pulled up in her truck, hopped down and stretched.

"Bumpy roads," she said, twisting her head to stretch her neck. She looked at his bandages. "If that's cosmetic surgery, you need to find another surgeon."

"If that's a joke, you need to find another writer."

"How's the arm?"

He lifted it. "Sore."

"How's the captain?"

"Fine," he said.

She hesitated. "He seems tired to me, Grady. Distracted."

"We all get tired."

"Not you and the captain."

Service felt tired, his arm was sore, and his face stung. Ten years ago he didn't need sleep or much time to recover, but this had changed. McKower was five-five, one hundred and twenty pounds, but it looked to him like she had added a few pounds and her dark hair was showing a few strands of gray. When he had been her training officer he thought they had sent him a cheerleader. She was twenty-four then, had spent three years as a USFS smokejumper, and was as tough as they came, mentally and physically. Later she had been promoted to sergeant, and last year to lieutenant. For one month, long ago, they had been intimate; when they realized their mistake, there had been some anger and a lot of embarrassment, but they had gotten past their indiscretion and had remained close as colleagues and friends. She was married now and had two daughters.

"How goes the el-tee life?" he asked.

She curled some of her hair in her fingers. "See the gray?"

"What gray?"

She smiled. "Seriously, I'm worried about the captain and you look like shit."

"Leave it alone, Lis."

She cocked an eye. "Whatever you say." She reached over and squeezed his wrist. "Be careful, okay?"

"Is that like safe sex?"

She walked through the door and Service turned his mind back to Harry Pung, but found no quick answers. He went back to his cubicle and started looking at the call-back slips.

Detective Jimmy Villereal in Benton Harbor had busted some people illegally harvesting ginseng near Van Buren State Park and wanted to know if he had similar cases in the Schoolcraft County coastal zone along the northern Lake Michigan barrier dunes. Ginseng? How the hell was he supposed to know?

North Trails Riders wanted an instructor for a snowmobile program. Somebody else could have that.

A female reporter from St. Ignace wanted a technical definition of hunter orange. Let her look it up for herself.

A man with a cabin on the Ford River wanted to lodge a complaint about a man in an ultralight aircraft, shooting airborne ducks and geese. Which county, Marquette, Delta, or Dickinson? He hated call-backs, wished Fern would take more information.

A magistrate in Marquette wanted to clarify some information on a ticket Service had written.

He threw the call-backs on the desk. All of it could wait.

McKower came into his cubicle and sat down in the chair next to his messy desk.

He talked her through the Pung case, including his need to ferret out more about the dead professor. She thought for a second, said, "Stretch Boyd."

"The departmental PR guy?"

"Budgets are tight, but I have it on good authority that he has access to LexisNexis."

"Which is?"

"About the best electronic library in the world. It's expensive, but you can quickly pull up litigation or news. Call Boyd and ask him to help."

"In exchange for what?"

"He's a trout-fishing addict. Give him a few spots and he'll bury your work in his budget. But don't give him any eastern Yoop spots."

"Because you've already done that," he said.

She smiled. "I'm keeping those for me."

He called Boyd as soon as McKower left the office and explained what he needed—any articles on Siquin Soong, White Moon Trading, or bear poaching.

"You understand there's a quid pro quo?" Boyd said.

"Yeah." Service gave him three spots, all of them good, none of them well known.

"Man, cool," Boyd said. "Talk to you tomorrow?"

Service didn't feel like cooking. He stopped at the Duck Inn, a tavern at a crossroad south of Marquette. It was a worn-out place favored by COs, loggers, cops of all flavors, a few lawyers, and a couple of judges.

He was not surprised to find Linsenman sitting at the bar, nursing a nonalcoholic beer. "The real stuff might help more," Service said.

"I gave it up for Lent," Linsenman said.

"You gonna eat?"

Linsenman nodded.

Service said, "I'm buying."

"This isn't a celebration."

"Any meal you can eat is a celebration."

Linsenman smiled.

"What the hell is your first name?"

Linsenman pursed his lips. "Weasel."

"Your parents named you *Weasel*?"

The deputy shrugged. "My mom said it was a difficult pregnancy. Call me Linsenman."

Newf jumped up, put her paws on his chest and stretched. Cat floated up onto a table in the foyer and extended her head so he could scratch her.

"Okay, okay," he said. "Don't overact, you two. I know I'm not Nantz."

He checked the room that Nantz used as her office. It was neat and orderly, reflective of a pilot's mind. He saw something in the fax machine and lifted the sheet of paper. It was from Nantz. She had scribbled a note:

"Can this be our Trapper Jet? NOT!"

Service studied the photograph underneath her note. "No way," he said out loud. People changed as they aged, but this was not a young Ollie Toogood he was looking at. He took the fax into the kitchen and got a bottle of Bell's Amber Ale out of the fridge. The beer was brewed in Kalamazoo, but only beginning to get into the U.P.

He popped the cap off the brown bottle and fed the animals, who ate like they were starved. Both of them were insatiable and would eat until they burst, but he and Nantz controlled how much they got. He watched Newf eat and pinched his own midsection. A year ago there was nothing to pinch. Now there was. McKower wasn't the only one adding pounds.

The Detroit *Free Press* and the *News* were out by the mailbox. He went to fetch them and settled onto a couch in the family room. Newf climbed up to take one end. Cat leaped onto the back and hissed to mark her own turf when Newf looked at her.

"Are you two finished?" he asked them. Newf dropped her head and wagged her tail. Cat began a paw bath.

He opened the *Free Press*. The polls on the gubernatorial race showed that Timms had moved ahead by five points, her rise called "unprecedented."

There was a blurb about the senator's bill to impose mandatory sentences for crimes that resulted in injuries to police officers. Sam Bozian was quoted: "This is a blatant play for publicity and an unnecessary statute." The governor was right on the last count but it was discomfiting to agree with Clearcut on anything.

The campaign schedule for both candidates was laid out for the next two weeks.

A sidebar talked about a party fund-raiser to be held at The Stage-coach Lodge in the Irish Hills in Jackson County. Senator Timms was to be "honored," whatever that meant. It was being organized by Siquin Soong. Service stared at the name and checked the date. Ten days. The people at the dinner would pay fifteen hundred a plate, the money going to the Democratic National Party. He called Nantz's cell phone.

"What?" she answered, sounding weary.

"Thanks for the fax. You want to talk dirty?" he teased.

She moaned. "Get real, Grady. My libido's still on the airplane."

"This photo sure doesn't look like Toogood," he said.

He could hear her wake up. "Lansing High School was called Lansing Central High School until 1943 when Lansing Sexton opened. The name in the record is a typo, I guess. They called it Old Central and the building is now part of Lansing Community College's downtown campus. I had to go to the Lansing Board of Ed to get a 1947 yearbook and they also let me look at Toogood's record. The records of most students from back then are now on microfiche, but Toogood's war record and academics make him one of their all-star alums. He was brilliant in math—a real whiz, which is how he ended up at Purdue. His father was a judge and it was a prominent family. Ollie was the only child and the father planned on his going to law school. When he chose math and Purdue, the old man was frosted. When the boy joined the air force they stopped talking."

"You learned this from the records?"

"No, Lori put me in touch with people at the Lansing *State Journal* and somebody there dug through their morgue and got some clips for me. There was a story about Toogood being on the dean's list in his first semester at Purdue, and another about him leaving school for the air force. More stories when he was captured, others when he was repatriated, and nothing after that. One of the reporters who wrote some of the stories is a retired columnist. He told me about the rift between the father and son."

"The father burned the bridge and the boy never went back."

"I don't know. The columnist was shocked to learn that Toogood has been in the U.P. all these years and he wants to see if he can do a story. He said several reporters tried to see him at the VA in Washington and Baltimore, but were turned away.

Service thought, where did he get his checks? "How much did you tell him?"

"Not much, but his interest is definitely piqued."

This could be useful, Service thought. "You did a helluva job," he said.

"Up to Grady Service's standards?"

"Exceeds," he said.

"I was going to call you in the morning. How's your face?"

"Okay." He made a mental note to call Vince and see if he could check the stitches. The cut above his upper lip kept seeping blood.

"And the rest of your body?"

"Sore, but getting better. The animals are tolerating me."

She laughed and he smiled. He loved her laugh, how she opened up and held nothing back when she was tickled. Her voice alone was a tranquilizer.

"How's Walter?"

"Good. I stayed with him last night."

"*Really?*" her tone said how pleased she was. He didn't offer details.

"How come Simon didn't meet us at the airport?" she asked.

"He said something came up," he said.

"I'm awake now, big boy. Wanna talk dirty?"

"Talking's not enough," he said.

"Don't I know it," she said.

"I don't like being apart," he said.

"Neither of us likes it," she said. "I dread the academy."

"How about if I come down and you can show me what you do."

She was silent. "Are you playing me?"

"Does it matter?"

"Probably not."

"The paper says the senator will speak at a fund-raiser for the party in the Irish Hills in ten days."

"I haven't looked that far ahead," Nantz said.

"Do you go everywhere with her?"

"Depends on how long the event is. Most of the time it's a whistlestop schedule, which means I usually wait at the airport and refuel so we can get on to the next place. She never wears down. What are you up to, Service?"

"I need to get into that dinner."

She grunted. "I'd like it better if you said you need to get into me."

"That's a given," he said.

"Why this sudden interest?"

He debated how much to tell her and decided to lay it all out. "Siquin Soong is Harry Pung's ex-wife."

"So?"

"She's organizing the foo-foo fund-raiser. I need to talk to her, but her lawyers are getting in the way. I figure I might get a chance for an informal chat during the dinner."

"Chat? That word doesn't fit your vocab. And Grady, she's a power broker and the senator's backer. I'm not sure Lori will buy this."

"The senator doesn't need to know."

"Are you asking me to lie to her? She's my friend."

"You don't have to lie. Just tell her we just want some time together. She can understand that, and it's the truth, right?"

"I don't like the position you're putting me in."

"I can think of some good positions," he said.

"Don't deflect," she said.

He took a deep breath and walked her through the case, the problems with Terry Pung, the body in Houghton, the AFIS hit, all of it.

"Are you suggesting that one of the most important people in the state's Democratic Party is doing something illegal?"

"No." The feds were, but he had no idea what that entailed yet. "I think she's just trying to shield her son. If she has nothing to hide, she has nothing to lose, right?"

"So you want to ambush her."

"What would you do if you were me?" he asked.

"Baby, I don't know. This just doesn't feel right."

"Get used to it," he said. "Cops follow the law and sometimes you end up in some funny places. If you could get the next day off, we can have dinner with Tree and Kalina."

"I'd like *that*," she said enthusiastically. "But I need to sleep on all this."

"No problem," he said.

"You," she said, laughing again. "I love you, Service."

"Even though I'm a busted-up old man?"

"Who said that?"

"Joke," he said. That asshole, Treebone.

She said, "I'll call you in the morning, honey."

Simon del Olmo called as Service was getting into bed.

"Sorry I had to leave the truck," Simon said. "Something came up."

"Thanks for dropping it."

"Did you hear about Dowdy Kitella?"

"She-Guy called me about it."

"He's in custody in the Iron River hospital."

"For getting his ass kicked?"

"No. Elza and I found steel cable in his truck. It matches the stuff she found. We also found a chemical the arson people said was the accelerant at Trapper Jet's place. We're headed out to his place with a search writ."

Simon and Grinda working together? That was interesting. "Have you asked him about Trapper Jet yet?"

"Not yet. The docs won't let us in. His head got bent pretty bad. We'll make the formal arrest tomorrow. You want to be here?"

"No, just let me know how it goes down."

"*Si, jeffe.*"

"Good work, Simon."

"Better to be lucky than good. An Iron County cop noticed the cable near where they found Kitella and called us."

Us? Service lay his head on the pillow and couldn't sleep. There was too much luck and too damn many coincidences in this case.

The phone buzzed at 4 A.M. It was Nantz.

"Good morning, love. I'm going to talk to the senator for you this morning."

"No concerns?"

"Some, but if Soong has nothing to hide, there should be no concerns about talking to you."

"Thanks, Mar."

"I'll call you later today, darlin'."

"You're the best," he said.

She laughed. "Damn right."

· 18 ·

The first thing Service did when he got to his office was to check e-mail. There was a note from Stretch Boyd of the department's PR group saying that DNR Director Eino Tenni had prohibited the use of outside electronic libraries and that he was sorry he couldn't help with the LexisNexis search.

"Great," Service muttered. He had traded for nothing.

The captain strolled by and looked in at him. "Are you familiar with Captain Richard Sorgavenko?"

"Should I be?" Service countered.

"Air Force Academy of 1963. Graduated at the top of his pilot training class and ended up in F-105s at Khorat in Thailand in 1966. He flew one hundred missions and volunteered for another tour. When he began to approach the end of his second hundred, he volunteered again and was turned down. So he began to destroy paperwork after every sortie and the planners lost track of where he was on his tour. He continued like this until he was shot down and killed on his two hundred and eighteenth sortie. What was his mistake?"

Service stared at his captain. "Pushed his luck, tried to do too much?"

The captain stared at his detective. "He got shot down," the captain said, walking away.

Service faced a quandary about what to do next. He finally decided he needed to get something started on Irvin "Magic" Wan. He had had the option of calling in a detective from the downstate Wildlife Resources Protection Unit; instead, he had called Treebone, who was supposed to have had a P.I. contact him. So far, not a damn word.

Service hung up and leaned back in his chair. He hated begging and depending on others.

The captain wandered into the office, sat down across from him, looked like he was going to say something, stood up and walked out without speaking.

He snatched up the phone as soon as it rang. "DNR, Service."

"Good morning. I'm Eugenie Cukanaw. I talked to Tree and I apologize for taking so long to get back to you. I was wrapping up a case."

Her voice was solid, neither high nor low. "Thanks for calling," he said.

"You must be a good friend to get Treebone to pull in a chit. I'm doing this gratis."

"We go back." Service wondered if gratis was why she was so long in getting back to him.

"What can I do for you?" she asked.

"There's an Asian guy who lives in Grand Rapids. He owns some clubs, said to be in the drug and skin biz. I know one club is in Kalamazoo and that's all I know."

"Magic Wan," she said. "We know Irvin pretty well. What is it you need?"

The question caused him to pause. What exactly did he want? "We are led to believe he works for a man called Mao Chan Dung and that Wan owns some sort of hunting camp in the U.P. What can you find out about his relationship to and dealings with Dung, and where's the hunting camp?"

"A hunting camp? Interesting. I don't know a man named Dung, but that doesn't mean anything. As for the camp, maybe I can get that information for you. Do you mind my asking why the DNR is interested in such a lowlife?"

"It's our specialty."

"I imagine it is," she said, her tone one of amusement.

"I have a potential international poaching case."

"Now *that* sounds interesting."

"An informant puts Wan in the business, but he's a new name and personality for us."

"Shouldn't U.S. Fish and Wildlife be involved in this?"

She knew the bureaucracy well. "At some point. Right now we're just taking a preliminary look at players, trying to figure out what it is we have."

"Fair enough—why get the feds involved until you have to."

"You've been there."

"Too many times to count. What sort of timeline am I on?"

"Soon as." He gave her his office, home, and cellular numbers. Once again, he owed his friend Tree.

Later, on his way to lunch, Fern LeBlanc said, "You have a visitor."

He looked around and saw no one. "Outside," LeBlanc said with a nod of her head.

There was nobody in the parking lot, but as Service got behind the wheel of his truck, the passenger door opened and Limpy Allerdyce struggled to get into the seat.

"Haven't seen much of youse, sonny," Limpy said wearily.

Allerdyce had shot Service during a scuffle and spent seven years in the State Prison of Southern Michigan for attempted murder. Allerdyce was one of the most notorious poachers in the state's history and the leader of a tribe of poachers, mostly his relations, who lived in the remote southwest reaches of Marquette County—the largest county west of the Mississippi and by itself larger than the state of Rhode Island. The summer after Allerdyce got out of jail, Service had found the murderer of the poacher's son and he and Allerdyce had reached a sort of agreement, which Allerdyce claimed to have had with Service's late father: no poaching in the Mosquito Wilderness, and he would provide tips from time to time. Limpy had made the deal to avoid going back to jail for parole violation, and last year he had helped Service break a major wolf-killing case. But it turned out that Allerdyce also had gotten money from the poachers, who were his competition. He had played both sides like a chess master.

"You're my visitor?" It had been months since he had seen the old man. He looked gaunt and sallow, his neck thin as a bird's, his skin yellow.

Allerdyce put a shaking hand on his belly. "Gives me the *wop-agita* gettin' so close to a cop house. Been too long, hey?"

Wop-agita? "Not long enough," Service said. "I'm on my way to a meeting."

"Don't bullshit me, sonny. You're goin' for grub. Limpy buys."

"I can't accept a gift from a felon," Service said. There was no policy that stated this, but he didn't want to spend time with the old man. "I'll pay," he said when Allerdyce made no move to get out of the Yukon.

They drove into the drive-through at McDonald's. Limpy ordered four large orders of chicken nuggets. Service drove them over to "the island," what locals called Presque Isle Park, a tiny and scenic peninsula jutting into Lake Superior. Sitting in the truck with Limpy's body odor would have been too much to bear. They got out of the truck and sat on boulders by the water's edge. The rocks were pinkish-red, showing their iron content. It was sunny and cool, clouds racing across under a brisk northwest wind, their shadows skating like sea creatures just under the surface of the frigid gray-blue water. The air had lost its summer softness and Service could feel fall coming.

Limpy put one nugget in his mouth and put the rest of the boxes in a brown shopping bag he was carrying. Service had a cheeseburger and coffee, and after the burger lit a cigarette and held out the pack to Limpy, who refused.

"Got a question for youse."

Service didn't look at the old man. Limpy never asked a question without a purpose, did nothing without intent. He was a predator in human form, a demon and shape-shifter, a crow pocketing a bauble at a five-and-dime, a wolf taking easy and helpless prey. He was cold-blooded and calculating, most of his children sired from his other children or their spouses, a dirtbag who took and did as he wanted, with no remorse. In Allerdyce's mind all that mattered was what *he* wanted, and if you disagreed, you were in deep trouble.

"What?" Service asked. The old man was acting strange. He couldn't put a finger on what it was, but something was different—the weight loss, some uncharacteristic fidgeting and nervousness.

"You let queers be game wardens?"

"Why? You looking for work?"

Allerdyce hissed, "I ain't one a dose, hey!" He screamed, "Don't youse never call me no queer!"

Limpy's face was red, his fists clenched, and he looked like he was going to strike out. Service kept his voice soft. "Why do you want to know?"

"Just wonderin'," the old man said. "You hear about Dowdy Kitella?"

"He fell down and hurt himself?"

Allerdyce cackled. "Got shit kicked out of him, is what."

Classic Allerdyce, always on top of everything that could potentially affect his business. Kitella was a longtime competitor and there was no love lost between the men, though for years they had avoided tangling directly.

"You confessing?" Service asked.

Allerdyce grinned. "A body wants Kitella outa da way, he just go missin', eh?"

Service waited for additional comment, but Allerdyce chewed away and stared at Lake Superior.

"How's Honeypat?" Service asked. Honeypat had been the old man's daughter-in-law. They had been sleeping together before his son Jerry died. Limpy and Honeypat had more or less hooked up until last fall when Service informed her that Limpy had hit on his grandson's girlfriend.

The old man didn't directly answer the question. "Fucked ole Honeypat right here on dis island many da time," Limpy said. "Could hear her scream all da way to da ore docks. You heard she got her own place over to Ford River?" Limpy added.

Honeypat had a place, meaning they were still apart.

"How's Aldo?" His grandson seemed a nice kid, totally unlike his grandfather.

"Up da college."

"He still seeing Daysi?" Daysi was Aldo's Ojibwa girlfriend.

"He don't say. Lives da college, nose in books." Limpy made a sour face and spit. "Guess I better get on."

When Service got to the truck, Limpy walked past him, heading down the narrow road that looped the park. "You're not riding?"

"Got the time?"

Service checked his watch. "Almost one."

"I'll walk," Allerdyce said. "Good for ticker, and good for da ticker's good for da pecker, sonny." The old man looked Service in the eye. "Ya know, Aldo's queer as da five-dollar bill. Like all dem Hershey packers down to Jackson." Limpy flashed a look of total disgust and spit a thick line of yellow phlegm.

"Three-dollar bill," Service corrected him.

Allerdyce grunted and shuffled on.

Service started the truck and followed and when he drew alongside, buzzed down his window. "You still in the bear business?"

Allerdyce gave him a dark look. "Give dat up long time back. No money."

"I hear it's major money."

"Not on da gettin' end of da business. Da Chinks make all da money dese days, eh?"

Allerdyce walked slowly, his pace barely a shuffle. Usually the old man could outwalk professional walkers. Service drove to the end of the island, found a parking place, and waited.

What the hell had Limpy wanted? Allerdyce always had a plan. Always.

When the old man passed by his parking place he stopped at a trash-can, took off the top and fished around in it, shoving some of the take into his bag. Then he walked slowly on, looking straight ahead.

Back at the DNR office Fern LeBlanc turned away and Service looked down at the captain's office and saw Aldo Allerdyce in his boss's office, both of them at a small round conference table. The boy wore a long-sleeved dress shirt and a red tie.

The captain waved for Service to join them.

"Hey, Aldo," Service said. The boy was tall and thin, his hair neatly trimmed and combed, his shoes shined.

"I came to ask the captain about careers in law enforcement," the young man said. "I'm majoring in criminal justice with a minor in wildlife management." Aldo paused. "Given my grandfather's predilections, I thought it wise to find out if his history would disqualify me."

The captain spoke. "Mr. Allerdyce has a four-point average and he's taken the state civil service exams and scored in the ninety-sixth percentile."

"That's great," Service said. "Does Limpy know about your career interest?"

"He said it's my choice," Aldo said grudgingly.

Typical Limpy, playing two angles. He tells the boy one thing, and goes behind his back to poison the well. "How's Daysi?"

"Fine. She's in school at Northern, too."

"Good to see you," Service said, excusing himself.

Later, Aldo came to his cubicle. "The captain says that what matters is my record, not my grandfather's."

"Limpy's trying to stab you in the back," Service said. "He showed up here at lunchtime and told me you're gay."

Aldo shook his head and smiled. "Would that matter?"

"Only to your grandfather," Service said.

"The captain thinks he can get me on as summer help—with one of the biologists," Aldo said.

"Say hi to Daysi," Service said. He watched Aldo walk away. The vision of Aldo with a badge confronting his rogue grandfather made him smile.

Simon del Olmo called on the cell phone later that afternoon. Service was in the parking lot, smoking. "Kitella's hired Sandy Tavolacci," Simon said.

"I'm not surprised," Service said. "Sandy only cares about how much cash a client has. Guilt's not a factor." Tavolacci often played the dunce, but it was all an act. He had put a lot of people back in the woods who didn't belong there. But Sandy was cagey and because he had to deal frequently with woods cops, there were times when he would signal something he didn't think was quite right according to his twisted interpretation of Hoyle.

Service thought, maybe Limpy had delivered several messages today.

· 19 ·

Until a year ago Grady Service had been petrified of dogs, any breed, any size, any temperament. The mere sight of one gave him the sweats. Proximity or a growl sent ice water racing down his spine. Since the arrival of Newf, a gift from his former girlfriend, the fears had begun to recede, but returned suddenly as he pulled into the driveway.

He saw a large red and gray dog come loping from the side of the house. It had a hyena-like snout, its neck hair hackled with spikes—a bowlegged, strutting, wide-bodied beast that looked like it could chew through a fire hydrant. Service had just cracked his door when he saw the dog. He immediately slammed it and felt something he had not experienced in a year. His friends and colleagues saw irony in his being a conservation officer and being afraid of dogs, but he found no humor in it. Fear was irrational and meant the loss of control. He hated not having control, or at least the illusion of it.

He saw Newf in the window of the house, barking and carrying on at the intruder, who showed no interest in leaving.

The cell phone buzzed while he was contemplating his predicament.

"Hey, it's me," Nantz said. "I called the house, but no answer. Where are you?"

"Almost home," he said.

"How close?"

"Not far."

"When you get home, open a beer and call me back."

"We can talk now."

"I don't hear any sounds," she said. "Are you moving?"

"I have the windows up."

"I talked to Lori about the fund-raiser. I told her about Siquin Soong."

The red and gray beast looked up at him and glared. "You *what?*"

"Don't get yanked. Lori's no fool. I told you that. She asked a lot of questions and I told her you want to talk to Soong. I told you I wouldn't lie to her."

He wondered if Nantz would change her tune after she had her badge. "What did she say?" The dog outside was still and seemed to be shaking. He wondered if it was rabid, but there was no drool, no foam.

"She thanked me for telling her the truth and said she's confident you'll use discretion and impressive diplomatic skills. Siquin Soong is one of her major supporters."

"Maybe she should rethink that."

"Grady, you don't have anything on the woman. You just want to ask about her son. What's for dinner tonight?"

"I haven't thought that far ahead."

"Get real. You always have dinner planned. What's going on? Your voice sounds strained."

"Nothing," he said. Which was true up to a point; he and the dog were at a standoff.

"Where are you now?"

"Almost in the house."

"Where exactly?"

"Close," he said.

She paused before speaking. "Jesus, you're in the driveway!"

"There's a goddamned dog," he confessed meekly.

She laughed. "And you're afraid to get out."

"Basically."

"It's a *dog*, Service."

"I know it's a dog, but there are dogs and there are *dogs*," he said. "This one might as well be a man-eating croc."

"Where is it?"

"Next to my door."

"It probably wants to play."

"I don't think so."

"Are his ears up or back?"

"Flat," he said.

"Is he looking at you?"

"No, he's looking off at about forty-five degrees."

"How's he breathing?"

"Panting."

"He's anxious."

"*He's* anxious?"

"You're probably making him nervous."

"It's *our* goddamn driveway, *not* his."

"Calm down," she said. "You're being irrational."

"Knowing that doesn't flip the switch to rational."

"Just get out of the truck."

"That's it?"

"This isn't number theory."

"You're not the one who has to do this."

"I know *that*," she said.

Service said, "When I was a kid I never thought dog and mail carrier jokes were funny."

"Just get out, but don't make eye contact. He'll read that as a challenge."

"So he can attack me blind?"

"Work with me, Service. I'm trying to help."

"Maybe I could shoot him."

"The animal hasn't done anything."

"You can't see what I see."

"Listen to me," she said. "Get out the passenger door, duck into the garage, and go from there to the house."

"He'll nail me before I get to the garage."

"No, he won't."

"He's right here, waiting."

"Have you got a better plan?"

He didn't, but maybe if he opened the door sharply, he could knock the dog away and scare him. "I could just stay in the truck until it leaves."

"And if it stays all night?"

Damn dog. "Okay," he said.

"Okay what?"

"Just okay. I'm thinking." If he got to the garage it was a short leap from there to the house. If he got into the house he could let Newf out and she could take care of the intruder. But what if the dog got between him and the garage? He could run for the house and if the animal attacked, he had no choice. He could give it a squirt of pepper spray—if he had a canister with him, which he didn't.

"Grady Service, you can't sit in your truck all night."

"I have a plan," he said.

"My plan, I bet," she said.

"Your plan, yes." With a modification: he would shoot the animal if he had to.

202 · JOSEPH HEYWOOD

"I think you can't do this," she said.

"Do what?"

"Get out of the truck with the pupper sitting there."

"It's sure as hell *not* a pupper."

"You can't do it. You're gonna sit there like a boob all night."

"Am not. I can do this."

"Standard bet?" she said. Standard bet meant the winner got their choice of time and place for sex.

"Really?"

"Sure. I'll win," she said.

"We'll see about that," he countered.

"Call me if you actually get into the house," she said, hanging up.

"Traitor," he said, snapping the cell phone shut.

He tried his door and the red dog immediately tensed. He pawed under the seats and found the remnants of some crackers, opened the window slightly and threw them onto the driveway. The dog took a step toward them, but stopped. A second batch sent the dog after them and Service went quickly through the passenger door, hitting the electronic garage door remote as he got inside, and out the back door, leaping onto the porch and into the house without looking back.

Newf was all over him, but he opened the door and yelled, "Get that red piece of shit!"

She charged out snarling, got almost to the marauding dog, stopped, wagged her tail, and the two animals began to play and roll around on the grass.

He opened a bottle of Bell's Amber Ale with a shaking hand and tried to steady his nerves. It took an hour for him to call Nantz.

"Have you been in your truck all this time?"

"No," he said.

"Yes you have," she said.

"I'm in the house and I win the bet," he said.

"There was a time limit," Nantz said.

"You never said anything about a time limit."

"There's always a time limit. You can't make a bet after the Army-Navy game's over."

"This wasn't a football game. There's no time limit."

"There's always a time limit, hon. Sorry."

"It's a mean-looking dog."

"Where is it now?"

He turned his back so he couldn't see Newf and the strange dog standing side by side on the lawn. "I can't see it now."

"Go see if it's still out there."

As he walked toward the door Newf and the red dog jumped up on the porch and lay down together.

"You see it?"

"Yeah."

"Where?"

"On the porch."

"*Our* porch?"

"Yes, our porch."

"Where's Newf?"

"Outside."

"Doing what?"

"They're taking a nap together."

"The *man-eater* and Newf?" She began to laugh hysterically and when she finally regained composure, said, "God, I love you, Service. But we still win the bet."

"We win?"

"Think about it, dummy."

He laughed. "Right."

"If the dog's there in the morning, how are you going to get to work?" she asked.

"Jesus," he said. "Did you have to bring that up?"

"It'll probably leave," she said.

More likely, it wouldn't.

"I've got to sign off, darlin'. We roll early tomorrow: St. Joe, Niles, Flint, Mt. Pleasant."

"In one day?"

"She has the constitution of a yeti. Be nice to that pup, Service."

"It's the hound from hell."

"You," she said, hanging up.

He thought about letting Newf in, but she seemed content and he didn't want to open the door. Instead, he called Simon del Olmo at home.

"Allerdyce came to see me today," he told the younger officer. "He wanted to know if I'd heard about Kitella. I suggested that maybe he had something to do with it, and he said if he wanted Kitella gone, he would disappear him."

"You buy that?"

"Allerdyce is into mind games."

"With no mind."

"He has a mind. It just doesn't work like ours."

"He's been violent before."

"It's not his style now. Too much risk, and believe me, he does not want to go back inside."

"Something I can do to help?" del Olmo asked.

"I'm not sure. Maridly got hold of a photo of Trapper Jet from high school. It doesn't look like him. Not even close."

"People change when they get older."

"Not this much. I got some of his military records and the start on a biography. He's from Lansing originally. When he was released by the VA, he came up to the Yoop and never went home. That makes no sense."

"He's loco," del Olmo said.

"Maybe he's smarter than we give him credit for," Service said.

"That wouldn't take much. You think he had something to do with Kitella?"

"He claimed Kitella burned his cabin."

"How's he gonna go after Kitella? He's blind. You think he'd hire somebody?"

"Not his style—and maybe we're the blind ones," Service said.

"You've lost me," del Olmo said.

"Okay, bye," Service said, abruptly hanging up. Why would Oliver Toogood want to lose himself in the U.P.? Had something happened in the camps in Korea? The rift with his father? The only people who could know for sure were those who had been POWs with him. How many were still alive? More to the point: was Trapper Jet Oliver Toogood? Service was having nagging doubts and had no idea how this could be.

All this had started with the body at the canal. He got another beer and called Treebone. Kalina answered.

"It's Grady. Is he there?"

"Parked in front of the TV—as usual. I'll take the phone to him. Don't want to get the man's blood pressure up."

"Yo," Tree said.

"Do you know where Teddy Gates is?" Gates had been their commanding officer in Vietnam.

"At this minute or over the past twenty-five years?" Luticious Treebone asked.

"Don't be a jerk."

"He's sucking the eagle's tit."

"Retired?"

"Ninety-four or -five, I think, after the Gulf War. He had a brigade over there, went out with two stars. Last I heard he was living in Alexandria."

"You got his number?"

"You know how to call information, right? They have that service up there?"

"Don't jerk me around. Did you get the information on Siquin Soong?"

"You a motherfucker, you know that? Takes time to get shit like this. What's crawled inside you and gone sour?"

"Ambiguity."

"My black ass. Cops breathe that shit."

"I need help."

"You're gettin' it. Just stay cool."

Stay cool with so many holes in this case?

He called information and found thirteen listings for Gates, but no Theodores and no retired generals. In the process he pissed off the long distance operator. Add unlisted phone numbers to your hate list, he told himself.

Newf was pawing at the door when he went downstairs. He looked out and saw that the other dog was gone and opened the door. Newf came in, looked up and wagged her tail.

"You're worthless," he said.

He got into bed, but couldn't sleep and got up again. It was 4 A.M. and Newf followed him downstairs, whining to go out. He decided to take her along—not that she'd be worth a damn if the red dog were still hanging around. But it wasn't. She settled into the passenger seat, went to sleep, and began snoring.

The DNR office in Marquette was dark and he let himself in with his key. The captain's truck was parked in the lot, which didn't surprise him. The captain's hours and rhythms were as erratic as his own.

He went to his cubicle, told Newf to take a nap, and turned on his computer to check e-mail.

Captain Ware Grant appeared in the opening to his cubicle, a bottle of Jack Daniel's and a folder in one hand, two glasses in the other. "I didn't expect company tonight," the captain said.

"Couldn't sleep. Things rolling around in my mind."

Grant set the glasses on the desk and poured a couple of fingers in each. "Ice dilutes." He eased a glass over to Service. "Does your dog suffer insomnia as well?"

They sipped in silence. The captain pushed the manila folder across to him. "The lab results," Grant said. "The fax came in after you left." Service opened the folder and read the summary.

Genetic testing verifies that hair samples, USF&WS—MI-4128–205 #B.1–3, are those of *Selenarctos thibetanus* (protected under Appendix I, CITES). *S. thibetanus* (Asiatic black bear) is indigenous to a variety of transasiatic climates and habitats, north to south in the east and west. The status of bears in heavily populated central China is unknown. While *S. thibetanus* is widespread, there has been minimal scientific study of the species and there are little reliable data about basic biology, etc.

NOTE 1: USF&WS has previously examined only one sample of *S. thibetanus* exhibiting the light color of MI-4128–205 #B.1–3. It has been theorized that this may represent an unknown color phase of *S. thibetanus*, or potentially (but unlikely) a previously unknown species of ursus. The previous sample was collected in Cambodia, and has been attributed to, but not confirmed as, a "golden" or "blond moon" bear.

NOTE 2: Tests confirm that galls in sample MI-4128–205 #s A.1–2 are that of *Ursus americanus*; all hair samples in MI-4128–205 #s B.1–3 are *S. thibetanus*.

CITES was the acronym for Convention on International Trade in Endangered Species of Wild Fauna and Flora. Appendix I listed endangered species and allowed no international trade. He knew from previous experience that North American black bears were in the less restricted Appendix II, which annoyed the hell out of wildlife managers. Not all states banned the sale of bear parts, and those that didn't served as havens for sellers and buyers.

Service looked up from the report to find the captain staring at him. "The historical intersects between you and complex cases remain unparalleled," Grant said.

"I don't pick the cases," Service said. "Especially this one." He had been visiting Gus when this one landed on him.

"That's what makes it extraordinary."

"A blond moon bear?" Service said shaking his head. "Live from the Upper Peninsula, it's the Twilight Zone."

Captain Grant flashed a rare smirk. "I have faith in your abilities, Detective."

Service opened a pad of yellow lined paper and began making notes.

FACT: Professor Harry Pung found dead at fish house, Hancock.

FACT: Pung poisoned with cyanide in chocolate-covered figs. COD confirmed by autopsy. Case classified homicide.

FACT: Two bear galls discovered in same package with the figs. Galls confirmed by USF&WS as *U. americanus*, our blackie.

FACT: Bear scat and hair found in victim's vehicle, species now verified as Asiatic black bear (but possible golden/blond moon bear, new species/color phase?). Different than our blackie.

FACT: Hair samples recovered at Harry Pung's rental home in Houghton, and at stainless steel cage in rented cabin on Lac La Belle. All hair samples confirmed as from an Asiatic black bear.

FACT: Lac La Belle cabin rented by Harry Pung.

CONCLUSION: The bear in Pung's vehicle was also in the rented house and cabin.

QUESTION: Did Pung possess and move these animals willingly?

QUESTION: Boat used to move bear from Hancock?

FACT: Second body discovered at house on shipping canal in Houghton.

FACT: Prints, documents, and immigration records confirm second body as that of Terry Tunhow. One witness confirms identity: Maggie Soper, the landlord.

FACT: A second witness (Enrica) says body is not Terry Pung, but a Korean student who was in her classes under the name of Terry Pung. Witness claims to have met the real (another?) Terry Pung.

FACT: Masonetsky confirms that Terry Pung was using a substitute to attend classes in his place and using his name and identity.

CONCLUSION: The actual Terry Pung is alive. Another Korean male was, with his permission and perhaps by his design, acting as Terry Pung. (Harry's role? Why?)

FACT: House on shipping canal in Houghton rented by the false Terry Pung, also confirmed by landlady.

FACT: Witnesses who found the body also report meeting another Asian male there (the "other" Terry Pung?).

ASSUMPTION: The second still-unidentified male—prolly the ersatz Terry Pung.

FACT: Witnesses at house saw smaller aluminum boat tied to a larger blue craft. Both boats sailed south.

QUESTION: Destination?

FACT: Harry Pung left all to ex-wife, Siquin Soong.

QUESTION: Why does she get everything?

QUESTION: When were they married, where, how long, reason for divorce, etc.?

FACT: Siquin Soong is major player in state Democratic Party, owns businesses in Detroit. Married to prominent lawyer.

ALLEGED: Per Tree, Soong suspected of illegal activities by the feds.

QUESTION: Which fed agencies interested, and why?

ALLEGED: The real Terry Pung transferred to U of M, Ann Arbor. No: A Terry Pung or somebody going by that name. Still not clear if either of the younger Koreans in Houghton was Pung.

FACT: The Pungs were members of archery *jung* in Oconomowoc, Wisconsin. Son's membership dropped. Why?

FACT: Per Pyykkonen, Soong's attorneys not playing ball with the investigation.

QUESTION: Why not? What are they hiding?

UNKNOWN: Why did Harry Pung leave previous position at Virginia Tech?

QUESTION: Fight, conflict between father/son?

UNKNOWN: What is known about golden/blond moon bears?

UNKNOWN: Why bring another species of bear into Michigan where blackies are more than plentiful?

UNKNOWN: What do feds think Soong has done?

UNKNOWN: What is relationship of Soong to Terry Pung? (Her son, Harry's son? Neither?)

Service set down his pen and read over his notes. In his mind he began to make a list of things he needed to do before meeting Soong at the fund-raiser downstate. He was surprised when he looked up to find the captain still sitting across from him.

"Lost in the case?" the captain asked.

"Just lost," Service said.

The captain held out his hand and Service gave him the notes.

Captain Grant sipped Jack Daniel's and read slowly, nodding now and then.

"Siquin Soong?" the captain said, looking up from the notes.

"Yessir. She was previously married to Harry Pung."

"She is a significant political force," the captain said.

"And a key backer of Timms," Service said.

The captain nodded. "What are the federals looking at?"

"I'm still waiting for that information."

"You may have to operate in concert with federal agencies."

Service understood, but wanted to avoid such cooperation as long as possible. Last year he had gotten mixed up with U.S. Fish and Wildlife and the FBI. The case had been resolved, but only after a lot of conflict and virtually no cooperation, which left a bad taste.

"Do you feel like you're making progress?" the captain asked.

"Very little, Captain."

Grant refilled their glasses. "Progress is progress," he said with a nod.

"Siquin Soong's political connections put us in a minefield," Service said.

"William Jennings Bryan told Democrats at their national convention, 'The humblest citizen of all the land, when clad in the armor of a righteous cause, is stronger than all the hosts of Error.' Don't let your imagination be restricted by raw fact."

Service took a sip of whiskey. Sometimes his captain acted like a man with his mind rooted in another dimension, one that always seemed to elude Service.

"The art of investigation," Grant added in his professorial tone, "once could be reduced to shoe leather. But we are in a new era, and the art now resides in the marriage of fingertips to the brain. You can't do everything alone, Detective. Your colleagues respect you and trust you. Use and depend on them."

"And if that doesn't work?"

"What have you found on the Internet?" the captain asked. "If Soong is culpable, don't be swayed by who she is. Let only what she has done be your guide."

"Are you telling me to go after her?"

"Go where the evidence takes you."

· 20 ·

S ervice knew that the Internet had been invented in the sixties by
government and university scientists who wanted to talk back and
forth in their insulated languages—and not waste travel money.
Now the Net was bastardized by commercial interests and expanding
like a newborn universe. In the early days, its use had been restricted;
now it was open to any fool who could afford a monthly fee. Service had
never had access to the original Internet, but wished it would come back
so he could be excluded in order to avoid frustration.

After the captain went back to his office, he took Newf outside for a
quick pee before the two of them settled back into his cubicle.

A cursory look at the Internet made it appear to be overflowing with
information, but more often than not his search engines dredged up and
regurgitated garbage. He first went to Switchboard.Com and got nothing, then two other telephone registries, with the same result. Over a couple of hours of Net searching, he snared a couple of leads, one to do with
Teddy Gates, the other pointing to a cultural anthropologist who might
know something about Asiatic black bears.

The first sweep took him into the organizational octopus that enveloped POW/MIA affairs. There was a lot of pent-up emotion surrounding the issue, a lot of anger and mistrust of government—though based
on his own experience last fall with the FBI, maybe mistrust of government agencies in some circumstances was not entirely unjustified.

He learned that there were more Americans killed in Vietnam than
in Korea, but only by four thousand or so. He had always thought the dif-
ferential to be much larger. He also found that about a thousand
confirmed American POWs went unaccounted for after the mass repa-
triation. He learned that there was a Senate Select Committee on
POW/MIA Affairs, created in 1991 and still in existence, though reports
since 1993 were few and far between. He also discovered by reading various reports that there was no central government clearinghouse for
POW/MIA information, no comprehensive, one-stop shopping data-
base, and that for a long time, gathering such material carried the lowest
of national priorities. Some agencies collected such information only if

they could justify it in connection with a national priority, but they did not routinely share. It was depressing, especially when he read that American soldiers lost during intelligence and secret missions were somehow excluded from overall POW/MIA considerations. Had he and Tree gone missing, they very likely would have been in this category. After rooting electronically for two hours, he discovered testimony from the Senate Select Committee's hearings of 1992 — and there he found his first lead. Major General Theodore Gates had testified.

Teddy's testimony bristled with indignation over troops left behind in Vietnam and Korea, but as strident and angry as his former commanding officer seemed, there was little in the way of actual information, and where his affiliation was to be listed, there was nothing but a series of XXXXXs. Looking at other testimony, he found the same technique employed. Okay, so they kept some personal shit secret. 1992 and Gates had been a two-star. The Gulf War was in 1991. Had Tree said Gates retired in ninety-four or -five? If so, had his testimony had something to do with it?

Two telephone calls to Washington, D.C., did not yield the general's phone number or address. An officious senate committee staffer informed him that what witnesses said was public domain, but their private lives — including their home addresses and phone numbers — were just that, private. This sent him scrambling for a back door.

During his Net scans he had developed a list of other witnesses from the date of Teddy's testimony, including one from a group called Reckoning Over Korea (ROK). The words of a civilian, the daughter of a missing naval aviator, struck home, and he had jotted them down: "The living bear the pain of not knowing until they die, and we can only hope that Almighty God will then reunite us." The offices of the operation were listed in Clyde, New York, and the witness's name was Augusta Rivitz. Teddy Gates was a gregarious softy in many ways, and if he had testified with others, there was a fair chance that the other witnesses would have his telephone number and address.

A woman answered the phone. "Mrs. Rivitz?"

"Oh, yes, it's Ms. Rivitz, and if you're trying to sell something I'm not buying," she said.

"Are you the Augusta Rivitz who testified before the Senate Select Committee on POW/MIA Affairs in February 1992?"

"Oh yes, that was me. Are you calling about my father?" she asked anxiously.

"No, ma'am."

"Oh, my," the woman said, obviously deflated. "The senators promised they would get back to me, but it's been over ten years."

Her voice faded, but quickly strengthened. "Darn government. Oh yes, they rip out your heart and throw it in the trash bin. My father, Lieutenant Barry Rivitz, was seen alive in his parachute and on the ground by his wingman, Lieutenant Junior Grade Edward Gisseler. My father was alive but never heard from again. We are still waiting, still waiting."

She did not identify the "we." The woman's father had never returned, the result being that she was mired emotionally and mentally somewhere between Clyde and wherever her father might be. He knew from his own experience and military training that the most dangerous time for a prisoner was immediately after capture—before transfer to a group camp of some kind. Ironically, this also was the best opportunity for escape. Even if her father had been seen, it didn't mean much. The invisible companion of every soldier was luck, both good and bad, but in this case, Ms. Rivitz was as much MIA as her father.

"You testified the same morning as Marine Major General Theodore Gates."

"Oh yes, I remember him," she said. "Such a southern gentleman, but he gave those senators the dickens. His older brother was also MIA in Korea, I believe."

This had not been in Teddy's testimony and he had never talked about it in Vietnam.

"Oh yes, a fine, lovely man," she went on. "Kind but fiery. Before we testified they put us all in a room and we could tell why he was a general. He was a born leader and of course, he had not been killed in a war. Oh yes, Mother insisted Daddy would have become an admiral."

"You wouldn't happen to have the general's number?"

"Oh, certainly. The general suggested we all exchange names, phone numbers, and addresses, and stay in touch. I get a Christmas card from him every year. He said I should call him if I ever needed anything, but I never have. Do you think he meant it?"

"I knew the general and yes, he meant it." Teddy Gates always meant what he said and said what he meant, which made it a miracle he had been promoted so high. If you crossed him, he could be brutal, and while his men loved him, his superiors usually harbored a different opinion. "Could I impose on you for the general's number and address?"

"Are you a friend of the general?"

"Yes, ma'am. I served with him in Vietnam."

"Oh yes, that dreadful mess; but you came back alive. Were you an aviator?"

"No, ma'am, mud marine."

"My father was an aviator. The navy calls them aviators, not pilots."

The navy did a lot of things Service considered stilted, pompous, and downright archaic. Marines called all sailors rust pickers, and swabbies called marines bullet sponges.

"If you're the general's friend, why don't you have his phone number? Oh yes, you men who have come home alive are lucky, but you need to be more attentive to your comrades and their loved ones. Lieutenant Gisseler, my daddy's wingman, doesn't call or write any more."

Service thought: Korea ended nearly fifty years ago. Presumably the man was dead. "Yes, ma'am, I've moved around some and I can't seem to find my book with the general's address. You know how that can happen."

"Oh yes—no, I don't know. I've lived my entire life in Clyde. I never wanted to live anywhere else. And oh yes, I never lose things. You really must be more careful," she said, chiding him. "Naval aviators are trained to be careful—all those dials and switches. But daddy said it was easy, a matter of simple logic and practice. Mother and I were to join him in San Diego when he got back. Mother was afraid to go so far from Clyde, but Daddy said he would come and fetch us. He never came back, did I tell you that? Oh yes, he was to leave Korea in a month but he didn't come back. . . ."

Ms. Rivitz was a few cards short of a full deck, but he couldn't blame her. "Is your husband there?"

"Please, you must listen better. I am a graduate of a class for active listening and the teacher said it is important to signal that we are listening, oh yes. I am Ms. Rivitz. I used to be Miss, but Ms. sounds more modern and I believe in growing with the times."

This was going nowhere. "My father was MIA in Korea," Service lied. "I read your testimony, where you said that 'the living must bear the pain of not knowing until they die.' "

"Oh yes, I assure you I do not plan to die until Daddy comes home," she said. "Was your daddy a naval aviator?"

"No, ma'am. We were both Marines."

"Oh my, the darn government let you both go to war? Your mother must have been devastated."

"My mother passed away when I was young. My dad raised me." Was it a sin to mislead the unbalanced?

"Oh yes, you poor boy. Mother didn't really love Daddy. She promised to wait, but she died before he could come back. I'll never forgive Mother."

"Ma'am, General Gates knows something about my father." This was not a prevarication. Specifically, Teddy knew he had been a marine in the Second World War and a conservation officer after that. Service and Gates had talked about families in Vietnam.

"Oh yes, your waiting might be over?"

"I don't know, Ms. Rivitz. It's been a long wait." Especially since he had gotten on the phone with her. "I really would appreciate the general's phone number."

"Oh yes, I have all the phone numbers right here in my kitchen. My Daddy said an aviator must always be organized. He calls me his little aviator. Just a moment, please."

He heard the phone clunk, listened to her opening and closing drawers, papers rustling, other drawers being rattled, and finally she was back on the line. "Oh, yes, here it is. Right in its place. Daddy will be so proud."

"I really appreciate this, Ms. Rivitz. It's a good thing for people to help each other."

"Oh yes, I agree," she said, "But what are you doing to help me?"

He shook his head. "I'll ask the general to give you a call."

"You would do that?"

"Yes, ma'am, absolutely."

She gave him the number and address, which was in Tidewater, Virginia. "You're certain the general will call me?"

"Yes, ma'am, you can count on it."

"Oh yes, I waited on Truman, Ike, Kennedy, Nixon, Ford, Carter, Bush, Clinton, and now another Bush. Do you know that Clinton did nasty things with girls in the Oval Office? And he never served our country in uniform."

"Thank you, Ms. Rivitz." He hung up before she could ramble on to whatever stop her train was rolling to next. Why in the hell had the Senate invited her to testify?

He dialed the number but got a recording telling him the area code was changing and to make a note of it. He was about to call the new area code when Fern LeBlanc popped into his cubicle, her eyes wide, her hands shaking like she had broken wrists.

"Come!" she said in a high, shrill voice. "*Hurry!*"

Captain Grant was on the floor of his office, his chair on its side. Service felt for a pulse and the captain's eyes fluttered open. "Not a stroke," he muttered. "Chair tipped over."

"I'm calling 911," Fern LeBlanc said, heading for her phone.

"Stop her," Grant said, but it was too late.

She was on her phone, tears welling. "This has happened twice before and he insists I not call help," she said, "but I'm telling you he's not well, Detective. This time I called."

It was the first time Service had seen anything other than professionalism or anger in her eyes. "You did the right thing," he said, but she was already on the phone again.

"Doctor Beaudoin, this is Fern LeBlanc. It's happened again." She nodded curtly and said, "Thank you, they're on the way."

She looked at Service. "His physician will be here soon."

The captain had his chair back up and was sitting in it when Service walked into his office. Grant's eyes were glazed and distant.

"Not a stroke," the captain said. "I was tipping in my chair, dozed off, and down I went." He rubbed his head. "Got a knot."

"She called 911, Captain." Grant looked dazed, a little disoriented, and clearly unhappy.

"She thinks I'm made of eggshells," the captain complained.

"Probably a good idea to get your head checked out," Service said. "She called your doctor too."

"Blast that woman!" the captain said.

Dr. Pope Beaudoin was six-four and close to three hundred pounds, with shaggy silver hair and rimless glasses. He arrived before EMS, went directly into the captain's office, and closed the door.

When they came out the doctor supported one of the captain's arms. Ware Grant was dragging his left foot and looking pale. Service walked out with them.

EMS met them at the front door. The captain and doctor got into the ambulance. "I'll be back," Captain Ware Grant said. "Don't get shot down, Detective." The doors closed, the siren came on, and the ambulance raced away toward the hospital.

LeBlanc came outside jingling her keys. "I'm going to the hospital," she said. "Will you cover the phones?"

When he finally got around to making the call to Teddy Gates, he got an answering machine recording, which said, "I'm not here and if that's not obvious, don't leave a message." Classic Teddy Gates, blunt as a fist hatchet, whatever that was. From tenth-grade world history Service had retained two terms, fist hatchet and Hammurabi's Code, both of which no longer had a context, but popped into his mind at odd times.

"This is Grady Service, calling the General." He paused before leaving his own numbers when a live voice intervened. "Sarn't Service, you asshole!"

"Captain?"

"Best damn job I ever had. Where the hell is that barbarian Sarn't Treebone?"

"Detroit Metropolitan Police, Vice Lieutenant."

"No wonder Detroit's so fucked up," the general said with a laugh. "You a cop?"

"Detective, Department of Natural Resources."

"Woods cop. I had a feeling. Just like your old man. What the hell do you want after all these years?"

"This may seem a little off the wall."

"That keeps it in character."

"I've got a strange old bird up here. He claims to have been a POW in Korea."

"Do I detect skepticism?"

"I got some of his records and used them to find his high school. The picture we found there, well—I know people age and change, but this can't be a photo of the man."

"Wouldn't be the first counterfeit POW," Gates said. "You want, I can poke around and see if anybody has anything. I've got writing utensil in hand, Sarn't. Fire for effect."

Service related Oliver Toogood's record. "The thing is, I can't find a place where he'd be getting a disability check."

"Maybe he's not. There have been a few men who turned them down. Or maybe your man's checks go to a bank somewhere else to accumulate and he draws against it. Money's like clay nowadays, you can knead it into just about any shape that suits you."

Service hadn't considered this. How did he get bank information? "There's one other thing. I got your number from a woman named Augusta Rivitz."

"Poor thing is totally bonkers."

"How did she get invited to testify?"

"Her organization sent her. They figured that the august senators should get a firsthand look at the personal cost to POW/MIA families, but politicians are reptiles. The only time they're warm, they've got their pampered fat asses plopped on hot rocks beside a donor volcano erupting cash."

"Her testimony seemed coherent." It had been the phone call that was at odds with what he had read on the Senate Select Committee's site.

"No doubt you saw her written testimony. The actual transcript is too fucked up to publish. You can't even dig it out of the Web site. Anybody wants it, they have to go the FOIA route, and you know how long that shit takes."

"Was her father a POW?"

"Technically, yes. Did she tell you about her father's wingman?"

"She told me."

"I checked it out at some length. The wingman saw Rivitz in his chute, but reported Rivitz wasn't moving or showing any signs of life, and when he hit the ground, he just lay there sprawled out. The Pentagon had no choice but to declare Rivitz MIA. In all likelihood, the enemy found him dead right where he hit the ground."

"She knows this?"

"Her mother was informed, and later Augusta was told on more than one occasion. She just can't seem to wrap her head around it. Can't or won't. That's a fine line."

"She said you send her a Christmas card every year."

"I do, and every one of them says the same thing: 'Happy Holidays. I am sorry for your terrible loss. Here's the name of a psychiatrist who can help you.' She's what the Pentagoonies call IUDCD—invisible unintended domestic collateral damage."

There was no love lost between Gates and the military. "When did you hang it up?"

"Ninety-two, the month after I testified. I'd already submitted my papers and I figured I went off the reservation a bit too far. They weren't sorry to see me go and I didn't let the door hit me in the ass on the way out."

"Rivitz said you lost a brother in Korea."

"She's dotty. What I said was that all the men and women dead and missing in Korea and Vietnam were my brothers and sisters. Did she tell you about her active listening training? Oh yes, Ms. Rivitz hears only what she wants to hear, which makes her like the rest of us who haven't been trained."

They both laughed.

"I do feel bad for her," Gates said, "but the living have to keep on keeping on. I'll get what I can for you on Toogood. If he's a fake, we'll nail his sorry ass. If he's getting a check, I'll find that out, too."

"Thanks, general."

"To you and that big black smiling sonuvabitch you call a pal, it's Teddy. Give that big bastard a kiss for me and watch your back, Sarn't Service."

"Yessir."

"Semper Fi, Sarn't. If I'd had a division of Services and Treebones we could have hiked up there to Hanoi and shot Uncle Ho and the rest of those red motherfuckers."

"You had a unit in the Gulf War."

"Not with the likes of you two. I'll get back at you."

It had been good to hear Teddy's voice.

He was ready to follow his second lead when Simon del Olmo called.

"Get this," del Olmo said. "That cable we found at Kitella's—it's a perfect match to the cable Elza found. In fact, it's off the same spool."

"What's Kitella say?"

"He don't know nuttin' from nuttin'. Insists it's a set-up."

"Any chance you guys can source the stuff?"

"Better. We have and you aren't going to believe this. It's aviation cable."

"Aviation cable?"

"To be precise, cable used in choppers, including the Enstrom 480B light turbine helicopter. A guy who flies told her it looked like aviation cable. The only aviation manufacturer in the U.P. is Enstrom down in Menominee. Elza drove down there and the company told her that the cable was indeed from a helicopter, and, in fact, is used in their 480B and another model. Further, they announced that a spool of cable had been stolen from the factory in July. They reported it and somehow the report made its way to the FBI, who got on the case and narrowed it down to an employee named Fahrenheit—spelled just like the temperature. Charley Fahrenheit. He's a former army chopper mechanic who served in Somalia and left the army honorably with the rank of staff sergeant. He joined Enstrom right out of the military and has always been a pretty solid employee, but there were a half-dozen thefts of various things over the past year and Fahrenheit was always the one with opportunity when stuff fell off the truck."

"Was he charged?" What the hell was this Elza stuff? Nobody called Grinda anything but Sheena.

"The FBI said all their evidence is circumstantial, and weak circumstances at that—opportunity and some motive, which amounts to smoke but no gun. The company canned Fahrenheit for poor attendance. The Feebs say he has a bottle problem and some financial troubles too, but there's no evidence of a sudden influx of cash to get him out of his situation. If he was ganking, either he's not moving the goods, or he has the money stashed."

Who fenced industrial goods? Service wondered. "In other words, that's the end of it."

"Not exactly. Enstrom has been served with a wrongful dismissal civil suit and MESC is involved." MESC, the Michigan Employment Securities Commission, takes care of labor problems in the state. "What's interesting is that Fahrenheit hired a big-ticket specialist from Midland. Even if he wins the case, he's not going to win big, so why would a lawyer of that caliber take an if-come job with marginal payback potential? What's even more intriguing is that the suit lists the name of an old friend of ours, Sandy Tavolacci. He's the attorney of record."

"Really," Service said. Labor law was way outside Sandy's usual browse. "Fahrenheit like the temperature, right?"

"You got it."

"Where's Fahrenheit live?"

"Marinette County, Wisconsin, a burg called Harmony. It's one of those places where the sign going into town lists the population number as 'sometimes.'"

"Sounds like home," Service said.

"There's no way for us to get into this one," del Olmo said.

"There's always a road in, Simon."

"If you say so."

"Thanks."

"*De nada.*"

Newf nudged his leg. He'd forgotten to bring food for her. He gathered his notes, drove to Donovan's Forest, bought two six-inch Italian meatball subs, and headed over to Harvey to the public boat launch on the Chocolay River to see if the salmon were in for the annual spawn yet. They were. Newf inhaled her sandwich and immediately splashed into the water chasing fish, whose minds were solely on sex, and easily avoided her clumsy lunges.

"You aren't a bear," he told her as she paddled around snapping at the fish and now and then looking up at him with water cascading off her snout.

While the dog splashed and barked, he ate and read the printouts he had downloaded at the office.

He had found a Web site called Legends and Species.Com. He had almost ignored the site, but was determined to dig until the lead went nowhere. Here he found a report by Tara Ferma, Ph.D., associate professor of cultural anthropology at Montana State University in Bozeman. The report dealt with parasites in *Selenarctos thibetanus*, the Asiatic black bear. The professor had written, "The incidence of parasites in Cambodian golden bears remains unknown, but given that the animal is a color phase of S. *thibetanus*, similar infestations seem predictable."

Service thought: Cambodian golden bear, same as blond moon bear. The information leaped out at him, but in truth it had been the professor's name that caught his attention. He liked unusual and nonsensical names. His favorite was Venus Dyke, a cop downstate somewhere, but Tara Ferma was right up there. His infatuation had paid off. He knew this find should have boosted his confidence in the Net as an investigational tool, but absent his interest in names he would never have gotten the lead. Serendipity was a piss-poor fuel for research, he told himself.

He opened his cell phone as he sat by the river. The professor's telephone number and e-mail address were listed at the bottom of the article, and after being transferred a couple of times he learned that Professor Ferma had left in August for a yearlong sabbatical in Cambodia and Vietnam. The departmental secretary advised him to try the professor's e-mail because she would be checking it daily, using a satellite phone to an uplink even when she was in the bush. She used her computer to upload research data and observations.

Service didn't want to wait for e-mail. "Does she have an assistant?"

"Cameron Gill is taking her classes this semester. Would you like to talk to her?"

He would.

"Ms. Gill," she said when she came on line.

"Professor?"

"It's Cameron or Cam. I'm a lowly instructor here." She sounded like a twelve-year-old unhappy with her lot in life.

"I'm a detective in the Michigan Department of Natural Resources, Wildlife Resources Protection Unit. I'm looking for information about blond moon bears."

"Are you with one of those insipid reality television programs?"

"No, I'm a cop."

"I can't help you," she said.

"Should I try to reach Professor Ferma by e-mail?"

"She's not amenable to interruptions when she's in the field."

"I really need to talk to her. We've found hair and scat samples here and the federal Fish and Wildlife forensics lab in Wyoming think it's *Selenarctos thibetanus*. The hair samples are blond, and definitely not from one of our bears."

"Where are you again?"

"Michigan."

"It's not possible for *thibetanus* to be there unless it's in a zoo. *Thibetanus* is translated literally to Tibetan moon bear, and the name alone gives flight to a lot of fancies."

"We have the hair samples and you know what Sherlock Holmes used to say."

"Sherlock Holmes?"

"The detective."

"In Michigan or Montana?"

"In fiction, in London. He was English."

"I don't have time to read make-believe," she said. "Did somebody kill the bear?"

"We don't know yet."

"Well, I can tell you the bear didn't kill a human. The Cambodians use *thibetanus* as entertainers. They're fairly docile when raised in captivity."

"The feds think that this may be a blond moon bear. They have a reference sample and the new hairs match."

"They're mistaken. It's no doubt a color phase of *thibetanus*," she said.

"From the little I've read, that's one school of thought. Is there any way to talk to the professor?"

"Not directly."

"This isn't a lark," he said. "There's a homicide involved, and I can always get in touch with Montana Fish and Game, get a judge, get subpoenas." No way this would happen, but it was worth floating as a trial balloon.

She said, "Look, I'll pass the word to the professor. That's the best I can do."

"That would be great." He gave her his phone numbers and e-mail address and hoped she'd follow through.

Back in his office, he rested his elbows on his desk and his forehead against his hands.

"You look like I feel," Fern LeBlanc said.

"How's the captain?"

"They're holding him overnight for observation. His doctor says it's not a stroke, but I don't believe the man. Either of them. Did you see the captain's leg?"

He had seen. "No sense letting our imaginations run wild," he said.

"Don't patronize me," she said. "Observation is not imagination. This has happened before. The captain does not take care of himself."

"He looks good."

"You can't see inside him," she shot back.

The combination of her concern and bullheadedness was interesting.

Her voice softened. "Has he said anything to you about retiring?"

"The captain doesn't confide in people."

"He admires you, Detective. He's logical and cerebral. You are emotional, impudent, and impulsive, Hyde to his Jekyll."

"Isn't it Heckyl?"

She rolled her eyes. "Everything is a joke with you," she said. "*Testosterone*," she added, as she whirled away.

He was tired and decided his next to last task of the day would be a call to Sandy Tavolacci.

"Hey Sandy, it's Service."

"What's the good word from the woods cop shop?"

"I've got two of them for you: Charley Fahrenheit."

"Don't get your balls in an uproar. He's a friend of a friend and I owed a favor. We gotta do favors in our business, am I right?"

"We're not in the same business, Sandy, and you're the attorney of record."

"That's a technicality. What's your interest anyway? Last I knew, woods cops didn't fuck with civil suits."

"We don't, unless there's some related criminal activity."

"You so low on work you gotta chase employment cases?"

"Bear poachers, Sandy. Bear poachers," he repeated, and hung up. Let the sleazy little bastard stew on that for a while.

His last task was a call to Wisconsin.

"Ficorelli," the Wisconsin warden answered on his cell phone, his voice barely audible.

"Wayno, it's Service."

"You still on that case?"

"Until I nail somebody," Service said.

"I hear what you're sayin'," Ficorelli said. "How's Limey?"

"Haven't seen her in a while."

"She's a hot one, eh?"

"Am I interrupting?" Service asked.

"No, I've got my binocs on a slimeball trolling for muskies on a closed lake. What's up?"

"There's a Wisconsin guy we're interested in. He lives in Marinette County, a place called Harmony. He worked at the Enstrom helicopter factory in Menominee. I know that's not your turf, but I thought one of your guys could —"

"My guys, my ass. *I'm* on it," Ficorelli said. "What's this dirtbag's name?"

"Charley Fahrenheit."

"That an alias?"

"Nope."

"Okay, I'll crank him through the computer and get back at you. This is a hurry-up deal, yes?"

"Kind of urgent."

Ficorelli laughed. "With urgent and pregnant there ain't no kind of. Is or isn't. Cut me a couple of days?"

"Thanks, Wayno."

"Am I just scratching for scent or do you want me to rattle cages?"

"Just scratch — for now."

"Not a problem. Remember, I'd like to join you guys up in da Yoop, be a real woods cop like you when I grow up."

He doubted Wayno would ever grow up, but there was something about his irreverence and spunk he liked. "I remember."

Newf looked up when he pushed back from the desk. "I've had enough fun for one day. How about you?"

She lifted her butt and stretched.

As they passed LeBlanc's desk he said, "If that red dog comes around tonight, I expect you to kick its ass."

Fern LeBlanc said, "What if I prefer diplomacy to warfare?"

Service grinned. "Sorry, I was talking to my mutt." It had been a very long day.

· 21 ·

It was nearly dark when he drove up the driveway and parked, his eyes alert for the marauding red dog. He was so focused on the dog that it didn't immediately register that the interior house lights were on. Had he forgotten to turn them out? Possible, he decided. He'd been less than alert when he and Newf left. As they walked toward the back door a low growl rolled out of Newf. Her ears were flat. At the back door he heard music inside, Norah Jones singing "Turn Me On." Nantz had discovered Norah recently, and her tunes always turned Nantz on.

He tried the door. It was open. He'd never failed to lock it before. His hand went to his SIG Sauer. He unsnapped his holster, and thumbed the safety off. No way he'd left the door unlocked. Somebody had gone inside; but if they'd broken in, why were the lights on, music playing?

Moving cautiously down the hall he heard a voice call out, "It's okay if youse gotcher gun out, as long as it's da right gun."

He peeked into the living room. Honeypat Allerdyce was seated on the couch, a glass of wine in hand. Her hair was cut short and done up. She wore a blue skirt and jacket, and navy blue stiletto heels. Gold earrings dangled from her ears. He couldn't remember ever seeing her dressed up. Usually she was wearing nothing or close to it. Now she looked like a stockbroker or something. The metamorphosis was astounding.

"Detective," she said, saluting him with her glass. "There's wine on the counter in the kitchen. I hoped you'd be here earlier. I didn't want to sit on the back porch. We wouldn't want the neighbors gettin' the wrong idea, hey? I hope you can forgive me for letting myself in."

"Honeypat," Service said. He didn't ask how she got in. The Allerdyces didn't need keys. In all the years he'd known her, she had never looked like this. She looked to be about 40 max, and this came as a surprise.

"Pour yourself a glass," she said.

Newf went into the living room and lay down, eyeing the woman. Service went into the kitchen. The wine was a 1994 Château Smith Haut Lafitte, a passable Bordeaux, and not one from his collection. Was this a gift or a bribe? And what did she want? He poured himself a glass and sniffed it. Good nose.

Norah Jones was starting on "Lonestar."

"Sweet tunes," Honeypat said. "Norah lights my fire."

He sampled the wine and sat down in a chair beside the couch. The wine was dry. "Thanks," he said. "This is smooth."

"You and your woman live good," Honeypat said, looking around.

He did not reply. Honeypat Allerdyce was nearly the savage that her father-in-law lover was, and she had always done as she pleased, her sexual appetite legendary.

"I owe you," she said. "That thing you told me last fall about Limpy and Daysi." She had slapped Limpy after Service had told her about the old man's moves on Daysi, and she'd stormed out of the family compound in southwestern Marquette County.

"I know youse didn't do it for me," Honeypat said. "I don't mind. I never went back."

"I saw Limpy," he said. Had it been yesterday? Time was jumbled.

"He tell you Aldo's queer?"

Service nodded.

"Aldo wants to be a game warden and Limpy's gonna do anything he can to shoot him down. I thought you ought to know, seeing I owe youse."

"Thanks," he said, lifting his glass.

"Wine okay?"

"Good," he said, even better than very good. "Limpy said you've got your own place now. Ford River."

"He was trolling to see what youse knew. He don't know where I am and I aim to keep it that way. He finds me, I'll be in for it. Does Aldo have a chance with youse people?"

Service nodded. "He spoke to our captain and the cap'n told him he doesn't care what his grandfather does. Aldo is responsible for himself."

"That's good," she said, taking another drink. "Make you nervous, findin' the lights on?"

It had. It was difficult not to stare at the woman. Dressed like this she looked almost elegant.

"Like my new look?" she asked.

"Do you?" he asked, turning the question back on her.

She smiled. "Nice clothes always get me going," she said. "How come you never took some off me? That time years back before Limpy went off to Jackson and you were hunting him, I'd've given it up."

"I was working," he said.

"I've got a job now," she said. "HPC, right here in Gladstone."

HPC was Hoegh Pet Casket Company, the largest maker of pet caskets in the country, maybe in the world. "They asked me to be a tour guide, but I didn't think that was too smart. I'm working as a bookkeeper on the night shift. It's boring, but it pays the bills."

It was surreal to hear her talking like a normal person.

"I've got a new name, too. Grace Thundergiver. Going back to my roots," she said with a laugh. "My mother was Mohawk, my father part Crow."

He'd never known this about her. "Does Limpy know you're Native?"

She smiled and shook her head. "Did, he'd have skinned me way back. Surprised I can hold down a job? I kept Limpy's books for years."

This was an interesting tidbit worth filing away for future use.

"Not surprised," he said. She was smart and tough, and dressed this way, more than presentable. "I'm surprised you're telling me all this."

"Wanted youse ta know," she said. "In case. Do you know Outi Ranta?"

"Ranta Lumber." Her husband Onte had died last spring.

"Outi and I go way back. I moved in with her after I left Limpy and before Onte got sick. We've been friends a long time. I was with her when Onte passed. I live in her guest house."

Rantas lived on The Bluff, less than a half-mile west, which explained why there had been no vehicle in the driveway. Onte had gotten sick in late winter, and died by the end of spring. Had Honeypat been there all that time?

"I come ta see youse once before," Honeypat said. "Your woman was ridin' your mule on the back steps."

Service remembered the night. He had begged Nantz to go inside, but she didn't want to.

"Got me going," Honeypat said. "Still does when I think about it. Tink your woman would go for a threesome?"

"Not a chance," he said. This was more like the Honeypat he knew.

"Too bad, eh. Would suit me."

"Not gonna happen."

"Your woman being out of town, I thought maybe youse'd like some company. I'd give it up now."

"Your largesse is appreciated," he said.

"We get dese clothes off, I'll give you somepin' youse can really appreciate."

228 · JOSEPH HEYWOOD

He didn't doubt it. "Thanks anyway."

She finished her wine, set the glass down with a flourish, stood up and primly smoothed her skirt. "Guess I'd better get along. No offense," she added, "but your woman's gone and you and me's not so different and I owe youse."

"The information settles the score," he said. "We're even." Were they really not so different? The comment bit deep, left him antsy.

Honeypat shrugged. "You know where I am, you want some."

Service nodded. He knew, and he was suspicious of Honeypat dropping in and laying all this information on him.

He walked her to the door. "Limpy comes around," she said, "one of us is dead."

She might be right about that.

She stuck out her hand and when he reached to shake, she grabbed his hand and licked his palm. "I'll keep it nice and wet for youse," she said. "Fact is, it's always wet," she said with a leer. "Flirtin' aside, thanks for Aldo. He's a good kid, not like the rest of his kin. I want to see the boy get out."

He watched her walk up the driveway into the dark. He almost felt sorry for her. If Limpy wanted her, he'd eventually find her. He was glad she had come, but not happy she lived so close. Her sensuality had shaken him. She was trying to do something good for Limpy's grandson. Aldo's chances of escaping the family were better than hers. Had he misjudged her all these years? Getting out was always tough.

There was a ville in the mountains of Vietnam. He and Tree were skirting it, en route to a recon job. They saw and heard kids playing, water buffaloes with bells around their necks were jangling away, and a flute of some kind keening across the landscape. They could smell shit from the fields and paddies. The place was small, a half-dozen hovels. To the east there was a range of low green hills. To the west were steep mountains with limestone outcrops.

"How do people get out of that?" Service had asked his friend.

"Most don't. Most don't want to. Those that do, have to learn to see over them." He pointed at the low hills.

"Can't be that easy."

"Didn't say easy, bro. Just what they got to do."

He hoped Honeypat and Aldo could see over the hills that were in their way. He also remembered that night on the porch steps. They were drinking martinis, watching the sun sink over Little Bay de Noc. He didn't blame Honeypat. The memory got to him, too.

Back in the kitchen he poured another glass of the gift wine and began to do the chopping and preparations for a quick dinner. He found it amusing that some food rags talked about quick dinners, referring to cooking time, and paying little attention to how long it took to get to that point. After he did the chopping, he dolloped some olive oil in a large skillet, added carrots and a half-pound of pork. He cooked it until the meat lost its pink color, dumped in pineapples and water, three table-spoons of Rasta Joe's barbecue sauce, a teaspoon of ginger, green pepper, and two cups of Minute Rice.

The cooking took only five minutes. He fed the animals while the rice cooked, then took his plate to the kitchen table, poured more wine, and ate slowly. Honeypat's wine was very good.

She'd come on Aldo's behalf. She'd also come because she was lonely and because of fear, giving him information and hoping without asking that he would keep an eye on her. Grace Thundergiver: No way could that be her real name. He grinned. Honeypat had a flair for the dramatic.

Maybe he'd keep an eye on her—from afar.

Nantz called as he was getting ready for bed.

"Long day," she said. "You?"

"The Cap'n's in the hospital."

"Oh no! Another stroke?"

"Doctor says no, but when the Cap'n went out to the ambulance, he was dragging his leg and trying to hide it. I think his doctor's covering for him."

He considered not telling her about Honeypat, but that's not how their relationship was.

"When I got home tonight, Honeypat was here."

"Did you invite her in?"

"She was already inside. She picked the lock."

"Wench," Nantz said. "She in her birthday suit?"

"Nope. She brought me information about Aldo." He related the events of the day.

"Limpy is a prick," she said. "Honeypat hit on you?"

"You remember that night on the back porch steps?"

Nantz laughed lustfully. "Every minute of it, and I'm glad we can count in minutes and not seconds!"

"She was out there, watching us."

"She told you this?"

"Wondered if you'd be interested in a threesome."

Nantz laughed gleefully. "She's a piece of work. What did you say?"

"I said I'd ask you."

She laughed again. "Liar."

"Right," he said.

"She wanted to jump your bones."

"Said she'd give it up."

Nantz said, "*Shuttt uppp*. I would too."

"She's on the run from Limpy."

"Is she safe?"

"Day to day, probably. Long term, who knows? Allerdyce usually finds a way to get what he wants."

"Would he hurt her?"

"First, then drag her back."

"She's playing a dangerous game," Nantz said. "Can you help her?"

"There's not much I can do."

"I'll be home late Friday night," she said. "I have to drop Lori in TC, and pop up to Esky."

"That will be a good thing," he said.

"No, baby," she said with a laugh. "It will be a *great* thing."

Service lay awake for a long time. Dealing with Allerdyce was like a chess game that sometimes resembled short-bus checkers and other times Kasparov against Big Blue. The key to dealing with Allerdyce was to understand that he orchestrated everything and to believe nothing. Limpy had only one motivation: himself. Aldo wants in the DNR so Limpy tells the DNR his grandson is gay. Then Honeypat shows up and says Limpy is lying and trying to undercut the kid. Was it this simple? Somehow, he doubted it. Maybe Honeypat was on the level, maybe not. One night soon, he'd do a little recon, see for himself.

· 22 ·

The phone rang at 4 A.M. and Service fumbled to find the receiver.
"Service, Ficorelli. How's it goin'?"
"I'm in bed."
"Not alone, I hope. I've been up all night. Your boy Charley Fahrenheit has never been busted by Fish and Game, but he hangs with a crowd my guys know well. Les Reynolds is the warden up that way. Bituva Boy Scout–tightass for me, but he gets the job done, and he's gotta hot old lady. How come the hot ones always hook up with the duds? I'll never figure that out."

"Fahrenheit," Service said, sitting up in bed and trying to get Wayno to refocus.

"A guy named Colliver's the leader of the crowd old Charley-boy hangs with. Colliver's been busted more than I've been laid. Les hasn't been able to get Fahrenheit, but he says Charley is part of the show."

"What kind of busts on Colliver?"

"Deer out of season, several trapping violations, felony theft of public timber, failure to register vehicles, trafficking bear parts."

"Did you say bear parts?"

"Les got him last fall on a deer case, three does out of season. He got a warrant and found bear parts at Colliver's camp—in a freezer. Les believes Colliver brings a bunch of Croatians from Chicago up to Iron County in the U.P. every year. They come up for three days each time and head home as soon as they have thirty carcasses in their freezer truck. They sell the meat around Chicago. The Illinois people are looking at it from their end. Colliver calls these weekends 3–30s and the Croats pay him big for putting them on animals. The Croatians always bring some hookers along for entertainment."

"Bear parts," Service said again.

"I'm gettin' there. Just trying to paint you a picture. Colliver's bear was tagged. He had a skin on the wall, minus paws. And there were paws in the freezer. Les wanted a DNA comparison done on the rug versus the paws, but our management didn't want to spend the money. He had the three deer and that was enough. I talked to Les last night and he wants

Colliver bad for his 3–30s. Said if you come over, the three of us can shake the trees."

"I'm not necessarily interested in Colliver. Just Fahrenheit." Although the information about bear parts might alter that.

"Les don't give shit-one about Charley-boy. You want, you and I can pay Fahrenheit a visit."

"When?"

"If not now, when? Am I right?"

Service thought for a moment.

Ficorelli said, "I can head up there this afternoon, poke around, check shit out. We can meet at the Hoar House in Marinette tomorrow—7 A.M. okay?"

"You want to meet at a whore house?"

"Chill, man. This is H-O-A-R: Hamburger, Oprah, Asshole, Rambo. It's a bar and restaurant owned by Frosty Gimble, one of our retired wardens. He's not a tightass like Les and he keeps his ear tuned."

"Seven at the Hoar House."

"Way cool. It's on Hosmer Street in the Menekaumee bar area. When you cross the river from Michigan, turn left. You can't miss it."

Newf jumped on the bed to let him know she wanted out, but he pushed her away and told her to lay down. "I'm not ready to get up," he said. He was awakened an hour later by Cat and Newf fussing with each other, and swung his feet down to the floor. "Goddamned animals. Knock it off!"

While the animals did their morning constitutional he went into the garage to work the free weights and found himself struggling to do his normal number of reps. All the damn office and phone time were killing him.

He called the office at eight. Fern LeBlanc answered.

"Cap'n in?"

"He's going to get out of the hospital at noon and be resting at home for the next two days. The doctor says it's a mild concussion. I'm going to pick him up. He would like for you to cover his calls in his absence. Are you coming in?"

"No, just relay his calls to me—either cell or the eight hundred. I'll monitor Channel Twenty." Lansing liked to brag about its technology. Let it prove its value.

"Please let me know where you are," LeBlanc said.

Service telephoned Vince Vilardo and asked to meet him at St. Francis Hospital in Escanaba. He wanted to visit Nordquist and get his stitches yanked.

He filled Newf's food and water dishes in the dog run built off the garage and told her and Cat they were on their own for the day.

On the way to Escanaba he drove past Outi Ranta's house. Her red Jeep was parked in the driveway beside an older gray Honda. Probably Honeypat's, he told himself. He called Station 20 and ran the plate on the Honda. It belonged to Outi.

Kate Nordquist looked sad and pale, but perked up when she saw him.

"I'm honored," she said. "Where's Mar?"

"Wild blue yondering. She'll be home Friday night."

"You smiled when you said that."

"Did I?"

"What's with your leg?" he asked.

"I'll keep it, but if the plastic surgeon doesn't work magic my miniskirt days are over. The doctors say I have to go on medical leave—up to six months. I'll miss deer season."

"There will be others," he said to reassure her. He understood how she felt. Deer season was the most intense and rewarding time of the year for officers. And often the most frustrating.

"Still a tough pill to swallow," she said. "This was to be the first on my own."

"You'll handle it."

"That's what Moody says too."

"You should listen to him."

"Did you stop by just to see me?"

"I did, and I asked Vince to come in and pull some of these stitches." He peeled the bandages back.

Nordquist appraised his face. "Looks like we both need time with the plastic surgeon."

"This face stays the way it is," he said.

"If Nantz agrees."

He nodded. "That too."

"How's your son?"

"Fine." How long had it been since they talked?

"Grady," the young officer said in a hushed tone. "I was sitting in the truck waiting for Eddie. A truck pulled up. The driver got out and went over to a trash can and knocked it over. Then he fell. I got out to see what was wrong and he came at me with a pipe or something. I never reacted. I went down and my head was swimming and then I saw the truck coming at me and I don't remember anything else. I think I fucked up."

"When you get hurt self-doubt is natural. Good officers always second-guess themselves. The dumb ones don't."

"Not you. They shoot you, break your bones, cut up your face, and you keep going like the Energizer Bunny."

"Appearances aren't the whole story," he said. "The feelings will pass, Kate. Your job now is to heal, rehab, and get your butt back in the woods with the rest of us. You can't leave Gutpile out there alone."

She smiled and reached out her arms. He leaned over and kissed her on the forehead.

"Mar and I will be over this weekend," he said on his way out.

Dr. Vince Vilardo stared at his face. "We should leave them in."

"The damn things itch like hell."

"That means you're healing."

"Get them out, Vince."

Vilardo smiled and set his jaw. "Not this time, pal. How's the finger?"

Service held up his hand, waved the taped-together fingers. "Good as new."

Vilardo shook his head. "You're a caveman."

"I thought the customer was always right."

"Patients are customers only to their insurance carriers. Where's Nantz?"

"Campaign trail."

"Timms is going to win," Vince said.

"We'll see."

"You're not voting for her?"

"Last I knew it was still a secret ballot."

"You want to come over for lunch?"

"I'm working a case."

"More like the case is working you," his friend said.

On his way back to Marquette he got a call from Lorne O'Driscoll.

"Chief," Service said.

"I left a call-back for you."

"Sorry, I got busy."

"How's Ware?"

"Fine. He fell out of his chair."

"LeBlanc says it was a mini-stroke."

"His doctor says it's a mild concussion."

"You wouldn't cover for him, would you?" the chief asked.

"Just handle his phone calls."

"Did Ware talk to you about the senator?"

"We talked." Was the chief going to thump on him now?

"If Timms wins, Tenni is out when his contract expires. In order to do this she'll probably have to replace some members of the Natural Resources Commission."

Eino Tenni was the director of the DNR and appointed by the Natural Resources Commission, not the governor. But the governor did appoint the members of the NRC, and Tenni had proven to be a rubber stamp for Bozian. A new governor would replace commission members with people more attuned to another way of thinking. They would not renew his contract, and would replace him.

"Politics," Service said.

"You understand that what Ware talked to you about is for the good of the force."

"Understood, Chief," Service said, grinning to himself. "I've got the job I want."

"Really?"

"Some days, more this year than last." Today wasn't one of them.

"Anything I need to know?"

Service toyed with telling the chief about Siquin Soong and decided against it. "No sir."

"Keep an eye on Ware, Grady."

"Yessir."

"How's Nantz? She ready for the academy?"

"She's ready."

"All right then. The other thing I want you to think about is this: Bozian's early-out program stripped us of a lot of good people. With all the retirements, and the lag in our replacement pipeline, we're short in most counties, especially up your way. I'm going to ask that all detectives and sergeants take on other areas in addition to their regular duties. This might last close to a year, but we have to do something. You'll probably be working the Lake Michigan fish runs this spring." The weather always sucked during fish runs, but it didn't stop poachers, and officers were out in the cold soup with them.

If the department's lawyers hadn't tanked the state's voluntary conservation officer program, COs would have VCOs in the vehicles with them, but the VCO program had been eliminated. Many COs could point to endless times where VCOs had kept them from serious injury, or helped make a case they couldn't have made alone. Management had ignored the pleas. "What about bringing retirees in to cover the holes? They already know the jobs and they're licensed to carry."

"Too many legal and civil service barriers."

"Be good to find a work-around," Service said. "The people of the state are going to end up paying one way or the other."

"Point taken," Lorne O'Driscoll said. "Talk to Ware about it."

"Yessir."

He was not five minutes off the phone with the chief, when Lisette McKower called. "This is frightening," she said. "Me reporting to you."

"You're not reporting to me. I'm answering phones—a receptionist."

She laughed. "How does it feel to have command responsibility?"

"Stop it, Lis."

"How is he, really?"

"Okay. His doctor says—"

"To hell with what the damn doctor says. You were there. What do *you* say?"

"I'm not a doctor."

"Jesus, you're talking just like a captain."

"Will my paycheck reflect it?" he asked.

"Not a chance."

Enough phone calls, he told himself. He called the office, got LeBlanc's answering machine, and left a message that he would be out of the vehicle. He needed time to think, time alone without interruptions. He pulled the truck into the trailhead of the Claw Lake Snowmobile Trail and parked next to some Japanese red pines.

He sat on a log and lit a cigarette and was two puffs in when two pickups came racing into the small parking lot and skidded to a stop. One man got out of each. They ran toward each other and went down in the gravel, swinging punches and cursing. He ran over to them and grabbed the first arm that came up. Which was when he saw a knife. Then another. Jesus!

He held up his badge, pulled his SIG-Sauer, and fired a round into the ground. The two men immediately stopped struggling.

"Conservation Officer! Put the knives on the ground, get down on your knees, and put your hands behind your heads. Now!"

"Dog," one of the men said.

"Fucker of dogs," the other one hissed back.

Service kicked both knives away. "Shut your mouths."

The men went silent. "What the hell is going on?"

"It's not serious," one of the men said.

"You almost wreck your trucks, jump out with knives, and start hacking at each other."

"Just his hair," one of them said.

They both had long hair tied into pigtails.

"We're pigtailing," the smaller of the two men said. It was hard to judge age.

"What the hell is pigtailing?"

"He's Sioux," the taller man said. "We drove them out of here a long time ago."

"He's Ojibwa," the shorter one said. "And some of us are back." He glared at the other young man.

"Let's see some ID," Service said. "One hand on your head, fish in your pocket with the other."

"We'd never hurt another person," the tall one said. "We're just trying to take each other's hair. You can't be a warrior without hair."

"What if you miss, hit his neck?"

"We know what we're doing. Our tribal elders approve of this as a way of settling disputes."

"What dispute?"

"It goes back?"

"How far?"

"Three, four hundred years."

"You want to scalp each other over something that took place centuries ago?"

"It's a matter of honor—like the Civil War."

"Sounds like a matter of stupidity," Service said.

He was reaching for the first wallet when he heard a thud and breaking glass down the snowmobile trail behind them.

"What the hell?" The two men joined him in staring down the trail. A man appeared and stumbled forward, caught his foot, and went down on his face.

"That dude's fucked up," the Sioux said.

The man lay on the trail, did not move.

"You two stay here," he said, adding, "Give me your wallets." He took them, checked to be sure they contained licenses, and stuffed them inside his shirt. You bolt and I will track your asses down and personally shave you as bald as Telly Savalas."

"Is that some kind of animal?" Sioux asked.

"You people are too stupid to be on Mother Earth," Ojibwa shot back.

All Service had wanted was some peace and quiet so that he could think.

"Stay," he ordered the two men.

They both nodded. "We're cool, officer."

When he got to the man on the trail he was on his knees and staring, his brow furled.

"You tough?" the man on his knees asked. His face was scraped. Blood was dribbling down his chin.

"Calm down, sir."

The man got to his feet, spread out his arms. "Let's see what you've got, big man."

"Sir!"

The man charged and was quicker than Service anticipated, crashed into his chest and wrapped him with his arms. Service tried to pry the grip loose, but his broken finger shot a pain up his wrist. The man lifted him in the air and Service looked down into eyes that were boiling blue fury. He pulled his head back and snapped it down hard, head-butting the man in the face. They both went sideways and hands were grabbing at him and pushing him away and when he rolled over, Sioux and Ojibwa were pinning the struggling man to the ground. Service crawled in with them, felt something cut into his knee, and took a hold by the man's neck until his eyes rolled in their sockets and he stopped struggling. "Roll him over," he told his helpers. "Get his arms behind him." He took his cuffs off his belt and did the man's wrists.

When things were calm, he sat back and fumbled for a cigarette. He offered the pack to his helpers. "Officer, you are like seriously fucked," Sioux said.

Service felt his face, looked at his hand. Blood.

"You got first aid in your truck?" Ojibwa asked.

Service nodded. The man ran off, his feet crunching against the gravel. The man in cuffs swore, began to scissor-kick his legs. "You got your knife?" Service asked Sioux, raising his voice.

The young man nodded. "This asshole moves again, cut off his balls."

Sioux grinned. "Can I have his scalp too?"

"Fucking eh," Service said.

The man rolled up on a shoulder and looked away.

Ojibwa stood by the truck, looking stumped. "It's locked." Service opened it, got out the first-aid kit, and handed it to one of the boys, who began trying to dab at Service's cuts.

"Man, you must do this a lot," he said.

"New cuts or did he open the old stuff?"

"Both. Most of the blood's from your nose and the head cut."

Service took gauze and began repairing himself. He looked at Ojibwa. "Go see what the hell the crash was, but don't touch anything, got it?"

"Yes, officer."

Service looked at Sioux. "Pigtailing?"

The boy shrugged and grinned. "We wouldn't hurt each other. We've been friends since we were eight."

"How old are you now?"

"Both twenty."

"Girls are a better outlet for hormones."

"That's the problem," Sioux said with a grin. "We both want the same one."

"Great. Take turns with her. It will be easier on everybody."

"That's like, totally sick, dude." He was grinning.

Ojibwa returned. "Ran his pickup into a tree. It's fucked. Guns on the floor, two fawns in the bed, neither of them gutted. Looks like a bag of weed on the floor, two vodka bottles, some in one, the other's empty."

Service nodded. "Stay with him." He got out his belt radio, clicked over to the District 3 frequency, called for help, gave his call sign 2514.

Peggy in the Escanaba office said, "Twenty-Five Fourteen, AVL shows Gary about three miles from your position."

Gary was Gary Ebony, who handled parts of Delta County and was built like an NFL linebacker. Violets in the county called him Agony because of the troubles he gave them.

"Rolling," Ebony reported over the radio.

Service lit another cigarette, got blood on it, wiped his hands on his pants, and waited.

When Ebony pulled up, Service helped the bulky officer secure the crashman. They collected weapons and evidence, the two dead fawns, took photos of the rest of the truck's interior, and called a wrecker. Ebony looked at him while they waited for a Delta County deputy sheriff to transport the prisoner.

"You need to get to the hospital," Ebony said.

"I need a new face," Service said. He ached all over, but the blood flow had been stanched.

Two deputies came in a patrol car and Service and Ebony loaded the prisoner in the backseat. Service stood with the pigtailers when the deputies and Ebony were gone. He handed them their wallets.

"We're really sorry," Ojibwa said.

"Leave your knives and get the hell out of here. Thanks for the help."

The two men ran to their trucks and raced away, their tires spitting stones.

Service went back to his log and sat down, his face and finger throbbing, his arm sore, his knee and trousers split.

Too many of these kind of days, he told himself as he began to run the whole thing through to see what he might have done differently. Find a different job was his final conclusion. He had hesitated when confronted by the boys and the man. Pain had made him hold back. Bad mistake, he told himself. He knew he should head back to the house, but he drove south to Menominee, called Jimmy Cosbee's house, talked to his mother and asked her to have Jimmy let Newf in tonight. He stopped at a party store near Cedar River, bought two bags of ice for his cooler, and continued south to find a room at a sleep-cheap.

The girl behind the reception desk at the Bayview Motel was blond, small, and meek. She wore a tanktop and her breasts looked like they might fall out the sides.

"I need a room," Service said.

"Your face," she said, giving him a look that was part fear, part awe.

"I know," he said. "One person, one room, one night." He put his badge and ID on the desk.

She hesitated. "You're not going to—"

"I'm not going to kill myself," he said. "I leave that to others."

She laughed nervously. "I, ya know, like, see a lot of shit in here, ya know?"

Service picked up his badge, held out his hand for a key. "Cops and receptionists," he said. "Birds of a feather."

"You want me to get some ice for you, officer?" she asked.

"Got some in my cooler. Thanks."

"I can call a doctor," she said.

"Faith will heal me," he said.

"Far out," she said, looking skeptical.

· 23 ·

The morning light hurt his eyes and it stung to stand under the hot shower water, but he forced himself. Dressing was equally uncomfortable. His knee was puffy, his broken finger throbbing, both eyes swollen and beginning to close.

He was coming out of his room when a voice sounded and he turned to find the kid from reception. She looked tired. "You okay?" she asked. "I've been worried all night."

He nodded. "Thanks."

Hoar House was on a block filled with several taverns, most of them sprouting Green Bay Packer memorabilia. The bar faced a channel in the Menominee River, barely qualifying it for a view, despite a red-letter claim in the window.

Service walked inside slowly, feeling cool autumn air cut through the slice in his pants. He was met by an old man in a pressed white apron and starched white jeans. "Do you just *look* like shit?" the man asked.

Service followed the man to a table near an electronic dartboard. The old man brought a pitcher of coffee and filled Service's cup. "You're the one Wayno's meeting."

Service nodded. "How did you know?"

"You got the look. I hope you got in a few good licks," he added with a sly grin. "You want to order now?"

He shook his head, checked the wall clock. He was ten minutes early. "Have you got a needle and thread?"

"Coming right up."

Service sewed clumsily, mending the hole in his pants while he waited. His run of luck had to change soon. It always had before.

Wayno Ficorelli arrived on time, marching into the bar with his hair combed, uniform neat and pressed, boots shined. "You meet Frosty?" the Wisconsin warden asked.

The man in the apron saluted with two fingers. "Frosty would be me," he said.

"Grady."

Ficorelli asked the proprietor to join them, and told Service, "I had a great night."

"Good for you," Service grumbled.

"Fahrenheit's old lady is named Mary Ellen and she's filed for a divorce. She hates Colliver, says Charley-boy will do anything for the man and she's sick of it. Told me she hasn't done the deed with Charley-boy in over a year. Can you believe that?"

Service looked at Ficorelli. "I suppose you helped rectify the deficiency."

"You could say we stroked each other's—"

"Spare us the details," Frosty said.

"Hey, sex is natural, like takin' a shit."

"We don't want those details either," Service said.

"You sure?"

Service rolled his eyes.

"We're sure," Frosty said.

"Okay, Charley-boy shot the bear on Colliver's camp wall. In fact, Charley-boy's shot six bears in the past two years. Mary Ellen says he and Colliver take the gallbladders and the paws and sell the carcasses down to Milwaukee. They hunt the U.P. in Iron and Gogebic Counties. They bring the bears back in coffins to Wisconsin, in a hearse, put a magnetic funeral flag on the fender to make it look legit, the whole deal. Never been stopped. They burn the carcasses. Colliver handles the transportation, Charley does the shooting. Colliver calls him Bear Boy. Last June they went up to Iron County to scout, and ran up against another hunter named Kitella. He beat the hell out of both of them, took their hearse, took them over the state line, and dropped them naked as jaybirds. Colliver got pissed, wanted to fight back. Charley didn't, but he does what Colliver wants, so they went back up to Michigan intending to mess up this guy Kitella's place. They never made it. Some old fucker stopped them in the woods, pointed a shotgun at Colliver. Turns out he doesn't like Kitella either, so he offers to help. Mary Ellen says Charley stole cable from a factory for this old man."

Service was suddenly interested. All sorts of intersections seemed possible.

"This old guy got a name?"

"Charley never told Mary Ellen."

"What about a description?"

"Vague. An old man, tough as moosehide."

Which could describe thousands of U.P residents, including Limpy and Trapper Jet.

"Mary Ellen blames Colliver for Charley losing his job. She confronted Colliver on this and he got Charley a lawyer. Now the lawyer says the case looks like a loser and Charley's pissed and Mary Ellen says if Charley will turn in Colliver, she'll drop the divorce."

"She make that declaration while you were porking her?" Frosty asked.

Ficorelli blinked a couple of times. "Sure. What's the name of that Frenchman, wrote if you'd talk to a woman till 4 A.M. you'd get into her pants every time?"

"Marcel Marceau," Service said.

Ficorelli frowned. "I'm serious. People get in bed, they run off at the mouth."

"They teach this as an interview technique in Michigan?" Frosty asked.

"No," Service said.

"Wisconsin, neither. We just got us a horny little wop."

Ficorelli took umbrage. "Right, put me down, but it works. I'm being serious here."

"Where's Mrs. Fahrenheit now?"

"I left her at the Muskie Motel on US Forty-One. She's gonna head over to her house in Harmony. She talked to Charley last night, told him she wants a meet. That's at noon. I figured we'd get there an hour before, stash the vehicle, and greet Charley-boy when he arrives."

This didn't sound like much of a plan, but Service was too tired and sore to argue or come up with something else.

"You want to see a doctor?" Ficorelli asked.

Service shook his head.

"Breakfast for you boys?" Frosty asked.

"Eggs over easy and hash," Wayno said.

"OJ, coffee, and dry rye toast," Service said.

Frosty left, shouting orders to his cook.

"Sleeping with witnesses isn't too swift," Service said.

"You're not my priest, and besides, we didn't sleep that much."

"Your priest would tell you the same thing."

Ficorelli laughed. "Yeah, sure, right after he gets out of the joint for buggering altar boys."

Service picked up his coffee and eyed his toast while the Wisconsin warden mashed his eggs into his hash. They ate in silence.

Fahrenheit's house was a large, fairly new ranch with an expanse of green lawn out front and a lumpy pasture stretching behind the house to a line of birch and cedars. A large garage sat beside the house, unattached.

"Charley-boy done okay with the chopper company," Ficorelli said.

They were in Service's Yukon. He pulled up to the house and Wayno trotted up to the door, talked to somebody, and came back. "There's a two-track behind the garage. You can park back behind the trees." Wayno pointed.

Service watched him go into the house, then drove around the garage, found the track through the field, and drove a quarter-mile back into the trees. He parked and walked into the field, didn't like the truck's positioning, went back and moved it again. He smoked a cigarette as he hurried across the field toward the house. He knocked on the front door but got no response. He tried the doorknob. Locked. He rang the bell, checked his watch: 11:30 A.M. No problem with time.

Wayno finally came to the door and opened it, grinning. "Sorry, didn't mean to lock you out."

Ficorelli's belt was undone, as was his fly. "Better shut your gate," Service said.

Wayno looked down, laughed, and zipped up as they walked into the kitchen where a woman in her mid-forties was standing at a counter, measuring scoops of coffee and dumping them into a brown paper filter. She was pear-shaped with an appealing, wholesome face, wearing a pale yellow short-sleeved sweater over a pale yellow skirt. Her hair looked mussed and she was barefoot. Some of her toenails were painted red.

"Mary Ellen Fahrenheit, Grady Service."

"Hi," she said, her cheeks flushed with color. "Sorry the coffee's not ready. I sort of lost track of time. Why don't the two of you sit in the dining room. The kitchen's a mess."

Service looked around. The kitchen looked anything but a mess.

Ficorelli remained in the kitchen.

Service went into the dining room. There was a red couch in the adjoining living room, its pillows gollywhompered. Pantyhose and a pair of women's flats were on the floor beside the couch.

There were prints of mermaids all over the walls, vases filled with plastic flowers, a crucifix.

Ficorelli and the woman came into the dining room with a tray of coffee cups, an urn, and a plate of cheese Danish.

"They're a day old," Mary Ellen Fahrenheit said.

"Are you sure about this?" Service asked her.

"To tell the truth, I'm a tad nervous, eh?" She glanced at Ficorelli and smiled. "Charley is basically a good man and we've had a pretty good life, but he follows that jerk Colliver. They go all the way back to high school. Colliver gets an idea and Charley does the heavy lifting, know what I mean?"

Service nodded. "You filed for divorce."

"I can't go on living like this. If Charley gives up Colliver, I'll try again. If not, I'm outta here. Sometimes you just gotta do what you gotta do. He's been a good provider, but. . . ."

"Did you tell Charley why you wanted to see him today?"

"No," she said. "Should I have?"

"It's okay," Ficorelli said, coming to her assistance.

The woman got up and rubbed her hands together. "I'd better pick up a little."

Service watched her go into the living room, scoop up the pantyhose and shoes, try to tuck them in front of her to hide them, and disappear down a hallway.

Ficorelli looked at Service. "I know what you're thinking. She was ready to lose it. I just helped her calm down."

"A man of high motives," Service said.

"That cuts, man. I'm tellin' ya, we got this guy for sure. Him and Colliver."

"We'll see," Service said. When Mary Ellen came back, she was wearing shoes and stockings and a light jacket.

"How long do you think you'll be?" she asked.

"We need for you to be here when your husband arrives," Service said.

"Then I can go?"

Ficorelli said, "That's fine. Just give us a number and I'll call you when we're done." The woman took off her jacket.

A little after noon a brown pickup pulled into the driveway and a lanky man with a mullet haircut got out. He wore a Packers hat facing backward and had a beer can in his hand. He took a swig and threw the can in the bed of his truck.

Service and Ficorelli stood on either side, inside the front door.

Charley Fahrenheit walked in and saw his wife standing a few feet down the hall. "What the hell's so important?"

"These fellas want to talk to you," she said, grabbing her jacket off a hook and heading for the back of the house.

Fahrenheit was a tall man, all muscle, with the opaque eyes of a cat. "What the fuck, dudes?"

Ficorelli held his hands up. "No problem here, Charley. I'm Warden Ficorelli and this is Detective Service."

"The bitch," Fahrenheit said.

"Why don't we take a seat in the kitchen?" Service said.

Fahrenheit's shoulders slumped as he walked into the kitchen, pulled a chair out and sat down.

"What's this about?"

"Mary Ellen told you if you give up Colliver, she'll drop the divorce?" Wayno said with a grin.

"What makes you think I want her ta drop it," the man said.

"For one thing," Ficorelli said, "as long as you two are married she doesn't have to testify against you. Divorced, she can sing like a bird. You know that song, 'Six Bears in Iron County.' "

Colliver looked puzzled. "That's not a song."

"We write the titles," said the Wisconsin warden. "You get to write the lyrics."

"I give you Colliver and what do I get, my job back?"

"The job's gone, Charley," Service said. "But you're still free. You give us Colliver and we'll try to cut you some slack on the bear killings."

"I won't do time."

"It's not up to us to make that decision," Ficorelli said. "But if you cooperate, it won't be nearly as bad. You've fucked up big time, Charleyboy. Why not spit it all out, get rid of it, give yourself a chance to start again? We can do this the easy way or the hard way—your choice."

Service thought someone should write a country song using all the one-liners game wardens used with violets.

"This is like a nightmare," Fahrenheit said.

"Always is when it comes time for payback," Ficorelli said.

"You worked with an old man in Michigan. He got a name?" Service asked.

Fahrenheit got up from the table and looked down the hallway. "My old lady gone?"

Ficorelli nodded. "At a friend's."

"I'm gonna tell you the truth here: I never met the man. Colliver knows him. I dealt with a woman."

"Does she have a name?" Service asked.

"She's Indian, man."

"What's her name?"

"Hannah."

"Are you telling us she set up the cable theft?" Ficorelli asked.

"She wanted the cable. She didn't say why."

"You gave it to her?"

"That was the deal."

"When?"

"July, about a week after I got it."

"See her since then?"

"Week, ten days ago."

"Was Colliver with you?" Service wanted to know.

"It wasn't business this time, know what I mean? Colliver dealt with the man, I dealt with Hannah."

Ficorelli rolled his eyes.

"Where'd you meet?" Service asked.

"Casino up to Watersmeet. She got us a room. She gets them comped."

"Why?"

"Don't know man, she just does. I think she used to work there or something."

"What's she look like?"

"Dark hair, pretty."

"Tall, short?"

"Little thing."

"Age?"

"I don't know. Thirties, forty, I guess. Listen, we didn't do nothing we didn't both want to do."

"You had a fight with a man named Kitella."

"Wasn't much of a fight. Fucker is crazy. Man, we're just walking around looking for sign and this fucker come out of nowhere with a base-ball bat."

"This was in June?"

"We were scouting for the fall."

"Were you on his land?"

"Hell no, it was state land, but this asshole says it's his, he's got the license as a guide."

"Guides don't get exclusive licenses for an area," Service said.

"I'm just telling you what the man claimed."

"He took your hearse."

"Ganked all our gear."

"You didn't report it."

"Man, it was our rig, understand."

"For poaching."

"Right."

"Colliver talked you into going back—to get even."

"I didn't want to go. Some guy kicks my ass, that's it, he wins, know what I'm sayin'. But Colliver, he wouldn't leave go, you know?"

"So you went."

"Yeah, we knew where Kitella's camp was, went to scope it out. This broad come out of the woods at me with a gun. Colliver run into the old man."

"Did you see him?"

"Just the woman," Fahrenheit said, shaking his head.

"She offer a deal?"

"No, Colliver heard that from the old man. Hannah had a radio. Her and me just sat there and when she got a radio call, she split."

"Then Colliver told you about the old man."

"Right, said he'd help us get Kitella, but he wanted some stuff."

"Cable."

"Right."

"Did Colliver ever meet the woman?"

"Not that I know of. I took the spool up there and gave it to her."

"Kitella ended up in the hospital," Service said.

"That don't break my heart," Fahrenheit said.

"Were the woman and old man part of your bear business?"

"No."

"You never saw her before this summer?"

"Not till that day in the woods."

"Hannah."

"That's the name she told me."

"Where did you sell the bears?" Ficorelli asked.

"Milwaukee."

"Got names?"

"Colliver handled all that."

"Bear Boy shoots 'em, his pal sells 'em," Ficorelli said.

"That's how it was," Fahrenheit said.

"You take the galls?" Service asked.

"Got them first, and the paws, but we took the whole animal. Can sell all that shit, you know?"

"How many?"

"Six the last two years."

"All in Michigan?"

Fahrenheit nodded.

"Here's the deal: We bust Colliver and you testify," Ficorelli said.

"I don't do time," Fahrenheit said.

"That's not the deal."

"Man," Fahrenheit whined.

"Where do we find Colliver?" Service asked.

"His place, up on the river near Porterfield. It's ten minutes from here."

"Does he have a job?" Ficorelli asked.

"He works at not workin'."

"Okay, Charley-boy, you're gonna call Colliver and tell him you're coming up. I'll ride with you. Service will follow."

"I don't got to call. I just show up," Charley Fahrenheit said. "We're pals."

"This time you'll call. We want to be sure he's there," Service said.

"I don't like this shit," Fahrenheit said.

Ficorelli went to the living room and made a quick call.

Service looked at Fahrenheit. His eyes showed no emotion, his shoulders were slumped.

"You use a rifle on the bears?"

Fahrenheitt nodded. "It's Colliver's. My old lady don't allow no guns. Always gotta have *her* way."

"Colliver has it?"

"No man, I told you. That Kitella guy took everything, wiped us out."

Ficorelli came back. "Make your call, Charley."

Fahrenheit used the phone in the kitchen. "Dude, I'm comin' over." He hung up, looked at the officers. "He's high."

Great, Service thought.

By the time Service retrieved the Yukon, Fahrenheit and Ficorelli were in the pickup and waiting. Wayno waved for him to follow.

The house was two stories and was built on the south bank of the Peshtigo River. It needed fresh paint and a new roof. The yard had a pile

of tires and the rusted hulks of four old vehicles, which had been canni-
balized for parts.

There was a man standing in the yard when the pickup pulled in.
The man turned to run, but Ficorelli jumped out of the truck, his
weapon drawn, yelling. Service parked behind the pickup.

"I want my lawyer!" Colliver shouted. "Right fucking now!"

Ficorelli pushed Colliver on to the steps of the porch.

Colliver stared at Fahrenheit. "Pussy!"

Colliver was five-eight and well over two hundred pounds, with a
bulging belly and long shaggy hair that hadn't been washed in a long
time. Service stood so he could observe both men.

"I'm Ficorelli," Wayno said. "He's Service."

"Fuck the both of youse."

"I had to tell 'em," Fahrentheit said in his own defense. "The old
lady put 'em on to us. They know everything."

"Keep your chow hole shut, Bear Boy."

Service walked around the house. There was a gutted deer hanging
in a tree by the river. He almost missed it, but a crow fluttered up as he
passed and caused him to stop and look.

"Got a deer out back," Service said.

"Out of season," Ficorelli said to Colliver. "And you don't have priv-
ileges if it was, asswipe."

"Put a liplock on my love muscle, you little faggot," Colliver said.

Wayno used his radio to call Les Reynolds and the county. He advised Reynolds to get a search warrant.

Colliver said nothing while they waited.

He was tense and looked like he would bolt at the first opportunity.
Ficorelli warned him, "Go ahead and run, you fat fuck. I'll break both
your fucking legs."

"You talk big with a gun, man."

Ficorelli started to unbuckle his gunbelt and Colliver hung his
head. Service glared at Wayno. The Wisconsin warden was a cowboy.
He'd never cut it in Michigan.

Warden Reynolds arrived with two county patrol cars right behind
him.

Service showed him the deer. Reynolds checked the opacity of the
eyes. "Late last night, early this morning," he said. Service had come to
the same conclusion.

Another deputy brought the search warrant.

Colliver whined but didn't resist when they went into the house.

There were three freezers in the basement, all of them filled with packages of meat. They found four bags of bear galls, a dozen of them. Two mason jars filled with weed were in plain sight on the kichen counter.

Ficorelli held up the bags with the galls. "Looks like you aren't his only Bear Boy," he told Fahrenheit.

Ficorelli and Reynolds read Colliver his rights, but he refused to talk and demanded his attorney. Service stood beside him while he made the call, noted the numbers, and grinned. It was Sandy Tavolacci's number.

It took two hours to search the house, log what they found, and transfer the men to the county jail.

Reynolds made a call to an assistant prosecuting attorney and explained what was going on.

He invited Service to sit in on the interrogation, which wouldn't start until Tavolacci arrived.

Ficorelli made a phone call, and announced he had to get back to his own turf.

Service called the Crosbees and asked that they watch Newf and Cat for another day.

The assistant prosecutor's name was Minerva Branch. She was in her fifties and wore thick glasses and spoke with a speech impediment. She said, "Leth ith really happy to nail thith one."

"He's not nailed yet," Service said. "His lawyer's good."

"I know Thandy," she said. "We've fenthed before. He lotht," she added with a wink.

"I didn't know he was a member of the Wisconsin bar."

"Michigan, Withconthin, Minnethota, Illinoith, Indiana, Ohio, a weal Midwetht legal forth."

A speech impediment made it tough to compete in a profession where speech was the primary tool. Service wondered if juries sympathized with her.

A deputy brought Colliver a tray of food. The prisoner threw it against the wall. "Fucking swill!" he said pushing the tray away.

Service and Branch ate hot dogs brought in by one of the jailers. "I keep tellin' them brath, but all they bring are dogth." She sounded resigned to gustatorial hell, and ate the whole dog.

"Lookth like you guyth went by the book," she said as they ate. "That helpth a heap. How'd you get to them?"

"Front door all the way," Service said.

She smiled. "You got inthide, thath all thath matterth."

Service tried to think about an old man and an Indian woman named Hannah. While they waited, he called Grinda and asked her to meet him in Watersmeet.

"It's on my way home," she said. "You want a bump?"

"No, I'm driving up there tonight. I'll TX when I get close."

"See you tonight."

When Tavolacci arrived he found Service sitting with Les Reynolds, the APA, and his client. Sandy looked at Service, and shook his head. "What the heck is this? You've got no jurisdiction here," the lawyer said.

"I'm an observer," Service said. "Remember what I told you on the phone?"

The lawyer frowned and stuck his nose in a notebook.

Minerva Branch passed a signed Miranda card to Tavolacci. "By the book, Sandy. Firtht item of buthineth, no bail."

"C'mon, for one measly deer?"

"Multiple offender, unemployed, a dothen bear galth in pothethion, and he'th a flight rithk."

"He'll walk," Tavolacci said.

"We'll see," the APA said.

Branch's speech problem seemed to fade when she got down to business.

Tavolacci wanted fifteen minutes alone with his client.

Service and Branch went outside. He lit up. She looked longingly at his cigarette.

"You want one?" he asked, holding out the pack.

"Like life itthelf," she said. "But I got kidth and they don't buy it. You got kidth?"

"One," he said, realizing he was getting used to the idea.

"Blow a little thmoke thith way," she said, leaning toward him.

He did and she inhaled and laughed. "Blathted kidth."

Tavolacci was somber when they went back into the room. "My client is pleading not guilty and he will not talk. We want bail."

"Not a chance," Branch said.

"The judge will decide," Sandy countered.

Colliver was booked and taken to the courthouse for arraignment.

Service walked into the courtroom with the APA, who saw the judge and whispered to Service, "Thith will be innerething."

The judge said, "Ms. Branch."

"Defendant has multiple convictions and is accused of going over the state line to kill six bears over two years and we have evidence of a dozen more. You can see the other charges as well."

No trace of a speech problem, Service noted.

"Mr. Tavolacci, it's your turn," the judge said.

"My client is a solid citizen, currently unemployed. He has not had a conviction in two years, he is not a risk for flight, and he did not kill any bears. Mr. Fahrenheit shot the animals."

"Save your arguments for trial," the judge said.

"This is a fuck job," Tavolacci said.

"One more word and you are in contempt, Mister Tavolacci."

"Holy cow," the lawyer moaned.

The judge's gavel hit the desk like a gunshot. "First offense is a fine. See the bailiff on the way out. The county doesn't take checks. Second offense you spend the night inside, am I clear?"

"Yes, your Honor."

She turned to look at the prisoner. "Are you employed, Mr. Colliver?"

"I work around my house," he said.

"What sort of work do you do?"

"This and that."

The judge raised an eyebrow. "Your annual income?"

"I don't remember."

"How long has it been since you had a paying job?"

"I don't remember," Colliver said.

"Bail denied," she said. "Remand to county until trial. Conference in my chambers, tomorrow at 11 A.M. See you then, counselor."

There was no sign of Fahrenheit.

"Did I miss something in there?" Service asked when they got outside.

"She'th Judge Marfug. She'th vegan, antivivithectionith, and a thufi master."

"Sorry?" Service said.

"Soo-fee," the APA said, forcing the word out. "She danth by thpinning. She hathe people who violate fith and game lawth."

"What happens to Fahrenheit?"

"Got to get him a lawyer."

"He opened the door for us."

"It will be taken into account," Branch said, touching his arm. "I won't fight bail on him."

Service visited Fahrenheit in the jail. "The court will appoint an attorney."

"I don't know if I can afford bail," he said.

Service gave him his card. "If you help us find Hannah and the old man, things will go easier for you."

"I told you everything," he said.

"If you think of anything else, call me collect. You're gonna have plenty of time to think."

"Can you let my old lady know?"

"Sure."

He swung by Fahrenheit's house. No lights on. He continued into town to the Muskie Motel. Wayno's truck was there. The feisty little warden had no judgment. Service went to the reception desk. "I'm looking for a man and a woman. The man's driving that truck." He pointed to the lot and held up his badge.

The man behind the desk looked through his register. "Room 28, ground floor on the end."

Service knocked on the door and said softly, "Wayno."

Ficorelli cracked open the door, peered out, his hair damp. "What?"

"Charley's in the county jail. If his wife wants to hire a lawyer for him, now's the time, otherwise they'll appoint someone."

"I heard," Mary Ellen Fahrenheit called out. "Let him rot."

"The APA won't fight bail," Service said over Ficorelli's head.

"I'll post bond when I get to it," the wife said. "Do him good to think about what he's done."

Wayno nodded and closed the door.

Service went into a McDonald's and got a cup of coffee. It was a long drive to Watersmeet and too late to call the office. Fern would be pissed.

· 24 ·

It would take too long to get to Watersmeet through Michigan. Service headed due west out of Marinette, and forty miles out swung north on W-32 just east of the Menominee Indian Reservation. From the turn it was pretty much a straight eighty-mile shot through the Potawatomie Indian Reservation and Nicolet National Forest to Iron River, and then another forty miles to Watersmeet, a total of about one hundred and sixty miles, all on two lanes in the darkness under a canopy of stars and a gray sliver of moon.

The road north passed through few villages and no towns of any size, the undulating terrain marked by rolling hills and occasional hogback ridges, both sides of the two-lane road covered with dense forests that grew down to within a few feet of the shoulders and threatened like a constrictor to cross and pinch the road closed. The air was cooling, inviting nightly freezes that would begin to sink a layer of permafrost into the ground for the snow blanket that would follow. Deer were still in their summer habitats, grouped by gender, bucks with bucks and does with fawns. Soon, when the weather turned cold enough, bucks' chests would swell with hormonal surges and they would separate, each male alone to begin hunting does to mate with. Tonight the deer were interested only in food, and were gathered in openings and along the roads, taking the easy grass, their eyes reflecting a witless green in his headlights.

After so many years in the north, Service was completely attuned to the rhythms and whims of the seasons, and he drove at night with two minds operating independently—one of them working actively and silently to assess the hazards and threats along the roads, the other buried deeply in the case that had propelled him all across the Upper Peninsula, east to west and north to south—a case that in many respects was not one case at all.

Harry Pung was the catalyst, and many things had happened since his death. But despite any glaringly clear connections, it felt to him that somehow it was all part of a whole. Siquin Soong might be part of it. That remained to be seen. Trapper Jet might be part of it. Dowdy Kitella's problems, too. The date-rape bozo in Wisconsin, and now

Colliver and Fahrenheit—each element leading in a certain direction and creating a path, but so far few of the paths had crossed. Even so, the tangents made it all very interesting.

In his twenty-one years in the DNR he had never considered investigation either art or science. It was, if anything, more like tracking, where you got on a spoor and followed it to the end, wherever it led. Such things never proceeded in a straight line. It was like waking up in a cedar swamp in a soggy floodplain, the trees thick and close together, whipped, bent and broken by wind, genetics and ice. And underfoot, tenuous ground, quicksand and sink holes, and you knew you had to keep walking to get out, and even when you had some vague sense of where *out* might be, there was no direct path possible. You advanced ten yards only to retreat the same distance or more in order to get a better angle around barriers. And in the process of finding safer footing and watching your step, you lost total awareness of where *here* might be—only that you wanted to get out, and that you could do it only one step at a time, forward, backward, sideways, doing whatever worked, while steeling yourself with perseverance and stubbornness until you finally emerged from darkness into light. In an investigation it was always the investigator who started out lost. The details of the case were irrelevant and served only as stepping stones to lead you out.

At the State Police Academy in East Lansing there had been a course in investigation techniques taught by Calvin Shall, then in his sixties and retired but still teaching. Cal Shall had taken a shine to Service and pulled him aside one day to tell him, "Ignore the theories and formulae. An investigation is about two things: luck and determination, and it is determination that makes your luck. When you deal with criminals you will ultimately find that greed is the engine that drives all crime. The shrinks will try to split hairs, but greed is the nexus. People want what they don't have or more of what they do. The feds will tell you to follow the money, but money can be hidden. I say follow the greed. It will always be there in plain view."

Following greed, Cal Shall's creed, had always worked for him, and in this case greed appeared to be the one constant in all the events that had transpired. Despite his efforts he felt no closer to solving anything, and as he drove north he felt increasingly irritable. He was still stumbling in the treacherous footing of the floodplain, still lost, the distance from the light not clear at all.

He called Grinda on the cell phone as he turned northwest out of Iron River to Watersmeet.

"Where are you now?" she asked.

"Leaving IR, should be over there in about thirty minutes. Meet at the casino?"

"We'll be there."

"We?"

"Simon and I are working together."

Simon, not del Olmo. Elza, not Grinda. Service grinned as he raced up US 2.

Duck Creek and the Ontonagon River joined near Watersmeet, which had been so named because of this by the Chippewa of the Lac Vieux Desert band. The Chippewa had once lived on South Island in the lake, now known as Lac Vieux Desert, but called *Ka-ti-ki-te-go-ning* by the Indians. Over time much of the band had migrated sixty miles northwest to L'Anse, on Keeweenaw Bay. There had been so much traffic back and forth that the route was called the L'Anse-Lac Vieux Desert Trail; Service remembered that nearly three hundred and fifty years ago a Jesuit priest was thought to have disappeared coming south from L'Anse. There were few Europeans in the area then, and it was unlikely much of a search ensued. Back then, if you were lost, you were lost, and life went on. It was not that life mattered more now—sometimes it seemed less valuable—but society, the value of life aside, was intent on being orderly. Disappearing was not acceptable.

The Lac Vieux Desert Casino Resort was two miles north of Watersmeet. The blinking neon complex featured a block building with a long portico, and the tribe's emblem in bright colors over the walkway. Like most tribal casinos in the state, it was open around the clock. There was a bar lounge, a restaurant, a motel with whirlpool suites, a golf course, and RV hookups for summer visitors. The parking was expansive, and as he pulled into the lot he counted three dozen tour buses. It was interesting to read constantly about the woes of the elderly on fixed incomes and then come to a casino to find busloads of bluehairs balancing themselves on walkers, working one-armed bandits with the intensity of John Henry bashing a vein of coal.

He smoked a cigarette, waiting for del Olmo and Grinda.

Grinda pulled into a space next to him and parked, and del Olmo got out of the other side and came around.

Sheena looked at his face and said, "Oh, my God."

Simon just shook his head. "You need to learn to duck."

He explained the reason for his visit and had another smoke.

"Pretty vague," Grinda said. "A woman who might or might not have worked here, no time frame known."

"She gets her rooms comped." Maybe, he reminded himself. From Fahrenheit he had scant information.

"Could be a player," Simon said.

Service grinned. She was a player for sure. The question was what game.

"We should call in a tribal," Grinda said. This was her territory, and the tribal police and game wardens, county, DNR, and Troops all worked hard to coordinate and help each other. Lansing often praised Gogebic County police agencies for their cooperation, as if they had chosen to get along. The truth was that there were few bodies, lots of tourists year-round, and without cooperation, there would be chaos.

"Who do we call?"

"Monica Ucumtwi is on duty tonight," Grinda said. "She just came over from St. Ignace. Young, but smart, and you can count on her."

The highest compliment one cop could pay another, an astounding comment coming from Grinda, who in the past had tended to trust only herself.

"Okay, give her a bump and let's get this going. I'll ask for the night manager, see if we can get a personnel weenie in."

Grinda smiled. "I think it's called Human Resources now. They have a complete night shift," she added. "People get hired and fired around the clock while the money cycles through."

The night manager's name was Laura Liksabong. She was in her late forties, smartly if a little too gaudily dressed for Service's taste, with silver and jade loop earrings. She greeted them as they stood in the lobby overlooking hundreds of clanging, clinking, wailing slot machines, and suggested they move to her office in back. Service saw video cameras at the entrance and assumed there were more above the gambling pit and at the exits.

Liksabong raised her eyes when she heard what Service wanted.

"Wild goose," she said. Her office was sterile, void of any personal items.

"Do you comp rooms?" he asked. There was a camera in her office, in the corner behind her desk. It would take in the whole room.

"Occasionally, not as a policy."

"For former employees?"

"It's possible, but being a *former* employee is not exactly endearing, is it?"

"We're just asking that you check your records," Service said. "I assume you have photographs of high rollers and troublemakers, and anybody who might warrant a comp room."

"We keep good records," the woman said. "But it's night shift and I don't have enough people."

How difficult could it be to check a few records less than a month old?

Monica Ucumtwi came into the office and smiled at Grinda. Liksabong didn't seem particularly glad to see her, but her attitude suddenly shifted to instant and fawning cooperation. "I'll take a look at the records and see what's there. Why don't you grab a coffee or something to nosh on in the Thunderbird—on the house," she said with a smile and a nod to Ucumtwi, who pulled Grinda's arm and led them to the crowded sports bar. There was a lot of conversation, but for a bar it was quiet, Service noticed. TVs were showing replays of a Packers game from the 1960s. The players looked almost comical. Few patrons were watching.

Service studied the snack bar menu, which listed muffins, gum, chips, candy, Rolaids, Tums, and cough drops, all under the category of "Other."

Tums and Rolaids with food? This wasn't irony; it was a sign of providence. He ordered a cup of coffee. Simon got a basket of jalapeño poppers. Monica Ucumtwi ordered a Coke, as did Grinda.

"The manager's attitude shifted when you showed up," Service told Ucumtwi.

"Tribal elections are coming. If she thought that I'd seen her being less than helpful, she'd be afraid I'd tell others. In our elections what people think about you is as important as your paper qualifications."

"All politics are local," del Olmo said.

"Tribal politics are the ultimate local event," Ucumtwi said pleasantly, "but they are taken as seriously as a second coming."

The decorations around the bar were more Indian-like than genuine, modern representations of all things Native rather than those of a particular tribe, which struck Service as tacky. Several elderly customers in motorized wheelchairs buzzed past en route to the pit. One of them had on a clear plastic mask attached by tubes to a large bottle of oxygen stuck in a pocket beside her. What kind of person would come to a casino to gamble when they were on their last legs? Wouldn't a prayer in church be a better wager?

Ucumtwi pushed up her brown uniform sleeve and checked her watch. "I'll go see how things are going," she said.

"Cameras all over this place," Service told Grinda and del Olmo.

Twenty minutes later they were in a room looking at still photos taken from videos, most from a camera positioned above the hotel's registration desk. Manager Liksabong explained that these were from the last two months, and if they needed copies made, she would take care of it for them.

The photos were in large, flat albums, in glycene sleeves.

"There must be four hundred people here," Service said. "Good thing they don't comp as a policy."

"What exactly are we looking for?" del Olmo asked.

"Native woman, dark hair, thirties or forties."

"That should make it easy," Grinda said, rolling her eyes. "How does one identify a native?"

Service ignored her sarcasm, and began leafing through pages. In the second book he found someone he recognized, but she wasn't obviously Native American and she wasn't in her thirties. It was Outi Ranta and she was dressed for a party.

When each of them finished their allotment of books, they pushed them to the next person so they could look. In this case, redundancy was essential, but the search revealed nothing more and Service was displeased.

He looked at the tribal deputy. "These are stills from a video. Can we also look at the video the stills came from?" He showed her the photo of Outi Ranta. There was a computer code along the bottom.

"I'll ask."

Thirty minutes later they were in another room with VCRs, and Service was inserting a cassette.

It took a while to find Outi Ranta, but he found her. Two cameras had captured her. One had her alone at the registration desk. Another had gotten her from behind as she walked toward the desk. The dress she wore barely reached her thighs, and walking beside her and looking back at something was Charley Fahrenheit.

Outi Ranta was Hannah. "I'll be damned," he said.

"You've got something?" Grinda asked.

"Something is a good word," he said, neither specific, nor with meaning. What was Outi Ranta doing with Fahrenheit? He was back in that swamp, and had just gotten to solid ground when it now appeared to be a patch of quicksand.

"I want a copy of this tape," he told Officer Ucumtwi, who went away to arrange it.

The night manager personally brought the tape to them. "If you need anything else, please call me directly." She gave Service her card.

"Do you have the registration card for the person in the photo?"

The manager smiled triumphantly and handed him a fresh copy. "Keep it," she said.

He scanned it quickly. Outi Ranta of Gladstone, and her address was correct. The box for a comp was checked and on the line beside *reason* someone had scribbled, "Gold Feather."

Service looked at the manager. "Gold Feather?"

"A special group of guests who spend at least two weeks a year at our hotel."

"High rollers?" he asked.

"Something like that," Liksabong said before she walked away.

Monica Ucumtwi leaned close to him and whispered, "Vendors."

Ranta and her husband had been in the hardware business for a long time. Service had never known they were gamblers. "Like hardware?" he asked.

"Personal service vending," the tribal deputy said.

Service was jolted. "A pro?"

Ucumtwi smiled. "The casino certainly doesn't comp amateurs."

It was 2 A.M. and Service was too tired to head back to Gladstone. He looked at Simon. "Okay if I bunk at your place for a few hours?"

Simon and Grinda exchanged a glance, and Sheena said, "You can crash with us."

Service looked her in the eye and she began to smile.

"Us, eh?"

She nodded and kept grinning.

· 25 ·

Service was first up in the morning, made a phone call to Walter, and started preparing for breakfast. Grinda and del Olmo came through the kitchen in sweats and running shoes. "Don't play in traffic, kids," Service said with a chuckle.

When they came back they showered while he started pancakes.

They were in uniform when they sat down at the kitchen table, their clip-on ties side by side between them. "A regular family breakfast," Service said.

"We're pleased to be the source of your amusement," del Olmo said.

"My, we're touchy today."

Grinda smiled. Service had no idea what was between them, but whatever it was, it seemed to agree with Sheena.

The three of them stood by their trucks in the early morning sun. "The light's getting flat," Service observed. "Winter's coming."

He didn't ask what they were going to be doing. Officers were expected to know their areas, make their own plans, and follow their own instincts.

Walter was waiting on the sidewalk outside his dorm, a backpack slung over one shoulder as he slid into the truck and looked at his father's face, flashing a questioning look.

"I know," Service said. "I know. S'up?"

Walter laughed, closed his eyes, put his head back. He seemed both relaxed and tense. "It's hard here. I'm in the books all the time."

"Are you feeling all right?"

"I've never studied so much or skated so hard. I can't keep up with these guys."

"You will," Service said.

They ate sandwiches at a shop near the campus. "You aren't saying anything about work," Walter said.

"There are more important things than a job."

"What I meant is that you aren't talking at all."

Service looked at his son and saw himself looking across a table at his father—in a bar, his father drunk and surly and putting him down whenever he tried to speak.

"Food, us, that's enough."

Walter nodded. "Gestalt."

Service said, "I didn't sneeze."

Walter laughed. "You can be funny."

"It wasn't a joke."

"*That's* what makes it funny," his son said.

Service started to say something, but Walter stopped him. "I know," he said. "It's cool. Is Maridly still flying?"

"She comes home Friday night."

"I like her," Walter said.

"It's mutual," Service said.

He took his son to a building on campus. They shook hands in the truck. "You all right for cash?"

Walter said, "Too busy to need money."

Service tried to hand him two twenties, but Walter pushed them back. "You know that commercial on TV?"

"I don't watch much TV," Service said.

"The punch line is 'priceless.' When you see it you'll know what I mean."

"Mar and I will call you Saturday."

"Make it afternoon. Rocky and I have a practice with our kids in the morning."

"You like working with him?"

Walter smiled. "He's different. He loves to get in the net to stop shots. I do all the power skating work. He's like an overgrown kid."

Father and son looked at each other, said in unison, "Goalie."

Service stopped to see Pyykkonen. She glanced up from her cluttered desk. "I thought you died, and by the looks of you, maybe you did."

"I know."

"You're gonna like this," she said. "I talked to a detective in Charlottesville who says they busted fifty-two people for bear poaching. They recovered three hundred gallbladders. One of the couples they got said they've been in the business more than ten years and have been selling three hundred galls a year."

"When?"

"The busts were made in 2001 after more than three years of digging. Virginia Inland Game and Fisheries worked with U.S. Fish and Wildlife and the Park Service. The ring was operating in the Blue Ridge Mountains, including Shenandoah National Park. The only regret here is that they never got the main money man."

"They ID him?"

"No, all they know is that he's Asian and fled the area before the grand jury came down with indictments."

"The timing coincides with Harry Pung's move to Tech."

"You must be a detective," Pyykkonen said.

He told her about Colliver and Fahrenheit and how Ficorelli had helped—but only his official role. "Wayno asked about you," he added.

She shook her head. "He'll get over it." Service wanted to ask her about Shark Wetelainen, but restrained himself. He didn't want his friend hurt, but it was none of his business.

"Did you run Harry Pung's name past the Virginia people?"

"They said all they know is that the money man is Asian. I don't think they were ducking."

"Be nice to know if Pung's son was with him in Blacksburg."

"He wasn't. I called the university and they said his records show no son. She handed him a folder. "From Virginia Tech, and the Michigan Tech papers are in there too. They don't square with each other. This whole thing is about bears," Pyykkonen said.

"I know," Service said. There were a lot of things he might have shared, but didn't.

He called Fern LeBlanc on his way past the Marquette office. "The Captain's calls are piling up," she said in a disapproving tone of voice.

"Tell the Cap'n I'm just not management material."

"Are you coming in?"

"No. Pass the most important messages to McKower."

"I already have," LeBlanc said.

Nantz's plane flared a little before 9 P.M. and settled for a firm landing, the tires squirting tiny jets of smoke as rubber struck concrete.

He watched her walk around the plane, making her post-flight inspection and talking calmly to a mechanic while glancing over at him, a smile dominating her face.

She came to him on the run and her clipboard clattered on the ground as she leaped and threw her arms and legs around him. He almost fell while they were kissing.

"Man, oh man," she whispered as she hugged him. "Man, oh man. There's a case of Bell's in the bird, and a case of wine."

They went out to get them. He carried them both and his arm and broken finger throbbed.

"You look like you got flogged with a frozen pork chop," she said. "I can't wait to get naked," she added.

He pulled into Outi Ranta's driveway and Nantz gave him a look. "What's this?"

The red Jeep was there, but no gray Honda. "I have to talk to Outi."

"Outi or Honeypat?" Nantz asked, raising an eye.

"You'd better stay here," he said.

He knocked several times on the door but got no answer.

He tried the door. It was open. "Outi Ranta?" he called into the hallway. Only silence.

He took one step inside and looked to the right into the kitchen and saw her, sitting at the table, her head on her hands. There was a large, empty glass in front of her.

"Outi?"

She looked up, her eyes glazed and distant.

"Outi?"

"Yeah, Grady."

"Have you been drinking?"

"What if I have?"

"I want to talk to you."

"Go away," she said, putting her head down.

"I want to talk to you about the casino in Watersmeet. And Charley Fahrenheit."

Ranta looked over at him. "What about it?"

"You want to tell me about it?"

"Get a warrant," she said.

"Outi, I'm just asking questions."

"Some things are none of your business."

"They are when they involve breaking the law."

"I didn't break no laws," she said, perking up.

"Outi, you were working with Fahrenheit. They were poaching bears. There's a whole chain of things and it all starts with a homicide."

"You mean a murder?"

"A murder."

She became animated. "I had nothing to do with a murder. I had a little fun is all."

"You got Fahrenheit to steal cable."

"He never said he stole it. Said he could lay his hands on some."

"For what?"

"Not my idea," she said, getting up and walking to an island in the kitchen where a bottle of vodka stood.

"It was like a big game, ya know?" she said. "Just some fun."

Service took the bottle and put it on a counter, out of her reach.

"Outi, listen to me! You got comped into a room as part of the Gold Feather Club."

"I'm a good customer," she said defiantly.

"My understanding is that Gold Feathers do more selling than spending."

Outi Ranta went back to her chair and sat down. "I knew when Honeypat showed up this would go in the tank. She was a big help when Onte died. I owed her for that, hey."

No tears, no breaking voice. Outi Ranta seemed to be a very tough woman. "Honeypat and I go way back—to high school. We dropped out, went with men. We didn't like school."

"High school where?"

"Detour." This was on the far eastern tip of the peninsula, across from Drummond Island.

"You're Tribal?"

"Same as Honeypat."

He didn't ask if she had been a prostitute.

"I left the life when I met Onte," she said. "Met him in Windsor. He didn't care about my past."

"Why Fahrenheit?"

She rubbed her fingers together. "Onte left the business in bad shape. I needed cash to pull it out."

Did this qualify as greed? Service wondered.

"You did this for Honeypat?"

"Her idea. She said I could make some money and have some fun, like the old days. And I was ready."

"She asked you to get cable?"

"Everything was her idea."

"Was Limpy involved?"

Outi Ranta made a sour face. "That *animal*? No way."

Service was not so sure. "Where's Honeypat now?"

"Gone."

"Where?"

"Don't have a clue," she said. "How'd you get to me?"

"Cameras at the casino," he said. "They tape almost everything."

"I told Honeypat that, and she said there was no way anyone would ever know it was me. Am I goin' to jail?" She looked directly at him, her eyes challenging and pleading.

"Not if you help me. If Honeypat makes contact, you call me first thing and you don't tell her we've talked. Can you do that?" He put one of his business cards on the table.

"I don't want to go to jail."

"Then help me," he said. She had received stolen goods and there was probably more, but if Honeypat had set up the whole thing, Outi was just a minor player. With his intercession, the prosecutor might agree to go easy on her.

"You really have to help me to help yourself, Outi."

"Yeah, like I'm supposed to trust a cop?"

"You don't have much choice."

"Honeypat," she said angrily. "I knew better than to let her into my life again."

He left her in the kitchen and went out to the truck. Nantz looked at him. "Are we going inside for a ménage à trois?" She was grinning.

They went straight up to bed, took off their clothes, and fell on the bed.

He woke up in the middle of the night. Nantz was sitting up next to him, light from the hallway illuminating her breasts in a pale yellow glow.

"Did we?" he asked.

"You fell asleep," she said.

"I'm awake now."

Her hand touched him. "That is a distinctly provable fact. I will try to be gentle."

"How am I doing?" she whispered after several minutes. "Wonderful," he said, wincing. Maridly's idea of gentle was somewhat different from that of other women he had known.

· 26 ·

Service awoke to find Newf where Nantz should have been. When he looked at the clock and saw that it was noon, he kicked off the covers and limped downstairs. He had more aches this morning than when he went to bed. He smelled something cooking, and Newf smelled it too as she bulled past him, nearly knocking him down the stairs.

He went into the kitchen, looked at the pot on a front burner, sniffed.

"White wine onion soup," Nantz said. "Twelve minutes to touch-down."

She put on a lavender oven mitt decorated with pale blue and yellow forget-me-nots, turned, hugged him, patted his butt, and gently hipped him out of the way. He stood with her, watching her stir in julienned carrots and remove a cookie sheet from the oven. She cooked as efficiently and confidently as she flew a plane. There were thick pieces of toast on the sheet and the scent of garlic engulfed the room. She took off the oven mitt.

"What can I do?" he asked.

"Pants would be a move toward civilized," she said with a smirk and a downward glance. She began to rub each piece of toast with the cut side of a garlic clove, drizzle on some olive oil, and add a small slice of Gruyère cheese.

She pointed the oven mitt at him once again. "Trou."

The meal was on the table when he came back downstairs. Bloody Marys in tall glasses were in place, with feathers of celery sticking out like flags.

They ate slowly, relishing flavors.

"Politicians eat miserably," Nantz said. "Always on the run, odd times. I'm surprised they don't all weigh three hundred pounds."

"Like Clearcut?" he said. Sam Bozian waddled with splayed feet.

"Sam's always had a metabolic problem," she said. She had known the governor since she was a child.

"He could jack up his rate by moving his ass once in a while."

She rolled her eyes and said, "Meow."

At the hospital Nantz and Kate Nordquist talked on about Lorelei Timms and her wardrobe and the practical concerns of campaigning day after day. Service went downstairs to have a cigarette.

Gutpile Moody rolled up in his truck, got out and yawned.

"All-nighter?"

"We had a plane over the Garden last night, bagged six shiners." Officers sometimes employed group patrols and sent a light plane overhead to look for jack-lighting activity at night. When lights were seen, the plane's pilot directed officers on the ground to the site. The method had become so effective that in some areas poachers had taken to working in broad daylight. But not in the Garden Peninsula, where poaching and violating were taken by many as inalienable rights.

"That time of year," Service said.

"It's *that* time year-round in the Garden," Moody said. "Rumor is that Lansing's gonna put you to work on the fish runs with the hired help this spring."

Service said, "Such decisions are above my pay grade."

"Don't be an asshole," Moody said with a sly grin. "You're Cap'n Grant's boy. How is he?"

"Bonked his head, slight concussion."

"If you say so. Way I hear it, Fern LeBlanc is telling everybody he's had another stroke."

"Is she now?" Service said. When Moody went inside he dialed Fern's home number and she answered on the first ring.

"You," he said. "You have to exercise some judgment in what you tell people."

"Ah," she said. "The prodigal detective trying to talk management. *You* will not tell me what to think or say," she said.

"Your thoughts are yours, but your words affect others. When you speculate, others take it for gospel."

"I am *not* speculating," she said, "and as you said, you are *not* management material. I intend to protect the captain."

"The captain can take care of himself."

"Like *you* would know," she said angrily. "You're never around! He wants to see you tomorrow night—at his home." She hung up on him, his point having found a fat vein, as his old man used to say after he had purposely antagonized someone.

Moody had joined Nantz and Nordquist and was regaling them with the tale of a shiner he had grappled with last night. Service and Nantz made their goodbyes and left the hospital.

Nantz called Walter on the cell phone as they drove toward Gladstone. "Hey, you," she said.

She listened and said, "Flying is flying."

Then, "He's driving."

More silence. "*Really*! No, I won't say a word."

"What was that about?" he asked as she snapped the cell phone closed.

"He's just checking up on us."

For dinner he grilled skirt steaks marinated in lime juice and zest, red wine, soy, ginger, garlic, sugar, and hot sauce. He cooked the meat rare and served it with a small tossed salad of Italian greens and grilled Spanish onion slices.

Nantz had opened a bottle of the new Italian wine, a 1996 Avignonesi Grifi, and poured each of them a glass.

"Mmm," she said, taking a bite of steak.

"Mmm," he said, tasting the wine.

After dinner, they loaded the dishwasher and Nantz camped at the dining room table with books from the academy while he put on the Norah Jones CD and poured another glass of wine.

Nantz snapped a book closed at 10 P.M. and said, "Hon, get me a two-gallon jar from the basement, okay?" For reasons he never understood, she collected jars and bottles and vases of all sizes and descriptions. The basement shelves were filled with bags and boxes of glassware.

He brought a jar to the the kitchen counter and watched as she put a strip of masking tape around it and wrote with a large marker, "4F."

"Okay," she said, pouring more wine for herself. "Give me five bucks."

He dug into his wallet and handed it to her. She took his five and another from her wallet, stuffed them ceremoniously in the jar, which she tucked under an arm, and picked up her wine. "Hi ho, hi ho, it's off to bed we go."

She made love with unusual tenderness and gentleness, lingering throughout, and when they had finished, he rolled to his own pillow and said, "I'm gonna let the mutt out."

She was breathing deeply when he returned. Newf flopped on a throw rug by the bed. Cat had gotten between the pillows while he was gone and opened her mouth with a silent hiss when he got into bed. He put his hand on Nantz's hip to feel her warmth.

"Go ahead and ask," she whispered.

"Four-F?" he said.

"Every time we fool around we'll each put five bucks in the jar. When it's full, it will pay for our honeymoon."

"Four-F," he said again.

"Frequent Fucking For the Future," she whispered.

They both began to giggle.

She patted his shoulder with a warm hand. "Sleep."

He fell asleep wondering if he had five dollars for the morning deposit to the jar.

· 27 ·

They made love at sunrise, put their money in the jar, went down to do their workout routines, and showered.

Nantz had arrived Friday night with only a small duffel bag, but packed a huge suitcase and garment bag after they got out of the shower. When she was done she ceremoniously opened her purse, took out a ten-dollar bill, and put it in the jar. She lay back on the bed and held out her arms. "This one's on me. Literally," she added lasciviously.

By noon they were at the airport. He loaded her baggage and followed her through her walk-around and preflight routine. There was nothing about flying and airplanes that he cared for, but she had it in her blood and treated an aircraft like an extension of her body.

"Meet you in Jackson Friday," he said.

"Plan on 2 P.M. We women will need time for construction before a big party."

"I'll bring a wad of fives," he said.

She smiled and kissed him. "Sorry I can't pick you up," she said. "Lori's schedule is awful again this week."

"I don't mind driving," which was true. "We'll need wheels down there. I'll call Tree about meeting him and Kalina for dinner on Saturday. You're sure your boss won't mind?"

"I suspect she and Whit are gonna be doin' just what we're gonna be doin'."

Whit was the senator's stay-at-home husband. "Ooh," he said. "Our aspiring governor likes nookie?"

She poked him. "All women *like* sex—with the right man." She paused and added, "And sometimes with the wrong man."

Before he could say anything she added, "You fit into both categories, big boy. You'll need a tux next weekend. I'll take care of it. Bring your good black shoes."

"The pumps or the sling-backs?" he said.

She laughed and rolled her eyes. He said, "The only black shoes I have are boots."

"You want to polish them up, that's okay by me."

He said, "I'll get some new ones. You sure a suit won't do?"

"This will be a deep-pockets crowd, very neufy."

They lingered in an embrace until she said, "Okay, gotta kick the tires and light the fires."

"This thing has propellers," he said.

"Whatever," she said with a wink.

She got into the Cessna, closed the hatch, and started the engines. He saw her focused inside the cockpit and talking on the mike when she looked over at him, snapped off a crisp salute, blew a kiss, released brakes, and taxied away.

He watched her take off to the west and bank southeast toward Traverse City, experiencing a surge of fear as he pictured her all alone in the cockpit; but she was happy and knew what she was doing, and if she wasn't worried, he wouldn't be either. Too much.

Next Friday night they would be in Jackson and he would meet Siquin Soong, he thought as Nantz disappeared from sight. He had no desire to see the captain tonight. Instead, he called McCants who was patrolling in the Haymeadow Marsh area. They agreed to meet at a picnic ground at Haymeadow Falls. He was to bring fresh coffee.

The days were shortening and the tamaracks, aspens, and birches along Haymeadow Creek were beginning to show the result of reduced light, which kicked in chemical reactions that turned needles and leaves a pale yellow or bright gold. Some leaves were beginning to drop, spackling the ground like a sloppy painter's palette. He breathed in the damp earth and decaying leaves, the perfume of fall hanging in the still air.

McCants arrived two minutes later. They sat at a picnic table, which had been chained to a tree, and enjoyed the silence.

"They flew the Garden two nights ago," he said, "Plucked six violets. How's the Mosquito been?"

The Mosquito Wilderness would always be his baby.

"Quiet. I think you scared everybody away, you big meanie. This last week has been quiet everywhere," she added. After a look at his face she said, "Almost everywhere . . ."

"This too shall pass," he said. "Just keep your feet in the dirt."

He remembered a Sunday of nearly twenty years before. It was snowing and raining and miserable outside and he had just pulled out his workbag when Sergeant Peter Slater had called.

"What're you up to today?" Slater had asked.

"Paperwork. You?"

"Thought I'd take a ride in the woods. Want to come along?"

The weather was beyond miserable, but Slater was a subtle man with a wry sense of humor, and he agreed to join his supervisor. By day's end they had written eighteen tickets for an unimaginable array of violations and problems, and the experience had taught him better than any lecture that the only way to enforce laws was to be out where they were being broken. After that he did paperwork at night or in little snatches of time.

He had known McCants so long that they were content to simply sit and drink in the sounds and scents of the changing seasons.

Service was pouring more coffee when McCants said, "Swans." He looked up to see four of the huge birds flying high above the creek descending toward the area where beaver dams formed several small ponds.

McCants lit up and stared at the creek glissading over gray and black rocks. "I still can't believe we get paid to do this," she said, adding, "I heard that sergeants and detectives are going back to the field to fill gaps after the first of the year."

"I heard that too," he said, leaving it at that.

"You think you'll work the Mosquito?"

"I doubt I'll get to choose."

McCants smiled. "You want to work it with me, I'd like that. Is Captain Grant going to be okay?"

"I hope so," he said. LeBlanc probably was right about it being another stroke, but if the captain said it wasn't, he would stick by his captain.

"What do you think of the senator's chances?" she asked.

"What is this, Twenty Questions?"

"I think she's a great choice," McCants said. "Be good to have a woman running the show. If she wins, you think Tenni's out?"

"After his contract expires," he said. "It will depend on the makeup of the commission."

"His departure alone will be a plus for all of us."

They were walking to their respective trucks when two shots popped over the hill toward the beaver ponds north of them. Instinct stopped both of them as they listened. The swans came back down the creek, lower now, flapping frantically to gain altitude.

Service counted three.

"One unaccounted for," McCants said.

He ran along behind her as she raced through the trees up a hill, pausing by a downed white pine and putting her binoculars up. They both scanned the ponds through the trees. There was no wind and the air was heavy, promising rain. Somewhere below they heard snippets of voices.

"There," McCants said, pointing. "Just inside that little peninsula. The blind's on the far shore and there's a camo johnboat against the bank."

Service glassed the area, saw what she saw.

"They must be parked on the other side of the creek," she said. "Up on the hill line." She pointed. "We can get in east of the ponds, curve our way in from the south, and come up behind them. They're probably parked further north. Got your waders?" she asked.

They'd been in the back of the Yukon at one time and maybe they still were—somewhere in the clutter. In his old patrol truck he had been pathologically neat and orderly because there was so little room, but in the Yukon he was becoming a slob.

They took both trucks and looked for and located a little-used two-track that led up to the hill where they wanted to be. The roads were pitted deep and rough, the frames bottoming out. After they had found a place to stash the trucks he rooted around for his waders, found them, kicked off his leather boots and slid into the waders. He strapped his gun belt over them.

McCants was ready before him. "Search first, confront second," she said.

He remembered the shy probie she had been, smiled at her confidence now.

It took twenty-five minutes to get down to the pond, its edge overgrown with tag alders, the bottom of the pond deep in black silt. They crawled through the dense cover, slithering along, easing over blowdowns, trying to avoid stumps left by beavers.

Eventually the trees ended and they were in brown grass. The cottony white entrails of cattails hung down like the exploded batting of ruined beds.

"I am so fucking wasted," a voice said.

"Shut up," a second voice said. "Voices carry."

"Yeah sure, what I'm gonna do, spook fuckin' beavers, eh?"

McCants was almost flat just ahead of him. She turned her head and nodded for him to come up to her. Service sank in sphagnum moss and black water up to his thighs as he crawled. The waders had a leak. Shit.

"Right there," she said, mouthing the words soundlessly. She held up three fingers, then looped her forefinger and thumb, lifted her foot out of water and touched it. Thirty feet. McCants delicately cleared a space in some mud and drew a picture for him. They would crawl forward about five yards apart, circle, and come back by different routes. Even the dumbest violet would not keep a swan in the blind. She wanted to find it before confronting the men.

The cold water coming in through the waders was soaking his pants, and it made him cringe as it seeped through to coat his legs.

"Goddammit, now I gotta piss," one of the voices said.

Service peeked through the grass, could not see McCants, but saw two men in camo clothing.

He could hear a stream of urine splashing in the marsh water at the base of the brown grass.

"You jerk!" McCants said with a yelp. "DNR!"

Service looked through the grass. Candi was standing up and angry. "You pissed on me," she said.

The man was trying to button up. "Serves youse right crawlin' around out here!" the man shouted.

The second man looked over, said, "What the fuck? Jesus!"

"Put that little thing away," McCants told the second man.

"DNR," the first man grumbled, eyeing her. He looked over at his partner.

"A cunt," the second one said.

They were weighing options, Service knew. He began to gather himself to intervene.

"Hey, what's the problem, Dickless Tracy?" this from the first man. "Little girl like you out here all alone."

"*God* is my copilot," McCants said calmly. "Let's see your hunting licenses," she said.

The second man grinned. "Mine's in the blind. I'll just—"

"Stay where you are," McCants said, stepping toward the first man. "Licenses," she repeated.

"Like Dray says, in the blind."

"Sir, move over here," she told the second man.

Service thought about standing up, but he was enjoying watching her work.

The two men were tall and rangy with triangular heads, ponytails, bushy black beards.

McCants stood at ease, but Service saw her hand resting near the grip of her SIG Sauer.

"Kneel," she said.

The men looked at each other and dawdled but eventually did as they were told.

"Okay, who shot the swan?" she asked.

"What swan?"

"Don't lie to me," she said. "I hate liars."

"Hey, you see a swan?" the first hunter said to his partner with a crooked grin.

She said to the first man, "Give me your hat."

The man laughed and took it off. She dropped it on the ground.

Service crawled closer so he could see what she was doing.

She reached under her tie and pulled out a green pouch.

"This is a lie detector," she said.

"Bullshit," the first man said.

"Shut up," his partner said.

"Now," she said. "You're hunting here, right?"

"If you say so," the first man said.

"You've got dope in the blind."

"No way."

"I smelled it," she said. "Don't lie. This pouch always reveals the truth."

"What's in there?" the second man asked.

"Truth," she said. "You shot the swan. Four came over, three came back. I was up there on that hill." She pointed. "Who took the shots?"

"We din't shoot no swan," the first man said.

"Swear to God?" she said.

"Swear to God."

She looked at the second man. "You swear?"

He nodded unconvincingly, said nothing. Service was fascinated, wondering what the hell she was doing.

"I'm warning both of you, if you lie over the bones you will have bad luck you cannot believe," she said. "The curse will be on you."

"You can't hurt us," the first man said.

"God will do it, not me."

"Did you shoot the swan?" she asked the first man.

He shook his head.

She dumped the contents of the pouch into the hat and nodded solemnly.

It began to drizzle.

"Did you shoot at the swan?" she asked, looking up at the man.

"I didn't hit it," he said.

"Shut the fuck up," the second man said.

"*You*," she said to the second man. "Did you shoot the swan?"

"No," he said, his voice faltering.

She shook her head and breathed in deeply. "You are in deep trouble, sir. God is about to punish you."

The man's face turned red and he started to stand.

Service stood up, trying to fight back a laugh.

Both men were startled by his sudden appearance. The second man screamed, "I did it, I did it!"

Service got up and walked forward. The first man looked up at him.

"Roll on your backs and take off your jackets," McCants said.

"It's raining," the first man whined.

Both men did as they were told. The second man was wearing a shoulder holster with a Colt 45.

"Hands out like you are on a cross," McCants said.

The men did as they were told. Service cautiously removed the .45 and pointed it toward the hill. "Safety's off." He pulled the clip, checked the chamber. "One in the boiler." He emptied the clip into his hand and put the rounds in his pocket. He removed the round from the chamber and put it with the other bullets.

"Shoot a lot of ducks with this?" he asked the second man. He grabbed the man by the shoulder and pulled him up. "Licenses. *You* get them both." Service went with him into the blind, was gone three or four minutes, and emerged with two shotguns, two wallets, and a wood duck decoy. "No plugs. There're fifty rounds of lead shot in there, two expended." He flipped wallets to McCants who looked through them and shook her head. "No hunting licenses, no waterfowl stamps."

Neither man spoke.

"A whole bag of these decoys inside," Service said. He turned over the one he was carrying and asked, "Which one of you is Bruce Mosley?"

"Neither," McCants said, holding the wallets.

"And the boat?" Service asked.

"Mine," one of the men said. "The decoys belong to a friend of ours."

"That's good," Service said. "There's no registration on the boat."

"Okay," the first man said, "I shot the swan. It was gonna fuck up our duck huntin'."

"No, it wasn't," McCants said. "This area's closed to duck hunting this year."

She walked over by the blind, took her 800 MHz off her belt, and called the driver's licenses in to Lansing. She gave Station 20 the name and phone number of the decoy owner and the driver's license numbers of the two men. It took ten minutes to get answers.

The first man was Dray Boekeloo, forty-one, of Thompson. He had two outstanding Schoolcraft County warrants, for possession of meth and contributing to the delinquency of minors. The second man was Jordie Rockcrusher, thirty-six, who was wanted for felonious assault in St. Ignace. The owner of the decoys had reported them stolen two weeks before. He'd never heard of Boekeloo or Rockcrusher.

"You guys hit the jackpot," McCants said. "Possession of stolen goods, killing a swan, lead shot, no plugs in your guns, a loaded, concealed weapon without a CCW permit, the unregistered boat, no waterfowl stamps or hunting licenses, and hunting in a closed area. I warned you not to lie over the bones. Where's your vehicle?"

Both men pointed north.

They cuffed the men and took the guns and decoys and started marching out of the swamp up the hill. It was easier going out than the way they had come in.

Up on the hill McCants called Delta County and asked for deputies to meet them out on the Rapid River Truck Trail to transport the prisoners. There was no way for a patrol car to get back to them. Service laughed thinking about this. Until a few years back all COs had were sedans, and they took them into places the manufacturers would never believe. Got them hung up and trapped a lot too. The trucks weren't perfect, but size and four-wheel drive had opened a lot of new territory to officers.

They took one man in each truck, made the handoff, and went back across the creek and along the hills until they found the men's truck. Service dropped McCants, who walked back to the beaver pond and started north in the boat. Service was waiting for her when she bumped the nose of the boat against the grassy bank. It was a struggle to pull the boat up to the truck, but they got it done, securing it with bungee cords. McCants drove it out to the main road to meet the wrecker driver, who hooked it up and hauled it away. Service took McCants back to her truck and called the captain at home. "I'm with McCants. Do you still want me to come by?"

"No. There are rumors in Lansing and Detroit that the feds are exorcised by a woods cop sniffing around one of their investigations."

Siquin Soong? Service wondered. He still hadn't heard back from Tree, which was unusual. "I haven't talked to the feds, Captain."

"Are you in tomorrow?"

He said he would be.

McCants said, "Want to grab a burger? I'm gonna sit on a field tonight."

"Want company?" he asked.

"Sure."

They bought burgers at the McDonald's in Gladstone and headed to a potato field not far from the Mosquito Wilderness. They backed the truck into some spruce trees and sat inside with the windows cracked, eating burgers and fries. "Good field?" McCants asked.

"Got a lot of shiners here over the years," he said. Too many to count.

At 11 P.M. a small buck walked past the truck, no more than ten yards away, sticking close to a wild olive hedgerow. McCants got antlers out of the back of the truck and rattled them together. The animal stopped and turned back to see what the sound was. The buck's brisket was not swollen. It would take colder weather to turn on the rut, but deer were naturally curious, which got a lot of them shot every year.

When the deer winded McCants, it sprang away and disappeared into the hedgerow with its flag up in alarm.

McCants got back into the truck, turned on a small red light, and started her paperwork for the day.

Service said, "Where the hell did you come up with that pouch routine?"

"Red Eacun," she said.

Eacun was a sergeant who had retired ten years ago, spent winters is Arizona, summers at his home in Cheboygan. He was a horseblanket, like his father, an old-time conservation officer who wore a full-length wool coat. Horseblankets were considered a breed apart by their successors.

"He said one of his guys used to use it. Works about ninety percent of the time if you size up the violets right."

"You read those two right," he said.

"It *was* sweet," she said.

"Total bozos," he said.

"Job security," she said, grinning.

"What exactly is in the pouch?" he asked.

"That, Detective, must remain a trade secret."

· 28 ·

As soon as Newf was free of the dog run, she ran into the side hedges, snarling and barking. Service tensed, thinking the red dog was back, but Newf soon came back panting and wagging her tail and made straight for the house.

"Miss Congeniality," he said to the dog, who looked quizzically at him.

There were two messages on the answering machine, the earliest from Pyykkonen, the latter from Treebone.

Tree's said, "Call you back from a Clark Kent. You probably just off making life miserable for your Bammas." A Clark Kent was Tree-talk for a phone booth. He had no idea what a Bamma was, but he could guess it related to rednecks. Tree's wanting to call from a phone booth was a distinctly negative indicator.

He tried Pyykkonen at her office and got a recording. He called her house and the line was busy. It took four calls for her to finally pick up.

"You been trying to get through?" she asked.

"Couple tries," he said.

"I've been on-line with Shark," she said.

"Wetelainen on-line?" It was unthinkable. Yalmer Wetelainen's life revolved around food, drink, fishing, and hunting—until recently.

"I showed him a site called Flyanglersonline.Com. It's got loads of antique fly recipes. He loved it, went right out and bought a Dell. Now I'm teaching him e-mail and Instant Messenger."

Service had no idea what Instant Messenger was, and didn't care. "You called," he said.

"I talked to the dean at Virginia Tech who was Harry Pung's boss. Just as the records showed, he was not aware of a son and had never heard Harry talk about one. I don't know what the hell to think anymore. I also put out a BOLO to the coast guard, county, and Troops for a blue watercraft. Nothing back yet. I called the locks at the Soo and asked them to scan the tapes. Anything on your end?"

BOLO meant Be On The Lookout. Cops rarely used the term APB anymore. "They have tapes at the locks?"

"Every boat that goes through." He hadn't known this and he was impressed that Pyykkonen had thought of it. He had assumed the blue boat had ducked into a harbor in the northern U.P.

"Irons in the fire here," he said.

"We're gonna break this," she said, sounding like she was singing in a graveyard.

He opened a can of Diet Pepsi and leafed through a copy of *Atlantic Monthly* that Nantz had left when he heard a siren pass in front of the house. He sometimes heard sirens below the Bluff on US 2, but rarely in the neighborhood. He put down the magazine, went out to the truck with Newf on his heels, and clicked on his 800 MHz. Nothing.

There were two radio systems in all DNR vehicles, the 800 MHz for talking to Lansing, all DNR field personnel and district offices around the state, and for talking to Troops. The county and city were on a separate system. With the 800 silent, he dialed in Delta County on the other radio and heard the dispatcher talking to a deputy. "Code 10-54X, Code 3," she said.

Code 10-54 was a possible suicide; X indicated a female. Code 3 meant get there fast. He depressed his mike button. "Delta, DNR Twenty-Five Fourteen, where's that Code 10-54?"

She gave him the address, which he automatically scribbled in the notebook he stored by the radio. His heart sank. It was Outi Ranta's house.

He let Newf into the truck and blue-lighted to the house. Two Delta County cruisers were just pulling in, along with an EMS Ramparts unit. A third county unit was on his heels. He grabbed a pair of disposable latex gloves from a box in the backseat, and got out.

The Delta County undersheriff, James Cambridge, pulled in beside him. Cambridge was sixty, overweight, had a chronic bad back, and would retire this summer. He was the sort of county cop who was gruff, unfriendly, and uncooperative with other agencies. His personality had cost him two runs at sheriff, and only the benevolence of the current sheriff allowed him to keep his job this time around.

"James," Service greeted him

"I hate calls like this," the undersheriff said. Service knew Cambridge would soon question his presence.

Service stepped into the house behind Cambridge. There was a young deputy in the hallway. The kid looked pale, about to be sick. Cambridge squeezed his shoulder, a gesture that caught Service by surprise. The undersheriff was not known for giving warm fuzzies to his people.

Service looked into the kitchen. Cambridge said, "Mind your step," and went back to talking to his deputy.

There were two lower panes of glass gone from the bay window. The rest of the glass and white wood were sprayed with blood and gray tissue. Service saw a body on the floor and leaned to look, not wanting to soil the evidence. It was Outi Ranta, her skirt hiked up around her thighs, one shoe off. She had a corn pad on the uncovered foot. A Colt Python with a four-inch barrel was on the floor. He guessed it was a .38. The two bottles of vodka were where he had last seen them, one of them unopened, the other one looking to have about the same amount as earlier. Ranta's chair was tipped over. It was the same chair she had been sitting in when he last saw her.

He stepped out of the kitchen and went outside for a smoke. A Gladstone cop pulled up and went inside. Then a Troop Service didn't recognize joined them. Cop lights always drew crowds. He walked along the side of the main house to the guest house in back. It was unlit, small. He tried the door. Open. He flipped on the light, saw the bed was made, no dirty dishes. It looked unlived in. He backed out, circled the small house, looked through a window into the bathroom. Clean towels, new soap in the dish. He sat down on a lawn chair and finished his cigarette.

He found Vince Vilardo stepping out of the house when he got back to the front. He was telling Cambridge and the deputy, "Body temp says two, three hours max. Who found her?"

Cambridge gave a soft nudge to the young deputy, who said, "A neighbor two doors down thought she heard a noise, but she was making supper for her kids. Later she come over and saw the broken glass and blood, and called."

"When did she hear the noise?" Vince asked.

"Suppertime," the kid cop said.

Cambridge said, "Go ask for an actual time — even if it's an estimate."

The young deputy took off on a run. Cambridge looked at Service and shook his head.

Vince nodded for Service to follow him. They went to the side of the house. "This wasn't a suicide," Vince said quietly. "Paraffin shows no traces of nitrates on either hand. The projectile appears to have traveled downward, right to left. Nitrate and appearance of the wound suggest five, six feet away. I'll verify all this in the lab, but I thought you'd want to know."

"You wondering why I'm here?"

"I gave up speculation long time ago."

"You're sayin' homicide, not suicide?"

"Ninety percent," Vilardo said.

"Thanks, Vince."

Cambridge drifted back to them. "Thanks for responding," he told Service. "We'll take it from here."

Translation, "Butt out and adios."

Vince leaned close to Service, whispered, "I'll call you in the morning."

When he got home there was still no call from Tree.

Why had Outi Ranta been killed? She and Honeypat had had a falling out. Was there someone or something else? He started to make a list but pushed the pad away. Not his business. Most victims knew their killers and most murders were crimes of passion, unplanned events that simply happened. He had not taken a close look, but it looked to him like there had been no struggle in the kitchen. Did Outi think she was alone or had she let someone in? Leave it be, he told himself. Let the process run its course and let the county do its job. Still, he couldn't help feeling that there was something he should have done to prevent this. He had seen her only two nights ago, and though she had been upset, he was sure she was all right and strong.

He fed Cat and Newf and let them out. Cat stayed out to hunt. Newf came running in and raced upstairs to the bed so she could claim it. He didn't bother pushing her off and slept fitfully.

29

U p before the sun, Service skipped the free weights and rode the stationary bicycle; his routines were always timed for maximum benefit, but today he just got on the device and pedalled, his mind still locked on the death of Outi Ranta. Sometimes sleep facilitated solutions to problems, but not last night, and not this morning. After an hour on the bike he showered and boiled water for instant oatmeal. He dumped a handful of dried Traverse City cherries on the powdered mix, poured on boiling water, sat down to eat, and found after two spoonfuls he had no appetite. He set the bowl on the floor for Newf to finish and grabbed the telephone.

Simon del Olmo answered, "*Wha?*" He sounded confused and still asleep.

"Where's Kitella?"

"Grady?"

"Is he still in jail?"

"I don't know."

"Find out, okay?"

Treebone called at seven, just as Service was getting ready to put Newf in her pen.

"Got my ass kicked," Tree began. "The commanding officer for Major Crimes landed on me like a five-hundred-pound wet turd, told me I got 'epizootics of the blowhole,' woompty woompty. Said the Feebs ripped him a new asshole because of me and that as far as he was concerned I should make like D. B. Cooper and disa-fucking-ppear."

"What the hell did you do?"

"I don't know, man. I was just trying to help you. I called my man at the Feeb house but he suddenly had lockjaw. You know Feebs, they always spooked by something, worse since nine-eleven."

"They've always been political."

"Never seen 'em quite like this. They got a new top dawg and he's changin' it all around."

"Change makes everybody edgy."

"Whatever. Couldn't get in that door, so I called Shamekia."

288 · JOSEPH HEYWOOD

Typical Treebone—once on a mission, he would not be put off. Shamekia was an attorney in the prestigious Detroit firm of Fogner, Qualls, Grismer and Pillis. She had once been an FBI agent who filed charges against the Bureau for discrimination and had won a huge settlement. Officially she was persona non grata in the bureau, but she had enough contacts to get inside whenever she needed to. Last year she had helped him solve a case that had gotten convoluted and polluted by conflicted police agency agendas. She was a striking-looking woman, intelligent and straight-talking, and had been a childhood friend of Tree's.

"Shamekia says she hit walls too, but she's got more juju with the black suits. She says she found out that the people most interested in Siquin Soong are out of Justice OCRS."

"OCRS?"

"Organized Crime and Racketeering Section."

"Mafia hounds."

"Not just. They track the old Cosa Nostra, what's left of them, Chinese Triads, Japanese Yakuza, and the Russians. They coordinate with DEA, FBI, others. OCRS squeezes all potential federal prosecutions through the prism of RICO."

RICO was the Racketeer Influenced and Corrupt Organizations Act, a broad statutory umbrella. It had only recently been used to apply to Fish and Game law, though the division's attorneys in Lansing predicted a lot more.

"Shamekia says the Detroit U.S. Attorney's Organized Crime Strike Force has a visitor from the Washington Litigation Unit. Apparently this is a signal that the strike force is getting ready to drop a bomb."

"On Soong?"

"That's her read. She says Justice doesn't send in the LU until it's time to pull the trigger. They like to make sure the target is directly in sight."

"Meaning they don't want anybody to disrupt their gig."

"There it is," Treebone said. "You and Nantz coming down?"

"Next Saturday."

"Kalina will be a happy woman."

"We're in Jackson Friday night. We'll call you Saturday morning, drive over that afternoon."

"Check it out," Tree said enthusiastically. "We're gonna hit Shinto for chow, then down to BoMac's for some late night tunes."

The BoMac Lounge was on Gratiot next to Harmonie Park, a downtown neighborhood that had undergone gentrification in recent years and now housed lofts, restaurants, clubs, and art galleries. BoMac's was famous for Detroit R&B and had been around for ten or fifteen years. It had once been the hangout of the Funk Brothers, whose music Tree was addicted to. The Funk Brothers were the studio musicians who helped make Barry Gordie's Motown frontliners famous—on call every day of the week, paid ten dollars a song no matter how many takes. The Funk Brothers were Motown's unseen backbone. He had first heard about them when he and Tree were in Vietnam, and they remained one of his friend's favorite subjects.

"Never heard of Shinto."

"You too far up in Bammaland. Serious money outta Tokyo opened it up on Lakeshore."

"In the Pointes?"

Tree chuckled. "Bought one of the old Windmill Pointe mansions, did it up, brought in one of those chefs you see on TV. Kalina's been dyin' to go before the locals shut it down. Some of the bluebloods got pissed, filed suit. We don't go now, we might never, sayin'?"

"Call you from Jackson."

"Word on the street here your senator gonna get the job. Kwami came out for her."

Timms. "We'll see." The opinion of the mayor of Detroit had the weight of a popcorn fart outside the city, Service thought.

"I hear ya. Sorry I couldn't get more for you. Gotta skate, dawg. Semper Fi."

Luticious Treebone, an original.

Service left water and food for the animals, put Newf in her run, and headed for Marquette. Fern LeBlanc ignored him as he headed directly to the captain's office.

Ware Grant looked the way he always looked, back straight, freshly pressed, hair combed, white Van Gogh trimmed.

"Close the door," the captain said.

Service closed it and sat down. The captain remained behind his desk, which was unusual. "It was not one of our people stirring the Federals," he said. "It was someone from the DPD."

DPD was the Detroit Police Department. Service waited for the captain to finish. He always spoke deliberately, letting his words loose only after they had been thoroughly processed, each one carefully considered for its impact. "Chief O'Driscoll is relieved. I believe if it were one of our people, that person would be in serious trouble."

"Feebs are always getting bent out of shape," Service said. Did the captain guess it was Treebone? Probably. He didn't miss much.

"Sometimes with justification," the captain said.

"Good thing we're not part of it," Service said.

"This is for your ears only," the captain went on. "If Senator Timms is elected there is going to be massive and profound change in the department."

"New party in Lansing."

"It's more all-encompassing. DNR and DEQ will be reunited under a single head. No more rubber-stamping on the environmental side. It will be back to the old values. There will be separate budgets, but the director will rationalize goals and priorities. Two budgets will allow lawmakers to track the costs of both parts."

"A total merger would be more effective," Service said.

"After all the budget cuts we've been through, improvement and stability are more important. But if the Senator doesn't win—"

"It will be Clearcut Redux," Service said.

"Yes, which means that the chief does not want anything to happen that might hurt the senator's campaign."

The captain's steely eyes drilled into Service.

"Are we becoming politicized?" he asked his boss. Was this meant to warn him off Soong?

"We always have been politicized at the Lansing level, and the chief does not want to be the author of our downfall."

"Does that mean we're to back off investigations?"

"There is backing off and there is assuring that evidence is solid and in place, am I clear?"

Not at all, but this wasn't unusual. "Make sure what we're shooting at."

The captain nodded once and looked down to the paperwork on his desk. Service had just gotten to his feet when he heard, "God has been reported on Spruce Street."

Service said, "Beg pardon, Cap'n?"

Grant looked up at him. "I didn't say anything."

Jesus, Service thought.

When he passed Fern LeBlanc's desk, she said, "Does he continue to insist it was a concussion?"

Service ignored her and continued on, but LeBlanc followed him and sailed a piece of paper on to his desk. "He gave this to me to type, just before you went in to see him."

The scribbles were unintelligible. Normally the captain wrote small in perfect penmanship, but this. . . .

"Did he mention God?" she asked.

"I thought I heard him say something about God and Spruce Street."

She nodded. "Yes, God has been reported on Spruce Street."

It was Service's turn to nod.

She said, "He told me the same thing, and when I questioned him he looked at me and said, "God can eat his desserts when he wants." LeBlanc glared at Service and left. His gut said he should do something, but he had no idea what. Was the captain's mind crashing?

A call from del Olmo interrupted his thinking.

"Kitella was released on bail the day before yesterday."

"Go see him, Simon. Find out where he was last night between four and midnight."

"What's going down?"

Service stared at the captain's scribbles, said, "Just fucking do it." And hung up.

LeBlanc reappeared, put another sheet of paper on his desk. Her eyes were teary and her hand was shaking. "I got this off the dictaphone tape he made early this morning."

Service read. "How's the cow? She walks, she talks, she's full of chalk. The lactine liquid extracted from the female of the bovine species is highly prolific to the nth degree. Go Army!"

"He shouted the last part, almost burst my eardrums," LeBlanc said.

Service said, "Come with me," led her down to the captain's office. The door was closed. He knocked once and walked in. The captain had a foot on his desk, the sock off. He was studying it through a magnifying glass. He looked up at Service, said, "If God inhabits our souls, he is in our toenails as well." He pulled his foot down and his tone changed. "What's the meaning of this? My door was *closed*."

Service put the two pages from LeBlanc on the captain's desk. The captain ignored them.

"Where are your keys, sir?"

The captain pointed at the corner of his desk. Service picked them up and handed them to LeBlanc. "Fern is driving you home, Captain."

The captain clutched his sock, held it against his chest, and looked confused. Service said, "If we can't go at one hundred percent, sir, the team suffers."

"Listen to him, Captain," Fern added.

The captain did not protest. Service walked beside him out to Fern's car, made sure he was buckled in, and watched them drive away, the captain staring straight ahead.

He went back to his cubicle and called Grant's doctor. "This is Detective Service. The captain is on his way home and he is not to come back here until he is ready. Concussion, my ass!" he added, slamming the phone down.

He was disgusted with himself and pissed at the captain's selfishness for putting him in this position. He had just turned on his computer to call up his e-mail when he heard a cough and looked up to see the captain standing just inside the cubicle.

"Writing utensil and paper," the captain said. He took a pen from Service, standing by the desk, and wrote, then handed the pad to Service. His handwriting was normal, flawless.

"It takes courage to do what's right," the captain said. "I never again want to hear that you lack management potential. Leadership is a burden few can endure and fewer are willing to do so. I will be in my office, Detective Service. Carry on."

Fern LeBlanc was standing behind the captain, smiling slyly. "Cash register," she said.

Service closed his gaping mouth. "What the hell is going on?"

"The captain is somewhat unorthodox in his methods," she said.

"I called his doctor."

"Exactly," she said, turning, swirling her skirt and disappearing.

He went directly to the captain's office and found him writing. Grant held up the pad of paper. "Do you wish to inspect?"

Service nodded, took it and scanned it. Normal, perfect. He handed it back.

"Excellent," the captain said. "Perfect. Good leadership: Assume nothing. Always follow up." He was smiling.

Service told LeBlanc he was going out. "Lunch," he said. Only when he got into the truck and pulled out onto US 41 toward town did he notice it was only 9 A.M.

30

Teddy Gates called on Service's cell phone. "I tried the office, but they said you'd gone to lunch. Lunch at *this* hour?" Gates asked with a chuckle.

"What is it?" Service shot back, still shaken over the captain's strange little performance.

"Oliver Toogood, Sarn't."

"He's a fake."

"On the contrary, he's very real and quite authentic. He receives a one hundred percent medical, which goes to a bank in a town called Ontonagon. He rarely draws on it and he has never made a deposit, the result being that he has accumulated a rather hefty nest egg."

"How can you get into bank records without a subpoena?"

"Work-around. It all depends on who you know," Gates said.

Trapper Jet was legit? "How can we be sure?"

"The bank has his fingerprints and they match the ones we have at DoD. I'm going to fax you some photos from his swearing in as an officer and another at the time of his release as a POW."

"When was the most recent withdrawal?" He was desperate for something.

"Three years ago."

If he was on the level, where the hell was he? "Thanks," Service said.

"Glad to be of assistance, Sarn't. You need any more help, you call."

"Yessir."

His mind drifted back to Cal Shall at the academy. The first day in investigations class Shall had given each student what he called a paint-by-number canvas. There were squiggles and geometric shapes all over it, but no numbers.

"What are you looking at? Please write your answer on the back of the board and pass it forward." Service still remembered what he saw. It was a message that said, "The obvious is only as clear as you allow it to be."

A second board was passed out. This showed the same black squiggles as the first one but this one had numbers in the shapes. "What are you seeing?" Shall asked. "Answers on the back, pass 'em forward."

A third board was the same as the second. Cadets were given blue and black crayons and told to use them to try to bring out a picture, write their answers on the back, pass them forward.

The fourth board was passed out, same as the last three, and an entire box of Crayolas was given to each cadet. "Color them in, write your answer on the back, pass it forward. You have ten minutes," the instructor said.

Not everybody finished their coloring, but Shall collected the boards and sent the cadets out for a break. "Back in fifteen minutes," he told them.

There was some laughing, but not much discussion of the exercise. Service thought it a foolish waste of time.

When they filed back into the classroom, they saw that Cal Shall had written on the blackboard:

LEVEL ONE: 1 of 30
LEVEL TWO: 2 of 30
LEVEL THREE: 5 of 30
LEVEL FOUR: 24 of 30

"Allow me to summarize," the instructor began. "Only one of you correctly visualized the unnumbered scenario. Only two decoded Level two. Five got the two-color work-up, which is excellent. Only three quarters of you got the full picture in color, though this particular result is related to individual working speeds. If you'd had enough time, you would all have gotten it," he said.

"Gentlemen, the first board is actually the second stage of most investigations. The initial situation consists of a crime and a few facts. Investigative techniques allow you to create level one, and from there you begin to ascertain how things relate and you assign them numbers, which equate to colors in level two. At this point you begin to try to relate the clusters, and often you do not have the full palette of evidence available, so your picture lacks full color and you are in level three. It is only at level four that full color enables you to easily decipher your situation. And it is from level four that the prosecutor will assemble the case for court." Shall looked at the clock on the wall. "Dismissed."

The instructor found Service outside and pulled him aside. "You were the one who got level one. Level one minds are rare; you'd better take care of and nurture your instincts and intuition."

"This is only an exercise."

"This exercise has predictive power. Looking back at scores of my students, I can see which ones were destined to become successful investigators."

"It's not realistic," Service said. "There are times when there are no shapes and the board is totally blank."

"You're mistaken, Cadet. There is always a starting point: a body, a theft, an accident, and so on. With each criminal event there is always the *fact* of the crime, and this becomes your point of embarkation. Even if you have nothing but suspicion—for example, in the case of a missing person—you have the person and the facts of their life. Do you understand?"

All of which brought him back to the present, staring at the seventy-five-foot-high Lake Superior and Ishpeming Railroad ore dock, where each week a couple of huge ships were filled with taconite pellets from the Tilden Mine.

He was back in his office at ten. A quick look at the fax from Teddy Gates confirmed that the Ollie Toogood he knew as Trapper Jet was indeed the officer being sworn in—and the released POW. What the hell was the story with the yearbook photo?

Wisconsin Warden Les Reynolds called while he was puzzling over the photograph.

"Thought you'd want to know, Mary Ellen Fahrenheit was killed in a vehicle accident last night."

"Really?"

"Thought you'd want to know because it happened up your way."

"It did?"

"M-35 at the Cedar River Bridge. She was southbound, lost control, went over the guardrail and into the river. A trucker behind her saw it happen, tried to pull her out, but failed. They had to call in a dive team. They recovered the body two, three hours after the accident."

Southbound? She had been a long way from home. "What time was this?"

"I think seven-thirty, eight P.M., your time."

"Where's the body now, Les?"

"Bay Area Med in Menominee. There'll have to be an autopsy. The roads were dry, she was thirty-nine and in good health. No reason for this."

Service looked at the map in his head. The next city north of Cedar River was Escanaba, then Gladstone, and she had been headed south. From where? Cal Shall's words came back to him: "The obvious is usually the right choice." Cedar River was thirty to forty minutes south of Escanaba and Gladstone. Mary Ellen Fahrenheit had taken up with Ficorelli as much for a payback to her husband as anything else, and when Service told her that her husband was in jail, she wanted to leave him there.

Could she have found Outi Ranta? He had done so, based on what Charlie Fahrenheit had told him. Mary Ellen seemed a determined woman — but to kill someone with a gun? His gut said no. This was not the sort of crime you attached to the average person, and even less often a woman.

He called Vince Vilardo at home and Rose said he was on the back deck, working on a report. She went to fetch him.

"Grady, I was gonna call you in a little while. Ranta was definitely a homicide."

"Have you got a time of death?"

"Temperature would indicate TOD sometime between six and seven P.M."

The time frame was more than intriguing. If Ranta died between six and seven, that could easily put Mary Ellen Fahrenheit around Cedar River at the time of the accident. "Do you know the M.E. in Menominee County, Vince?"

"Blaize Jenner. She's the only board-certified forensic pathologist in the U.P. right now."

"She the cooperative type?"

"Yeah, but I don't think you ought to be lookin' for a date."

"This is professional. There was a fatal accident near Cedar River last night, a woman named Mary Ellen Fahrenheit. The body is at Bay Area Med and there will be an autopsy." Service explained what he wanted.

"Blood tox is standard," Vince said incredulously, "why the heck do you want paraffin tests for a car wreck?"

"Please humor me, Vince. I'm in the middle of a convoluted case and I'm desperate to nail down anything."

"Desperate, eh? Okay, I'll do what I can. You at your office?"

He wanted to correct his friend and call the office his cell because every day he felt more and more like a prisoner.

Vince called back thirty minutes later. "Jenner will do it tomorrow, but she'll do the paraffin today and then let us know about the tox results when they come back. You coming over for supper soon?"

"Soon. Thanks, Vince."

Fern LeBlanc poked her head in his office. "The Secret Squirrels are outside."

The Secret Squirrels were Egon Spurse, the outdoor reporter for Marquette's Channel 22 ("For the latest Yooper Sports and News, Tune in The Double Deuce!"), and Mia "Midge" Private, who had an outdoor radio program at a small station in Munising. Private's station might be tiny, but her weekly thirty minutes of anti-DNR vitriol was syndicated by tape across the U.P. She called her show "Sporting Voices," but the only voice heard on the program was her own: angry, shrill, and filled with righteous indignation over "the gray-shirted Nazis who usurp our rights as Yoopers and Americans."

Spurse was a bit more restrained and attempted to cover various sports and goings on in the U.P., but every program carried at two- to three-minute "DNR Report Card," at the end of which he flashed a letter grade for the department for that week. The grade rarely got as high as C-minus.

The two often worked together and were known throughout U.P. law enforcement circles as the Secret Squirrels. Both were married—to other people—but had engaged in a not-so-secret years-long affair. The source of their well-known animus for the DNR stemmed from a time when Lisette McKower, prior to her promotion to sergeant, caught them in flagrante dilecto in a van parked by the Rock River in Alger County. Shortly thereafter, the rants against the DNR began, and every U.P. officer except one had at least once been the subject of their on-air scorn. The only exception was McKower.

Spurse was short and wide with a bushy red beard and always dressed in camo, which he strong-armed from various sporting goods stores in return for "editorial consideration." Mia Private was not quite five feet tall, and had abnormally large breasts she displayed to maximum effect in tight blouses. She was a tiny woman, which had given her the nickname of Midge (a very tiny insect), and she had long straight black hair and looked like an aging hippie. She also had a concealed weapons permit that had been granted because of numerous alleged death threats.

The two had room-temperature IQs, huge egos, and excessive ambition. Their audience was said to be largely comprised of the mullet-and-militia crowd, those locals across the peninsula who claimed to love their country and hate their government.

"The captain asks that you talk to them," LeBlanc said.

"Have they asked for someone?"

"Not yet. They're out by our sign."

"Crew?"

"One camera operator with Spurse. Midge has her recorder over her shoulder."

"Get me a tray with three cups, sugar, milk, and a jug of coffee. Is Romy working today?"

Romy van Essen was a Northern Michigan graduate student who worked as an intern with the wildlife biologists. She was in her late twenties and had worked several years as a TV reporter in Mt. Pleasant before deciding she needed a life of more substance, and returned to school in Marquette. She would go to Alaska-Fairbanks to start her Ph.D. in the fall. She was a great kid, and a friend of Nantz's. Though no longer in the TV biz, she carried a small video camera everywhere and shot footage of everything.

"Okay," Fern said, heading for the canteen.

Romy came to his office and looked in, "Wass'up?"

"The Secret Squirrels," he said. "Grab your camera."

Fern met him at the door with the tray of goodies, including a plate of Pecan Sandies. Romy came with her camera. "Just follow my lead," he said. "Make sure you keep pressing tight on Midge's face. She's got a lot of wrinkles and she covers them with enough makeup to ski on."

"Not to worry," Romy van Essen said.

Midge Private saw them coming and turned to face them. Spurse was talking at the camera pointed by his operator, a man with a port wine stain on the right side of his face.

Service held out the tray. "Coffee and cookies?" Romy van Essen pointed her camera and began to record. It made no sound.

"Bribes won't do you any good," Midge said.

"Sound level," Romy said.

"We thought you'd probably like a snack and a pick-me-up," Service said, raising his voice. He looked at Romy. "Sound okay?"

Romy said, "Perfect."

Service turned back to Private. "We call this hospitality, not a bribe."

Midge Private glared at Romy's camera.

"What the hell do you think *you're* doin'?"

"Recording for the record," Romy said politely. "To keep the record accurate. You shoot and edit your tape. We show ours in its entirety, let people see what we're seeing."

"Like the DNR has budget to buy air time," Midge Private shot back sarcastically.

"Not the DNR," Service said. "Outside donors."

Egon Spurse had finished his bit and turned to join them. "Hey, Service," Spurse said. "Thought your office was over ta Newberry."

"I moved."

"At citizen expense, no doubt," Midge Private said.

Spurse saw the tray, grabbed a handful of cookies and stuffed his mouth.

"What can we help you with?" Service asked Midge, who immediately thrust her microphone at him. "I have a source inside the DNR who has shown me a memorandum directing gray shirts to make life miserable for bear- and deer-baiters this fall."

Service smiled. "The baiting rules are designed to protect the herd," he explained. "When the animals congregate, they can pass bovine TB, and I'm sure you and your listeners are just as concerned about the threat of Chronic Wasting Disease coming across the state line fromWisconsin."

Romy stepped forward, her camera up.

"Get that outta my face!" Midge snapped.

"Camera off," Romy said. "I'm sorry, Ms. Private." Service saw a green light still illuminated on the side of the camera. "You've got something on your blouse," Romy said.

Midge stared down and began brushing herself. "Keep that camera off."

"Since the camera's off," Service said, "You and Igor ought to take a ride over to the Rock River. Our officers have come across some extremely interesting situations over there—you know, people who've gotten themselves into unusual positions."

Midge glared at him. "You egotistical asshole."

Egon Spurse said, "It's Egon, *not* Igor," and took more cookies.

"In fact," Service said, "you should talk to Lt. McKower about Rock River. She's got a great story to tell. Pictures, too."

"What about baiting?" Midge Private asked, trying to regain control, but the mention of pictures had clearly put her off balance.

"I believe in baiting," Service said. "As long as the rules are followed." He looked down at her. "By the way, are you carrying? You know the new CCW law requires you to declare yourself when you encounter a police officer."

"Do I look like I'm carrying?"

"I'm just following the rules," Service said.

"That's harassment," Private said. Her color was red and it was showing through the layers of pancake.

"Are you carrying?"

"You gonna strip-search me?"

"If we do that and discover you're carrying, you'll have a problem."

Midge Private grabbed Spurse's thick arm. "Let's go," she said. "*Nazi*," she said over her shoulder.

Spurse grabbed the rest of the cookies and stuffed them into his mouth as he waddled to catch up with her.

"She's a little touchy," Romy said as the van pulled away. "Does Lis really have pictures of them?"

"My lips are sealed. Your camera was on, right?"

"The whole time."

Romy handed the tape to him as they walked inside. Service went into the office kitchen, washed the cookie dish and set it aside to drain, threw away the paper cups, put the milk and sugar away, and set the plastic coffee urn on the break table.

The captain came in and dug through the Pecan Sandies bag on the counter. "What's their angle this time?"

"Baiting rules. She claims to have a Lansing directive."

"Undoubtedly she does," the captain said. "Is she going to blast us?"

"Not with what she got today," Service said.

Vince called a few minutes after five. "Paraffin was positive for nitrates, prelim tox results tomorrow," he said.

"Was a weapon recovered from the vehicle?"

"I don't know the answer to that."

"Tell your M.E. friend that Delta County will be in touch, and tell her thanks."

"Delta?"

"This is more than a simple accident."

Simon called a few minutes later. "I just pulled out of Kitella's. He was home all day yesterday. He's on vicodin and can hardly move."

"Witnesses?"

"His girlfriend and his daughter say they were with him the whole time. What's up?"

"Outi Ranta was shot last night in her home. Mary Ellen Fahrenheit was killed in a vehicle accident at Cedar River last night. I was at Ranta's. It first looked like a suicide, but it wasn't. There was a revolver and the paraffin was negative on both her hands. I just talked to Vince. The M.E. in Menominee got a paraffin positive on Fahrenheit."

"Geez," del Olmo said. "What more can I do to help?"

"Not sure yet. I'll call when I know something."

Service called undersheriff James Cambridge at the office. "James, it's Grady Service."

"Yes?"

"There was a fatal vehicle accident in Menominee County last night. The vick's name is Mary Ellen Fahrenheit. The M.E. down there is Dr. Blaize Jenner." He spelled the name for him. "Outi Ranta was involved with Fahrenheit's husband. The doctor did a paraffin test on Fahrenheit and it was positive. I don't know if there was a weapon in the vehicle.

"What's the DNR doing in County business?" the undersheriff challenged.

"We're not in your business," Service insisted. "I assisted a Wisconsin warden in arresting the vick's husband and his friend for illegally taking bears in Iron County. We interviewed the wife during the investigation and the warden called me to tell me about the accident. I asked Vince to ask the M.E. down there to do the tests—just in case. Outi Ranta admitted she was fooling around with Fahrenheit's husband."

"Paraffin doesn't confirm anything, and why the bloody hell didn't you tell me this before?"

"Do what you want with it, James. I'm just sharing what I know."

"Jenner, right?"

"The body's at Bay Med."

"Okay then," Cambridge said, hanging up without further comment.

"Okay then," Service said, putting the phone down. Cambridge was a crab and still bitter over having lost the most recent election for sheriff, but he was close to the end of his career and would be all over this in order to close the case and go out with a feather in his cap. Tonight he would get a photo from Menominee and deputies would be checking around Escanaba and Gladstone to see if anybody had seen Mary Ellen Fahrenheit or her vehicle. Chances were good the answer would be yes.

Why the hell hadn't the private detective from Grand Rapids called? He dialed her number, got her answering service, and asked for a callback as soon as possible, even if she had no results.

Having left the message his attention went back to the photo of Ollie Toogood. What was the deal with the yearbook?

· 31 ·

Nantz called when he was on his way home, but McCants came up on the 800 MHz at the same time. "Twenty-Five Fourteen, Forty-One Twenty-Eight."

Service said, "Stand by one, Mar," to Nantz, set the cell phone on the other seat, and picked up the mike for the 800. "Twenty-Five Fourteen."

"You remember that place where you and your friend had a picnic before she went off to Lansing last fall?" With so many police scanners in the public, officers were careful to disguise locations and destinations. They tended to use a code that referred to places only the other officer would know.

"I remember."

"I've got a situation," she said.

She was in the Mosquito and he felt an immediate surge of adrenaline. "Rolling," he said. Then to Nantz on the cell. "Did you catch that?"

"Your end," she said. "I'll call you tonight around midnight. Be careful, hon."

Service drove faster than the speed limit allowed, stopping briefly at a country store to refill two thermoses with coffee. Candi wouldn't have called unless she had something serious, and she was in the Mosquito, *his* Mosquito. And it was already dark.

Her truck was parked exactly where he and Nantz had found it last fall when they walked back from their afternoon visit to the Mosquito River.

McCants was sitting in her truck, smoking. He handed her a thermos.

"There is a God," she said with a smile as she took off the top of the thermos and filled it with coffee. "I've got a wounded bear and a dead hound. I found a couple of dirty baits two days ago and I was moving in to sit on them tonight. Two shots," she said, her words clipped. "I heard the dog, the shots, and then the bear came flying by me and veered south into the swamp." She pointed.

Service knew the swamp intimately. It was nearly twelve miles across to the next road and he had hiked it all over the years.

"The dog's in back," McCants said.

He went to look at it, cringed, and came back. "Beagle-Redbone mix?" Even dead the animal left him feeling uneasy.

She nodded, took a sip of coffee. "Grady, I got a good look at the bear. His lower jaw was gone. He left a big blood trail."

"Size?" he asked.

"Big," she said.

Shit, Service thought. A big wounded bear was not something officers liked to deal with.

"Just like you said, the action started to pick up over here. There's been five veeks in the area over the past three days, three North Carolina plates, one Tennessee, one Kentucky. Station 20 ran all the plates. No warrants."

Which didn't mean much. Some elements of the bear-hunting crowd were rough, competitive, and lawless, and those who came up from the South were among the worst. "Who has the baits?"

"Kentucky truck," she said. "It's owned by Lefton Valda, out of Bailey's Switch."

"Kennel?" Most of the hunters from the South were dog men.

"No. Classic dirty baits, hanging anise and some hummingbird juice, ground piles of gummy bears, waffle cones, stale donuts, chocolate-covered raisins."

"Spare no expense in the hunt for glory," Service said.

McCants patted his arm. "We don't want to leave a wounded animal out here."

Service agreed. "Did the shooters start tracking?"

"I don't know. They're east of us in the swamp. I just heard the shots. Their truck's parked just to the north of here. The blood trails are pretty easy to follow. The dog must've run some distance before it bled out."

"Somebody's gonna be pissed," Service said. Most serious bear hunters treated their best dogs better than people. "How do you want to play it?" he asked.

"I don't want to do any tracking with shooters still in the swamp."

"They should be out of the woods by now."

"Shoulda, coulda, woulda," she said, getting out of the truck.

There was a blood trail about a hundred yards below their trucks. Service looked at the blood and tracks, followed it to the edge of the cedars and went several paces inside, using his light. "Steady flow. Big animal, eh?"

"Biggest I've seen in a long time."

This was bad news. Big bears rarely climbed trees when pursued by dogs, preferring a running fight on the ground. "No dogs pushing it," he said. "It may lay down."

She said, "Let's deal with the shooters before we go looking."

They took her truck and circled around to where she had seen the Kentucky truck parked.

It wasn't unusual for hunters to drive up from the Appalachians to hunt Michigan bears. The laws in many of the southern mountain states forbade baits, and their often-mountainous terrain was imposing, with few roads. Here in the U.P. it was relatively flat with numerous dirt roads. The usual dog-hunting procedure was for hunters to drag dirt roads clean at night, then go back in the morning to check for crossing tracks. They would drive around with their best dog, the strike dog, sitting in a basket welded to the front bumper or grill and a kennel with another four or five dogs in the truck bed.

When the strike dog caught a scent, it would make a ruckus. The hunter would dismount, release the strike dog and the pack, and follow them on foot. Other hunters in the group would chase around on nearby roads guessing where the bear would cross and hoping for an intercept. Ultimately they'd try to get the dogs to tree the animal, then kill it at their leisure. In some ways it was like a small military operation, with trucks fishtailing and bouncing all over the back roads, the hunters all jacked up on adrenaline and sometimes on alcohol or more, and all of them with primitive eyes beamed in on the kill to come. The hunters communicated by CB or FRS radios and talked like a bunch of infantry wannabes.

He had encountered a few bear hunters in the Mosquito from time to time, but not many. The terrain harbored a sizeable population of animals, but it was wild and almost totally roadless, which made dog-hunting demanding. Owners valued their dogs too much to risk losing them in bad country. Mostly he had found baiters in the wilderness area.

The Kentucky truck was dark, its hood cold, no sign of the hunters.

"They should've been out thirty minutes ago," McCants said.

"Doubt they'll sit in there all night," Service said. Bear hunters were an odd breed, a blend of fearlessness and superstitions, coupled with some shining examples of pure stupidity.

"Their trail's clear as a highway," she said.

They walked up the trail in the dark, moving slowly and listening. When they got to a small rise that faded gently down to a cedar swamp, they stopped and squatted. Service heard his knees creak but ignored the sound. The weather was cooling, damp. There were pieces of bait along the trail and four beer cans, one of which McCants toed with her boot. "Wingnuts," she said, adding the can to others she had picked up.

"The river's about three hundred yards," he said, remembering the terrain like it was his own skin. Bears nearly always traveled in heavy cover and preferred creek- and riverbeds near swamps with access to hardwoods and mast crops.

Service wanted a cigarette but didn't light up. Smoke traveled in the forest and the ember could be seen in such darkness. The first skill of officers was the ability to remain invisible until they chose to appear magically.

"Good place to wait," McCants said.

He agreed and stretched, feeling achy. Stopping hunters at night always entailed risk, more if alcohol was involved. McCants showed good judgment in calling for help. If the department had the people they needed, somebody else would be here. Maybe this was a preview of the year ahead, he thought. With Nantz at the academy, how was he supposed to look after Walter? This was worrisome.

"Need more beer," a voice growled below them.

"Less be more," a second voice said. "You missed that sumbitch."

"Hell I did," the first man said.

Service could hear the sloshing of slush, probably in an ice chest. One of the men crumpled something, threw it in the grass, where it struck a rock or stick and pinged with a metallic sound.

When they were within ten yards, McCants stood up and said, "DNR, Conservation Officer, you fellas have any luck?" She didn't turn on her light.

The walkers stopped. One of them grumbled, "Law."

McCants turned on her light. "Any luck, guys?"

"Bejayzus," one of the men said.

Service stood and illuminated his own MAG-LITE. "You heard Officer McCants. Any luck?"

"Sheeit," one of the men said. "Me and Dermid heared you-un. Gut nuthin'. Fust tahm, come all ta way up here. Got more bars back ta home, I'd say."

"I'd like to see your licenses," McCants said.

The men grumbled, shuffled around. "Musta left 'em in ta rig."

"Mr. Valda?"

One of the men said, "How you-un be a-knowin' ma name?"

"Are you Mr. Valda, Mr. Lefton Valda?"

"I be."

"And you?" McCants said, swinging her light to the other man, who squinted and held his arm up to block the light. "Dermid Atbal. Gittin' thet light outten my face, womarn."

Service saw that the men wore jackets over full camo jumpsuits, no hunter orange. They each had hold of the end of a large ice chest. Their rifles were slung over their shoulders, barrels down.

"Handguns?" Service asked.

"Huntin' bar, fool," the one called Atbal said. "Cain't a-swing a long-gun own a bar in ta blind, kinya now?" The man lifted his arm and Service saw a shoulder holster.

The other man said, "Under ta coat."

"Handguns loaded?" McCants asked.

"Not much good they ain't," the one called Atbal said.

"Rifles loaded?" McCants asked.

"Same ting," the man said. "You-uns walk aroun' with unloaded pieces?"

Service said, "Put the ice chest down," and stepped forward, keeping his light on Atbal. Both men had jumpy voices, the kind of nerves on the surface that he'd learned over the years to treat with extreme caution.

McCants moved up at the same time, keeping her light on the other man.

"Okay, gentlemen," Service said, "Unsling your rifles and place them on the ground. Then take a step back and remove your coats."

"I speck we kin unload 'em," Valda said.

"On the ground," McCants said firmly, reinforcing Service.

Service picked up Valda's rifle, kept his light on the two men while McCants shone her light at the rifle in his hands. The safety was off, clip in. He clicked the safety on, popped the clip, checked the chamber. There was a round in it, which he extracted carefully, letting the bullet fall to the ground.

He set the rifle down and repeated the process with the second weapon, same result.

"Okay," he said with a steady voice. "I'm going to unholster your handguns."

Both men carried .44 Mag revolvers with six-inch barrels. Both weapons were loaded and had a round in the chamber. He popped the cylinders and dumped the bullets, quickly scraping them up and putting the ammo in his pocket. He collected all four weapons and flashed his light around until he found the can they had thrown away. He told Atbal to fetch it and carry it out.

McCants said, "Okay, guys, grab the ice chest and let's go back to your truck and talk about things."

"What about our guns?" Valda asked. "We paid cash money. Ain't cheap."

"We'll talk about that," McCants said.

The men moved slowly, water and the crumpled cans sloshing in the cooler, both of them complaining about the other man's gait.

From the trail that ran between large sumac clusters, Service saw that more trucks had pulled into the area. He saw trucks, no people. There was no moon, no stars. Clouds had moved in, threatening rain, and he could feel the humidity.

A voice called out, "Which of yas shot ma Winston."

"I'm Officer McCants, DNR," Candi said. "Who is Winston?"

"Winston be my strahck dawg what's a-stretched out day-id in ta back thet rig," the voice said. It sounded to Service like the man was emotionally between grief and blowing up. Service heard clothes rustling. Something scraped the side of a truck _____.

"No good, shot ma strahck dawg," the voice said. "Somebody gone pay, thet's fact."

McCants said, "Everybody out where we can see you," she said, pointing her light ahead.

"She Injun?" a voice asked.

"Cain't you be a-seein', she's gook?" another voice challenged.

"You got weapons?" Service asked. The situation was feeling increasingly uncomfortable.

"We plan to far 'em we halfta, donchu know," the original voice said.

McCants said, "We'll find out what happened to your dog. Everybody just *chill*."

Service counted five men, ponytails, full beards, camo shirts and muddy pants, faded orange vests and hats.

They all had slung rifles.

"Place your weapons on the ground and step back from them," he said, trying to make it sound like a neighborly suggestion.

"Damn fine gook womarn," one of the voices said.

"Weapons on the ground," Service repeated, this time not trying to impart anything other than precisely what he wanted. "*Now*."

"Okay, boys, you-uns don't be peartin' off. These-uns is the law," the first voice said.

Too many people for two officers to handle, Service thought. Way too many.

The men put their rifles on the ground.

One of them complained, "I just done cleaned hit."

"Handguns?" Service asked.

"In ta trucks," the first man said. After his initial challenge he was sounding calmer, and like the leader. Service said, "Hold up your coats."

The men did as they were told. McCants had reached her truck. Service went over and put the first two men's weapons on the passenger seat and turned to the weapons on the ground. None were loaded, but he put them in the truck anyway. McCants was on the driver's side, reached in and picked up a mike. "Delta County, DNR Forty-One Twenty-Eight is requesting backup. Code Two." This meant urgent, but no lights or sirens. She gave the location and hung up the mike. "Twenty minutes," the dispatcher said. McCants turned on the truck's headlights and blue flashers before she got out, and left her door standing open.

The huge size and geography of the Mosquito was such that police agencies from any of four counties might respond. A voice on the radio chirped, "ETA, five mikes." Service recognized the voice and the call sign. It was Linsenman from Marquette County.

McCants said, "Everybody stay calm."

Service felt edgy, glad backup was close.

Dogs started barking in one of the trucks, and a man said, "I'll fetch 'em some water, Eulik."

"Never mind water." Service said. All they needed was for dogs to get released in this and they would have total chaos.

"They's a-callin' for water," the first man said, adding, "Who shot my dawg?"

"Eulik?" Service said.

"That be me, Eulik T. Somcoc."

McCants said, "Okay, Mr. Somcoc, let's just relax so we can do our jobs."

"I be waitin'," the man said.

"Yankee justice," one of the men near Somcoc groused quietly.

McCants said to the first two hunters, "Okay, let's see your licenses." She followed the two men over to their truck. Valda leaned in, moved and tossed things around, cursing under his breath. He went on for two or three minutes, then straightened up. "I speck they be back ta camp."

"Mind if I look?" Candi asked.

"I done looked," the man said, standing his ground.

Service looked at Atbal. "You got something to hide in there?"

"Hay-il no. Ain't ma truck, is all."

"Mr. Valda," McCants said.

"They in camp," Valda insisted.

She looked at Atbal. "Sir, I can smell alcohol on your breath. You were in the woods with loaded weapons after legal shooting hours, no hunter orange, no licenses, littering. It's just gonna keep piling up. A little cooperation will go a long way here."

Valda said, "Ain't mine. Belongs ta Dermid."

"May I look inside?"

Valda stepped aside. McCants pawed around under the seats, found a one-gallon freezer bag, lifted it out, held it up for Service to see, and held it up for Valda. "A little weed—as in half a pound?"

"Done said ain't mine," he said. "Talk at Dermid." He added, "Tole you don't be smokin' that shit!"

"Best you-un be a-shuttin' thet mout," Atbal said.

"Okay," Service said. "Mr. Valda, please join Mr. Atbal and have a seat."

"Ground's cold, maht rain any minute, I speck," Atbal said.

"Bear hunters are tough," Service said.

When neither man moved, Service said, "Put your ass in the grass, *now!*"

The two men did as they were ordered. Service looked at his watch, said to McCants, "Fifteen." The law required a fifteen-minute observation period before sobriety tests could be administered. Usually this applied to the testing that went on at the station after the preliminary evaluation in the field, but Service had always followed the rule, wherever he was, and years before, he had taught McCants to do the same.

"*Capisce*," she said.

They heard Linsenman coming down the road, bottoming out as he raced along. His vehicle needed a new muffler.

His patrol car jerked to a stop and aimed its headlights from behind the second group of men. Linsenman got out and stood by his patrol car with his door open to shield him. "You want me over there?"

"You're good to go right there," McCants said. "Thanks."

Now that they had everyone lit, Service began to relax.

"We busted?" Valda asked.

"Sir, it's illegal to possess drugs," McCants said.

"Din't possess nothin', the man said. "Was thet nitwit dere who done hit."

"Who shot the dog?" McCants asked.

"Weren't no dawg ta be shet at," Atbal said.

"Was a she-bar an' cub," Valda said. "Sumbitch missed 'em both."

"Din't miss," Atbal said.

"Did you shoot at both of them?" McCants asked.

"Hit 'em both, d'ya know."

"You shot at a cub?" One of the men from the second group asked, his voice strained.

"Make no sense ta pop mama bar, leave thet babe all to itseff," Atbal said in his own defense.

Valda nodded agreement.

"You shot after dark," McCants said.

"Did not," Atbal said immediately. "'I'was still shootin' light.'"

Service refrained from rolling his eyes.

"What took you so long to come out?" McCants asked.

"Din't want no wounded bar a-jumpin' us," Atbal said.

"Weren't no wounded bar," Valda said.

"Was," Atbal insisted.

After fifteen minutes, McCants got her preliminary breathalyzer test kit out of the truck and stepped over to Valda.

"Stand up," she said.

"Thet a lie detectin' thang?"

"No, sir. Please hold your hands out level with your shoulders, then touch your nose with your left index finger."

He did as he was told, the finger striking above his left eye. "Okay, other hand."

Same result. "Sir, I want you to walk forward *exactly* nine steps, heel to toe, turn on one foot and return to me; do you understand?"

As often happened with people who were high, Valda started walking before she finished the instructions, stumbled, went down to one knee, tried to get up, and fell on his side.

McCants let him get up on his own. She held a penlight in front of his eyes and moved it slowly from right to left.

"Give me a number between nineteen and twenty-one," she said.

"Twinny-two," he said.

Service cringed.

"Okay, sir. Take a seat."

She repeated the same tests with Atbal, who did better on the walk-and-turn, but had the same impairments in the HGN test. Horizontal Gaze Nystagmus tested the subject's ability to track a moving object. Neither man had passed.

McCants removed the PBT device from its carrying case and took out a plasticized card and read Atbal his test rights under the Michigan statute. "You do not have to take this test," she said after she had finished reading the card, "but you will have to take a test when you get to the station. That's the law."

Valda said, "Din't have thet much ta drink."

"How many?" McCants asked.

"Four cans."

She didn't hide her irritation. "There were four cans on the trail and one of you dumped another one on the way out."

"Each," Valda said. "What's ta trouble? We wunt drivin'."

McCants looked in the bed of their truck, saw two empty twelve-packs.

"How long were you in your blind?" she asked.

"Since ta sun got own high," Valda said.

"You weren't here at two and I saw your truck at four."

Valda shrugged. "Four each is all we had, swear to God. I ain't takin' no test."

"Me neither either," Atbal said. "If we ain't gotta, we ain't gonna."

"This is only a preliminary breath test—a PBT," McCants said. "There will be another one at the station."

"We wunt drivin'," Valda said. "Why we gettin' took ofe ta jail?"

McCants got out her Miranda card and read the men their rights. The onlookers were all listening intently and quietly. When she finished, she said, "Here's what we have: hunting while impaired, no orange, no licenses, littering, carrying loaded weapons after dark, shooting while impaired."

"You-un ain't sayed nothin' 'bout ma dawg a-bein' kilt," Eulik Somcoc said from the group between Linsenman and the two conservation officers.

McCants said, "We're going to take care of it, sir."

"Best you do," Somcoc said. "Winston a-been with me onta five year."

The dogs in the truck kennel started barking again. McCants said, "Go ahead and give them a drink, but don't let them out."

She looked back at Valda. "Anything you say can be used against you in court. I suggest you say nothing more until you talk to a lawyer."

"Where we get a lawyer up here, you-un?"

"Sir, the state will take care of that for you." She read Atbal his rights as well, then asked each man to sign a form verifying that they had read and understood them.

Two Delta County deputies had arrived; the whole area was illuminated now. Above them lightning was flashing inside the cloud cover, turning the night sky a ghastly yellow.

"Deputies," McCants said.

The two Delta deputies came forward. McCants put one-time cuffs on each man and the four officers took the prisoners to the patrol cars and put them in the backseats. She gave the deputies the weapons and drugs and had them sign evidence custody cards. One of the deputies looked at the bag of dope and grinned, "Chocolate Thai make an elephant fly." They drove away silently with flashing lights.

McCants took off her hat, ran her hand through her hair, and turned to the group. "We need to look at your licenses, boys."

Eulik T. Somcoc said, "I want thet dawg a-mine."

The licenses were all in order.

"I'm sorry. I can't let you have your dog yet," McCants said. "Your dog is evidence. Where's your camp? Soon as we're finished, I'll bring him to you."

"Ain't right," Somcoc said. He told her where their camp was. "How long you be? We expected down home next week."

"Sir, do you want this taken care of or not?"

"I surely do."

"We'll get Winston back to your camp as soon as we finish with him."

"We be leavin' Thursday."

"Okay, your licenses are good. Why don't you and your friends head for your camp."

Service and McCants watched the trucks drive away.

Linsenman came forward. "You want coffee?" Service asked.

"Works for me. Man, that was some dicey shit. That bunch looked like they'd creep out the squeal-like-a-pig crowd," Linsenman said.

McCants said. "We need to go find their blind, pick up cans."

Service nodded.

"Thanks for coming," McCants told Linsenman as he poured coffee from her thermos into his travel mug.

As soon as Linsenman left, the two COs got a plastic trash bag, hiked back to the swamp, found the hunters' blind, and recovered twenty-three empty cans. The overarching canopy kept most of the rain from penetrating, but Service said, "If it turns into a downpour, we could lose the blood trail."

They got back to his truck at 10:30 P.M., and McCants grabbed her poncho and her rifle case.

"What're you doing?" he asked.

"Rain. We need to track that bear."

He looked at her. "I've been thinking. If he keeps going it could take us hours to find him, and if we lose the blood trail, he's gone. Better to wait for daylight. There's nobody around for him to blunder into."

He saw skepticism in her eyes. "Grady Service using discretion," she said. "Meet you here at sunrise?"

"Okay," he said.

When she was gone, he got his rifle out of its case and walked down into the cedars and began tracking alone, his natural state, nobody to worry about but himself.

It was raining steadily in small cool droplets, but the canopy captured most of it and would keep doing so until the foliage was completely saturated. Only then would the rain penetrate, and it would be like standing under a waterfall. For now the ground was damp but not soaked, and the blood trail still reflected black under the beam of his light.

The trail remained obvious all the way to the river. As wounded deer often fled to water, so too did bears, and this one had come south in a straight line, never veering. Thunder rattled like snare drums in the northwest, rolling steadily. Not close, he told himself. Even the lightning had little effect, creating muted pale green flashes through the gaps in the canopy.

As he tracked he tried to stay focused, but he was tired and his mind was jumping around. They needed the animal to recover the bullet, assuming it was still in it. If he didn't find the bear tonight, the coyotes or wolves would tear it apart. It had to be tonight, he kept telling himself, and suddenly he was at the river's edge, his head down. He had to lean back to keep from walking into the shallows and cobble bottom. Break, he told himself. He poured a couple of fingers of coffee in his thermos top, swallowed it, and felt the plume of warmth bottom out. He put the thermos back in his pack and stood up, aiming his light across the river, trying to pick up blood on the other side—but the rain had soaked the rocks along the river and it was impossible to determine blood without fording across.

He wanted a smoke, but a cigarette here would quickly disintegrate. Focus, he said over and over. Retrace your steps, shit-for-brains. He had come to the river. No . . . he had suddenly arrived at the river. En route, he had reached a spot where if he stayed directly on the trail he would have to crawl over a blow-down, or scramble over upturned roots and relocate the trail. The bear had not once deviated from its course, so he had veered right by two or three steps, then cut back and found himself at the river's edge, too tired to think, cold and wet. His teeth began to chatter and he willed them to stop, but knew in time the cold would have its own way.

He left the river and went back to find the obstacle he had skirted, stood there, aimed his light two or three feet out, and turned slowly like a radar beacon, totally focused on the beam against the littered ground. On his second revolution, he extended the light beam to five feet, but there was nothing. The animal had come straight to the river and ten feet from the shore had disappeared.

A coyote barked to his west and was answered by another, their voices trailing off into whines that suggested their noses had something. If the bear was dead they would eventually tear it apart. Maybe not tonight, but soon. He was tempted to cross the river, to keep moving, but when you tracked you didn't move on until you had sign that told you where the animal had moved. He pulled the light into two feet, narrowed the beam and started again.

Only a bobbing light to the north broke his concentration. It was coming down the blood trail, clambering over the same obstacles he had crossed. He turned his light off, squatted. Raindrops bounced from the canopy to things below, beating a heavy tattoo. The bobbing light came forward, all sounds absorbed by the damp ground and unrelenting patter of raindrops. Thunder overhead exploded with a sharp clap that left the air sizzling with ammonia.

"Fuck!" a voice bellowed.

It was McCants. He turned on his light. "Here."

"Grady?" she asked.

"Me."

"Asshole," she said. " 'Wait till *tomorrow*,' the man says." There was no anger in her voice.

"No sense both of us drowning."

"Bullshit," she said. "You'd think a father would think about somebody other than numero uno."

"Spur of the moment," he said, knowing this was not true and that she knew it too.

"Right," she said. "The trail was pretty clear all the way in."

"It stopped here," he said, explained what had happened, how he had let his attention lapse.

"Okay," she said. "Let's both offset to the left and work our way east. If we come up empty, we'll come back here and try the west side."

She got into position without asking his approval. He watched her set herself fifteen feet to the east of him, turn on her light, start turning slowly. He moved five feet off the blood trail, did what she did. The rain continued to fall, the thunder back in the distance, some of it crackling like a pine fire.

"Here," McCants said. The rain was picking up and he could barely hear her.

"Drops," she said, pointing her light down.

The animal had cut due east, paralleling the bank.

"I've got it," she said.

He followed, making sure to stay two paces off her steps to avoid fouling anything they had missed.

"Here," McCants said. "Pretty heavy splash. I think it's close."

He eased toward her, watched her bend over with her light, studying the ground. "The river's right there," she said, "maybe four feet in front of me." He could hear the water flowing over the rocks, rain peppering it. Her light suddenly turned back toward him and her rifle jerked up. He ducked and looked over his shoulder. They had passed another upturned cedar. The animal was slouched over the lip, its hind legs facing them. Its fur glistened in the light beam, shining deep black, looking ratty from the rain tendrils of steam rising off the body. Not down that long, he told himself, putting his light beam on it. No movement.

He reversed around the upturned roots, pointed his light. The animal's head was over the edge, staring down. He picked up a stick, touched its eyes, got no response, exhaled. "Candi."

He waited for her to join him, lit up, didn't care if the rain destroyed it.

She looked at the bear's head. "Youch," she said.

"Big," just like she said, the word an understatement. This was a five-hundred-pound animal, huge for a U.P. black bear.

He put his light beam on the head, on the lower jaw, which hung down.

"Not hit there," he said. "No blood. Could be congenital or from a fight."

"How in God's name did it live with half a bottom jaw?"

"Same way we would," he said, "No choice, but do what you gotta do."

He had never seen a deformity quite like it, but black bears were the ultimate omnivores, eating everything and anything; vegetable matter, larvae, insects, fruits, and nuts. Rarely did they hunt other creatures. Whatever its limitations, this guy had found a way to get what he needed. Service dug in his pack, got out a Leatherman tool and a small knife and pried out a molar he could pass to the area biologist to age the animal.

McCants slid into the crater made by the roots of the cedar. He saw her light on the other side. "Looks like two entry wounds," she said. "Let's get it down, do what we have to do."

Her heard her grunting. "Are you gonna help?"

He pushed on the head, but one of the legs was slung over the top and the animal was hung up. He used a knee to get up on a thick root, pushed, slipped, fell in the slick mud below him. He crawled around to McCants. "It's stuck up there. We need leverage."

She stared at the animal for a moment, thinking, then said, "It crawled up there for a reason."

"Last legs," he said. "He was ready to defend."

"All that time with those hunters turned out to be a good thing," she said.

"Just how it worked out," he said. "Don't be groping for divine signs."

They located a small log, about six feet long with a four-inch diameter. Service hoped it wasn't dry, climbed up the side of the roots, planted the bottom of the limb under the animal's wedged shoulder, and heaved upward.

"Any movement?" McCants asked.

"Shit," was all he said. He pushed harder, lifted more, moved his foot, braced to get a better grip, and heaved. The harder he pushed, the more he felt his traction giving way, until he lost it completely and suddenly bounced off some roots and slid down into the crater. The bear flopped awkwardly and came to rest against him.

McCants held out her hand to help him up. "Born engineer," she said.

He looked at the smelly animal and said, "Use a toothbrush."

He wiped rain from his eyes with the back of his muddy hand, grabbed the bear's front paw and jerked, but the animal moved only slightly.

McCants grabbed the other paw in her hands and pulled until the body shifted.

Service sat in the muddy crater, rain soaking him, running down his neck. "Check it," he said. He was getting tired and cold.

She got on her knees on the bear's other side, said, "One entry." Then, "Two."

He breathed relief.

"We should get a four-wheeler," she said, "haul it out, dig out what we need in the open."

"Let's just do it," he said, "I'll gut it. Help me get it on its side."

He tugged on his gloves, got his knife from his pack, made an incision at the neck, slid two fingers into either side of the opening and cut steadily down the animal's belly to its genitals, where he made a cut to the right and another to the left. Making the first incision was simple, but warm air rolled out into the rain and the fetid smell of blood and broken organs enveloped him.

He reached into the bear's neck cavity, up to his shoulders, severed the wind pipe, put the knife aside, reached in with both hands and ripped down on the viscera, tearing them loose en masse until there was a slippery, steaming heap at the bottom of the animal. He shined his light into the rib cavity and saw immediately where one bullet had penetrated.

"One got through," he said. He knelt and used his knife to separate the organs, found the heart, intact, and examined the lungs. Nothing. He looked at the stomach, found it badly broken. "Gut shot," he said, making a face. He pawed around until he found the gall, cut it out and handed it to McCants. "Evidence bag," he said.

She gave him a questioning look, but bagged the organ and turned to her own work. "The second round is higher," she said. She took out her knife and started probing through the hide on the other side of the carcass while he checked the other side of the rib cage. The bullet that hit the stomach had not gone through into the other side. McCants said, "Got it! Low neck by the shoulder." She held up the bullet, "Pancaked."

"The other one's got to be somewhere in this slop," he said. "Toss me a couple of trash bags from my pack."

She threw them to him and he stuffed one inside the other, then opened the double bag and began piling viscera into it. When the body cavity was clear he rubbed his hands around the bottom, which acted like a reservoir, illuminated the interior with his light, looked for a bullet, found nothing. She gave him a small hatchet from her pack and he hacked through the pelvic bones, began scooping pooled blood out of the reservoir like he was paddling. When it was as empty as it was going to get, he raked slowly through the liquid with his fingers several times, felt nothing.

"Are those bags going to hold?" McCants asked.

He said, "Go back to your truck, grab one of my canvas tarps and more trash bags, back your truck down to the swamp edge. We can work better out there." He handed her the spare keys to his Yukon.

"I'll be quick," she said.

He cut a stout stick, wrapped the end of the plastic bag around it, fixed the handle with duct tape from his pack, tested it. Hefty but moveable. The guts weighed close to a hundred pounds, more with the rainwater that had gotten in. He put on his pack, lifted the handle toward his chest with both hands, and started the haul, centering the load between his feet, bending his knees, lifting and sliding sideways six to twelve inches at a time. Lift, move, stop. Lift, move, stop. His broken finger was throbbing, his bloody, sopped glove slipping on the handle. He had to stop frequently to wiggle his fingers and bend his wrists to release cramps.

McCants met him halfway to the clearing. He was kneeling, legs splayed, the bag between them, rain pecking relentlessly at the plastic.

"Tarp and bags," she said, holding them out to him.

She helped him jam the original bags and contents into the new ones. They pulled the bags onto the canvas tarp and used duct tape to reattach the handle, looping twisted tape through a couple of metal grommets.

"Side by side?" McCants asked.

"I'll drag, you push," he said. "You'll probably have to straddle it."

"Ah, face to face," she said, "and me on top—my favorite." She began to laugh.

"Get serious," he said.

"It's always serious when I'm on top," she said, laughing harder, and soon they were both laughing, neither of them sure why, neither of them caring.

They had not moved from where she had found him when his cell phone buzzed. He tried to reach into his coat, but dropped the phone.

McCants picked it up from the mud. "McCants," she said. "He's right here." She handed him the phone.

"What the hell is going on?" Nantz asked. "Candi can hardly talk."

"We're in the Mosquito."

"Still?"

"Bear hunters," he said.

"You're breathing like—"

"Working," he said, cutting her short.

"Let me talk to Candi."

He handed the phone back to McCants.

She said, "He's tired, Mar," added, "count on it."

McCants put the phone in her own pocket. "She said I should keep an eye on you."

He got to his feet, started pulling on the tarp. "Let's do it."

"No foreplay?"

"Shut up, Candi."

It took close to thirty minutes to drag the remains into the open field beyond the cedar swamp. McCants reached inside her truck and turned on her lights, including the spotlight on the driver's side. The rain continued to fall, varying in intensity, but never stopping as he knelt in the grass and mud, reached into the plastic bags, and began searching for the second bullet.

McCants filled a cup with coffee for him and held it out. He stopped working, took the cup and sipped.

"Some nights, it's just not a pretty job," she said.

They drove their trucks to Guilfoyle's near Cornell, which was across a road from the Escanaba River. Guilfoyle's was one of those Upper Peninsula taverns that kept its original name and decor while it went through revolving owners. The current proprietor was D. J. Reardon, a retired tool company executive from Wisconsin. He had owned the place going on seven years, and welcomed cops of all flavors. There were fewer vehicles in the gravel parking lot than usual, but it was a weeknight and the rain continued to come down.

Their work done, Service and McCants had checked off duty with Station 20 and gone looking for hot food. It was late, but Reardon played loose with last call, especially for cops coming off patrol.

The juke was low. Two men were watching a TV on a pedestal above the bar. Riordan's wife, Susie, was holding down the cash register.

The conservation officers sat at a table, stripped down to their soft armor vests. "We reek," Candi said.

Riordan's wife came over to the table. "Kitchen's closed but I can whip up grilled cheese."

"Thanks, lots of pickles on the side," Service said.

"There are some Troops in the back room," Susie said with a smirk. "Poker night with D. J. and open to all badges. But by the look and smell, you two already had way too much fun tonight."

The sandwiches came within fifteen minutes and they ate in silence. "You ever sleep in your truck?" McCants asked.

"Too many times."

"Bear hunters," she said, shaking her head. "I may sleep in my bathtub tonight."

"You could drown."

"That would be a *bad* thing?"

"Only the paperwork afterwards."

She grinned. "Thanks for being there tonight."

He flexed his injured hand. "You'd do it for me."

"Sooner or later, more and more people are going to discover the Mosquito," she said. "It's inevitable, Grady."

He nodded, knowing she was right, but he was not in the frame of mind to talk philosophically tonight.

"We should have gotten a four-wheeler, hauled the animal out and taken it to town for an X ray, then pulled the slug," she said. "But you didn't want anybody to see the size of the animal, and know it came out of the Mosquito."

"I stand moot before the court," he said.

"It's mute."

"It was a pun," he countered, knowing that a rotting carcass in the Mosquito was not likely to be discovered. If seen in town, word would spread wide and fast.

McCants lifted her arm and sniffed. "Eau de *ursus*. I may need an acid bath."

They collected their gear after eating, left some cash on the table, and walked out to their trucks.

"I'm going to put the dog in the evidence locker tonight, extract the slug tomorrow."

McCants opened her cooler and took out an evidence bag. "What do I do with this?" she asked, holding up the gall in the plastic bag.

"Put it in the freezer. We might use it for a buy sometime down the road."

"Always thinking," she said.

Not long thereafter he was in his old cabin, taking in how barren it was. He peeled off his bloody, muddy clothes and dropped them in a heap. He grabbed a blanket and stretched out on the footlockers that for so many years had served as his bed. He no longer lived in the cabin, but kept it maintained year-round. A thin cushion served as the mattress, and tonight he could feel the hardness of the footlockers pressing against him, but he was tired and set his wristwatch alarm for 7 A.M. Discomfort was part of the job, always had been, always would be. It was fine to sit in an office talking on the phone and looking at a computer, but discomfort and pain told you that you were doing something real. Tonight he felt like he had done real work and he went to sleep almost immediately.

He awoke to the buzz of his watch alarm, heard and felt his knees and shoulder pop when he got off the footlockers and went into the shower, which was built against the wall on the ground floor in the main living area. The upper floor of the cabin remained unfinished. He stood in the shower under scalding water, watched his skin turn red. When he finished rinsing off the soap, he grabbed a towel he'd slung over the shower wall and stepped out, drying his hair.

"Geez-oh-pete, youse shoulda done that last time we talked, hey."

He pulled the towel from his eyes and saw Honeypat holding up his blood-drenched pants and smiling. She was wearing cutoffs, and a charcoal gray tank top. Her hair stuck out at angles and badly needed combing. She wore ankle-high hiking boots that had seen a lot of use. She was dressed but looking more like the Honeypat of old.

His nose told him that coffee was brewing. He glanced over at the pot.

Honeypat said, "It's stale, but what the hey. Good to start the day with a jolt. I seen youse at Guilfoyle's last night."

He had not seen her.

She made a face and dropped his clothes on the floor. "I like a man isn't afraid ta get bloody," she said with a lecherous smile.

"You saw me last night?"

"With McCants. But I'm gettin' me a better look here, hey."

"What do you want, Honeypat?"

She winked at him. "What I need youse ain't gonna give up, so I'm tellin' youse, word's goin' 'round some tootsie from Wisconsin killed Outi."

"The radio said it was a suicide."

"Youse were at da house, you seen her. Don't it strike you a bit odd, a woman killin' another woman just 'cause she give it up?"

Had she been watching his cabin? "I expect you have a theory."

"What I know is ain't many women gonna drive that far and use a pistol in cold blood. In ta heat, sure—pow. But cold blood?" She grimaced and shook her head.

"What do you care?"

"She was my friend and it worries me that maybe Limpy learned about us."

Service considered confronting her with what Outi had told him, but held back to hear what else she would say.

Honeypat walked over to the coffeepot, blew dust out of a couple of mugs, filled one of them, brought it to him, held it out.

When he took the cup her other hand shot under the towel and pressed firmly between his legs.

"Oh, what I could do with that guy!" she said.

He tried to turn away, but she pivoted with him, kneading and laughing until he twisted away, spilling some of the coffee on the floor.

"You broke into my cabin."

"Door was unlocked," she countered.

Probably true. He rarely locked it. "Get out," he said.

She pursed her lips, shook her head, and walked toward the door where she stopped and looked back at him. "Youse don't use that guy, youse could lose him. That's medical fact."

"Thank you, Doctor," he said, following her. "I thought you were on the run from Limpy."

"No way the old bastard's findin' me now. I been with him too long, know all his ways."

He watched her get in the gray Honda and drive away. The license plate was missing.

He went to his truck, called all channels, asked for a BOLO on the plateless Honda knew it was a waste of breath. She'd not be found, but it was worth the off chance of hassling her.

There was nothing to eat in the cabin. He dressed in fresh clothes he kept in the Yukon and told himself he had to get home to Gladstone. Home: The word made him smile. The cabin no longer felt familiar. It was the skeletal remains of a former life he had no desire to return to. Home was Gladstone. Walter? No time to think about the boy now.

Newf pouted when he let her out of her run. No sign of Cat again. He threw his dirty clothes in the washer.

What did Honeypat mean, she'd been with Limpy too long, knew all his ways? Did she believe she could outthink and outmaneuver him? Was she telling him she saw Limpy go into the house, that he had killed Outi? He doubted that. Limpy was a lowlife, but he wasn't a killer.

He and Newf drove into Escanaba and parked in the lot facing Little Bay de Noc and went inside to the sheriff's office.

Undersheriff James Cambridge was at his desk.

"Don't think I like the look on your puss," the undersheriff said.

"I've been thinking about Outi Ranta."

"That case is all but closed."

"Do we know if Outi Ranta knew Mary Ellen Fahrenheit?"

Cambridge said, "There was no sign of a struggle."

"What if Outi didn't know she was there? We don't know that Outi even knew the woman, so why would she let her in?"

"What the hell are you getting at now?"

"I don't know," Service said. "I'm just thinking out loud."

The undersheriff followed him outside and grabbed his arm. "Fahrenheit was positive for nitrates, her blood full of alcohol, too much to drive without killing herself."

"What if somebody gave her to us?" Service asked. He had just connected some dots that left him feeling very uneasy. "James, have you requested Outi's home phone records?"

"Why would I?"

"Find out who she called, who called her."

"Seems like a waste of time and energy—and budget," he added. "Counties don't have the budgets, thanks to Clearcut."

"What if Fahrenheit was set up?"

"That's a reach at best."

"So is a woman driving this far to shoot another woman in cold blood."

"It happens," Cambridge said. "We don't need you to go complicating this on me."

"I'm not trying to complicate it. It just seems a bit strange. I'm thinking maybe there's something in the phone records to put our minds at ease."

"Like a call from Fahrenheit?"

"That would suggest they had at least talked."

Cambridge considered what he had heard. "I guess that's reasonable. I'll talk to the prosecutor today. It'll take a couple of days to get phone records."

"Just as long as you see them," Service said.

Service sat in his truck, thinking. Outi insisted Honeypat had engineered everything. Charley Fahrenheit had dealt only with Outi. Colliver had dealt with an old man Fahrenheit never saw or met. What was Honeypat trying to accomplish?

Follow the greed, Cal Shall had told them long ago· wanting something you didn't have, or more of what you did. Kitella, Colliver, and Fahrenheit were all linked by bear hunting. Kitella had attacked the Wisconsin men to drive them off turf he considered to be his own. Trapper Jet believed Kitella burned his cabin. Was Trapper Jet the old man?

He called Les Reynolds as he departed Escanaba heading south, and told him that he wanted to talk to Charley Fahrenheit and Colliver in the Marinette County Jail in Wisconsin.

Fahrenheit was morose.

"I'm sorry about your wife," Service said.

Charley shook his head, a response Service couldn't read.

"Hard to believe she'd drive all the way up to Michigan to shoot Outi Ranta. She have that kind of temper?"

"Flash and done," Charley said. "I told youse she hated guns. Tried for years to teach her so she could protect herself, but she wouldn't have none of it."

"Sometimes a wife's temper goes into overdrive when another woman is involved."

"This wasn't the first time," the prisoner said.

"Not the first time her temper flared?"

"Not the first time there was another woman."

"She'd caught you before?"

"A few times."

"And she didn't get mad?"

"Mad enough to go right out and find a man to take to bed. Said fair was fair."

"You were okay with this?"

"*Hell* no! It's just how she was. She'd go off with some guy, come home and tell me all about it. Said getting even was better than getting mad."

"Did she ever threaten any of your girlfriends?"

"Said it was all my fault, not theirs."

"How was Mary Ellen's mental health?"

"You mean, like, was she off her rocker? No way."

"Do you know the names of the men she went with?"

"She always told me. She wanted me to know."

"Friends or strangers?" Service asked.

"Both."

"What friends?"

"Colliver for one."

"She did Colliver and you two remained friends?"

"It wasn't his fault. I forgave him. Him and me go way back." So too had Outi Ranta and Honeypat Allerdyce, Service thought.

Sandy Tavolacci was not happy about being dragged down to Wisconsin again.

"Hey, Sandy," Service said. "You're looking spiffy."

"Up your ass," the attorney said.

Colliver was seated behind a table, looking sullen.

Service stood over him and pointed a finger like a sword. "Why'd you and Charley go after Kitella?"

Tavolacci said, "My client is charged with an illegal deer. This is a buncha bullshit and you have no jurisdiction here."

Warden Les Reynolds said, "The deer put him inside, counselor, but it's the bears and other stuff keeping him here."

"We're just trying to have a friendly chat with your client," Service said.

Colliver had crossed his arms, his hands clenched into fists under his arms.

Uptight, pissed, defensive, Service thought. "I asked you a question, Mr. Colliver."

"I don't know no Kitella."

Service said, "He beat the shit out of you and Charley."

"Don't usually get no name from some asshole when you're in a fight."

Service sat down to bring himself to Colliver's level, a calculated move to even the ground and go eye to eye. "Your payback sort of backfired."

"What payback?" Colliver asked, looking over Service's shoulder.

"There's all kinds of payback," Service said. "Charley's told us a lot, said he's had too much on his chest, like how you balled his old lady."

Colliver couldn't hide his surprise. "She threw it on me."

"And then she told Charley."

"Why'd she do that?" Colliver asked.

"This interview is concluded," Tavolacci shouted. "This is over—finito!"

"She wanted to hurt him. Payback, right?"

Colliver looked sullen.

"How do you think we got to you? Mary Ellen gave up her old man and Charley gave us you, how you set him up with Hannah and the old man to get Kitella."

Colliver sneered. "Charley never met the man," he said.

"I'm telling youse to remain silent," Tavolacci said, grabbing Colliver's arm.

Colliver jerked free and flashed a nasty look at his attorney.

"Charley can't testify to what he don't know," Colliver said.

"Are you saying he lied?"

"Damn straight."

"Okay," Service said, leaning back to break tension. He looked up at Reynolds. "Let's scratch that off. Charley never met an old man." Service bent forward suddenly. "Who is he?"

"Fuck off," Colliver said, looking away.

"This just gets deeper," Service said. "Poaching, assault against Kitella, theft, homicide."

"Nobody got killed," Tavolacci said, his voice turning shrill.

"Mary Ellen Fahrenheit," Service said. "And Outi Ranta."

"Car wreck. Mary Ellen was a lush, eh?" Colliver said. "Been busted for it. I don't know no Ranta."

"A car wreck after she shot Outi Ranta," Les Reynolds said, looking down on Colliver and sounding like the voice of God.

Colliver looked confused.

Service said, "She drove up to Michigan and shot Ranta. Outi Ranta was Hannah, the woman who worked with the old man, and you worked with the old man. We're looking at conspiracy here at the least."

Colliver smirked. "Who's she gonna tell now?" His voice was icy.

"The old man's free," Service said. "You and Charley are in lockup and it looks to me like it's all gonna land on the two of you. And I can tell you right now, Charley wants company."

Tavolacci sprang to his feet. "Shut up!"

Service asked, "Did the old man have one leg?"

He saw in Colliver's eyes that he had no idea what Service meant, so he pressed on. "The theory is that the old man set up Mary Ellen. Ranta's dead, Mary Ellen's dead, you two are inside, and the old man's out there laughing at you both. What's his name, Mr. Colliver?"

"Wasn't no old man," Colliver said. "I just told Charley that shit. Man was my age and he never give no name. He had a streak of white hair right here." He reached to show them. "Like a skunk or something."

"You gave the cable to him?"

"Said Kitella was cutting in on his territory and needed to be taught a lesson. Charley got the cable and I give it to the man and I *swear* that's all we done, man."

Outside the jail Les Reynolds asked, "Do you know who he's talking about?"

"Possibly," Service said. Skunk Kelo was a sometime enforcer in the Allerdyce clan, and he had a prominent patch of white in his hair.

"You're not talking," Reynolds said.

"Can you pull Mary Ellen's driving record? Let's see if she had priors."

"What will you be doing?"

"Trying to connect some dots and fill up a canvas," Service said.

"Is that standard procedure over there in Michigan?" Les Reynolds asked.

· 33 ·

olliver was right about Mary Ellen Fahrenheit. Wisconsin records showed she had been stopped twice, the first time in 1992 when she blew .095, and in 1994 when it was .08. She had been clean since.

"I'd say she got her act together," Les Reynolds said.

Some people managed to do just that, Service knew, but stress sometimes made them to do stupid things, including fall off wagons. Had this been stress or pure bad luck?

He was back in Escanaba by mid-afternoon, and stopped to see the undersheriff. "You see the prosecutor?"

Cambridge nodded. "Phone records in forty-eight hours and then we can put this thing to bed."

Service stopped to give Newf water and let her run, put her in the house and headed north, trying to sort out what he knew about Skunk Kelo. The man had done a stretch downstate for aggravated assault and had returned to the Allerdyce clan a month or so after Limpy was released from Jackson Prison two years ago.

Retired CO Steve "Ironhead" Southard had once patrolled southwest Marquette County, where the clan's compound was located. Southard had busted Kelo several times on snagging cases and had sent Kelo to prison after he had beaten Southard senseless with a three-pound priest made of ironwood. Southard had gotten his nickname as a result of the attack, but had retired a year later. He lived in Palmer, south of Negaunee, and was self conscious about his nickname.

Ironhead had a dense, curly black beard that was beginning to salt and smiled when he opened the door and saw Service. "Must be business," the retired officer said. "Neither you nor your old man were much on social calls."

"Skunk Kelo," Service said.

"What's that cretin done now?" Southard asked.

"I'm just looking for information. Have you seen him since he got out?"

"No, and I don't want to," Southard said. "I did hear he went after She-Guy Zuiderveen over to Champion. Talk about your basic lapse in judgment. Zuiderveen gave him a helluva going-over."

"When was this?"

"Sometime last winter. Kelo was in the bar yappin' about bear guides and She-Guy took offense."

"You busted Kelo several times."

"One time too many," Southard said. "That last time, he was the one doing the busting. The bastard tried to kill me, but the prosecutor went for a plea bargain because he didn't like the looks of the jury. One of us gets killed they'll plead it down to verbal abuse or something."

The man's bitterness was palpable and justified. Over the years a lot of officers had been injured making arrests, but few perps ever got the full fist of the law.

"What's Kelo like?"

"Limpy's muscle, cold as a lamprey on ice. Limpy gives an order, it gets done, no questions asked."

"Blood kin?"

"Good as. He took up with one of the clan's women and made his bones with the old man."

"Took up with which woman?"

Southard grinned. "Hell, all of 'em is my guess. You know how that bunch is down there in the Sinai. That's what I used to call it. Fuckin' desert with trees."

This stop had been a waste of time. "I did hear one thing," Southard said, "but I'm not sure if it's important. Kelo and Limpy had some sort of falling out."

"Over what?"

Southard held up his hands. "You just heard all I know. I heard this late last winter."

"Before or after She-Guy and Kelo had their scrap?"

" 'Bout the same time, now that I think on it," Southard said.

"This from a source or bar talk?"

"I gotta be retired a lot longer before I can go into bars around here," Southard said. "I heard it from a source—a reliable one. When I retired, he retired. I promised he'd never get bugged by the department."

"Your word's your word," Service said. "Any chance you could talk to him, find out what the beef was about?"

"Sorry, Grady. I'm outta that shit now and happy to be out. Not fair to ask me that. Cecilia's happy I'm out and she wouldn't like me crawling back in."

Cecilia was his wife, a beautiful redhead who was a fine singer. She had never been a big supporter of his CO work.

"You into something heavy?" Southard asked.

"Just trying to help a Wisconsin warden close a case." Heavy was a relative concept with too many interpretations.

"Huh," Ironhead said. "Most of the cheesies were a good lot in my day. I guess I could maybe have a chat with my man. What's the harm, eh? It's all in the past now."

"Thanks, Steve."

"Hey, it true you've got a son?"

"Looks that way." He gave Southard one of his cards.

Southard studied it and shook his head. "Cell phones, e-mail—you got more bloody numbers than a banker. Technology," he added with obvious distaste. "I'll call you soon."

"Give my best to Cecilia," Service said.

"She's at the church tonight—choir practice."

He called Pyykkonen from Palmer and got an immediate pick-up. "Uncanny timing," she said. "I think we've got the blue boat."

"No shit?"

"A couple of wading salmon guys found it hung up off Laughing Fish Point," she said. "Looks like she was scuttled further out, but broke loose, drifted in, got hung on a boulder fifty feet off the beach in six feet of water. Ten feet north and it would have drifted east into the big lake. Fate, I guess, hitting that rock. I guess the guys who found it didn't think much about it, you know, with Superior spitting stuff up every now and then. Locals take what they can use, leave the rest to rot. Turns out one of the men has a son who's coast guard in the Soo. He came home for a day of fishing with his dad, saw the boat out on the point, and remembered the bulletin. I got the call yesterday, asked the Alger County marine safety officer to pull it out and put it in the vehicle impoundment in town, but Alger kicked the job over to Marquette. I got a call an hour ago. It's in Marquette now. No registration number. Maybe somebody obliterated it to make sure it couldn't be identified."

"I'm near Negaunee. I can get over there and take a look."

"I was gonna drive over in the morning," she said.

"Let me take a look and give you a shout."

"I'll be at Shark's tonight," she said. "He's a hoot, you know."

Hoot wasn't the word he'd select to describe his friend.

The Marquette County marine safety officer was Guy Bartoletti. He had been a longtime road patrol officer and a sergeant who retained his stripes when he was shifted into the current job in preparation for his retirement. Service had known him a long time, as had his father before him.

The vehicle impoundment was nearly in the middle of downtown Marquette, inside a double chain-link fence topped with razor wire.

Bartoletti said, "This should be Alger's, but their sheriff called in a favor from my boss, so here we are."

The wooden craft had a blue hull and a gaping hole in the bottom.

"Looks like it hit something," Service said.

"More likely an insurance job," Bartoletti said with a smile. He started to reach for the hull, but Service blocked his arm, gave him rubber gloves.

"You're a hotshot detective now, eh?" He put on the gloves and grabbed the broken edge. "See, when you hit something, most of the damage goes inward. Not all of it, 'cause the boat rocks and so forth, but mostly, see? This one's all outward. I'm guessing a sledge. Somebody wanted this thing on the bottom."

Service looked at the damage, saw the marks, agreed with the assessment.

"Twenty-six-foot Miltey Commander," Bartoletti said. "Built in 1995. Not many of them around."

"Miltey Boat Company," Service said. "Chassell."

"That's it."

"There's no registration."

"Don't matter," Bartoletti said. "You need a sign on a whitetail's ass says it's a deer?"

Bartoletti stepped into the hole in the hull and flicked on his flashlight. "See there? Joe Miltey burns the serial number into the hull in six or eight places so nobody can mistake his work. New, this rig went for nearly twenty-five thou. Twin Chrysler inboards, wide beam, high gunwales—she'd plane good on the lake and go like a scalded dog in a pretty good sea."

Service wrote down the serial number, checking two of them to be sure they were the same. "I want to get inside," he added.

Bartoletti got a ladder and they climbed up into the boat. The aft deck was small, but below decks was deep and there was plenty of room for a four-by-six cage. There were four holes in the floor. Bartoletti saw him looking at the holes and said, "U-bolt holes. The bolts probably got lost."

Service called Pyykkonen as he drove west. "The boat's not registered, but there are serial numbers. Maybe the owner didn't know about them. The boat's a 1995 Miltey Commander."

"Blue?"

"As a pretty girl's eyes," Service said.

"Miltey Boat Company?" she said. "So we've circled back to where we started, eh? Joe Miltey's daughter was the one who found Harry Pung. You want me to visit him?"

"Let's both go. I'm going to see my kid tonight. We'll go over there in the morning. Pick you up at Shark's at eight."

"Works for me," she said.

He called Walter's dorm room and Karylanne Pengelly answered. "Is the hockey player there?" he asked.

"At the rink," she said. "He's *always* at the rink."

"Seems late for practice."

"Not hockey. He goes over there every night with that fly rod."

Service laughed inwardly. His old man had given him his first rod, just as his old man had gotten his first one from his grandfather. "This is his father," Service said. "I'm going to be there in seventy minutes. Thought I'd pick him up, see if he wants a late-night snack. Would you like to join us, Karylanne?"

She laughed. "I never pass up food. My mom always tells me to eat now while I've still got my metabolism."

"I'll pick you up in front of the dorm and we'll go fetch him," he said.

The girl had an infectious laugh and a soft voice, gentle but strong. Probably Walter and the girl would not last as a couple, but at least he had picked a good one for now. Or she had picked him. In his own day, his picks had been anything but stellar. "There in sixty-seven minutes," he said.

Later he passed the Shrine of the Snowshoe Priest. Father Frederick Baraga had been a Slovenian member of the powerful Hapsburgs, who had sworn off wealth and power for a life of the cloth—and in the bush. Baraga had come to the U.P. in the nineteenth century as a priest for an Austrian missionary society and had founded missions as far south as Grand Rapids and west to the Apostle Islands in Wisconsin. Baraga was known as a priest who would always be where he was needed, and there were plenty of stories of him snowshoeing a hundred miles in snowstorms. What Service liked about the priest, who eventually became the

U.P.'s first bishop, was his total dedication to his work. In recent years a movement for his canonization had been organized to find and document two miracles in the priest's past. News reports said the group was having a hard time—that while the priest's life had been filled with good works, miracles were still in question. It was a classic case of seeing trees and missing the forest. Baraga had traipsed the entire U.P. and into Wisconsin, almost always on foot and alone, and he was a great model for the horseblankets, the old COs who had blazed the trail for him. As he drove under the monument, he flipped a salute, said "Father Fred," and smiled.

The L'Anse-Baraga area south of Chassell had seen a lot of history—Indians battling Indians, priests, fur traders, loggers, Lake Superior fishermen. Much of the area had been settled by Finns who had married Native Americans, their offspring called Finndians—as resolute a cultural blend as he had encountered.

On the way into Chassell he saw a new house being built. Floodlights from the driveway lit it up to show the Finnish roofing style called *walmdach*, which featured a distinct and different angle in every quarter, helping to spread the weight of the snow pack and shed snow as it melted.

Come Christmas he could take Walter up to Pequamming where Norwegians lived, surrounded by Finns, Swedes, and French Canadians, and treat the boy to sweet rye bread and *lutefisk*. Nantz would have a week off from the academy, and the three of them could use some of the time to see and do—if he could get her out of bed. The thought made him laugh out loud.

Karylanne was waiting on the sidewalk and waved as he pulled up.

"He was supposed to be back by now," she said.

"Is he late a lot?"

"He just gets interested in things and loses track."

In the bloodline, Service thought.

McInnes Arena was still open. Intramural teams played all night, while classes, the varsity, and the public used it at more convenient hours.

They found Walter in a yellow hallway. There was a red rubber donut about forty feet away and he was flicking a tag of fire-pink yarn at the target. Using reach casts, which Service had not taught him. Where the hell had he picked that up? The casts were near the target all the time, the technique designed to throw a mend into the line to help the fly drift parallel to an obstacle with little drag. Many fishermen never learned to do it correctly. Walter looked like he had control of it.

"Where'd you learn that?"

Walter tilted his head, showed a flash of surprise, said, "Book, by the wall."

Service walked over to the wall, picked up a casting guide by Lee Wulff, one of the old masters and too advanced for most beginners.

"He's cleaned out the library," Karylanne said. "Walter," she said sharply. "Your father's gonna feed us."

"That's cool," he said, making one last cast.

With few restaurants open late, they ended up at Sundog's Seiche, a coffee house and college hangout run by the wife of an astonomy professor. Service had an avocado and tuna sandwich and listened to Walter and Karylanne talking back and forth. The boy was more at ease with her than he had ever been with a girl at that age, and when the girl talked, Walter paid attention. When he looked at the boy's face, he imagined he could see Bathsheba's eyes.

"Are you staring at me?" Walter asked.

"Not staring at, just staring."

"Right. Who do you see, Sheba or you?"

"I see somebody who looks pale and needs to beef up."

"So I can clog my arteries?"

Karylanne said, "There's a training table for jocks. It's run by a full-time special health nutritionist."

When Service played at Northern, hockey players had lived on burgers, beer, and pasta — especially beer.

"When did you learn to cook?" Walter asked him.

"My old man was a lush and he'd go days without thinking about food. Somebody had to remind him, and I was always hungry."

Walter nodded. "What did you call him?"

Karylanne said, "My father will always be my daddy."

Service smiled. "If I'd called him Daddy he would have backhanded me through a wall. I called him, Old Man. And Sir."

"He didn't mind?"

"I don't think he noticed. Mostly he thought about violets."

Karylanne said, "He liked flowers?"

"Violet, violator," Service said.

There was silence while they ate.

They dropped Karylanne at her dorm and headed for Walter's room. "How's my casting look?"

"I'll tell you that after we see your grades. Got a place where I can bunk tonight?"

"Sure, and my grades are fine. It's not easy, but I'm keeping up. Are you going to give me some fatherly advice about Karylanne?"

"She looks like she can take care of herself."

"Kinda like Maridly," Walter said. "You want to grab breakfast in the morning at the training table?"

"Gotta work."

"Whatever, old man."

Service saw that the boy was grinning. "Stop busting my balls."

"That's Maridly's job," Walter said as he clicked off the lights. "Good night, Daddy."

"Consider yourself backhanded," Service said, smiling in the dark.

Service, Gus Turnage, and Pyykkonen went to the Miltey Boat Company in two vehicles. Gus knew Joe Miltey, said he'd be less belligerent if they came in force.

The Miltey Boat Company was built on the banks of the Pike River, where it flowed into Pike Bay, the southernmost feature of Portage Lake. Five aluminum hulls were lined up at the garage door of a large pole building. Three finished boats were at the other end of the building, one of them not entirely shrink-wrapped, the plastic hanging off like a partially shed skin. There were piles of cans and pallets with boxes everywhere. Service looked at a dock by the building, saw the technicolor swirls of gasoline in the river.

Joe Miltey was in his late forties, with a red face, veins showing in his cheeks and nose, and red hair starting to gray. His office was inside the production area. He sat at a desk in the middle of a circle of desks. Windows looked out on the production line and Service counted only three people working. There was one clerk in the office with Miltey, who was scribbling on a clipboard and did not look up. Miltey's company didn't look like it was thriving.

"I get tree of youse?" the man finally said.

Service put a piece of paper on the marred and distressed desk. All the furniture looked like it dated to the time when the company was still building fishing tugs.

Miltey looked at it, said, "Is this supposed to be a winning lottery number?"

Gus said, "That depends on if you can keep your big foot out of your big mouth."

"Those are serial numbers off one of your boats," Service said.

"You bring a subpoena?"

Gus winced. "Joe, you've got piles of epoxy and paint cans outside, and a fuel storage tank is leaking into the river. You want to play games, we can send over DEQ and let you talk to them. In the end, Joe, we'll still get what we want."

"Maybe he's got something to hide," Pyykkonen said. "This is a homicide case and I don't think you want to be obstructing it, Mr. Miltey."

Joe Miltey went to one of the file cabinets and came back with a piece of paper he dropped on the desk. "Irv McCrae bought da boat in nighny-six."

"Got an address?"

Miltey shoved the paper across.

The address was Freda, a village fifteen miles west of Houghton on the Lake Superior coast.

"Thanks," Gus said.

"Yeah, right," Joe Miltey said.

Service called McCrae from his truck. The man had a sandpaper voice and claimed he sold the boat to Margaret Soper in Painesdale last July and asked if Service wanted her number. Service wrote down the name, thanked McCrae, and showed his notebook to Pyykkonen.

"Round and round we go," she said, shaking her head.

Gus followed them to Painesdale. Maggie Soper came out on her porch.

Pyykkonen said, "You bought a boat in July from Irv McCrae in Freda, a twenty-six-foot Miltey Commander with a blue hull."

"I sold a boat to da professor," she said.

"You didn't mention that the last time we were here."

"Youse was askin' aboot real estate, hey. I don't read minds."

"How long after you bought it did Pung buy it?"

"I never even seen it. The professor called me up and said he found dis boat for a good price and he wanted it for fishing. Said since nine-eleven, foreigners can't get registrations and stuff. Said he'd give me the money and he'd buy it in my name."

"How much?" Pyykkonen said.

"Four thousand plus a thousand."

"Where's the boat now?"

"I thought youse had it," Soper said.

"Have you got a bill of sale? Did you register the boat?"

"He said he'd take care of all that, but he never got the paperwork to me."

"But you got the cash," Pyykkonen said.

The woman smiled smugly. "I don't care for your tone of voice."

"We'll talk again," Pyykkonen said, "and next time you're gonna *hate* my tone of voice."

Service called Station 20 for a title and registration check. The boat had last been registered to McCrae two years before, which meant it was good for another year, unless it was sold. The Certificate of Number had not been surrendered to the secretary of state as the law required when a boat was sold. A search showed no new registration had been filed for.

Service called McCrae again. "The secretary of state says your registration hasn't been turned in."

"Geez, I give it to da fella picked it up. Said he'd take care of it. Is this a ticket?"

"Who picked up the boat, Irv?"

"Asian fella. I tink 'is name was Harry. Teacher up ta Tech, said he was picking it up as a favor to the Soper woman. Am I in trouble?"

"Was Harry a young guy?"

"Everybody's young compared to me. I'd say mebbe he was fifty, ya know."

"We'd like for you to look at a photo for us."

"What's this all about?"

"Relax, Irv. Just look at the photo when the detective comes, and we'll leave you be."

Service looked at Pyykkonen. "Looks like Harry picked up the boat himself."

"He didn't want a paper trail," she said. "Sounds like he didn't expect to be a boat owner long."

"He wasn't," Service said. "Have you talked to the ex's lawyer yet?"

"Three of them, never the same one twice. They insist there's no son. We've gotten nowhere."

Every case had a key, and more and more it looked like Soong was it—but he couldn't stop wondering why the boat had been scuttled near Laughing Fish Point.

"I guess I'd better get on out to Freda," Pyykkonen said, but he wasn't listening.

He ended the day with a call to Nantz, explaining the Toogood photo mystery. She said she would have time soon, and would check into it.

· 34 ·

He was hungry but not in the mood for a sandwich, and settled on an old recipe for quick black bean and hominy stew. He heated olive oil in a big pan and added green peppers, onions, and garlic. When the vegetables softened, he poured in chicken broth, added the hominy, ham, cumin, coriander, minced chipotles, and a can of black beans. As the stew was thickening he got a call from Ironhead Southard.

"Honeypat left Allerdyce last year before Christmas. The word is that she hooked up with Kelo and Limpy didn't like it, which as far as I know is the first time that old reprobate's been bothered by anything like that," the retired officer said.

Service stirred the stew halfheartedly and thought. Ironhead had basically told him what he already knew—that Honeypat had fled in December—but Ironhead didn't know that he had stimulated the split by telling her that Limpy had been hitting on his grandson's girlfriend. Outi Ranta blamed Honeypat for what she had gotten involved in, and made the point that Honeypat would never change. These words felt indelible. Outi needed money and she was looking for some fun. Honeypat had come up with a scheme. Outi had dealt with Charley Fahrenheit while Colliver dealt with Skunk Kelo. What was Honeypat's angle?

The more he thought about it, the tougher it was to imagine Limpy going off the wall because Honeypat had hooked up with another man. It had never bothered him before, and Limpy's alleged reaction didn't fit. Where was the greed in this, wanting to keep something that was exclusively his? Possible. Honeypat had sex with the ease that most people took a drink of water, and with about as much meaning. The flow of men and women in Limpy's clan had always been hard to pin down, and by and large, who was with whom never seemed to matter to Allerdyce, who had always been about money and the power that came to him through his poaching enterprises. In many ways he was a feudal lord operating on values that dated back centuries to a world he defined as black and white, with little gray. He took care of his clan; they did what he ordered, like some sort of lowlife, plaid-and-Carhart-mafia. Was the break with

Honeypat real and permanent, or something else? No matter how hard he tried to think it through, there was no reasonable conclusion. Limpy had actively tried to undermine his grandson's interest in the DNR. This certainly amounted to some form of greed: keeping what he had. The salient point was probably that Limpy thought he was losing Aldo and had moved to prevent this. Did the same apply to Honeypat? Had Allerdyce tried to find her and bring her back? Had he been involved in Outi Ranta's death?

Service scooped the finished stew into a one-gallon plastic container, made sure the lid was tight, and called Les Reynolds. "I'll fax you a photo first thing in the morning. Show it to Colliver, see what he has to say."

"Do we have a suspect?"

"Maybe."

"No problem. I'll call you back as soon as I've had the talk with him."

Service took the container and drove to the Marquette office. He went through the files to find a photograph of Skunk Kelo, and faxed it to Reynolds at his office.

Why would Honeypat go after Kitella? What was the old Arab proverb, the enemy of my enemy is my friend? He wasn't sure if it was from the Koran, or who for certain used the saying—only that it was some group with a beef, of which there were plenty in the world. By this logic, Kitella was a potential ally for Honeypat, but her actions made no sense, lacked context. Service called the sheriff's department and learned that Linsenman was off duty.

He called the deputy at home.

"How about we take a nice hike in the autumn woods?"

"It's night, Service."

"The best time to see animals in their native habitats."

"Nature?" Linsenman said. "I have squirrels in my yard. I don't need anything more. You scraping the barrel for help?"

Something like that. He had seen Linsenman hold his ground and his cool in a shootout a few days before. Such nerve was uncommon. "Meet me at Da Yoopers Tourist Trap and we'll take my truck."

"In uniform?" Linsenman asked.

"No need for that. This is a social call."

Linsenman exhaled and said, "I bet."

Service said, "You might want to bring your sidearm."

"Oh, boy," Linsenman said.

The deputy got to the Trap on US 41 a few minutes after Service, got into the Yukon with a thermos, and looked over his shoulder into the backseat.

"What?" Service asked.

"Wanted to see if you had a rocket launcher back there."

"We're just going visiting."

Linsenman didn't ask who or where, but as they made their way south into the western part of the county, Service saw the deputy's uneasiness growing.

"I don't much care for this direction," Linsenman complained.

"I thought we'd pop down to Limpy's, see how he's doing."

They were moving at fifty mph when Linsenman opened his door.

Service looked at him.

"I'm thinking of jumping."

"You'll get hurt."

"What difference does it make when or how we get fucked over?" He pushed the door open and slammed it. "We can't make social calls in daylight?"

"Limpy likes the night," Service said.

"So do vampires," Linsenman mumbled.

"We'll just walk in, offer him some stew, and have a nice visit. It's a beautiful night. We're lucky to work in the Yoop."

The deputy said grimly, "The issue is, will we collect our pensions here."

The Allerdyce compound was built on a narrow peninsula between North and South Beaverkill Lakes, a long distance from anything that might be termed a town, much less civilization, and it was not the sort of place you just stumbled on to. With water on two sides and swamps on both ends, it was difficult to reach, even if you knew where it was. There was a two-track from a USFS road down to the compound's parking area, and a half-mile hike from there along a twisting narrow trail through dense and interlocked cedars, hemlocks, and tamaracks. In terms of isolation it was a fortress, and since Service had led police officers into the area the summer before last, Limpy had beefed up his defenses, sprinkling sound sensors and motion detectors along the entry road and adjacent forest.

Service knew that as soon as they got out of the vehicle they would be under surveillance, and if Limpy didn't want them in the compound, they would not get that far.

The two men carried flashlights, but did not turn them on. Service had spent so much of his life working in the dark that his eyes always adjusted quickly. Even as a boy he had never been afraid of the night, one of the few things his old man had ever complimented him on.

Halfway to the compound they heard a wolf howl in the distance. Too far away to be one of their watchers, Service thought.

The final approach to the camp was dark, and as they squeezed out of a dense grove of cedars he could see dim light and the outlines of the shacks where the clansmen lived. One step further and Service stopped.

Linsenman whispered, "I can't see shit. What?"

Service remained still, rotating his head slowly to the side and back again. There was movement along the ground, dark shadows stalking. He looked around deliberately and realized that they were surrounded by whatever it was.

"Oh, boy," Linsenman said.

Service felt the hairs stand up on his arms and neck, his breathing quicken. "Walk in my steps," he whispered to the deputy, "and don't look around. Keep your eyes up and on my back."

"This is crazy," Linsenman said.

Over the years Limpy had resided in different cabins, but the past few times he'd seen him, he'd been in the same one. Service led them directly to it, his eyes on the tree-based horizon, moving steadily, neither slowly nor quickly. The ink sky was filled with stars, but the light did not penetrate trees.

The cabin was dark, which was not unusual. Service stepped onto the porch and Linsenman plowed into his back, muttering, "Shit."

Powerful spots came on, splashing light across the area they had just crossed. Service looked back, saw more than a dozen pairs of eyes gleaming on the edges of the illuminated area. The eyes moved slightly and he finally saw what they were: dogs—dark, squat animals, all of them staring up at the porch, watching. He felt a wave of panic and pushed it away. They were on the porch; the problem was off the porch. Old Vietnam training: isolate the problem, and focus on the problem you have, not the one you had, or what comes next. Now counts, nothing more. Limpy was inside, waiting, and Service knew that the dogs had been a reception committee designed specifically for him. Limpy might look like he couldn't add snake eyes, but he had an amazing cunning, quick to ascertain and exploit a foe's weakness.

He rapped on the door and waited.

Limpy himself opened it, grinned one of his toothless smiles and cackled. "I'll be damned, sonny, youse comin' all the way out here."

"We happened to be in the neighborhood," Service said. Allerdyce's cackle deteriorated into a wheeze, which terminated in a wracking cough.

"Come on in, come on in," the old man said, clearing his throat and holding the door wide.

Service felt Linsenman pressed up against him as Limpy closed the door and engulfed them in black.

They waited motionless as a kerosene lantern hissed to life, throwing a dull pink-orange glow into the middle of the room, enough to render shadows, but not enable sight. Service heard faint movement to his right, someone brush against something, suck in air.

"Take a seat, sonny," Limpy said from a chair directly across from them.

"When—" Linsenman started to ask, but Service nudged him to be silent. Limpy usually moved like a wraith in the dark. Not tonight. He had tracked him all the way to his seat.

Service and Linsenman sat in wooden chairs facing Limpy, who sat in an old rocker of heavy wood.

A young woman stepped out of the shadows and Service gave her the container. She took it and withdrew. She looked to be fourteen or fifteen, a child only in her face.

"Brought some stew," Service told Limpy.

"Kind of you, sonny. More like yer old man every year."

"This is Linsenman," Service said.

"I know," was all Allerdyce said.

Service smelled the stew warming. He had rehearsed several ways to open a conversation but concluded that his presence alone would signal Allerdyce that he was interested in talking. He would leave the old poacher to pick the subject and deliver whatever message he was hoarding.

The girl brought stew in bowls. She served Limpy first.

"Dis little piece is Lixie," Allerdyce said. "Youse want some, help yourself. She's a good one."

One, a piece of property. "Good as Honeypat?" Service asked. The girl was just one more possession, Service thought. Was Honeypat different? Did greed and ownership require Limpy to be the one to share, and that it was not the property's choice? Probably.

Limpy stared over at Service and glared. "Bring up dat name."

Allerdyce sipped his stew, made a face, bellowed angrily, "Hotter, you bitch!" He held the bowl out, his hand shaking, the stew spilling onto the floor.

The girl sheepishly rescued the bowl and disappeared. When she brought it back Limpy took a spoonful and made a face. "*Hotter*, Goddammit! Hot, hot!" She took the bowl and the process was repeated. When she brought it back he sampled one spoonful, stopped chewing, and placed the bowl on the floor. The girl didn't fetch it.

At least this kid was dressed, Service thought. He had always been offering Honeypat to visitors and now it was this young girl. If he'd offer Honeypat and this girl, why would he come down on Kelo?

Allerdyce stopped, looked over at the detective. "You make dis?"

Service nodded, tasted the stew, put the spoon back in and set the bowl on the floor, mimicking Allerdyce. Linsenman's spoon was clicking busily against his bowl.

"Youse come out some day, teach Lixie to cook. She knows what ta do in da bed, hey, but her cookin's bad. Never gets nothing hot but her pussy!"

Linsenman ate faster.

Service said nothing.

"Youse seen da mutts," Allerdyce said.

"Beautiful animals," Service said, his stomach immediately beginning to knot up.

"Rescued 'em," Limpy said. "Got da fight in 'em—all scars and broke stuff, hey. Been beat, shot, kicked, cut, but you gotta kill one to stop it. Born ta be what dey are, hey. Don't know nothin' else. Born in dere blood, fight till youse can't fight no more. One gets jumped, dey all fight. Like family's s'posed ta."

"Just like NATO," Service said. He squinted to see better and caught the outline of a pile of books off to his left. He could read a couple of titles. Cookbooks. What was going on here? Books for the girl?

"Da town?" Allerdyce said.

Linsenman sniggered quietly. Nadeau was a village in Menominee County.

"Like the treaty organization in Europe," Service said.

He had never seen Limpy eat so lightly; tonight he had barely touched his food. When he'd taken Limpy to McDonald's, he had eaten one nugget, put the rest in his coat, and later he had seen him dig through a trash can. Something was definitely going on.

Allerdyce stared at him. "Youse know I'm not stupid, sonny," he said. "Lixie," he added. "Fetch da mutt."

Service heard claws scraping the wooden floor. The girl emerged from the dark with a rope attached to a short-haired, low-slung dog with piles of loose skin, only one ear, and scars crisscrossing its fur. Some of them looked new. "Youse take 'im," Limpy said. "Got no fight. It stays I got to put it down. Don't earn da keep in da family, don't get to keep da take, hey. Don't want to waste lead."

The animal did not look at Service or Linsenman. It watched only Limpy. Service took the rope from Lixie, let it hang slack, wishing it was longer. The animal didn't cringe, it just stared at Allerdyce, who grinned and rubbed his whiskers.

"Youse don't act like family, youse gotta go," Allerdyce said. "Dat's da law here."

Lixie placed the empty plastic container in Service's lap. It had not even been rinsed.

Limpy put his hands on his knees, tried to get to his feet, but couldn't seem to manage it. Lixie held out her hand and helped haul him upright. He shuffled unsteadily on stiff legs to the door with his visitors, straining for breath, wheezing like he was exhausted.

"Good grub, sonny. Youse best be careful dem mutts out dere. Dey don't much like dis one, ya know."

Service and Linsenman stepped onto the porch and the door slammed behind them. They heard a bolt click.

"What . . . the . . . fuck . . . was . . . that?" Linsenman whispered.

Service ignored him. The spots were no longer lit; the dog on the rope was pulling and growling low like he had a bee trapped in his throat.

"Side by side this time," Service said. The dog was surging, straining to go.

When they stepped down from the porch the area erupted in snarls and barks and growls, and dark forms pranced around herky-jerky. Service's hand was shaking, his heart pounding.

"Give me the leash," Linsenman said calmly.

For the first twenty yards the dogs charged in to snarl at them and retreat, snapping their jaws.

As soon as they were in the trees they could hear the animals crashing en masse through the underbrush on either side of them.

From time to time, the dog on the rope would snarl and lash out, or freeze suddenly until whatever captured his attention moved away.

The last hundred yards they heard nothing, and the dog on the rope settled into an easy walk until it saw the Yukon and balked.

"You can let him go," Service said.

"So that old asshole back there can kill him? You don't want him, I'll take him."

"Let's get out of here," Service said.

The dog snarled when Linsenman opened his door, but the deputy talked softly to the animal, reached down, and hoisted it into the truck.

"I think I'll call him NATO," Linsenman said. "You see how those other dogs danced at him, but none of them had the balls to take him on. I think Limpy is dumping him because he couldn't handle him."

NATO lay his head on Linsenman's knee.

"You get what you want?" the deputy asked.

"Maybe," Service said. "Understanding Limpy is like trying to read hieroglyphics."

"That's good," Linsenman said. "That stew was great, but I'm never ever going on another night hike with your woods cop ass."

The deputy rubbed between the dog's ears, said, "If this man ever comes to our house, you can bite his balls off."

Service was happy to see that the dog didn't respond.

At least one of Allerdyce's messages was clear: Animals that refused to run with the pack and pull their weight were *out* of the pack, and Limpy was the alpha male. Did this refer to Kelo, Honeypat, or Aldo? The subtext wasn't clear at all. What really rubbed at him was Allerdyce's curious qualification about a family acting the way it's supposed to—all for one and one for all.

Ten minutes after Linsenman departed with his new pet, Service realized that while his decision to go to the compound had been an impulse, his reception there was not, and such a reception meant that Allerdyce had been expecting him, which made the message even clearer. Or was the message one of misdirection? Limpy's mind was unconventional and anything was possible. Superficially, a reasonable person would assume that Honeypat and Kelo had been thrown out because they wouldn't abide, but Service knew that it had been Honeypat who chose to walk. The circulating story made it seem like she had hooked up with Kelo and been thrown out. That didn't fit facts or history as he understood it.

More importantly, the man he had met the last two times was not the man he had known and battled for so many years. If Allerdyce was sick, it wasn't a passing bug.

· 35 ·

Cambridge was patiently watching him go through the phone calls in and out of Ranta's house. Cambridge had thoughtfully hand-printed a name beside each number, but there was no Kelo, Colliver, Fahrenheit, or Honeypat—no nothing.

Cal Shall had always preached to his students: "There's always something in every case that's not clear or obvious until it's over. Sometimes that something is nothing."

"Satisfied?" the undersheriff asked.

"Can I get a copy?"

"Keep that one."

"What about her business calls?"

The undersheriff rolled his eyes. "It just goes on and on with you."

"James, we're trying to get to the bottom of this."

"No, Detective," Cambridge said with a snarl. "This is *my* jurisdiction, *my* case, and *I* am trying to get to the bottom, but you keep trying to dig the basement deeper."

The undersheriff did not say he would seek the business phone records.

Les Reynolds called at 10 A.M. while Service was driving north toward Marquette.

"Colliver says that photo is the guy he dealt with. You got a name?"

"Jukka Kelo, but most people call him Skunk."

"I think we're going to BOLO the man, all agencies, detain for questioning in connection with a felony investigation."

A good lawyer would have Kelo on the streets in a blink. All they had were claims, and those only from Colliver. Fahrenheit thought Colliver was working with an older man and would not be able to corroborate. "Whatever floats your boat, Les. I doubt you'll find him." There was no point in telling the warden about the Allerdyce clan and all that entailed, including their ability to disappear when they needed to.

Fern LeBlanc called right after he finished talking to Reynolds. "You had a call yesterday from a doctor named Ferma and she sounded rather unhappy you weren't available. She said she's in Cambodia and would e-mail you some information."

Tara Ferma. Service smiled. "I'm heading back to the office now."

He found the captain in his office staring at a computer screen. "Cap'n?"

Grant swung his chair around. "You found your way back."

"I'm here, somebody wants me there. I'm there, somebody wants me here. I feel like a dog always on the wrong side of the door. I can't be everywhere."

The captain smiled. "You seem to manage: McCants and the meth lab, coming to the assistance of a Troop when shots were fired, swan killers, a junkie, Indians trying to scalp each other, and McCants and bear hunters."

"Those things aren't getting my case solved."

"I agree. Everything you've done is commendable, but how many of these diversions *required* your participation? McCants is a good officer with a fine mind. The county and state were coming to the trooper's aid. There are times when the bad guys are going to get away with things. If they repeat, as many are wont to do, the odds swing to us. You have to husband your time, Detective. And your energy. A detective's beat is his mind, not geography."

"I don't think I'm cut out for this."

"What you're doing is trying to recalibrate your expectations. You used to work the Mosquito. Even when you had a quiet day, you were physically there, acting as a deterrent. Detectives don't deter. They can only react to what is passed to them and go from there, to dig out the facts, find and assemble evidence."

It was not a satisfying conversation, despite what seemed like sympathetic words.

Service returned to his cubicle and called up his e-mail. The blinking mail icon indicated a lengthy message coming through and after five minutes, he left the machine to download on its own, got coffee in a paper cup, and went outside for a smoke. It was sunny and cool, Lake Superior a dark green and fading to its winter color. By November it would be the hue of spent charcoal and treacherous, the most dangerous time to be on the water. Traffic raced by on US 41, mostly trucks bristling with antennae. Without trucks life in the U.P. would be even more hard-pressed than it was. The U.P. tended to lag behind most states in choices for people, but they always got here sooner or later, both the good and the bad, and most of it by truck.

Four consecutive automobiles went by with women talking on cell phones. Nantz was *always* on the cell phone, and while initially he had not been receptive to having one, it had proven its value. He mashed his cigarette in a red bucket filled with sand and went back to his office. The e-mail was still downloading and he hoped a power interruption wouldn't knock it off-line. He picked up Outi Ranta's telephone record and studied it. She averaged six or seven incoming calls a day: the bank, power company, standard fare. Three or four calls went out, the two main recipients S. Imperato and L. Ranta, her sister-in-law. Lenore Ranta had worked for years at Marble Arms in Gladstone, selling knives, and was married to a knife-maker at the factory. Not many calls between sisters-in-law, but some. Service looked back to the spring. More then than now, few since Onte's death. Significance of the reduced frequency? The Ranta brothers had been partners in the business at one time, but Onte had ended up with the whole shebang at some point. Hard to say what any of this meant, just numbers to look at. Still. . . .

Cambridge needed to get hold of her business records. If there was nothing more to this case, they all needed to know. It was tangential to his interests, but a tangent was like a small hole in a tooth: it felt larger than it was. Why weren't there calls from Ranta to her own business? There were until June, but after her husband's death, none, which was when she took over the running of the business. Most small business-people lived their work. Odd. He looked through the records. No calls to the store, absolutely none. That seemed unusual at best.

Ranta's work reminded him that Honeypat told him she was working at HPC as a bookkeeper on the night shift. He had somehow ignored this, maybe thought it was bull, but it was a detail and he had time.

He called the pet casket company in Gladstone and asked for Mac Loireleux, the manager. She was well known in the local business community and reviled by employees who called her "Mae Not" because she insisted on doing things her way, and wasn't open to innovation unless the idea came from her. He knew the woman enough to exchange greetings and not much more. She had a loud voice and an in-your-face style that kept most people at bay. Her husband had bailed years ago and as near as Service knew, she was alone and likely to stay that way.

"Mae?" he said when the receptionist got her. "Grady Service, DNR."

"How's your business?" she asked. To Loireleux all life was reduced to business.

"Steady," he said.

"Wish ours was. Little dips in the economy we can get past, but this economy is like the bloody Grand Canyon, eh? You'd think people would be consistent in their affection and concern for their pets, but it isn't so. Times get tough, people cut back. I can understand that; I mean, we do it with our kids, right? Are you a father? No, you're the bachelor with the trail of broken hearts. I have a daughter, she's sixteen and not sweet. She's been bugging me for a cell phone. I said, 'We live in Gladstone, your friends aren't but two blocks away, why do you need a phone, eh?' I told her times are tough and we have to cut back, and my ex, of course, he's no bloody help. He said it's up to me, so I told her no more talk about cell phones, end of subject, we don't need surprise bills at the end of the month. The girl can't pick up her room or keep gas in the car, eh. So that's a week or so ago and she gets quiet and yesterday she pipes up at breakfast, and she's got the solution—a *prepaid* cell phone, like those cards you can buy at the convenience store. She said she'll make the payments with her babysitting money and it won't cost me anything. I told her I'd think on it."

"That's nice," Service said, wishing she would shut up.

"Sorry," she said, "I guess my daughter's got me all worked up. You called me."

Finally, he thought. "Do you have an employee named . . . Grace Thundergiver?" He'd almost said Honeypat Allerdyce.

"I wish I still had her," Mae Loireleux said.

"Still?"

"She worked here for a week and left, no explanation. Just disappeared and never come back, not even to pick up her paycheck."

"She was a bookkeeper?"

"At night. Said she didn't want a public job, insisted she'd be happy with numbers. You don't find many people that good with numbers, but she was one of them."

The woman sounded impressed. "She left, but you'd still like to have her back?"

"Well, I wouldn't hire her again based on the way she left, but she knew all about phones and computers. She used one of the prepaid kinds and talked several of the girls here into doing the same. With her mind for numbers, I figured she could tell me if it was a good deal."

"When did Ms. Thundergiver leave?"

"Musta been coupla weeks ago. I can check if you want. Why?"

"I'm just doing some follow-up on a case. How did she come to HPC?"

"Just walked in one morning and started talking. The woman has the charm for sure, especially with the men, but the women thought she was nice too."

"Did she leave a number?"

"Just her cell phone. Said she didn't have a phone where she was staying, that the cell was all anybody needed."

"Do you have record of it?"

"You betcha."

She left the phone, came back and gave him the number, and he wrote it down.

The area code was in Colorado. He dialed the number, got a no-longer-in-service recording.

He looked in the phone book and found the name of a business in Marquette that sold prepaid phones and asked the clerk who answered if all prepaid numbers were in Colorado.

"No," she said, "Georgia and some other states too, because the tariffs are lower there, which is why the businesses are there. In the telecom business you look for any advantage you can find."

"So you could live in Michigan and have a number from one of those other states?"

"Of course. Everything is managed by computers," the woman said, not sounding particularly happy about the reality.

"Is it possible to get a record of all calls to and from a prepaid number?"

"Not without a subpoena, and the rules on that vary by state. Most of these businesses run out of states that are pretty protective of privacy. That's another reason they're there."

More than interesting, Service thought. Allerdyce had never had a telephone and the nearest pay phone was a long way off. How he communicated with his people had been the subject of considerable speculation in the division over the years. While Allerdyce's competitors were going electronic, there had been no evidence of Limpy following suit until last year when Service was certain he'd seen Limpy using a Family Radio Service device. He also knew that Limpy had installed a complex advanced warning system at the compound. Maybe the old poacher was more up-to-date than people thought. Honeypat sure seemed to be keeping up with the times.

The Marquette office had phone books for the entire Upper Peninsula. Service got out the Delta County book, called Marble Arms, and asked to talk to Lenore Ranta, sister-in-law.

"Lenore, Grady Service."

"I heard youse found Outi," she said.

"I didn't find her, but I was there."

"Too selfish to commit suicide," Lenore said. "All that woman cared about was money and men. If Onte hadn't died I think he'da left her, the way she fooled around."

"Someone in particular?" Some of the things you learned after a person died were not all that flattering. Mourning passed quickly except for those closest to the dead.

"Strangers, one-night-stands, never local. I give her that, not putting out in da back yard."

"Onte knew?"

"Was what killed 'im, ask me."

Her interpretation.

"She was a pro, ya know, down to Windsor when Onte met her."

"He told you this?"

"We hired a detective, cost us a heap, but worth it, hey. She just kept spendin' and spendin' and da business was goin' down da tubes."

"Did the two of you talk much?"

"Before Onte passed, ya know, da right ting to do for family, but since den, forget it. She never liked family, just money. Her idea for Onte to buy us out, hey. We needed cash back den, and we couldn't stand da woman, so we took da offer. My hubby never really wanted out. We'd like ta buy 'er back, but da bank's gonna get it now, and dey don't offer good deals, hey. Onte left a will. She din't."

"Did Outi use a cell phone?"

Lenore snorted. "Had two of 'em, one for da business and one for her other stuff, ya know."

"Do you have her number?"

"Only way to get one of 'em was sleep wit 'er."

"Do you remember when she started using a cell phone?"

"Last spring when Onte was sick, I tink. Yeah, I'm sure, it was den."

"Do you know what brand or service it was?"

"She never showed it to me, but I seen 'er usin' it plenty. Was purple, I remember."

Service immediately called the store in Marquette again and got the same clerk. "I don't have the brand, but the phone I'm interested in may be purple," he said.

She laughed. "They almost all make a purple phone now, and there are companies who make colored covers. Purple doesn't tell us anything. Sorry."

He noticed that the e-mail had finished coming in, and saw that the note, along with an attachment, was from Ferma. Her address was: <u>bear woman@worldnet.com</u>. The message was to the point:

Dear Officer Service: I regret the untoward delay in responding to your inquiry. A colleague was derelict in informing me. If the samples of S. *thibetanus* are as purported, they represent invaluable scientific evidence of what may be a rare color phase of S. *thibetanus*, or more likely, and in my opinion, a new species of *ursus*, heretofore unconfirmed, but long rumored. Reports of the animal have persisted in Southeast Asia for the past century. During the Vietnam War there were several serendipitous reports, but the Khmer Rouge was in brutal and absolute control of the target habitat, and no on-site scientific inquiries or expeditions were possible. A live animal has never been confirmed by a reliable source, and the sole evidence consists of the hair sample preceding yours. As a conservation officer you are undoubtedly aware of the global animal parts market; in this regard, a live specimen of a new mammalian species would be scientifically invaluable. Commercially such an animal would bring a price beyond imagination, one estimate being in the range of $200K USD. Everything must be done to ensure the safety of a live specimen. That you collected samples in Michigan may suggest that a live animal has been captured and maintained there. There being no modern photograph extant, I am attaching a copy of a rare nineteenth-century print (of poor quality) from Southeast Asia. You will note the hanging cage. We believe this species to have been decimated over the centuries. Its flesh is said by practitioners of various cultural traditional medicines (China, SEA, etc.) to possess significant medical properties, which is what drives the current market in bear parts. More importantly, it is thought that the consumption of the animal's flesh will cause good fortune and power to accrue to the consumer. Specifically, it is believed that if the animal is eaten immediately after being dipped *in vivo* into boiling oil that the meat and tissue provide advantages beyond medicinal powers. The heart is, of course, the most valued part. The rarity of the animal, we believe, stems from these and similar beliefs fostered in part by those who seek commercial gain. If through some fluke there is a live specimen, we must do all in our power to see that it is protected, or a species may pass that will never be seen again. The animal is thought to range in size from 45 to 65 kilos, which places it at the lowest end of the ursine spectrum. Males, of course, are larger than females. Please keep me informed of further developments.

Sincerely, T. Ferma, Ph.D.

He checked the top of the note. No copies. The professor apparently didn't wish to share her speculations with others—or share credit if her hunch was right. Goddamned metrics. He got out his dictionary, looked under the listing for measures, converted kilograms to pounds, which worked out to ninety to one hundred forty.

He looked at the sepia print for a long time. A light-colored bear (nearly white against the brown background) was locked in what looked like a huge birdcage, suspended in the air. Despite the print's poor quality, the animal's terror seemed palpable.

The captain came over after Service called him, read the note without comment, and studied the photo on the computer. When he was finished, he looked up at his detective and said, "Siquin Soong?"

Service forwarded the e-mail to his home computer before leaving the office, and called Les Reynolds, who was just leaving his house for night patrol. "Can you talk to Colliver? We need to know if he ever called Kelo, and if so, the number. Otherwise, how did they communicate?"

"Consider it done," Reynolds said.

Les Reynolds was a pro, unflappable, thorough—very unlike Wayno Ficorelli.

36

Nantz called at 5 P.M. "Did I catch you eating?"

"Thinking about thinking about it," he said. His mind was too occupied to be hungry.

She laughed. "You're not thinking about food. I'm hungry for you, Service, what about that?"

"That's different," he said.

"Jackson on Friday, right?"

"We're all set. I talked to Tree. He and Kalina have a plan for us. Fourteen hundred hours at the airport, right?"

"I'll have to be handcuffed to not attack you on the tarmac."

"I'm ready," he said.

"I talked to the people at the Lansing Board of Education and they did some poking around. It turns out that the yearbook photographs of Toogood and another kid got flipflopped by mistake that year."

Service sat back and put his hand on his forehead. A mistake?

"You're not talking. Do you want the right photo faxed up to the office?"

"Yes, to tie off the loose end. Thanks."

"You're still not talking."

"Stuff on my mind."

"Hope it's the same stuff I have on mine," she said. "How's our kid?"

"Good. I stopped to see him the other night."

"I know, he called me. He was really pleased, Grady."

"Is this a conspiracy?"

"Of the best kind, honey. Nothing but the best."

Her voice made him smile, did something to his chemistry. "I love you, Mar," he said.

"Friday, babe," she said. "Gotta scoot."

Service greeted the sun, sitting on the back steps with Newf and Cat, who had decided to grace them with her presence. They shared a raspberry Pop-Tart.

Les Reynolds called later that morning as Service sat in his office, staring at the photograph of the blond moon bear on his computer screen.

"We got a number from Colliver. It's a cell phone."

"Prepaid?"

Reynolds paused. "Just a cell phone. We called the number, but no answer. The vendor gave us an address in Nelma, Wisconsin, that's Forest County. I'm there now with the county people and the Wispies. There's a body."

Wispies were members of the Wisconsin State Patrol, the state's equivalent of the MSP.

"Who does the phone belong to?"

"It's registered to an Oliver Toogood of Iron County."

Service sat back and blinked. Trapper Jet? "Did you find Kelo?"

"The deceased is an elderly male with one leg. There's gonna be an autopsy."

"That's Toogood," Service said. "He claimed that Kitella burned his cabin."

"You don't say."

"Get the autopsy results to me soon as you can, okay?"

"One of the Wispies used to be a registered nurse. He says the old man looks like he starved to death."

Service went outside to walk around and clear his head and the captain followed him.

"Are you all right, Detective?"

Ollie Toogood had not been the only nearly blind man.

Trapper Jet and Honeypat had teamed up against Kitella. Skunk had helped. This made sense, he tried to tell himself, but there was something still gnawing at him. The cell phone in Nelma had not been disconnected. Somebody wanted them to find Ollie. They would not find Kelo, Service expected, dead or alive.

The fax from Lansing came in just before noon. The student photo was definitely Ollie Toogood.

Service wished Eugenie Cukanaw would call back with information on Magic Wan, but after their one brief conversation with the investigator, she had not returned his call. He pulled up the picture of the bear again. The blue boat had been scuttled off Laughing Fish Point for a reason. The bear could have been moved with a lot less trouble, but Terry Pung had taken the boat there, and sunk it. Why?

Irvin Wan allegedly had a camp in the U.P. His connection to Pung, if any, was not apparent. He couldn't just sit around. He needed to start preparing to look, and western Alger County looked like the only logical starting place.

He hoped.

37

Six-foot-six Jake Mecosta pulled on his rain slicker, uncapped a tin of Marvil Hot, and tucked a pinch between his cheek and gums. Mecosta was one of a few Native American officers in the DNR, a Baraga-L'Anse Chippewa. Mecosta and Service were the same age, longtime friends who shared a love for wild brook trout.

"Hope I can find the way," Jake said, eyeing the angle of a steep ridge overgrown with beech and maple.

Service grunted. "We'll just have to walk a little more. You take care of your feet and I'll take care of navigation."

Jake Mecosta grinned and nodded. He had long been an effective officer, but he had a couple of weaknesses—he was both clumsy and had an amazingly poor sense of direction. Fellow officers teased him about it; he had laughed at himself, and said it just caused him to walk a little more than his colleagues, so he kept himself in better shape. Neither man was perfect: for Service it was dogs, for Jake, direction.

Service did not know western Alger County well enough to make a one-man search. The boat had to have been dumped in this area for a reason. Last night he had studied maps and plat books and given up. Nothing fit, and his time was limited. He had called Jake Mecosta who covered western Alger.

"Let's talk to Santinaw," Jake had said after hearing the problem.

"He's still around?"

"Eighty-five and still going. Walks down to Eben and back once a month, eight-mile round trip."

Santinaw was Huronicus St. Andrew, a Munising Ojibwa who had served in the Pacific in World War II, and come home in 1946 after some time in Japan. As a boy, Huronicus pronounced St. Andrew as Santinaw, and that had been his name ever since. He lived alone, never married, and occasionally worked as a hunting or fishing guide. Service's old man had known him well, but Service hadn't thought about Santinaw for at least fifteen years.

His cabin was in the deep ridge area of the headwaters of the Rock River, east of the Laughing Whitefish, and they were getting ready to hike in to find him.

"Santinaw's been living here since he come back from the war," Mecosta said. "If anybody knows the area, he'll be the man." But you did not call St. Andrew on a telephone. You had to go to him, and before you got to him, you had to know where he lived.

Service studied the ridge. "This doesn't look too bad."

Jake Mecosta grinned. "Isn't too bad—for a bit—then she turns nasty. This rain and all that slate, we'll be lucky not to break a leg."

"How far?" Service asked.

"Mile, maybe two," Jake said. "It twists around a lot."

"Your route, or Santinaw's?"

"Santinaw never walks the same way twice; claims it keeps his footprints out of the forest."

The rain was falling steadily and it was cool.

"Let's do this," Grady Service said.

If Santinaw would allow it, Jake would remain with him in order to use the 800 MHz radio to maintain contact with Service, who would hike out and head for Jackson for the meeting with Siquin Soong.

The first quarter-mile was uphill, through a relatively clear maple and scrub oak forest, until they came to the lip of a ridge, where the terrain dropped straight down into an alder and cedar swamp bottom with braids of a small stream wandering through.

"We can climb down here," Mecosta said, moving to Service's right. "Further along, we might need our ropes." They both had harnesses and safety lines in their packs.

A man in his eighties walked around here year-round, Service reminded himself.

After an hour's walk along the cluttered streambed, Mecosta stopped. "I think we gotta climb back out somewhere around here."

Service looked up at the rock ledges that seemed to stick to the cliff wall like a five-year-old's Legos.

"You got a favorite route?" Service asked, looking up into the rain.

Jake sighed. "Seems like I always take a different one."

They used their green lights to climb, so they wouldn't be throwing wide, bright beams all over the woods. It was dark.

Sweat was pounding out of Service when they got to the top. "Now where?"

"East, down a bit, south over a ridge, and there we are."

Which translated into two sweaty, tricky hours, and a small cabin built near a rock shelf looking down on what was the beginning of the Rock River.

They smelled smoke before they got to the cabin, and as they approached, a small bear came hurtling past them. Even in the green beam its fur was deep black and shiny. Both men laughed.

"Santinaw, me and Service came to talk with you," Mecosta yelled from the front of the cabin.

The old man stepped outside, holding a pipe. His loose, shoulder-length hair was bright purple and lime green, and he was smiling.

"Young Service," he said with a big smile. "Lucky you got here at all, following Jake. Come in, come in."

The interior was tight and dry and warm, a small fire going in a wood stove. There were cured furs on the walls, tools, rifles, a honed crosscut saw, a shelf filled with old crocks and bottles, and a rack with fishing rods. The wooden floor was shiny from use, no dust.

Jake and Service put their packs on a small table, opened them, dug out the contents. Coffee, tea bags, brown sugar, snuff, pipe tobacco, matches, aluminum foil, duct tape, smoked whitefish, some cigars. "For you," Mecosta said.

Santinaw ignored the goods, asked them to sit. "Just about to make some tea," he said. "I took honey off a bear."

"We saw a bear on the way here."

Santinaw smiled. "That's him. The tyke's been hanging around ever since I took his honey, hoping I'll share. I might, but don't be tellin' him. Good to keep bears and women guessing."

St. Andrew put on a teakettle and sat down with his visitors.

Mecosta touched his own hair, said to the old man, "That the new look in Rock River country?"

"Got a woman over to Eben. Her idea. Said it makes me look like a rock star, whatever that is."

Mecosta smiled. "How old, twenties?"

Santinaw pursed his lips. "She's a mature woman—thirty at least."

Mecosta looked at Service and rolled his eyes.

"We need help," Service said, and told the man the whole story of the murders, the blue boat, the bear, everything.

Santinaw listened without interrupting.

"You think they brought this animal up into the Laughing Whitefish country?" he asked when Service had finished.

"I'm guessing," Service said. "They sank the boat off the point for a reason. If they were going to transfer it to a truck, they could've done that elsewhere." In Hancock, for example.

"You say this is a sacred bear?" Santinaw asked.

"Not sacred—rare. And if it's real, maybe the only one of its kind that anybody's seen."

"That makes it sacred," the old man said.

"You've been all over the area," Jake Mecosta said.

Service said, "We're looking for a camp, not sure of the size, but we figure it's isolated, not that easy to get to. Probably not on the lake."

"Be easier if you knew the owner," Santinaw said.

"We think the people we're looking for are Asian: Korean or Chinese. They've brought the animal here for a reason, maybe to sell it."

"I'm not a holy man. I don't see futures," Santinaw said. "Except in bed with that woman in Eben. I always know what she's going to do."

"Like dye your hair?"

"I didn't see that one coming," Santinaw said with a wink. "You know *maw-wi-win a-tik-a-meg.*"

"Weeping whitefish," Service said.

Santinaw nodded. "Your father taught you well, young Service. We fought together, you know; Guadalcanal, Okinawa, all those places, a long time ago. Too much blood, too much blood."

Service thought they were about to lose him, but the old man recovered, heard the teakettle whistling, filled cups, added tea bags, let them steep. "*Ja-ga-nash*, the English, could not read a brown face. They came here and found many whitefish in the river, took the fish, did not offer to share, saw some of our people crying and thought they were laughing."

He paused. "They cried not for the fish. *Match-i manito* lived up the river, above the lake in the canyon *ma-da-gam-ish-ka ni-di.*"

"Where the water moves quickly?" Service said. "I'm a little rusty. *Match-i man-i-to?*"

"I can't speak it at all," Jake said.

"Yes, fast water, above the lake. *Matchi manito* is the one *ja-ga-nash* called the devil. To us that is *matchi* or *wa-ni-sid*—unclean."

"An evil spirit."

"For Christians, *the* evil one, but our people knew him since time began. He would come to that place above the river to do things that would make our people cry."

"But there's no place for a camp up that way," Mecosta said.

"Now," Santinaw said. "Now."

He got up, added honey to their tea, dumped two huge spoons of sugar into each, and gave the cups to his guests.

"It is true," Santinaw said. "*Nin ba-ba-mosse, ond-jish-ka-osse, bi-ji-ba-osse, qwai-a-kosse, be-dosse, ki-ji-ka, nan-do-dish-kig.*"

Service had to concentrate hard to understand. St. Andrew had said something like, "I walk about, into the wind, slowly and fast, in circles and straight ahead, feeling my way."

"You walk a lot," Mecosta said.

Santinaw laughed. "Enough Ind'in talk. My memory is better with tobacco."

Service opened the outside pocket of his pack, took out two cartons of Marlboro Light 100s in boxes.

Santinaw opened the first pack delicately, tapped a cigarette out of the pack, put a piece of dry spaghetti in the wood stove, used the pasta to light his cigarette.

"You want me to talk *nish naw-be?*" St. Andrew asked Service.

"You've taxed my vocabulary already."

"The Iroquois, the *na-do-we,* used to go up above the lake and eat their enemies. Long ago some of my people met the Iroquois down near the lake and killed them. We never saw *na-do-we* again. This isn't in many white history books. My people avoided the above-the-lake because they wanted to let the *manitos* there have their peace. They had seen too much. But there was a time when the whites had a camp up there, a big cave." He made a shape with his hands.

"A grotto?" Service said.

"Yes, grotto. It goes deep into the side of the canyon and it is dry. Some white trappers lived there for many years and then a sickness came and they were gone."

"I think we're looking for something a little more recent than a grotto," Service said.

"I will leave in the morning, walk around, see what is to be seen."

"I'd like to stay and go with you," Jake Mecosta said.

"A man is free to choose," St. Andrew said.

Following his own route, Service was back in his truck in just over one hour.

How the old man had lived so long in such punishing territory was impossible to comprehend.

Service was almost home when the cell phone buzzed. It was Teddy Gates.

"I've been calling all day, but I didn't want to leave this message. Toogood withdrew all his funds from that bank up there."

Ontonagon. "When?"

"The day after I talked to you."

"Did he go there himself?"

"No, he was up there earlier this fall and asked for a cashier's check to be picked up by a friend. He even gave them a photograph of the guy."

Service sighed. Had Trapper Jet been to Ontonagon before Betty Very stumbled on to him? Was this why Toogood had been up there? If so, what was he doing wandering around the Firesteel River?

"Toogood's dead," he told his old commander. "The body was found yesterday."

The general cursed. "The check was for just under a half a million smackers."

Service hung his head, did not think, listened to the rain thumping the cab, mocking him: "You dumb fuck, you dumb fuck."

He called Betty Very and asked her to make a run to the bank in Ontonagon.

· 38 ·

Jackson was eight hours south of Gladstone, thirty degrees warmer, and as different as a Traverse City cherry and a durian. Service sat in his truck outside the general aviation building and talked to Treebone on the cell phone. Eight shiny corporate jets were parked on the apron, and a sign on the fence said, GOD IS BUSY. ATTENTION PILOTS: EYES UP FOR DEER ON TAXIWAYS.

"You understand what I want?" Service said.

"Got the what, not the why," Luticious Treebone said.

"Need to know, man."

"How it is, dawg."

"Your best man, right?"

"Sterling's our own Motown strike dog. Can follow a fart off a motorcycle seat with a five-day head start."

"He's so good, how I'm getting him?"

"The man is in the drawer, you know, Idi Amin shit. He shows you his stuff, maybe you can bring him over."

Idi Amin was Treebonese for IA or Internal Affairs. "Must be some most serious shit."

"No, man. He breathed some on the wrong brother, lipped his script."

"English, asshole."

"He's a hunter, Grady, got his ass in somebody else's patch, changed his story couple of times when he was talked at. His time here could be short. You like what you see, you might want to put a gray shirt on him."

"He's a brother?"

"Yo, he's a flyboy brat, grew up near the Soo."

"So you're asking me to audition a man when I need your best."

"He is the best. He does the job and then we talk.' "

"Your Grand Rapids P.I. hasn't delivered," Service said. "Is your man carrying a cell?"

"That's not like Eugenie," Tree said. "I'd better check on her. My man carries two cells." Treebone gave him the numbers.

Service explained what he wanted, said, "We tight?"

"Semper Fi, bro."

Service needed help and his friend was talking up his man, but Tree wasn't past a little scamming to get what he wanted for his people.

The plane came in from the northeast, nose into a light wind, touched down without a smoke puff on the five-thousand-foot runway, and taxied in. Lorelei Timms got off the twin-engine aircraft looking tired, a wrinkled trench coat slung over her shoulder. She was followed by a burly silver-haired man with a beaming smile. Timms walked toward Service and nodded. The silver-haired man followed with two bulging suitcases and a battered leather garment bag. The senator said, "Grady Service, this is my husband, Whit."

Whit Timms set the bags down and shook Service's hand. "Mostly I'm her pack animal," he said.

The couple walked toward a waiting tan minivan and driver. A State Police SUV was behind the van. Two young women and a young man got off the plane carrying cardboard boxes and headed toward a second van.

Nantz stepped into the hatch opening, looked down at Service and smiled. "Permission to come aboard," she said. "I'll show you around my office." She wore black trousers, a white short-sleeved shirt with epaulets, a thin black tie, a black wheel cap with wings.

There was not enough headroom for him and he had to stoop.

"There's no security here," he said.

Nantz stopped and pointed out a window at the threesome loading boxes in a second van. "The guy is Troop Sergeant Toby Robinette and there are three more in the detail in civvies. It's covered, Service."

"Sergeant? He looks fourteen," Service said.

"Everybody looks fourteen to you," she said with a laugh. "He works older than he looks."

She squeezed past him, pumped the hatch closed with a hydraulic arm, and latched the door.

They went back through the bird to a bench seat on the starboard side.

"What happened to my tour?" he said.

"It's about to begin," she said, tossing her tie over her left shoulder, unsnapping her trousers, letting them fall and stepping out of them. She pushed him onto the bench, put her hands on his shoulders, squatted over him.

Someone began banging on the hatch.

"Somebody wants in," Service told her.

"Only one person's getting in right now," Nantz whispered.

The outside noise continued.

The sound on the door blended with her movement and faded. When she came she collapsed on him, her arms tightly around his neck. "God," she said, her hips and thighs spasming with diminishing after-shocks.

There was no one near the plane when she opened the hatch.

He carried her bags to his Yukon. She sat beside him with her hand on his hip. "That just blunted my edge," she said. "Why am I so horny?"

"Why is air invisible?" he said.

She shrugged. "You're supposed to say something earthy and carnal," she said.

"My brain's not working."

She smiled. "Well, at least one part of you is. I need a nap this after-noon."

They drove twelve miles south to the Indian Road B&B on Devil's Lake. It had a gray brick facade, with neatly mown lawns and fingers of peony beds down to the lake.

Nantz hung up her evening gown, got out her shoes for the dinner, took off her clothes, and collapsed on the bed.

Service took a tux out of a plastic bag and hung it up. He had not worn a tux since his wedding. He tried to imagine himself in it and groaned, remembering he had forgotten to get black shoes.

He went down to the Yukon and dug out his Danner boots. At least they had once been black.

A woman named Hazel Slack owned the B&B. She was dressed in tight slacks and a red cowl-necked sweater.

"Got a shoeshine box I can use?" Service asked her.

"Sure," she said, scampering away.

The voice of Lorelei Timms said, "Out here, Detective." Service stepped onto a glassed-in porch holding his boots. She had a cup of cof-fee, a cigarette in an ashtray.

"You have your woman all to yourself in a beautiful room and you're going to shine your work boots?"

Service didn't respond.

"She's missed you," the senator said. "Have you been following the campaign?"

"Not really."

"You don't care who wins?"

"I care, but I'm just one vote."

"Do you think I have a chance?"

"I usually don't follow politics," he said.

She smiled. "You're priceless. Did Maridly give you her *special* tour of the plane?" she asked, arching an eyebrow.

Hazel Slack intervened with a shoeshine kit in a wooden box. "This is all we have."

Service went outside and did the best he could to bring the leather back to life, using old military spit-shine tricks, and carried the polished boots up to the room.

"You forgot black shoes," Nantz said groggily from the bed.

He shook his head. "I told you my brain isn't working and you said the boots are fine."

"They are," she said. "C'mon, we have an hour to rest and I want to spoon."

She patted his hip and sighed. "Don't let us oversleep, hon."

After the nap and a long bath, she dressed slowly, finally dropping a gold georgette gown over her head and adjusting the spaghetti straps. The dress dragged on the floor until she put on her shoes. "New," she said, holding up pointy-toed shoes by their tiny straps. "This is one of my weaknesses."

She added two strands of pearls and pearl drop earrings.

He dressed beside her and when he sat down to put on his boots, she rolled her eyes and smiled. "Are you going to tuck them or wear the pants over them?"

"What do you think?" he asked.

"Over," she said. "Unless you want to look like G.I. Joe."

Out in the Yukon she said, "Turn on the overhead light."

"We're gonna be late," Service said.

He watched her apply lipstick and examine her work.

"I can do what I gotta do while you drive," she said. "Thin lips," she added. "Collagen can fix them."

"Your lips don't need fixing." He couldn't understand why when she looked in the mirror she didn't see what everybody else saw.

"We're not going to be late," she said. "Stop worrying."

"Late's not an option for fifteen hundred a plate," he said. "Thank God we're not paying guests."

She looked over at him. "That's not exactly accurate."

He looked back at her.

"I made a little donation?" she said hesitatingly.

"How little?"

"Twenty K to Lori's campaign, and fifteen hundred each for us tonight."

"Good God, Mar, you can't be doing things like this! You're going to be a CO and we're not political."

"When I'm a CO I promise not to make any more political donations," she said. "Cross my heart."

She had money, but he had no idea how much and rarely thought about it. She was not ostentatious. She owned a nice home and a private plane and spent generously on food and wine, but she rarely bought clothes or jewelry, and she never talked about money. Yet, she had coughed up twenty-three thousand for the senator and her dinner, and done it with as much thought as he would in leaving a tip for a bartender. "You didn't make the sign," he said.

She made a sour face, halfheartedly waved her hand over the center of her chest, said, "Okiiy?"

"It better be a great meal," he griped.

She laughed and shook her head. "Just go with the flow, baby."

Betty Very called when they were stopped in the line of vehicles at the security checkpoint, a half-mile from the Stagecoach Lodge. The area was lit by portable floodlights and blocked by a zigzag maze of Troop cruisers and trucks.

"The bank president looked at the photo," Bearclaw said. "It's Kelo."

"Did he talk to Toogood when he made the request for the withdrawal?"

"For better than an hour. He tried to talk him out of it, but the old man wouldn't hear of it. His mind was made up and he insisted on a cashier's check to be picked up by somebody else and he left a photo of the pickup man."

"Kelo."

"Yes, the president said the photo that Toogood left with him matched the man, but he wasn't about to give it away without some security. They had quite an argument and, in the end, Kelo grudgingly agreed to a fingerprint as a receipt."

"Did he use his name?"

"No. He said the photo was enough and he refused to give a name."

"You have the fingerprint?"

"And the photo. The fingerprints have been transmitted to AFIS already."

"Great job," Service said. "Thanks, Betty."

"I'm sorry about your friend," she said.

Service turned to Nantz and told her about Trapper Jet and Kelo and all that he had learned and gone through. "I think Kelo's a dead man," he concluded. He didn't know for sure, but almost everyone in this case was turning up dead.

"Why would he agree to give a fingerprint?" Nantz asked.

"The bank president boxed him in. He probably figured he was there to get the check and there was no way to run a single print through the system and, in any event, the bank president didn't have his name. Kelo's never been known as a bright bulb."

Two state troopers stood on either side of the vehicle. Nantz showed her ID and invitation; Service flashed his badge. They got the nod to move on.

The Stagecoach Lodge was a low, sprawling, red brick building that looked like it had undergone a lot of additions. The parking lot was in front of the building and full of expensive vehicles. Service parked along the driveway and locked the Yukon.

They walked under a canopied portico to the main entrance, presented their invitations and IDs, and gave up their coats. Nantz wrapped a gold and scarlet georgette wrap around her bare shoulders. The main area was filled with women in shimmering gowns and pointy high heels.

A young woman in a short black skirt and white blouse offered a tray of champagne flutes. Nantz took one; Service refused.

"What's with you?" she asked.

"Later," he said.

She took a swig and grinned. "That's a ten-four, big boy. I might get a little drunk tonight."

There was a reception line leading down a corridor to the dining room. It moved too slowly for Service, who said "Baah," just under his breath and got a poke from Nantz. They moved through, shaking hands with various politicians Service didn't recognize until they got to Lorelei and Whit.

The senator looked down at his boots, but her expression remained even. "Siquin, these are my friends, Grady Service and Maridly Nantz."

Whit Timms leaned toward Service. "Great kicks, man."

They had not had a chance to talk at any length, but Service instinctively liked the senator's husband.

"Yes," Soong said. "Detective." She held out her hand, gripped his momentarily, and used it to guide him to face an old man standing with the assistance of two metal canes hooked to his wrists by metal bands. "My husband, Buzz Gishron."

Soong looked barely forty, her husband at least twice that and not likely to last much longer.

Gishron said, "Twinkie man," and smiled, nodding like a bobble head.

The dining room was massive with a head table on a raised dais and in front of it a sea of round tables covered with white linen cloths. Candles burned at each table beside small arrangements of red and orange fall flowers in shiny brass vases.

They found their placecards at a table in the center of the white sea and sat down as others filed in and took their seats.

A string quartet and a piano were making music in the corner. The music was white noise to Service.

Nantz said, "Dutilleux, 'Ainsi la Nuit.' " She closed her eyes, seemed to let her mind flow with the music.

Nantz smiled and greeted everyone who came to their table, making small talk. Service grunted politely and watched the room, looking for Soong.

The younger men in the room wore their hair cut short on the sides, longer on top, shiny with gel and prickling with little spikes, like their bodies gave off electrical charges. Many of them wore Lenin goatees.

"Hair," he whispered.

"It's called 'faux hawk,' " she said.

"More like punks-with-money," he said.

She tapped his arm and took his hand in hers. "Be nice. Having money doesn't make people assholes."

"Younger crowd than I expected," he said. "Where does the money come from?"

"Professionals, dot-com survivors, and trust-fund babies," she said. "Most of them are so leveraged their finances would collapse under a fart." She squeezed his hand for emphasis and dragged a fingernail along his palm. He felt a spark and saw her blue eyes gleaming.

A relatively tall and muscular Asian man helped Buzz Gishron to his place at the head table. After he was seated, the others joined him, five couples in all, including Lorelei and Whit Timms. The Asian had the same gleaming spiked hair and wore a black suit, not a tux. His suit said he didn't belong; his attitude said something different. Service could feel the arrogance.

Service thought they looked like ravens on a power line scoping the world for food or mischief, whichever opportunity came along first.

One of the men on the dais stood up and held up his hands for silence. He made introductions without fanfare. Senator Timms got a standing ovation that went on for five minutes, but she did not rise to speak.

"Okay, team," Service whispered, "let's all haul out our bank books and buy us a candidate."

Nantz kicked him under the table. "It's a *party* fund-raiser, dummy," she whispered.

Siquin Soong studied the audience with a practiced smile and intense eyes. Service looked back and saw that she was looking at him, but she showed no emotions and moved her eyes on.

"She's gorgeous," Nantz said.

"Like those neon-colored frogs that draw in their victims to poison them."

"She's Lori's supporter."

"How do you separate support from ownership?" he asked sarcastically.

"Pish," she said.

He ignored Nantz and watched Soong. She was attractive and he could still feel her hand—not just cold, but frigid, like she had no blood flow at all.

The menus were delivered to the table. They were printed in gold on linen paper that felt like pressed cloth. It said, "A Tribute to Michigan's Bounty." Five courses were listed. "Walleye Pie with Sautéed Dickinson County Morels; Asian-style Medallions of Free-Range, Farm-Raised Venison with Chartreuse Medley of Vegetables from "The Mitt" (baked in a fresh pastry shell); Puree of Kalamazoo Small Roots; Central Michigan Sour Cream Drop Biscuits; Toffee Pudding (a thick nutmeat roll with caramel sauce); Demitasse Café and Tea (Chocolate-Dipped Ginger, South Haven Blueberries Florentine, Truffles).

"They got baloney?" Service asked, loud enough for others at the table to hear. Several of them snickered.

Dinner was brought one course at a time with long pauses between.

After the fourth course Soong left the head table. Service excused himself, and followed her onto the back patio.

He stood outside the fringe of light from the dining room.

"I am pleased to find you alone," Siquin Soong said from the darkness. She stepped forward, her face obscured in shadows. Light bathed her shoulders and lit the angles of her breasts, which were barely contained in the strapless black gown. He saw a red ember.

"A dreadful weakness," she said. "I tried any number of times to quit, but frustration alone guarantees failure." She made a *tsk*ing sound. "There are things we cannot change about ourselves, do you agree?"

"I'm sorry," he said to bait her. "You are—?" She had no accent, spoke English like she had been raised in the States.

Soong laughed without mirth. "Don't play games, Detective, especially when you don't know the rules. You came here specifically to meet me and I have made it possible. A little gratitude might be in order. I have nothing to hide."

"At the moment?" he said.

"I was warned you could be abrasive."

Warned by whom? he wondered. "I wanted to ask you about your son. Your lawyers aren't playing nice."

"My dear Detective, you're misinformed. Fate and biology have decreed I have no children, a burden no woman should have to bear."

"Your ex-husband's son," he said.

"My former husband had no son. In fact, he lacked the wherewithal, if you understand."

"There is a man posing as his son," he said.

"Ah," she said. "You have evidence of this?"

"Not yet."

She sighed dismissively. "An alleged imposter, then. I admire our country, but the culture encourages outrageous behaviors."

"Eventually we will find the man and then we'll find out."

She straightened up, pushed her head back and her breasts forward. "Are you a Mountie, Detective, one of those policemen who always get their man?"

"Not a Mountie, ma'am, but I tend to get who I am after."

"Well," she said, "I have no doubt that you have no trouble getting any woman you choose," she said, pressing her breast against his arm and maintaining the pressure. "You must be proud of our mutual friend. She is certain to be elected and that will be a great day for our state."

Our country, our state—she played the immigrant citizen role well. "I think the people will have to vote before that happens."

She pulled away from him. "I expected more sophistication," she whispered.

"What are we talking about?" he asked.

"We always hope to meet interesting people," she said. "Thank you for allowing me to monopolize a few moments of your time." She stepped into the light, looked back at him, and lowered her eyes. "I should attend to my guests now."

"You'll be at Harry's funeral, right?"

Siquin Soong's eyes widened momentarily, then narrowed. "Pardon?"

"You heard me," he said as he slid past her and through the door.

He found Nantz with Lorelei Timms. "Where were you?" Nantz asked. Dessert had been served.

"Grabbing a smoke," he said.

Lorelei Timms was holding her shoes, standing on the carpeted floor in her stocking feet.

"I wish I could wear *my* boots," she said. "*And* have a smoke."

Service checked the room. Most people were standing around tables, talking and laughing.

Buzz Gishron was still seated at the head table and Whit Timms was talking to him.

Service touched Nantz's arm to let her know he was slipping away again, went out to the patio, and circled the building.

There was a guard at the side entrance, a Lenawee County deputy. He showed the man his badge.

"Some soiree," the deputy said. "You on duty?"

"Just hoping to get laid."

The deputy laughed. "Not a problem in this crowd. They've been going back and forth to the vehicles all through dinner. You can smell weed in the air over in the lot. We're in the don't-ask, don't-tell mode."

"Have you seen the senator?"

"No, but I seen that big-shot Asian bimbo who came in with her and the old guy."

"Where?"

"She's out in that white Mercedes stretch."

Service crossed the lawn, making sure to keep a good distance from the vehicle. He came up in its blind spot, saw two heads in back, no driver. He immediately stepped into the shadow of another vehicle and waited. Siquin Soong got out of the limo and made her way quickly into the building. A man got out of the rear door opposite the building and started to open the driver's door, but Service bumped him hard to get his attention. The man froze and tensed. Service leaned over and looked directly into his eyes.

"Sorry," Service said. "Guess I had a coupla suds too many, hey?"

He felt the man's eyes on him as he crossed in front of the limo and went back into the lodge.

Timms and Nantz were still talking. Some of the crowd was beginning to drift out of the building.

Service said, "Senator, who was the young Asian man that helped Soong's husband to the dais?"

Lorelei Timms looked at him suspiciously. "The man is her driver and her pilot. I once heard someone call him her brother, but I doubt that. I think he serves other purposes. Do I need to be more specific?"

"Aren't you worried about a scandal?"

"She's a political supporter, not my friend. What she does is her business and she is an extremely independent woman."

"Do you know the man's name?"

"No, why are you interested?"

"He's plagued by curiosity," Nantz said, tugging him away.

"Are Soong and her husband staying nearby?"

"I assume they're returning to their home in Detroit," Timms said. "I'm not comfortable with these questions, Grady."

"I get paid to ask questions."

"You're not on duty tonight."

"A cop and a governor are always on duty," he said.

Lorelei Timms glared at him. Nantz grabbed another glass of champagne and pulled him away.

Service said. "I think I screwed up. Let's split."

"Now?"

"Now."

They got into the Yukon and he saw that the white limo was still there. Service punched a number into his cell phone. "Sterling?"

"You got 'im."

"Where are you?"

"Entry road, only way in and out. What's going down?"

"White Mercedes stretch limo, driver and two passengers." Service gave the man the license plate number. "You stay with the driver, no matter what."

"Give you a bump when he lights?"

"Yeah, good luck," Service said.

"Don't need it," Sterling said.

· 39 ·

Nantz got out of the vehicle and walked unsteadily up the walk into the B&B, waving at him to let him know she was okay. Service turned on the 800 MHz, clicked to Channel 3, called, "Thirty-One Eighteen, Twenty-Five Fourteen," repeating the call twice, then waiting.

He tried again five minutes later and still no response.

Five minutes after that Jake Mecosta radioed, "Thirty-One Eighteen is up."

"What's your status?"

"We may have something. We found that place our guide told us about. It looks like somebody's been there."

The "guide" was Santinaw. "Any critters?"

"No sign of that, but somebody's done some sprucing up."

"Kids?"

"Possible, but our guide picked up a trail at the north end of that body of water we discussed. We followed it up to a tote road, about half a click. Somebody ran a four-wheeler down to the river. Old tracks, in and out. Just one trip."

"How far from that trail to the hole we talked about?" Service asked. The body of water was Laughing Whitefish Lake. The river flowed into the top of it and out the bottom. The hole was the grotto Santinaw had told them about.

"Two clicks maybe."

"Isn't much."

"Wasn't, but last night somebody left a voice mail for me and urged me to take a look at a cabin on a small lake east of the chute, above that body of water. We're there now. Lots of activity, five males, three four-wheelers, and a canoe with a motor. Lots of crates and gear, but we haven't gone in close to find out what. I sent Dort to the county clerk, see if we can find out who owns the place now. She'll TX me soon as she knows one way or the other. These people here are most definitely not from Kansas—all from way east of our Far West, copy?"

Dort was Mecosta's wife. "Copy." Service understood.

"Anonymous caller, male or female?"

"Female, no name, and I didn't recognize the voice. You know how it goes."

He did. Most Yoopers didn't abide law-breaking, but also didn't want to get involved because they feared testifying or getting crossways with neighbors. It had always been so above the bridge.

Mecosta was being extremely circumspect in telling him what was going on, but it boiled down to the fact that an anonymous tip had pointed him at a cabin where they had seen five men and a lot of gear, five men east of west, meaning across the Pacific—Asians. An anonymous call could mean somebody had a beef with them, or was worked up over what appeared to be so many foreigners in one place, one of the legacies of September 11.

"How's your guide holding up?"

Mecosta said. "Ought better ask how I'm doing. I've never seen a walker like him, up hill, down hill, same pace, hours on end."

"I'm going to alert backup in case we need them. See any weapons in the group?"

"Long guns in cases."

"Got a meet-site in mind?" Service asked.

"You know the next little burg west of where our guide has his lady friend?"

"I remember." Mecosta meant a place called Rumely.

"There's a road runs north out of there, same name as the place. It T's three miles north."

Rumely Road, Service thought. "Hides?"

"Some fields with some hardwoods right before the T. Right or left is fine, rocky ground."

"Okay, I'll make calls. Let me know what you find out about ownership."

"TX or 800?"

"800 is best, but either will work."

"You coming back?"

"Let's see what we have in the morning."

"Thirty-One Eighteen clear."

Maybe this was something, Service thought, then decided it rated a probably. Five Asian men in the same area. A definite probably.

He called Captain Grant at home. "Service." He laid out the situation and what he needed.

"The T north of Rumely on Rumely Road?"

"Right." The captain sounded wide awake.

"Four more people do it?"

"Should."

"Count me in. I'll be there. Any feel for what's in the offing?"

"Nossir, just something."

"Soong's copilot?"

"That's what I was told."

"This would be Pung?"

"I don't know," he said. He had seen the man, but had no photo.

"But you don't know."

"It's gut and circumstance at this point, Cap'n."

"Keep me informed."

He locked the truck and went up to the room. Nantz had dumped her gown on the carpet and was asleep, breathing steadily.

He put his handheld and cell phone on the night stand, undressed and eased in beside her, not wanting to wake her, but suddenly he heard a buzz and groped for his cell phone.

"Service?"

"Yeah." He glanced at his watch: 4:30 A.M.

"The driver dropped the couple at a house near White Lake, spent fifteen minutes inside, brought out some boxes and drove the limo over to Oakland County International where he met four Asian males at the Horizon Lounge. They had several drinks, he dropped them at a Holiday Inn Express, and drove out to the airfield to the transient parking area. He moved the boxes from the limo into an aircraft, a Cessna Citation Ten. Got something to write with?"

Service reached down to the floor, fumbled for a pen from his pants. "Okay."

Sterling gave him the tail number.

"Where's the guy now?"

"He went to operations, was in there twenty minutes. I watched him back to the bird, went into ops and flashed my shield. He filed a flight plan for Sawyer International, open departure for tomorrow morning."

Sawyer was the old air force base twenty miles south of Marquette and about the same distance west of Mecosta and Santinaw. This couldn't be coincidence. "How big is this bird?"

"Twin-engine jet, looks to me like it can handle six to eight pax, and crew."

"Where's your man now?"

"On the bird, lights out, either napping or choking the chicken," Sterling said. "You want me to stick here?"

"Call me as soon as he moves."

"You got it."

Nantz was awake when he closed the cell phone. "What's going on?" she asked sleepily.

"Jake got an anonymous tip. He and Santinaw are sitting on a camp right now."

"Will this happen today?" Nantz asked as she got out of bed and went into the bathroom.

"Maybe," he said.

Service called Grant, gave him the report and the aircraft tail number so he could alert the authorities at Sawyer and try to run down the bird's owner.

The captain said, "Our people are set: McCants, Moody, Ebony, and Mecosta. I haven't talked to the Troops or Alger County yet."

"Let's hold on them," Service said. "We don't want a false alarm. This thing is iffy enough."

Nantz came out of the bathroom holding a glass of water, picked up her purse, sat on the edge of the bed, dug around for a bottle of ibuprofen tablets, took three, and washed them down with the water.

"Did we overtrain?" he asked.

"I'm fine. I was counting on having all day to recover."

"Change in plans. I need for you to fly me to Munising."

"Today?"

"Now," he said.

"What about your truck?"

"Leave it. We'll handle details when we're done."

She put her head back and said, "God," stood up, got her clothes, and started dressing.

"What's the flight time to Munising?" he asked her.

"Depends on weather. It's not like driving a car, babe." She pulled on a sock, added, "Two and a half hours if I firewall it and the wind and weather cooperate. That's from gear-up here to over Hanley," she said.

Service called Treebone at home while Nantz finished dressing. "Raincheck on tonight. We have to fly back to the U.P."

"Fly? Man, you must be onto something big. I keep trying Eugenie's number, but all I get is her machine."

Service had always been uncomfortable in aircraft. "Tell Kalina we're sorry."

Nantz stopped to see Lorelei Timms.

Service was waiting in the Yukon. "What did she say?"

"Wanted to ask questions, but I told her there's no time and that I'd get back to her. She and Whit were planning to stay until Sunday. Campaigning starts again Monday morning. I'll come back Sunday. Soong's chauffeur's name is Irvin Terry."

Service thought, Irvin Wan, Terry Pung: One and same?

They were at the plane in twenty minutes.

Nantz got out. "I'll do the pre-flight, make sure it's fueled and ready."

Service sat in the Yukon, waiting.

Mecosta called on the 800. "These people are getting ready to move stuff down to the river on their four-wheelers."

"How will they get the stuff upriver?"

"Slate ledges and low water. They can run it like a highway."

"Get down to the river and monitor."

"What about the camp?"

"Only one radio, I don't want Santinaw on his own. We're coming north."

"Now?"

"Soon."

Service hung up and the phone rang. Mecosta again: "You didn't let me finish. Dort called. The cabin is owned by White Star Properties, a subsidiary of White Moon Trading Company of Southfield. Mean anything to you?"

"Thanks, man," Service said.

Nantz came back.

"I need one more call-back," he said.

"I need coffee," she said. "I'm going to find a vending machine."

"Don't dawdle."

She laughed. "I thought that's what we'd be doing in bed about now." She gave him an exaggerated wiggle and strode away.

The field was silent and there were only a few lights. He got out of the truck and began piling the gear and clothing he needed on the tarmac.

Nantz brought two coffees and looked at the pile.

"Let's get all that stuff out to the bird," she said. "We can wait in the plane as comfortably as here."

He agreed.

He sat in the copilot's seat, half-seeing the bewildering array of instruments and gauges.

The cell phone buzzed. "Service."

"They just filed for an 0745 takeoff," Sterling said. "Same destination."

"Stay with them until they're off the ground and call this number when you see them lift off." He gave Sterling Captain Grant's cell phone number.

"Thanks," Service said, checking his watch. It was 5:23 A.M. If the other plane took off on time, he and Nantz would have more than a two-hour lead. He opened his cell phone and called the captain.

"Treebone loaned me a bird dog and he's going to call when the plane leaves Oakland for Sawyer. His name is Sterling. He's stuck in some sort of bogus IA mess and Tree thinks he'd make a good man for us. He's done the job for me. He's a pro."

The captain thanked him, said they would talk about Sterling later.

Nantz said, "I checked weather when I got coffee. There's a cold front coming down off Lake Superior. Should make landfall midday. We should be fine if the advance winds aren't too stiff."

Service buckled his lap harness and nodded. "Let's roll."

The phone rang again as they paused at the end of the runway. Nantz nodded for him to answer it as she adjusted the throttles.

"This is Eugenie Cuckanaw. I'm sorry to take so long. Wan doesn't own a camp in the U.P., but he uses one in—"

"Alger County," Service said interrupting her. "Thanks." He hung up.

Service held up his 800. "Can I use this?"

She nodded. "Be quick."

"Jake, we're on the runway, ready to go. Cap'n Grant is arranging backup. Give him a bump and have somebody meet us at Hadley. You've definitely got the place. ETA . . ." He looked over at Nantz who held up three fingers. "We'll be there zero eight forty-five. See you later."

"Copy," Mecosta said.

Nantz said into her headset, "Roger, Four Niner Mike Juliet Mike is rolling."

She pushed the throttles up and Service felt vibrations in his ass as she taxied onto the runway, went to full power, and took off into the wind, pulling the nose up steeply and leveling at eighteen hundred feet. When they finished climbing to their assigned cruising level, she put the bird on autopilot and dug through her flight bag for let-down charts. "Hadley's a grass field," she said. "It field closes tonight until May 15."

She looked at a calendar on her leg-board and said, "Boo!"

"What?" he said.

"Today's Halloween, big boy."

· 40 ·

S ervice was on the 800 as soon as Nantz set the plane down on the grass. The sky was gray and roily, with an erratic light wind sending leaves fluttering in bunches from trees ringing the perimeter of the field. He saw the captain parked and waiting, and radioed Jake Mecosta. "We're on the ground, where are you?"

"On the rim, directly above the target."

"Where do you want us?"

"These guys are back and forth on the route I told you about. Best you come in from the up-water drop, and make sure you stay on the Reagan side."

The up-water drop was Laughing Whitefish Falls. Reagan side meant conservative, therefore the right, which meant the east as they would come in. "Copy. We'll call back when we start in."

Mecosta responded, "Get set and I'll come to you."

Service acknowledged receipt with two clicks of the mike button.

Nantz helped him load his gear into the back of the captain's truck. "I should head back," she said.

The captain said, "I could use your help first."

She smiled and got into the backseat.

McCants and the other officers were waiting in the small gravel parking lot at the trailhead that led to the falls. There was a green porta-john, a picnic table chained to a tree, a barbecue pit, and a sign with a map of the walking trail through the area. All of the officers carried packs and MAG-LITEs. McCants and Moody carried their recently issued rifles, Gary Ebony a shotgun.

The captain exhibited his usual calm. "I'll take keys. This is too public to leave the vehicles. Ms. Nantz and I will move them to the original hide. There's bottled water in back. Help yourselves." They each took three one-liter bottles of water and put them in their packs.

Nantz looked like she wanted to hug him, but simply looked into his eyes and nodded. They had reached a point in their relationship when words weren't necessary.

She and the captain left in two of the trucks as the group started the almost one-mile hike to the falls. It was a wide, groomed trail through second-growth beech and maple. The leaves of the maples ranged in color from red to orange.

There was a wooden stairway at the top of the falls that went down nearly two hundred feet into the canyon. The falls at the top dropped fifteen or twenty feet straight down onto a limestone and slate slope that sent the water cascading at a forty-five-degree angle. Ahead they could see open sky and canopies of forest, the leaves ranging from lavender to red and pink. The air smelled earthy and fishy. They stood on the top platform and Service laid out the situation for them.

"Pairs?" McCants asked.

"You and Gary, Gut and me. I'll hook up with Jake later. Remember, we're looking for a bear, one of a kind." He let that thought sink in, took out the wrinkled computer image and passed it around. "It probably looks like this—blond, ninety to one hundred and forty pounds or so, with a mane like a lion."

"I think I used to date her," Ebony joked.

"Right tense on all your women," McCants said, grinning.

Ebony grimaced.

"Focus," Service said sharply. "These people have killed twice so far."

"I don't like the so-far shit," Gutpile Moody said.

"Use it to stay on track," Service told him.

McCants was studying the photo. "What's with the cage?"

"I don't know that," he said.

"Lotta unknowns here," Ebony said.

"The scene looks medieval," McCants said. "Creeps me out."

"That was the nineteenth century and a lousy photo," Service said. "This is now." He took them through the case again, in more detail, concluding, "I think they're testing the waters. If they can bring this animal in, they can take out what they want."

"Bring the animal in for what?" Moody asked.

"We'll find out," Service said, thinking about the picture but not sure what it meant.

None of the officers asked what they would do if this was not the group he was after. They came up empty lots of times and simply regrouped. Failure was part of the job.

Light rain began to fall when they got down to the riverbed. The water was still angling down, moving fast, and there was a light mist from the falls, the river about seventy-five feet across. Service had no idea how wide it was below, but they needed to move down the right wall and he led them across. He stopped on the other side and put on his rain jacket and gloves. The temperature had dropped fast since they left the trailhead, as it always could in the Superior watershed, especially this time of year.

"Cold front coming across the lake," he told them. "Supposed to hit the area around noon."

Moody sniffed the air. "I smell snow. She'll be wet and slippery."

McCants looked at Service and winked, got no response, rolled her eyes, said, "I know . . . focus."

"Have you seen the grotto?" Gutpile asked.

"No, but Jake's been there with Santinaw. They've been scouting the area for a couple of days."

"That crazy old Indian's still alive?" Moody asked.

"Candi, you and Gary will set up closest to the grotto, then Gut, and I'll be last so I can maneuver to meet and talk to Jake. Everybody on 800s, earphones. Only Jake and I will talk. Acknowlege with clicks."

The canyon was more of a gorge and the river wasn't deep, but it moved with force, driven by gravity and slope. The rocks all along the way were slick and they had to be careful of their footing. The sides of the gorge were nearly vertical, in shelves twenty to thirty feet high, stacked on each other. Here and there was some greenstone and exposed strata. Shards of broken stone littered the river, having been snapped off by the cycles of freezing and thawing. At one point, McCants raised her fist and they all squatted. A beaver came swimming up the river toward a two-foot-deep pool, carrying a six-foot-long aspen toward a small dam in the making. The structure wouldn't survive the winter, but failure never deterred beavers. Service thought about how far the animal had to drag the aspen and sympathized.

The rain fell heavily for nearly an hour, then let up, and as the temperature continued to fall, turned to snow. Snow wouldn't raise the river level, which wouldn't impede the movement of things up the river. Service was almost glad to have the snow, knew the ground was too warm to hold it, that it would hit and soon melt.

They got into their hides just before noon. Service met with the group one final time and told them he didn't know how long they would be there, but to get comfortable and be prepared for a long wait. There were no smartass remarks now. They had all done surveillance and stakeouts many times, understood what had to be done, and were getting their minds into the zone where time would pass and they would stay attentive only to the moment. Some people never developed the ability to do this.

Service found a place under an overhang that afforded some protection from the wet snowflakes and got on the 800. "We're here," he said.

The captain said, "Might get two inches tonight. Our friend says that bird is not yet on the ground. Nantz got off safely."

Service toggled his transmitter twice, click click. Where the hell was the other aircraft?

He needed to talk to Mecosta, but would let him take the initiative.

The snow intensified around three o'clock, coming down so heavily that it was impossible to see across the river, which was about ten feet from where they were. Leaves were shooting down the river, brightly colored wrinkled rafts. The river level had risen, but not much. A mature bald eagle came soaring down from upriver, got almost to the surface, saw one of them and lifted off, scattering feathers. Service could hear its wings batting the air as it struggled for altitude and safety.

Behind him a mink pussyfooted along the rocks, saw him, and reversed direction. He could smell the animal's musk.

In a pool by his hide he saw four steelhead on a gravel bed. A chrome female flashed in the low light as she finned and shook to clean the area in preparation for putting out her eggs while the three males bumped and chased each other behind her, jockeying for position.

A gray jay came down to the river to drink and looked at him. Gray jays lived in Canada, came down to the U.P. for winters, which in Service's opinion, put their intelligence in question.

Mecosta made contact just before dark. "All subjects are out of the grotto," Service heard in his earpiece. "Going back to camp. Takes them about twenty minutes to get to the trail, thirty minutes up to the cabin, load time if they're bringing more stuff, fifty minutes to be back in the grotto."

Service radioed, "New arrivals at the cabin?"

"Don't know. Santinaw is with me."

This was good. They didn't need anybody without a radio wandering around until they knew what they were dealing with.

"Santinaw says there's another entrance to the grotto," Mecosta said. "Somebody ought to get inside while they can."

Another entrance? "Where are you?"

"On top."

"I'm coming up."

"No elevator," Jake said. "Just climb up where you are and Santinaw and I will find you."

Service looked up at the rocks above, figured it was between one hundred fifty and two hundred feet. While he had light he had visually marked several routes, but in darkness it would not be an easy climb and there was a lot of loose rock and stone to contend with all the way. "I'm climbing," Service said.

It took an hour to make the climb, with only a few times where he had to backtrack for safer footing. It was steep but he stayed at it, and when he finally crawled over the top he was drenched in sweat. He sat on the edge and took a drink of water.

"You have the grace of a turtle," Santinaw whispered from the dark. "We could hear you coming for thirty minutes."

"Three minutes for me," Jake Mecosta said.

Santinaw chuckled. "Don't understand how you two could catch anything."

Service was tired and beginning to chill. "While we're bullshitting, nobody is in the grotto and nobody is covering their route. We have people down there. Let's *move*."

The entrance was nearly two hundred feet back from the rim, beside some large oaks and between two boulders. Service used his penlight to look into the hole. "This looks like an old copper pit," he said.

Santinaw said, "From those who came before the people."

Service didn't say anything. To every Native American, their own tribe was "the people" and other tribes something less. The old copper pits had been dug out by Indians who lived in the area thirty-five hundred years ago, where they found surface copper, dug around it, building fires to break off the metal. Copper from the Great Lakes had been traded all over the continent. He had never seen such a pit east of the Keeweenaw, but there were patches of copper here and there in the central U.P. and this was not a total surprise.

"Why didn't you say something about this earlier?" he asked Santinaw.

"If you get to be my age, you'll understand."

"Have you ever been down this?"

"I don't think so," Santinaw said. "It's hard to remember."

"But it goes down to the grotto?"

"It will or it won't."

"Goddammit, old man."

"I'm old, the earth is older. Things move around. Perhaps it went all the way once, maybe it still does."

Service heard an urgent whisper in his earpiece. "Hey, up there, we have traffic down here." It was McCants.

Service answered with two clicks. "They're back," he told Mecosta.

"I'll go down with you," the other officer said.

"No, somebody has to sit their trail, monitor traffic."

Service toggled his 800. "Give me a count, how many visitors." He got back five clicks, evenly spaced.

"Five," he told Mecosta. "Others will come."

Service radioed the captain. "Bird down?"

"Five straight up."

Five? What the hell had taken them so long?

Service sat and put his feet in the hole, shone his light down into the darkness, and saw rocks jutting out. "The angle doesn't look too bad," he said, hoping it would stay that way.

"The earth moves," Santinaw reminded him.

The tunnel was a tight squeeze in some places, wider in others. Generally he could make steady progress downward. At one point he took out his compass, but the needle refused to settle. There was iron ore in the rock as well. He climbed down with his face against the wall and did not lift one foot until the other one had purchase. He checked his watch periodically and a minute or so after the forty-minute mark, he saw light below him. Faint, but definitely light. He could feel air coming up the shaft. The light was reflected against a boulder at the base of the hole right under him, maybe five feet down. He carefully lowered himself to the bottom and belly-crawled forward toward the light source. He was moving horizontally now and there was some rubble on the floor, but the sides of the tunnel were smooth; he felt them and guessed it was an old mineshaft. He hoped it was through hard firm bedrock, not soft and porous limestone. At the end of the horizontal shaft there was a large boulder blocking the exit and lights moved and bounced beyond his vision, spilling over the top: flashlights. He undid his pack, took a swig of his water, closed the pack up again. He got to his knees and stood in a crouch. Training: never try to see it all at once from concealment. He would make minor adjustments, try to see what was ahead of him in quadrants, assemble the whole picture in his brain.

He was about to take his first peek when he heard voices, men shouting happily, boisterously. He froze against the rock, waited. Heard some crashing not far in front of him, wanted to look, needed to. He took a deep breath, let it out slowly, started to push up again.

A flash lit the tunnel, sent him down hard, banging his elbow, causing the arm to go numb. Jesus! In front of him there was crackling, popping, and smoke began to roll in across the blocking rock. Fuck, a fire.

He lay with his feet away from the grotto, moving his arm, trying to unfreeze it, get feeling back into his hand. The smoke was rolling in, but sliding over his head in a visible line, like a layer of gauze. It reminded him of mosquito netting in a barely detectable breeze.

When something touched his leg, he kicked instinctively, but his leg was caught and he looked back.

"I remembered it comes through," Santinaw said. The old man patted his leg affectionately before releasing it. The old man tapped him again and Service looked back. He handed a cloth to Service and took one for himself and poured water on it and tied it over his nose and mouth. Service understood. Makeshift filtering for their lungs.

Service followed suit, told himself he had to look, had to do something.

Santinaw crawled up beside him.

There were voices in on the other side of the rock, two, three; no, he couldn't differentiate. Not speaking English, heard movement, things being dropped. Wood crashing on a fire—logs being added. The clanging of metal, something heavy being wrestled around. A voice was singing some sort of high-pitched thing, no tune, just sounds that grated at him.

Santinaw said, "Death song."

"That's not Ojibwa," Service said.

"Death song," Santinaw repeated.

"Where's Jake?"

"It was boring with him. I like to look around."

Jesus Christ. Metal grated metal, made a screech. Above. Then another sound, a new one, high to low, anguish, fear. Also above.

He looked up at the flow of smoke, knew he couldn't break the stream or it would cascade down and choke them. Right now the smoke was moving smoothly through the tunnel and up the back shaft like a chimney. They needed to keep it that way.

Santinaw tugged on his jacket. "*Makwa*," he said.

Mak-wa, Ojibwa for bear.

"*Pa-gid-ji*," the old man added, pointing upward.

Bear above. Bear above?

"The picture," Santinaw whispered.

The picture, bear in a hanging cage. No fire in the picture. Fire here, bear above.

Shit, he thought.

"Its *man-i-to* is afraid," Santinaw whispered.

So is mine, Service thought. He studied the smoke, had to get up there to take a look.

"*Be-ka*," the old man said.

Slowly, don't disrupt the smoke.

More chain sounds, sharp, pained squeals.

He got up, turned his head sideways, looked under the smoke, saw several men dressed in saffron robes, like *bonzes*, the Buddhist monks who burned themselves in Vietnam to protest the war.

Chain sounds again, overhead but closer. He looked again, slightly downward, saw a huge stainless steel vat. What the hell?

Then it hit him: Christ! What had Tara Ferma written in her e-mail, that bears would be lowered into boiling oil? Shit shit shit.

Now the animal screamed a long, angry cry and banged the cage. As the chains rattled, Service understood that he had run out of time.

He looked again. Now he could see the animal, blond, almost pale pink in the glow of the flames. It was shaking the cage, its eyes wide, as it began to scream and bash its head against the steel bars.

Eight feet off the ground and descending. Protect the animal, he told himself. He took out his 800, hissed, "Go now!" and slithered over the rock, falling four or five feet to a stone floor, got up, saw the huge fire under the vat, huge boulders around the whole thing to render it a cauldron, heard McCants screaming, "DNR! Police!" Saw the cage descending, ran forward, sprang off a boulder to wrap the cage with his arms, driving it sideways, momentarily weightless, almost flying, then crashed on something hard, his feet in the fire. He jerked them out, stomping his feet to dump embers and something struck him hard on the left shoulder and he felt warmth on his arm. He rolled to his belly and got up, a cacophony of voices surrounding him, English, another language, none of it making sense, men with their hands up and shouting, the beams of flashlights knifing around, the sound of cuffs being fastened. Gary Ebony was holding a guy by the collar, yelling "Stop kicking me, asshole!"

Santinaw pushing him aside, grinning. "It's a beautiful animal. Your pants are on fire."

Service slapped at his trousers, watched Santinaw kneel beside the cage, begin speaking to the bear in a quiet voice.

His shoulder was burning, something not right. He went outside, breathed in the fresh air, saw the snow was still falling. Gutpile suddenly beside him, holding him up. "Steady, partner."

"How many?" he yelled at McCants.

"Nine," she said.

"There should be ten."

He grabbed for his 800, but he had lost it somewhere, and yelled at McCants, "Call Jake, tell him we're at least one short here!" Moody helped him sit, offered him water.

"The whole lot of these buggers are swacked on something," Moody said. "Girl scouts coulda took the whole lot of 'em."

Santinaw sat down beside Service, held his hand. "*Mak-wa* was frightened. His spirit decided to leave."

Service looked back at the unmoving animal.

"It was a beautiful animal," Santinaw said. "Someday I will have to leave, but not until I see the woman in Eben again. It's hard to leave when you have a good woman."

Service took another swig of water. "What's Jake say?"

McCants said, "He's on the way to the cabin."

Santinaw patted Service's hand. "It was brave what you did. I think this animal's spirit will honor you."

Service shook his head, offered the bottle of water to the old man.

"*Mig-netch!*" Santinaw said "You're a lot nicer man than your father was."

They were standing in the cabin with Mecosta and the captain. Alger County deputies were moving prisoners to Munising. Someone had placed a call to the regional agent for U.S. Fish and Game. He lived in Grand Rapids and tried to cover the U.P. from there, which was a joke.

The body on the floor was face-down in a pool of blood. Service put on latex gloves, reached down. The head was blown off, leaving nothing.

"Shotgun," Jake Mecosta said. "Close range."

"Preserve the site," the captain reminded him.

Fuck the site.

Jake said, "I found him this way."

Service lit a cigarette and walked outside with Mecosta. "Jake, do you still have the anonymous voice mail message?"

"Sure." Mecosta opened his phone, punched in the numbers for his mailbox, held it up for Service to listen.

"Familiar?" Jake asked.

It was, but not the voice he expected.

· 41 ·

The apartment was a duplex in the student shopping district on Third Street. Next door was DuPendre's Café. The sign on the glass had weathered, lost some letters, read, DUPE D CAFÉ. The irony wasn't lost on him as he rapped on the door of the apartment.

"Daysi," Service said when Aldo's Ojibwa girlfriend opened the door. He had met the girl a year ago and she had been pretty, but plump. Now she was thinner, older looking, with huge eyes, long black hair.

"You called Jake Mecosta," he said.

"Who?"

"No bullshit, Daysi. I'm not in the mood." His left shoulder ached from the fall. His right shoulder burned where it had been stitched. The bear had clawed him during his grab of the cage, a reminder of the un-Disney-like reality of nature.

She looked him in the eye, her shyness gone. "I made the call for Aldo. He just gave me words to say. I didn't know what it meant."

Service said, "Where is he?"

"At the hospital with his grandfather."

She pointed toward College Street and Marquette General Hospital, the regional medical center.

· 42 ·

Aldo was alone in the hall outside ICU. He looked at Service with red eyes and pointed to a door. "He's dying."

"What happened?"

"I don't know. He was just getting sicker and sicker. I brought him in the night before last. The compound is gone. Burned."

"Where's the family?"

"Scattered."

Service pushed open the door, saw Allerdyce in the bed. Monitors on the wall flashed vital signs. He had a clear plastic mask over his face, two I.V.s, one in each arm. He looked small in the bed, his skin yellow.

Service felt the old man's eyes track him as he moved around the room.

He leaned over the bed. "When you went to prison, you left Honeypat in charge. When you came out, she wouldn't give it up and the family wouldn't back you. She let you play the role, but she ran the show."

Allerdyce's eyes hardened.

Les Reynolds had called last night. The preliminary read on Ollie Toogood's autopsy showed that he had been starved and his heart had given out. Allerdyce looked the same as the photos of Toogood that Les had faxed to him.

"It was going along fine until you made the move on Daysi. People thought Honeypat left in a snit, but she never left, did she?"

Allerdyce blinked, said nothing. "She was trying to crush all the competition and she wouldn't give you anything unless you went along with her. That day you came to see me I saw you squirrel away your food, barely eat, grope in the trash. You were hoarding, afraid you'd never eat again, fighting back the only way you could."

Service continued, "It was Honeypat's idea to get Aldo into the department. She sent Aldo to us and she sent you to make it look like you didn't want him with us, but that's what Honeypat wanted. She came to see me, said you were lying. If she cancelled your lie, Aldo gets in, her idea all the way, her plan."

He had the old man's attention. "I think she started out to drive out all her competition, but she got a couple of surprises. First, she recruited

Ollie Toogood to help her take down Dowdy Kitella, but then she found out about Ollie Toogood's money and figured out a way to get it: starved him, just the way she starved you. She wanted to create the impression of a war up here over bears and somehow she learned about outsiders coming in and she figured a way to make something from that, too. You were good in your day," Service said, "but you're not in her class. You ruled by fear. She kills and leaves no witnesses."

Allerdyce glared, struggled to pull down his mask.

Service helped him. "She burned your camp, scattered your people. They were afraid of her. You were nothing compared to her."

Allerdyce cackled, coughed. "Look at youse, son of da boozehound, hey? Dey used ta call Jake Jacobetti King of da U.P. Dat's bullshit. I'm da king. I own it. I get out of here, I hunt da bitch down, sonny." Jacobetti, the longtime politician from Negaunee, had made sure a lot of pork flowed into the Upper Peninsula through the state legislature.

"You and who else?" Service said. "You're alone and Honeypat's free, and she's got cash to do what she wants." He put the mask back in place and walked into the hallway.

Aldo stood up. "Your grandfather and Honeypat tried to get you into the department. They figured they could use you inside. I know Honeypat was running things. I'm still not sure what your role is in all this, but in time I will."

Aldo straightened his back. "I'm an Allerdyce."

Service nodded at the room across the hall. "That's how Allerdyces end up—if they're lucky."

· EPILOGUE: LIGHT
AT THE START OF
THE TUNNEL ·

The atmosphere in the Marquette office was partylike, DNR and DEQ personnel alike walking around with insipid smiles and lingering in the break room. It was election day and Senator Lorelei Timms was the favorite. By and large, DNR law enforcement personnel were geeked. Fern LeBlanc had shown up for work in a slinky dress that had all the men gawking. She was hosting an election open house tonight and inviting everyone.

It was unsettling for Service to see so many giddy people in a government office, many of them carrying on like it was a holiday; but this was finally the end of Sam Bozian's reign and the methodical destruction of the department over more than a decade. The people deserved to celebrate, he knew, if only for a day. Meanwhile, he kept fretting: Had he taken the rabbits out of the freezer yesterday for tonight's dinner? Damn memory.

While Grady Service found himself surrounded by happy people in the office, there remained legions of pissed-off parties in the wake of the case just finished. U.S. Fish and Wildlife was livid for not being brought into the bear case. FBI and Immigration had lodged formal protests for his failure to inform them of potential illegal aliens.

DNR Director Eino Tenni had reprimanded him for attending a political fund-raiser and promised "further discussions." Lorelei Timms could not dump Tenni because the DNR director was the hire of the Natural Resources Commission, and he had about a year to run on his contract.

Justice and the DEA had gone ballistic because he had interfered in a long investigation into drug trafficking and smuggling by Siquin Soong's White Moon Trading Company. It didn't matter that breaking the bear case had also brought White Moon Trading crashing down; DEA wasn't getting the credit and in government circles, credit was what mattered most. Predictably, Soong had hired a high-profile defense lawyer out of Los Angeles and was denying all allegations.

Professor Tara Ferma had written him a scathing e-mail accusing him of gross incompetence in the rare bear's death, and his reply that the carcass would be turned over to her had not mollified her.

The identity of the dead man remained a mystery that was likely to stay that way. Fingerprints and DNA had been sent to the government of South Korea, but the South Koreans were pissed at the Bush administration, and cooperation, while promised, was unlikely to materialize soon, if ever.

As near as they could make out from the men arrested in the grotto, the bear was to be lowered into boiling oil and then eaten—its fear supposedly magnifying the therapeutic effects of its flesh. The men had paid fifty thousand each to partake in the so-called bear feast. None of them were U.S. citizens. One of them had begun to talk in the grotto, but now had a lawyer and had recanted. All had been charged by the feds and eventually would be deported. The money had not been recovered and Service was pretty sure that Honeypat had it. The Regional Fish and Wildlife man told him such bear cases were almost always open-ended and untidy.

The captain had informed him that a freeze on replacements was in place until further notice, and this news made Treebone unhappy. There was no way for his man Sterling to move over to the DNR right now.

Service had spent hours with Dulin, Marquette's prosecuting attorney, trying to pry loose warrants for the arrest of Honeypat Allerdyce, but Dulin "respectfully declined." The case was too circumstantial and Service had no real evidence against her. He didn't blame Dulin, and he admired Honeypat, not for what she was, but for her total dominance of events. She had started out trying to manipulate the clan's competition, but she had gotten greedy. Her lack of discipline suggested that she would always be driven by greed, which according to Cal Shall was a lethal weakness. There was a federal BOLO for Honeypat, but in this day and age of terrorists, it was not likely to get much attention. In the long run, though, she would fall.

Wayno Ficorelli had been calling him every day to see if he could get a job in Michigan and Service had put him off, explaining the freeze, but Wayno was a bulldog in his own self-interest.

Maridly had flown to Traverse City last night to be with Lorelei and Whit Timms for the election results. She had wanted him along, but he had begged off, telling her he needed to vote. She had already cast her ballot by absentee and she had left last night in a huff. This alone made his mood dark. He and Nantz had never let a parting end this way before.

Yesterday the captain had put out a directive for all sergeants and detectives to pick up slack in coverage due to retirements from Bozian's early-out program. Service had talked to the captain about it and would be taking Kate Nordquist's turf in western Schoolcraft and eastern Delta Counties. The Garden Peninsula was part of the Delta duty and he was looking forward to renewing acquaintances with some of the violets he had busted during the Garden Wars in the seventies and eighties. His boots were going back into the snow, mud, and dirt, and nothing could make him happier.

He drove to his polling place in Gladstone by mid-afternoon, stood in line for twenty minutes to vote, and then headed for the grocery store. Walter and Karylanne were coming over from Houghton for the night and he was looking forward to seeing them.

It felt like he hadn't cooked a good meal in a long while, and he was ready for it, tempered by the fact that Maridly would not be with him.

The sun was out and the temperature in the mid-fifties with only a slight wind, a perfect fall day. Newf and Walter and Karylanne were roughhousing on the lawn when he returned.

He carried the groceries into the kitchen and began to organize his thoughts. Walter and Karylanne came in. "Either of you know diddly about cooking?"

"Some," Karylanne said.

"Sheba didn't cook," Walter said.

"Time you learned," Service said. He opened a '95 Amarone, poured a glass, and quickly made assignments. Soon the three of them were bumping into each other and laughing as the kitchen swelled with the aromas of good food: infarinata, corn meal soup; rabbit in sweet and sour sauce; sautéed dried morels in parsley and garlic; a dessert of rice custard cake with cherry compote. Karylanne turned on her boom box, put in a disk, Tom Petty's *Learning to Fly*.

Captain Grant called at 5 P.M.

"I talked to Allerdyce's doctor," the captain said. "They've taken him off the critical list. He's still extremely ill, but it looks like he will pull through."

He wondered how Limpy would handle seeing the burned-out compound, and how Honeypat would take the news that Limpy would live.

He'd been tough on Aldo, but he was in no mood to revisit the case tonight.

A few minutes after the captain called, Moody arrived with Kate Nordquist, who was on crutches. Moody was carrying a cooler. "Venison tenderloins," he said. "Where's the grill?"

Service looked at them incredulously. "What're you two doin' here?"

"Party," Moody said.

Gary Ebony and McCants arrived next. Then del Olmo and Grinda, Rose and Vince Vilardo, and soon the house was filled with the sound of beer bottles being uncapped and people shouting and laughing and looking for things to eat.

Service tried to keep a nice face, but he just wanted to sit with Walter and Karylanne, eat and watch the election returns. That wasn't going to happen.

Linsenman came in lugging a case of nonalcoholic beer. He was followed by his new dog, which in the light was the ugliest thing Service had ever seen. Naturally Newf welcomed the animal like a family member.

Service was closing the door when he saw Fern LeBlanc and Captain Grant coming up the walk arm in arm. He was dumbfounded. "Open house at your place," Service said to Fern.

"We changed the venue," she said.

We?

By 11 P.M. pollsters were calling the election a Timms victory.

At 11:18 the news programs broke from their regular reports to go live at a hotel in Traverse City. Lorelei Timms, her husband, and three kids walked onto a floodlit stage, smiling and squinting amidst thunderous cheers. Service shouted, "Everybody shut up!"

Gutpile Moody said, "I don't think the people in TC can hear you, partner."

Timms looked directly at the camera with her disarming smile and said, "I've been waiting for ninety minutes to make this announcement," she said. The people in the hotel erupted and she held up her hands to get them to settle down. "We are a great state, filled with wonderful people," she said. "We don't all think the same, but we all nurture dreams. The election is over and now it's time for the state to pull together, all of us, not just some of us, to use our differences to strive for our mutual goals. These are difficult times and we are going to need the thoughts, prayers, and interest of all citizens, from Gladstone to Temperance."

The crowd cheered again. "It is my fervent hope that we will accomplish a lot of things over the next six years. I am sure there will be disappointments ahead, but on this first night, I can sure as heck get at least one small thing right. People who love each other should be together at important moments," she said looking directly into the camera.

"What the hell is she talking about?" Service said disgustedly.

Walter Commando said, "Dad, look behind you."

Dad?

A hand touched the small of his back and he turned to look down into the intense blue eyes of Maridly Nantz. "No way I'm in Traverse City alone and my family's way up here," she said, flinging her arms around his neck.

"I'm sorry," he said.

But she put her hand over his mouth, wouldn't let him speak as Lorelei Timms talked on.

The kids excused themselves at midnight and got up to leave. "We have to leave early to get back for classes," Walter said.

"Separate bedrooms," Service told his son.

"Not a problem, Dad," Walter said with a grin.

The rest of the crowd trickled out and Linsenman had to carry NATO out to his truck because he had played so hard with Newf they were both worn out.

Much later when they were alone, Service and Nantz sat on the couch, sipping wine and reflecting. The state had a new governor. Nobody had any idea what Clearcut would do with the rest of his life and Service didn't care. In January Bozian would be gone, a burden lifted.

Nantz said, "God, I adore you, Service."

Service said, "I love you, Mar."

They sat close for several minutes, saying nothing.

"You never said who you voted for, Dad," she said.

He had written in the name of Zoltan Ferency, the perennial candidate for the Democratic gubernatorial nomination, a former state Democratic chairman who resigned in opposition to LBJ's war policies—the only politician in Service's life who had quit over principles. Ferency had been dead nine years.

"I'll never tell," he said.